TWELVE TO ONE— IMPOSSIBLE ODDS

Hyde dropped beside the vehicle. A bullet careened off the hood making him leap with tension.

He heard a voice summoning others and hurriedly slipped his arms through the straps of the backpack, his breathing hard, preparatory. He rested his weight against the side of the Land Rover. Another shot struck, thudding like a blow and burying itself in the upholstery. Then the silence flowed back, and Hyde flung himself to his feet only to be thrown forward by the wave of a detonation. As his hands clamped over his ears and the ground lit up to receive the impact of his body, he heard the explosion of a grenade, then a second, immediate detonation of the gas tank. The rocks flared red as if dyed and the ground quivered beneath his body.

"Offers action and intrigue in full measure."
— *Publishers Weekly*

"One of the more satisfying stories around."
— *Rocky Mountain News*

"[Thomas'] best yet . . . a pulse pounder."
— *Marlboro Enterprise-Hudson Sun*

Also by Craig Thomas

EMERALD DECISION
FIREFOX
WOLFSBANE
SNOW FALCON
SEA LEOPARD
JADE TIGER
THE LAST RAVEN
RAT TRAP
FIREFOX DOWN!

Published by
HARPERPAPERBACKS

CRAIG THOMAS

A HOODED CROW

HarperPaperbacks
A Division of HarperCollinsPublishers

If you purchased this book without a cover, you should be
aware that this book is stolen property. It was reported as
"unsold and destroyed" to the publisher and neither the
author nor the publisher has received any payment for this
"stripped book."

This is a work of fiction. The characters, incidents, and
dialogues are products of the author's imagination and are not
to be construed as real. Any resemblance to actual events or
persons, living or dead, is entirely coincidental.

HarperPaperbacks   *A Division of* HarperCollins*Publishers*
10 East 53rd Street, New York, N.Y. 10022

A hardcover edition of this book was published in 1992
by HarperCollins*Publishers*.

Cover illustration by Bill Schmidt

First HarperPaperbacks printing: March 1993

Printed in the United States of America

HarperPaperbacks and colophon are trademarks of
HarperCollins*Publishers*

❖ 10 9 8 7 6 5 4 3 2 1

This one is for

Babs and George, Joy and John,
Chris and Tony, Beryl and Nev.

for all the good times.

But Eden is burning, either brace yourself for elimination
Or else your heart must have the courage for the changing
   of the guards.

       —Bob Dylan, *Changing of the Guards*

                    ... sun destroys
The interest of what's happening in the shade.

       —Philip Larkin, *The Whitsun Weddings*

PRELUDE

And thus do we of wisdom and of reach,
With windlasses and with assays of bias,
By indirections find directions out.
—*Shakespeare,* Hamlet, *II, i*

The noise of the official reception billowed out of the open doors of the St. George Hall like a reproof as Andrew Babbington strode down the gallery toward Kapustin. The midday sun struck through the long windows which overlooked the Moskva. Kapustin's shoulders were hunched belligerently, his hands clasped behind his back as if he, too, were flinching against the hubbub of the reception for David Reid and his entourage of British businessmen and civil servants, all come with their loans and their arrogance to help bail out the Soviet economy and Mother Nikitin and his *perestroika*. Babbington realized that his mouth mimicked his disdain—and perhaps the ironic, shivery nervousness he felt—as he glimpsed Nikitin and David Reid laughing together. Should Reid turn now, he would recognize Babbington, even with his beard. Had Kapustin, the deputy chairman of the KGB, summoned him for just such a small, bitter humiliation?

Rich stucco graced the walls behind the British Secretary of State for Trade and Industry and the Soviet President, and there were huge zinc columns supporting a row of statues of the goddess of Victory, each crowned with laurel. What sort of victory was it, Babbington wondered, when representatives of the British government were entertained so obsequiously for the sake of some scrubby little trade deals and short-term loans? Marble slabs in niches commemorated the names and units of officers and men of the Russian armies who had been awarded the Order of St. George—as he himself had been. Now they might strike a new St. George medal to commemorate what was happening in there at that moment! Perhaps Kapustin had intended this humiliation. There was a certain, wormlike bitterness twisting in Babbington's stomach—people he knew, even some whose careers he had furthered, and the British Embassy across the river; he walking between the two. That room had celebrated the victory over the Nazis in 1945. Nikitin had barely earned the right to be in it!

Kapustin's head snapped up, as if he had sensed rather than seen Babbington's proximity. Yes, he was aware of the irony of Babbington's presence, but had not engineered it for his humiliation. He was still—and always would be—the traitor to his country who had fled to Moscow after Aubrey exposed him. Useful, promoted to the rank of general in the KGB. And *used*. Trusted only because they were certain he had no alternative. A constant diet of humiliation and rancor.

Kapustin's broad, peasant's face was alive with anger, determination and the ubiquitous calculation. The old-fashioned suit he wore was generously bemedaled. Kapustin caught his glance, and grinned. "Some of them I actually deserved, General," he murmured, then tossed his head. "Unlike some recipients I could name."

"Deputy Chairman, why do you suddenly require

my presence here—at this humiliating farce?" He caught someone in the room, near one of the doors, studying him, before shaking his head and turning away. Mistaken identity. As always, his habitual, aloof disdain of Kapustin was forgiven out of the benevolence of superior power.

"I summoned you because there is something that must be discussed now, at once. Walk with me—the noises of our mutual countrymen grate."

At once, they began to patrol the windowed gallery, Babbington keeping his glance toward the river and away from the doors. Even that much nervousness dismayed him. Glass-roofed tourist pleasure cruisers invested the river like floating greenhouses. The laughter and chatter boomed out at the two men as they passed each pair of open doors; empty, calculated gestures and the clink of glasses. Babbington gripped his hands behind his back, as if parodying Kapustin—two starlings on a lawn, he thought, then quashed the Englishness of the image. Kapustin's blunt head moved beside him at shoulder height, pecking occasionally at present concerns and toward the doors that seemed to divide them both from a certain past, even as they were, evidently, to discuss an unexpected, though already planned future. Kapustin appeared uncomfortable; angry, but wary. He looked up at Babbington. "Andrew, I must instruct you to a course of action you will resent and mistrust—but which is necessary."

"And that is?"

Kapustin's spadelike hand gripped his sleeve. "Andrew, do not be languid with me. I have just spent a very uncomfortable fifteen minutes in an anteroom of that hall with Mother Nikitin and a quorum of his—and our—supporters in the Politburo. I was summoned there and given my orders. Comrades Lidichev and Chevrikov would not, apparently, divert his attention. Perhaps it is the appearance of the British Secretary for

Trade that has stirred the mud at the bottom of his mind—I do not know. Our friends—our Chairman in particular—agree with him, on this occasion—"

"Kapustin, what is it we are talking about?" Dealing with these people was often like another and more tense secret life than the one he had led in London, before Aubrey had exposed and usurped him. "What the devil is this business?"

"We are talking about—toys, trinkets, shiny objects. We are talking about seeing a *return on our massive investment,* as he put it to me." Kapustin waved his hands in the air, as if engaged in some spell-casting or martial arts ritual.

"What do you mean?"

Kapustin's eyes were bright with anger, even as he squinted in the sunlight coming over Babbington's shoulder. "I mean proving to Nikitin and others that we have not run off with the money!" His hand tightened on Babbington's sleeve once more. His words hissed. "They are afraid—all of them, including our Chairman—of the amount of money and investment and goods that are about to be lost to us, since you informed us that Mr. Shapiro is about to be arrested—and seems prepared to discuss a way out of his difficulties with the FBI and the CIA."

"I've already made my feelings clear. Shapiro's usefulness is at an end. The material he supplied from the Reid Group has dried up. He can only do harm now, should he talk. I have already suggested that Shapiro be dealt with before he reaches that position. He's skulking in London now, afraid to return to America. So, let me remove him as an obstacle—"

"He is not the only obstacle! Much of our operation in California has been uncovered by the FBI—the companies in which we have an interest, the bank in Fresno, the banks and holding companies in the

Caribbean . . . and the fact that Aubrey's people have not been put out to grass, as you assured us they would, when illness removed Sir Kenneth."

"Everything else is secure!"

"No, it is *not* secure." Kapustin glared at Babbington. It was the accusing glance of a pedagogue severely disappointed in a once-lauded pupil. "The London Rezident is monitoring the activities of that small group of people around Aubrey. They are continuing with their investigation of the Reid Group and its subsidiaries. And they are not as purposeless as a chicken with its head chopped off. Godwin, Hyde and the others might, at any moment, find the tripwire that sets off all the alarms, Andrew. *That* cannot be allowed to happen."

The sunlight dazzled from the river's surface and from the floating greenhouses. Babbington rubbed his forehead, which prickled with the heat of his anger. Or perhaps it was a reaction to that heavy blanket of noise that kept billowing from the room as if orchestrated for his chagrin.

"You're panicking needlessly," Babbington said.

"*I* am not panicking—but Mother Nikitin and some of his supporters *are*. What they desire is the advanced wafer scale integration technology and the transputer technology that could be obtained from the Reid Group—*now*, not when *you* feel the time is right."

"You want to waste all those *years* with some operation that stinks of looting a bazaar?" Babbington involuntarily threw up his hands. "I don't believe I'm hearing this, Kapustin. The material you require must be brought out piecemeal, if at all. You want to deliberately attract the attention of Aubrey's people? Why not *telephone* them, if that's the case!"

"Nikitin has fixed his mind," Kapustin whispered fiercely, "on acquiring this wafer scale integration technology from the Reid Group to assist our dash into capitalism, which has already taken us four years and shows no signs of working!" He bent closer to Babbington, so that the taller man had to lean down toward his mouth. "Just at this moment, *we* are disposed to please him, to satisfy his childish lust for these new toys. Do I make myself clear, Andrew?"

Waiters moved as in some vast hotel ballroom, with trays of canapés and bottles of champagne, refilling glasses. Guests rubbed well-cut suits against cocktail dresses, comparing mutual luxury. A blue cloud of cigar and cigarette smoke hovered over the vast room.

"I understand you—I don't agree with you, however. In fact, I violently disagree—"

Kapustin moved his hand in a flat, dismissive gesture. "I am not concerned with your disagreement. There is to be no more continuation of risk. Just one final risk. You will get the richest, ripest pickings out of the UK, especially WSI and transputer technology. You will do it *now,* as quickly and ruthlessly as possible. Then you will shut down the UK operation until it is deemed safe to continue penetration of high-tech companies. You can move your focus of operations to Germany or France, until it is safe to go back. Until Aubrey retires . . . or dies." He smiled grimly.

"A consummation devoutly to be wished," Babbington growled.

They began to retrace their steps down the long gallery. The traffic seemed heavy on the nearest bridge, and the pleasure cruisers cut small wakes on the glittering river. Dots of color strolled the far bank.

"See to it, Andrew. You have—"

"If we asset-strip the UK operation, then we will simply be shooting ourselves in the foot," Babbington persisted with whispered, hoarse rage. His fist clenched and unclenched at his side in emphasis. "We would have to start more or less afresh to penetrate high-tech companies—"

"Do it, Andrew. We are seeking to maintain our influence with Nikitin, and this—at *this* moment—is our way of doing so. Time presses. To minimize any additional risk, the timetable that has been proposed—" it was, so evidently, Kapustin's timetable "—culminates in the VIATE fair in Venice, which will be your cover—"

"Impossible!"

"—culminates at that fair at the end of the month. It is not impossible. It must be done. Get rid of Shapiro, and then move swiftly." He patted Babbington's sleeve. "I'm sorry it has to happen, Andrew. The penetration of the Reid Group, the shareholding we have acquired so covertly . . . a great pity. But other priorities make their demands. For the present, we have to placate Nikitin and the Politburo, and they are more or less united in demanding a return on their investment. Where are the toys you promised us? they cry like children. We need them to perform our economic miracle! Ridiculous—but necessary." He shook his sleeve again. "You *do* understand, Andrew?"

Babbington nodded stiffly, after an interminable silence filled with the billow of laughter and chatter from the St. George Hall. "I understand," he said thickly. Then, clearing his throat, he repeated: "I understand my instructions. They come from—" He broke off, as if surprising himself in the act of betraying a secret.

Kapustin smiled with knowing satisfaction, then he said: "Of course you do. Good . . . now, off you go to get this business organized. Shoo!" He waved his arms as if to scatter chickens in some peasant farmyard.

Babbington's cheeks were hot with anger. Even with shame, he thought, as he turned away and began to walk down the long gallery with as much indifferent dignity as he could employ to stiffen his shoulders and his gait. *They come from*—he had blurted, wanting to say that all Kapustin's spoken arguments were merely specious. *They come from* those pug-faced generals and defense people we are forced to consort with and call our friends. Those *peasants* in braid-covered uniforms whose eyes and tongues have been slavering ever since they saw the first news footage from the Gulf. All those shiny *playthings!* All that obscenely glamorous Western military technology. Get it for us, we must have it!

He reached the end of the gallery and turned out of sight of Kapustin, who he knew would be watching his—*retreat*. He retained the stiff, military posture.

The generals and the other hardliners—all the contemptible, powerful little people—had raised the game's stakes; they had to have this new technology. They'd been rendered ten years out-of-date by weaponry, tactics and skills displayed in the Gulf, and they wanted, yet *again*, to catch up.

The stakes were dangerously high now—they would be ruthless with someone who failed them.

PART ONE

SELLING ENGLAND BY THE POUND

I never think you should judge a country by its politics. After all, we English are quite honest by nature, aren't we?

—From Hitchcock's The Lady Vanishes

1

THE ENVY OF LESS
HAPPIER LANDS

There were too many sensations in the room, too many people, all moving as black shadows against the summer light coming through the opened vertical blinds. He was angry, and his mood jolted against the smooth, closed business of the room, its finality. Shapiro was the only person missing, inactive. *For God's sake, how the hell had it been allowed to happen? The bugger was on the point of being arrested and extradited, and now he'd killed himself!*

Daniel Garrison, CIA Station Chief, signaled to him, and he stumped on his heavy crutches across the deep, blue carpet. Through the multiplicity of windows of the hotel suite's lounge, the traffic shunted or moved with matador grace and suddenness around the Wellington Arch.

Tony Godwin was there by virtue of a gesture, almost as if he were being rewarded—with a bloody consolation prize—for good work; a star in his school exercise book. Shapiro had committed suicide in the bedroom of his suite at the InterContinental. The frock-coated management representative looked like a premature undertaker, especially since he seemed to find hand-wringing a comforting exercise. His look obscurely accused Godwin as he moved through the small crowd of Special Branch officers, a Customs official, the forensic team, others. Godwin clapped his crutches together as if saluting Garrison and looked toward the half-open bedroom door. He glowered at Garrison's people posted there. Shapiro, to put it bluntly, had fucked up six months' work by killing himself!

And he had never appeared the suicidal sort. Only likely to be talkative, once he'd been pinned down.

"Well?" he snapped at Garrison, who shook his head lugubriously. "Dan, how the hell could it have happened, just now, when he was about to have his collar felt? He was even putting out little feelers for a deal with us, for God's sake!" He rubbed a large hand through his fraying fair hair, catching sight of his untidy appearance in a long mirror: awkward and crippled, furiously angry like a frustrated child. He clenched his hand into a fist. The sun burned on the blue carpet and, despite the purr of the air-conditioning, the room seemed hot. "Why the hell did he do it?"

His anger had fermented in the heat of the taxi that had brought him here from his flat. Hadn't even paused to feed Dubcek, the black cat he'd brought from Prague years ago.

"Calm down, Tony, you'll blow a fuse." There was no mockery in the remark. "Look, we don't know why. He *was* beginning to sound like he wanted to play ball, tell us everything he knew. Now, this—" He gestured at the two officers from Special Branch. "Your people saw him come in last evening, with a high-class hooker on his arm and a smile on his face. She left about—"

"There was someone else here? Then he didn't necessarily help himself to oblivion! What does the doc say about time?"

"Anywhere between one and three this morning."

"How?"

"Sleeping pills, washed down with Krug champagne. He'd had sex—the girl must have left and he got depressed. Perhaps he didn't like the idea of ten years on the prison farm, after—"

"The more he'd have told us, the shorter the sentence. He understood that! Who was this tart he brought back?"

"No one knows. He didn't arrange anything from here or over the telephone."

"She picked him up, then. Where did he eat last night?"

"Your people watched him. He went to some club, came out with her."

"Then she could have killed him!"

"We don't *know,* Tony!" He rubbed his forehead. "Look, I'm just as mad as you are. But it really doesn't look like she shoved a bottle of pills down his throat! I'm sorry, I guess the guy just chickened out at the last moment—who knows?"

"And maybe—just maybe—it's better for Langley and Washington that he's said good-bye?" Garrison's eyes flinched at the accusation. "No one really wanted another fuss about the KGB, did they? Not with all those loans on the table and Nikitin visiting America next September. *Very* inconvenient, a scandal!"

Garrison ignored the blunt sarcasm and said: "You want to take a look at him? He looks kind of—"

"You sound like a relative! Doesn't he look peaceful! There's months of hard, patient work up shit creek because fat Mr. Shapiro of Shapiro Electrics of San

Jose, California, has either killed himself or been done in. Nothing changes *that,* whatever happened to him." The room had fallen silent, the shadows posed in stillness against the blinds. He was the actor, they merely the audience—too true, he thought bitterly. Their play was over, after a lengthy run, while his had closed for lack of support! "Oh, *shit!*" he bellowed at the top of his voice. They could have had so much out of Shapiro. The details of the web, the methods of operation, the loans, the smuggling, the extent of KGB penetration of the Reid Group—bloody everything! Especially the details of the pipeline and how much Malan was involved. Bugger it! The operation was dead now. "Was there a note?" he asked.

"A short one—his handwriting, on hotel notepaper."

Godwin sniffed in disbelief. "True. He blamed our harassment, business worries, the fear of prison—or worse. The usual paranoia."

"He had nothing to worry about!" Godwin exclaimed.

"Maybe he was too scared to talk?"

"And maybe they killed him because he was about to."

Garrison shrugged. "Whatever, it's over now. We'll pick over the bones. Maybe we've frightened the Russians into laying off for a while. So long as we stay alert—"

"Christ, they'll own Saks Fifth Avenue before we get a better chance to see what they're up to!"

"I'm sorry, Tony—really sorry." He cleared his throat. "Look, I have to report to your Director General, Sir Clive—"

"Great. It's just the excuse he's been looking for to redeploy us—ever since Aubrey chucked us back in his lap and went on sick leave."

"Sorry. I'll try to make it sound as if you should be allowed to go on with it. Do what I can."

"It's stuffed, Dan—it's all stuffed!" He glared at the bedroom door. "Thanks, Mister Bloody Shapiro—thanks for nothing!"

The sunlight glowed through the leaded glass of the pub window behind him and spilled across the faded, dusty carpet from the open door. Customers entering were solid black shapes without feature for a moment, as he glanced up from the *Evening Standard* as each one came in and took on slow substance in the yellow gloom. Godwin was wetting himself over Shapiro, and the phone call from Kellett had given him kittens. Patrick Hyde's attention was slow, incurious. He seemed more attentive to the soundless cricket on the television screen behind the bar.

David Reid, HM Secretary of State for Trade and Industry, occupied much of the newspaper's front page. There was a large photograph that seemed placed especially to irritate Hyde. Reid was shaking hands with Alexander Dubcek, in the Hradcany Castle in Prague. The frail, smiling figure of Dubcek, more substantial than a mere ghost from the past, was potent, and a reminder of change. *Othello's occupation gone . . .* Aubrey that was, being lugubriously clever when he'd accused the old man of seconding them to the DTI for all the real bloody good they were doing! Smuggling microchips and maybe transputers and wafer scale integration technology for all they knew—not all that different from selling them laptop computers, telecommunications, microwaves and bloody fridges. Who *really* gave a shit, anyway? Not even paranoid capitalists like the Yanks, it seemed, now that Shapiro was dead. Besides, in a year, we'll be *selling* them WSI and transputers and anything else they want, because we're all pals now and they pay in hard currency bought with their massive gold reserves.

David Reid's picture . . . on his tour of newly democratized Eastern Europe, drumming up business. Hyde recognized the faces of at least four of the party surrounding Reid and Dubcek. Managing directors and chairmen of large UK companies. Christ, what a comedown. He rubbed his stubbled cheek and sniffed loudly, turning to the back page then folding the newspaper at the racing section. Royal bloody Ascot. He fished in the inside pocket of his grubby cotton jacket for a ballpoint pen and began marking his selections from the afternoon's races. Glanced up at a shadow flung through the door—no—and then looked down once more.

Reid Electronics Group. If they were going to do the job properly, they needed to bug the company offices in the NatWest Tower. But Orrell wouldn't let them. Hyde shook his head, smiling sardonically. Prissy old bugger. Can't upset a company like Reid, or its former major shareholder and founder, the Secretary of State for Selling England by the Pound. Reid had made another fortune when he'd sold his shares in the Reid group in the aftermath of the Harrell business. Of course he didn't know anything about it, and of course his shares were in the hands of his stockbrokers while he served in the government—all very proper—and he was even more decent and only made another ten million or whatever out of publicly divesting himself of the family holding in Reid.

Oh, stop moaning. He looked up at the television behind the bar as he sipped the glass of lager. Someone was walking back, head bowed, from the wicket, bat dragging. The scoreboard appeared, showing 57–4. It could only be England batting. He grinned. Against his lot, the Aussies, too. Perhaps he could skip off for a couple of hours that afternoon and watch some of it. Plenty of blokes he knew would be there, corks on their hats, the beers going down like ninepins. More of a laugh than waiting here for Kellett. He returned his concentration to his betting permutations. Godwin was obsessive about the Reid Electronics Group, but he wasn't wrong. His contact inside Reid, Kellett, was already—he looked at his watch—twenty minutes late. *Urgent*, Kellett had said. *I think I've really stumbled on something this time.* Kellett needed to justify the money that had been spent on him. Christ, I'm bored.

He rose in search of a refilled glass, then sat down again as Kellett, his contact, resolved himself from the black lump he had appeared in the doorway. Young, yuppified, with too much expenditure on a salary required to stretch twice its capacity. Back in April he'd persuaded Shelley to pay off his most pressing credit-card bills and supply enough pocket money to last a couple of champagne-and-smoked-salmon weeks, and they'd had a man inside Reid Electronics' head office who couldn't be helpful enough. Falling over himself to offer them the information—most of it duff. Until now, perhaps? Hyde willed the younger man to go straight up to the bar. Instead he hesitated, nodded to Hyde, then moved to order a drink.

Did Kellett have something, at last? He appeared tense, but that was usual when they met. Part of the game—the game Aubrey had worn himself out playing, so some quack in Harley Street diagnosed nervous exhaustion and a touch—*only a touch, mind you, nothing to worry about*—of angina. *Take a month's rest.* So Aubrey was sitting, feet up, in his flat or dawdling around the garden of his Oxfordshire cottage, while this operation he'd started trickled on, tired and aimless.

Another shadow in the doorway. Hyde hardly glanced at the man because he was with a young woman and they were talking loudly and laughing as they came through the doorway. His accent, as he asked for two glasses of white wine, was faultlessly upper-middle class, Oxbridge, Julian-and-Nigel. Baggy suit, loosened tie, fashionable haircut; there were another six just like him in the pub at that moment. The woman was smiling—too much, Hyde realized. And her eyes were hardly still for a moment; except when she glanced at his corner of the room. She leaned against her companion as in sexual conspiracy. Kellett paid for his half bottle of red wine and began moving toward Hyde, who nodded his head with one small, abrupt gesture and waggled his newspaper toward the open door. Keep away, the signal announced. Just in case. Was the woman anything but overconfidently vain, arrogant with money or narcissism? It was like cleaning a rusty old garden implement suddenly and unexpectedly required, trying to decide. He gripped the newspaper tightly. Kellett went to a table on the other side of the doorway. The girl's head kept moving, smooth as a typewriter carriage. She seemed unconvinced by the distance between Hyde and Kellett. But Hyde *was* convinced. The man with her was her cover. She glanced across the pub once more at Hyde's corner. She was, presumably, one of Priabin's new intake, fresh from some Moscow training school. Priabin ordered ersatz yuppies and Sloanes by the barrowload to blend with his image of London; the training school was doing a good job. Hyde did not recognize her. That's because no one really bothered anymore; the Heathrow photographs arrived from the Branch, via MI5, weeks late these days—one long bloody holiday while the container trucks packed with microwaves and televisions queued at Dover, all labelled Prague or Warsaw or Bucharest.

He picked up his empty glass, rose and walked toward the bar, even as the woman, chin raised, continued to scan the room as if seeking items for a gossip column. Her arrogance was a little too perfect, her condescension toward the pub's occupants clockwork in its precision. Hyde waved the newspaper stiffly behind his back, warning Kellett to leave. He reached the bar and placed his glass on it, ordering another pint.

The woman was in her early twenties, dressed in a wide floral skirt and black, shiny cotton top, her narrow shoulders and small breasts drowned in a baggy designer jacket. The cricketers drifted off the miniature green field of the TV, for lunch. The room seemed more smoky, noisier, and Hyde admitted the tension that the tiny, unimportant proximity of himself and the woman generated. A casserole hissed on a hotplate with the smell of cheap red wine. The woman's companion laughed at something she appeared to whisper, but the sound was tight in his throat. The woman studied him with deliberate indifference, then lit a cigarette. Hyde raised his filled glass to his lips, picked up his change—

—the lager poured over the designer jacket and the cotton top. The woman had nudged his elbow. He looked round momentarily. Kellett, alert, remained seated.

"You drunken pig!" the woman screamed at him, the accent perfect and perfectly outraged. She brushed frantically at her jacket, her cheeks reddened with anger, her eyes glittering with calculation. The man acting as her cover and minder moved purposefully closer to Hyde. "Look what you've done!" There was an almost-silence in the pub.

"I sorry, I—my fault," he muttered, drawn into the charade as the man pressed against him.

"It's *you* again!" the man shouted into Hyde's face. "I've warned you before to stay away from Nicky!" His accent, too, was studied and under control, despite the simulated anger.

Serious. The artificially created situation was being hurried, deepened. Kellett was watching them now, bemused, hardly afraid—yet.

"I don't know you," Hyde muttered thickly, swaying slightly, half-raising one hand. The barman leant over and clutched his wrist.

"None of that in here. You've had enough, friend. Apologize." He sounded puzzled, as if his expert judgment had been compromised. Hyde was suddenly drunk. "You know this bloke, Miss?"

"A neighbor. He's a drunk. Pesters Nicky all the time," the cover man explained. He was taller than Hyde, his frame tensed against the necessity of sudden movement. He knew who he was dealing with, it was obvious—the type if not the individual.

Kellett had become just another member of the audience, all of whom were beginning to settle for an intriguingly unfolding drama. Sexual inadequacy, drunkenness; a soap opera in miniature. The two Russians were working to a good script. It had depth, needed an audience. Hyde, forced to comply, swayed more deliberately, aggressively, hoping that Kellett would understand and would leave.

"Piss off!"

"Watch the language," the bartender warned.

The woman had removed the designer jacket and was regarding it with appalled fascination.

"Four hundred it cost me! You've ruined it! Jimmy, get him to pay for it!" Someone laughed.

"You jogged my elbow," Hyde protested.

"I did *not!* You lurched against me. Why can't you leave me alone—stop following me everywhere!"

"Is he—?"

"Fuck off," Hyde snapped at the bartender.

"Mate, if it's trouble you're looking for . . . " said a bulky figure who rose from one of the bench seats under the window, purple, ruby and gold falling from the stained glass onto his clothes and face like diamonds, then sliding off like oil as he moved. No, there were two of them . . . not

Russians, just the unofficial bouncers for those times when yuppies start throwing empty bottles and plates and throwing up.

"Trouble, George?"

Kellett was sitting like a rabbit in front of a car's rushing headlights. Go on, bugger off! Go home, go anywhere—I'll find you. It was more serious than he had recognized. It was a deliberate separation ploy, to get Kellett on his own. Isolate him.

I think I'm really onto something. It's important— worth a lot—I know it is. Oh, yes, Hyde had replied, bored. Kellett had called him at Centre Point. Godwin had handed him the phone. Kellett exaggerated, they all did when they were on the hook and greedy. Now he knew the man really did have something valuable. So did they, though God knew how. The information was so good they'd worked like mad to get this dangerous, complex charade organized in less than a couple of hours. Followed Kellett, yes, but they must have checked out the meeting place, even to spotting the potentially useful bouncers—who were poised on the tip of the inexorable progression of the situation as it moved on oiled wheels. *I'm sure it's what you've been looking for.* He hadn't believed Kellett—

—who had to get out now, while Hyde could still keep all of them occupied. Kellett was tense and bemused and suspicious but still seated. The woman was still dabbing at her sodden top and jacket, convincing Kellett that this was arbitrary, accidental. Hyde gripped the edge of the bar with one hand, lurching to attention.

"I don't know either of you."

"You lying pillock! You hang around the flats, watching Nicky. You've been doing it for months. The police have even warned you off—" The man's eyes gleamed, darting once to the bulk of the two bouncers. Gog and Magog, the Brothers Grim. They looked eminently capable of inflicting efficient, brutal damage. It was almost bloody laughable, the way he'd been pulled into the situation.

"I bloody don't—!" he protested to the bartender, extending the fiction, attempting to hold the Russians within the circumstances they had created for long enough to allow Kellett to decide to leave. Bugger off! He waved his arms at the room. "I don't bloody know either of them!" The bouncers despised him and, where he had been comic to the rest of the pub a moment before, the sexual innuendo had made him arachnid, something that scuttled for the express purpose of being trodden upon. The woman glared at him, shaking her head violently.

"He does! He's known to the police—I had to report him to the police for watching me!" Oh, bloody hell, but you're *good*. Her voice was one a genuine Sloane would have had to practice assiduously to acquire. Perfect. It convinced the loose suits and vivid ties, the louche young men and the langorous girls. The trap was beautiful in its architecture, speed, manner of execution. The Russians now controlled the whole room.

"Oh, piss off, darling—I don't know you! Who'd fancy you, anyway, with tits that small?" He leaned toward the cover man. "I don't know *you*, either!" The situation had to degenerate quickly into violence, which was inevitable, anyway. The bouncers intended to be the *deus ex machina,* the nemesis. They stirred like Rottweilers barely under leash. "I'm bloody off, then, if my custom's not—"

He turned from the bar, staggered a little to giggles from the room, shoulders seedily sloped, acting the role they had created for him, even wiping a loose mouth with the back of his hand. He saw the woman and her cover exchange a quick, suspicious glance. The man looked toward Kellett. The sunlight glowed through the open door. Kellett was on his feet at once, but still hesitating, not realizing—

"What about my *jacket?*"

And the nearest of the two bouncers was in front of Hyde, his large splayed hand thrust against his chest.

"You heard, mate. What about the lady's jacket?" The mock-Victorian veneer of the place came away like old paint. The bouncer's eyes were wary but confident, the swollen stomach bulging over his waistband irrelevant when dealing with a drunk of much smaller stature.

"Piss off—now!" Hyde growled, staring beyond the bouncer, directly at Kellett—

—who nodded, wiped his lips and turned through the door. Black in the sunlight. Now, just get past this oaf and catch up with—

He head-butted the bouncer, who staggered back— noise of breaking bone drowned out by his squeal of pain. The second bouncer struck Hyde in the kidneys before he could turn, and he staggered and was hit again, then a third time. Glancing blows. No one believed he was drunk now, but it didn't matter. Blood covered the first bouncer's face, a larger, uglier badge than the lights from the stained glass on his clothes as he lay slumped near the door, a table overturned beside him, beer puddling on the carpet. Someone was complaining their trousers had been stained.

Hyde turned, but his legs were kicked from under him. The woman was struggling into the sodden jacket, and the man's shadow already blocked the doorway. They were going after Kellett and he couldn't get out—

A heavy shoe in his ribs. He rolled away. Noises of an audience pleased at the violence happening to a stranger. His ribs burned, his kidneys ached. The first bouncer staggered to his feet and came lurching toward him. As his foot swung, Hyde grabbed and twisted the man off balance. The second bouncer kicked Hyde in the thigh as he climbed to his feet, and he lurched against the bar. A glass fumbled itself into his grip. The bartender was already on the telephone, the damage mounting to unacceptable levels, too high just for the pleasure of seeing him get a kicking. Hyde broke the glass and thrust it forward. The bouncers hesitated, then someone encouraged them. The woman and her cover had disappeared. Christ, what a mess—

"Come on sport!" he taunted. "I'll have your face off!"

Hurry up, you idiot! he yelled silently at the bartender who was gabbing into the receiver and staring at him. There were others stirring now, like the beginnings of a pack, as if they wore fur, not suits and frocks. Everyone wanted a little taste of the concoction the Russians had manufactured, the dangerous, heady flavor of violence. Except for the broken beer glass in his hand, they'd be circling him now.

Hurry up . . . Godwin's last lead into the Reid Group has just walked out of here with the KGB on his tail! Bloody hurry it up—

"Look, I couldn't get here any sooner!" Godwin roared at Hyde, lurching round on his crutches to face him. "Terry Chambers has the Malan surveillance, young Darren is otherwise engaged, and I've been trying to cobble together a report that will persuade Orrell to let us carry on with this bloody mess of an investigation! All right?"

On the television screen behind the police station's sergeant's desk, a late news program was repeating film of David Reid toasting his Czech hosts in an ornate room, beneath chandeliers. Everyone was smiling and appeared content to the point of smugness.

"I've been sitting in a bloody cell all afternoon, for Christ's sake—because P. C. Plod and his mates didn't believe me without ID. And I didn't have my bloody

ID, did I?" Hyde tugged his jacket over his shoulders, wincing at the renewed pain in his kidneys and ribs.

"Are you all right?"

"Nothing broken," the sergeant at the desk murmured without looking up from his newspaper. "The doc had a good look at him." He glanced up then, malevolently. "That car got there before *he* did any more damage—to himself or anyone else." He glowered at Hyde. "You will tell your friends you *can* find a copper when you need one, won't you?" Then he tossed his head and returned to his crossword, sucking the end of his pencil. A drunk sat slumped against the opposite wall, smelling of beer and vomit, his face gray with stubble and decline.

"What's what, then?" Hyde asked, then called back over his shoulder: "I peed on the blanket before I left!" and laughed.

"Christ, Patrick, no wonder you put people's backs up!"

"Look, I was in there for hours and no one was in the slightest bit interested. They were too busy looking for witnesses!"

"Shame about democracy, isn't it? Gets in the way."

"They were about to charge me with actual bodily harm, for Christ's sake!"

"Oh, calm down. What happened to the Russians?"

"They went after Kellett. What would you expect? What have you done about it?"

Godwin looked intensely glum. "Nothing, yet—except get you out of jail."

"Christ, I sometimes wonder about you!" Hyde exclaimed. "Either Kellett has something—a lifebelt—or he hasn't. But we'd better grab hold of something! Come on."

The car that had brought Godwin was parked fifty

yards along Old Jewry from the police station. The driver sat upright from his dozing slouch as Hyde opened the door. Godwin struggled into the rear seat and Hyde slumped in beside him.

"Kellett's flat—Docklands." Hyde gave the address. "I told you on the phone, when I finally managed to reach you and you deigned to take my call, that he might need protection. But you've been too busy watching your own ass to bother!" He sat back against his seat, feet thrust up like a child against the front passenger seat, and looked at his watch. Eleven.

"I didn't do anything because I was too busy trying to salvage something from this bloody mess!" Godwin snapped.

"All right—don't throw a fit. Kellett is about all we can salvage from this fiasco, mate. You should have realized that."

The bulk of the Bank of England disappeared in the sideview mirror.

"Is he in any real danger?"

"God knows. He got out of there, eventually, as if his trousers were on fire. But they went after him. Let's hope they didn't catch him. Christ, it was a smooth enough operation."

"And you fell right in."

"Kellett didn't call the office until ten-thirty. By twelve-thirty, they had the whole thing up and running."

Eastcheap, then the Tower, strange as a dream, a folly beached amid the concrete and lights.

"What could he have turned up, all of a sudden? He wasn't just scared, was he?"

"What of?"

"I don't know! It's just that he hasn't been much use to us before."

"How did they even *know* about him?" Hyde asked. "Unless they've got the tap into Reid Electronics that we're not allowed! What a bloody laugh if that's true. Turn Sir Clive purple, that will—have to order an extra-strong apératif before dinner." Hyde turned to Godwin. "It's fucked, isn't it, if Kellett's dead?" Godwin nodded lugubriously. The Royal Mint loomed ahead. "Shit."

Eventually, Limehouse intruded on their oppressive silence. New flats along the river, which was skeletal with lights, the buildings crowding above newly fashionable streets and smart alleys. Hyde was wound like a spring as the driver turned right and began to patrol the walls, the ornamental gates, the brick-paved causeways and mock jetties. Porsches, though fewer than before, BMWs clustered like flies, the noise from wine bars and discos coming into the car through the window Hyde had opened. Smell of the river. Hyde sniffed as a leggy girl sprang from an Escort Cabriolet, laughing, long hair moving as in a shampoo advertisement.

"This is it," he announced, tapping the driver on the shoulder. "That one over there."

The driver rasped on the hand brake opposite a geometrical, subdued brick block of flats, jutting and crenellated like the wall of a castle; as if the place required defending from the surrounding countryside and its inhabitants. Hyde got out and breathed deeply. Kellett lived on the seventh floor, overlooking the river. He couldn't afford the flat and his lifestyle, especially his cocaine intake, not with high interest rates and the BMW and the very expensive hi-fi. Godwin stumped along beside Hyde toward the foyer. Hyde pressed the video entryphone for Kellett's flat—again, then a third time. He looked darkly at Godwin. "Police ID?"

Godwin nodded, and Hyde pressed the resident porter's bell. Eventually:

"Who is it?"

"CID. Let us in. We want to see Mr. Kellett. He's not answering his bell." Godwin dutifully held up the warrant card at the eye of the entryphone.

"Very well." The doors buzzed and Hyde pushed against them.

"Careless sod—either that or he's got wonderful eyesight." A closed, stale, cooking scent in the foyer, and in the lift. "I'm glad he's not my porter."

"Ros hardly lets *you* back in."

The lift sighed up. Hyde said, quietly, "I should have warned you—you're right. I should have."

"We're here now," Godwin replied, acknowledging what appeared to be a grudging apology. The door of the lift soughed open, then clunked, the noise announcing the silence of the carpeted corridor. Another stale smell. "Which one?"

"Flat 62—this is 61 . . . " Hyde walked down the corridor.

"You look like a man dying for a pee," Godwin remarked, leaning against the wall.

"Here we are."

The noise of music more appropriate to the lift sounded in Hyde's ears as he pressed the bell of the flat. Coming from inside. The bastard was in. Godwin clumped softly toward him across the carpet, speckled with marks and a lack of vacuuming. Black dustbin bags outside a farther door. The noise that could come only from satellite television from somewhere else—an American football commentator. Hyde pressed the bell again, and heard the buzzing just above the volume of the hi-fi. Twenty thousand quid to play that rubbish, he thought. A right idiot, hardly in the real world, just holding on lightly to it by his fingertips.

"He hasn't put his bags out for the porter, then."

"He bloody hasn't."

Hyde knelt down and lifted the letter-flap.

"Well?"

"Fancy half-stairs—can't see a bloody thing."

"Well?"

"Smell gas, can you?"

"Quite possibly."

Hyde kicked the fragile door—compressed shavings, by the look of the inside of the letter-flap, and no Banham locks. It opened at the third attempt, and he stumbled into the flat. Four stairs led directly into an open-plan lounge. The smell of still-new carpet and half-dried plaster, and the whiff of static in his nostrils from the hi-fi. Pictures on the walls, posters and abstracts.

"Who in hell told him to invest in this stuff?" Godwin asked. "No wonder he's hard up. All from Bond Street and Mayfair galleries—look, all signed, limited editions." The enlarged, monochrome print of a moonrise over an open field which Hyde had noticed and which Godwin now recognized. "You know how much the old bugger sells prints of *that* for, don't you?" he murmured. "Whatever his bloody name is . . . ?"

Hyde shrugged. He glanced around the room. Leather furniture, Chinese rugs that were hardly less expensive in Hong Kong than Mayfair. The hi-fi's large speakers and perhaps a dozen boxes to produce the noise that was coming from them. And the prints and posters and limited editions on the walls . . . and the old, leather-bound books—he picked a Dickens from a shelf and checked its date; first edition, naturally. The room was a library, a gallery, a means of exhibition and investment. With borrowed and overspent funds. Hedging against a rainy day and creating bad weather at the same time. The room was—greedy, too. An octogenarian's pride belonging to a boy of twenty-five who couldn't wait. Perhaps his parents in the country had endowed him with the taste, and the appetite. It was empty, too, and silent except for the noise from the hi-fi.

"What sort of life does he think he's living?" Hyde asked. "Who is he trying to impress?"

"A string of birds or doting parents?"

"Or not doting—or not even well-off," seeming to gain some other insight from the room, before he saw Kellett's ankles and shoes protruding from behind the huge leather Chesterfield. "He won't be doing much of either any more, will he?"

"Oh, shit," Godwin breathed, his look accusing.

Hyde knelt by the—body it certainly was. The young features stared up at him uncomplainingly. There was the spillage of nausea and his whisky glass near his cheek and dribbling on his chin. No pulse. Flesh warm, soft. The small sheet of foil, the lighter and the inhaler were not simply casually or of necessity on the coffee table, then. They were evidence, they were deception. The smell of the crack in the room was deliberate—that bloody Russian-actress-Sloane-cow!

Godwin loomed over him, breathing heavily.

"He'll have had a heart attack, as well, I expect just to, complete the Trinity—it's so bloody clichéd who could resist believing it?"

"Not Orrell, that's for certain," Hyde murmured, as Godwin stumped away on his crutches, muttering: "Someone's nailing up the exit doors one by one, before they set fire to the cinema."

Hyde stared at the pale, young face, then turned toward Godwin, who was dialing a number on the cellular phone he had picked up from the coffee table, where it had been lying beside the silver foil and the inhaler and the white granules that looked like chips of almond.

"What did the tart look like Shapiro took up to his room?" Hyde asked.

"What? Oh, the tart—white about catalogues the description in detail."

"In this case, tell that old fart Orrell he'd better let us bug Reid Electronics—or find us something else to do!"

*   *   *

It was a DC–3, an old Dakota, in desert camouflage, still and broken. The starboard wing was cracked like a broken arm. A gouge in the red earth of the Bush stretched behind the wreck, stenciled by a line of broken trees and spread-eagled bushes. The crash was recent. A thin, last skein of oily smoke rose from the port engine.

Richard Anderson slowed the Land Rover some sixty yards from the dead airplane, on the crest of a dunelike rise, and leaned his forearms on the steering wheel, studying the Dakota. He was prompted by no sense of possible survivors, certain that the crew was dead. His beard scratched his neck as he repeatedly shook his head. He could picture the plane's interior vividly, ribbed, skeletal, half-made-up. Birds climbed into the heat of the early morning, and his arms were reddened by the sun rising behind him, throwing the bulky shadow of the Land Rover and himself down the slope toward the wrecked Dakota. There was dust on the fuselage, dulling the glint of metal and glass. Eagles and their prey, hunters and songbirds, moved above him. He heard the noises of wings and throats as the shock of his discovery became tangible. Why had the plane crashed out here? There had been no storm the previous night in Windhoek. The old aircraft lay as if beached by some great wave on the reddish, sandy soil. He could smell the slow, safe leakage of aviation fuel on the hardly stirring morning air.

From the vantage of the rise, he could see for miles in every direction. He was alone in that part of the Bush. The gouge that the plane had excavated pointed west, toward the coast and Walvis Bay. Curiosity finally itched in his frame, and he put the Land Rover into gear and the vehicle bumped and heaved itself down the shallow slope. The blue flash of a lizard crossed his path and disappeared. A long, dappled neck swerved away from the far side of the DC–3, then the giraffe glided into view, only half-startled, loping away with an easy stride. He passed dry, baked, gray trees.

A white blob that was an expressionless face hung as if thrust against the pilot's side window, staring blindly down at him through the dust-smeared perspex. There was a dark stain across the man's cheek, from his ear. He was alone . . . ?

The Dakota's camouflage paint might have been military, but the fuselage carried no insignia or company logo. Where had it been heading, then? It was at least a hundred miles off-course if it was flying from Walvis Bay to anywhere in South Africa, carrying whatever freight. Black hair draped stickily across the broad forehead of the dead face in the cockpit.

Anderson climbed out of the Land Rover, muscles creaking. His right hand stroked along the fuselage. Dust on his fingers. He moved to the starboard engine. The pool of leaking aviation fuel was still wet. The aircraft must have crashed just before dawn, little more than an hour earlier. He studied the sky with a movement as involuntary as a nervous tic. Empty. Cautiously, he moved around the silent plane until he reached the main cabin door, which had lurched open during the crash. He gripped the door frame with both hands and pulled himself into the hold. No one. Only boxes and crates emerged from the gloom as his eyes adjusted to the blackness of the interior. Stenciled lettering on the lashed-down cargo, even torn labels. As he remained poised in the doorway, the silence of the hold seemed more oppressive than that of the Bush around the wreck, as if a great charge of electricity had been left unearthed. The hair on his forearms and neck prickled with it.

A lizard, already intruding, scuttled away from his boots as he moved forward toward the cockpit door.

His hand hesitated on the handle. Scraped-away words and instructions on the metal, in Afrikaans and English. Military? Carefully, he pushed open the door and ducked into the narrow cockpit.

There were two of them, he realized, flinching against the mass of flies that rose from the bodies, then settled slowly again to feed. The pilot's face was pressed against the side window while the co-pilot's body was folded over its seatbelt like an abandoned ventriloquist's dummy. His head was down, his neck resting on the cup of the control column's wheellike grips; a man waiting for some imagined guillotine blade's descent. The flies were congregated around the mouths and noses and ears of the two men, making the streaks of blood black and viscous. He studied the invested faces, and the almost identical clothes on the bodies. Sandy-colored bush jackets, pale corduroy trousers on the pilot, grubby cotton slacks on the other man. Not military, then. He leaned forward, his hand hesitating above the co-pilot's bush jacket. Flies drifted toward him, inspecting the perspiration on his forehead and beneath his arms. It was many years since he had seen any dead body other than that of the occasional elephant poacher shot by the patrols. Swallowing, he patted the pockets. A small bulk in the co-pilot's back pocket. He raised the body, growling as if to keep the flies at bay, and removed a scuffed, misshapen leather wallet. Then, with the flies and the smell of blood slowly nauseating him, he searched the pilot's body. Nothing. Strangely, nothing at all; no identification.

Growling again at the flies, he flailed his arms at them and slammed the cockpit door behind him. If the clock on the instrument panel had been stopped by the impact, the Dakota had crashed no more than forty minutes earlier. The flies that had accompanied him slowly dispersed. It was hotter in the hold, now. Nothing on the instrument panel had appeared to explain the cause of the crash. A dry breeze puffed and threw dust in through the cabin door.

He knelt on the floor of the hold beside a crate stenciled in English. A name and a company logo had been all but obscured with a smear of black paint. In the light from the open door, he opened the wallet. Namibian currency, some high-denomination rand notes. A snapshot and a piece of folded card. A photograph of a young woman holding a baby in her arms, with the drab, wide desolation of some city square behind her. He turned over the snapshot. The woman's name, that of the child, and the place and date, all recorded in a flourishing hand. Church towers, he had noticed, onion-domed in the distance behind the woman. NOVGOROD, 1989. The snapshot quivered in his hand. The piece of folded card was red. The co-pilot's photograph and name, the same as that of the woman. A sort of passport, or warrant card. He understood Russian. He'd seen such things before. It was a KGB warrant card.

The legend on the crate nearest him was distinct enough to recognize. REID ELECTRONICS GROUP, PLC. UNITED KINGDOM. His eyes glanced from the snapshot to the KGB identification, to the crate—snapshot, card, crate—

The pilot, presumably, had been intent upon concealing his identity. Was he South African? The Russian had not wanted to leave his wallet or his wife's image behind, or his official identity. *Novgorod, 1989. Reid Electronics, United Kingdom.* He stood up stiffly and quickly, thrusting the card and snapshot into the wallet and the wallet into his back pocket. He was seized, momentarily, by a desire to escape from the hold, to leave the place; only slowly did he understand the resurrection of old impulses, old instincts, as if his present self had been elbowed roughly aside by the younger, trained person he had once been. He was sweating again and could hear his heartbeat in the silence of the hold.

He calmed himself gradually, breathing deeply. The crate had been loosened from its restraints by the impact, had moved and become damaged. It contained television sets, the crate claimed. Color televisions. Other crates contained microwave ovens, others portable hi-fi sets . . . ridiculous to find a mystery here. He glanced at the cockpit door. A KGB guard for microwaves, televisions? He pulled at a long splinter of wood on the damaged crate, then another, exposing—

Not television sets. What, he was not certain. He snatched the emergency axe from its clips on the fuselage, and chopped crudely. The wood splintered, came away.

Stout polyethylene and polystyrene chips protecting the contents. Their unfamiliarity, as he tugged and ripped open one package, disappointed him. Transistorized units, a tiny personal computerlike keypad. Another package—something like a transceiver. INFRA-RED, he caught on one package. His younger self urged him. He snatched up packages wrapped in bubbly polyethylene or in cardboard. He did not know what they contained, only that they were—

—proof. Of something untoward. The temperature was becoming unbearable in the hold of the Dakota. His present, fifty-three-year-old self attempted to protest, *this is simply a crashed old aircraft filled with civilian freight,* but he was aware of the bulge the Russian's wallet made in his back pocket. Ridiculous, this, he told himself as he carried the armful of packages to the Land Rover, his frame slightly stunned from the small jump from the hold onto the reddish, sandy soil. He flung the packages into the back of the vehicle and whirled round giddily. Hot. An eagle soared, but the sky was otherwise empty. They would be looking for the aircraft.

He hurried back to the Dakota and climbed with a great effort into the hold. Stumbled forward to the cockpit door, hesitated, then opened it onto the ascending cloud of flies. He searched the pockets of the doors, the nets above the dead men, the shelf beneath the instrument panel—nothing. No flight plan, nothing. Further proof. He looked balefully at the Russian, obscurely blaming the man for his panic. He swatted and flailed at the flies, then fled the cockpit and jumped down once more onto the sand, aware for the first time of the crowded scuffings of his footprints, of the tire tracks of the Land Rover leading down the rise to the Dakota. He brushed his forehead, at a loss.

Soon they'd be here. The black dot in the sky was still an eagle or a vulture, not an enlarging aircraft or helicopter. A KGB officer as co-pilot for a civilian flight carrying freight without a flight plan. He had no idea what it meant, though he did know he was afraid, was panicked by what he had found. He shook his head like a wounded bull.

The dry breeze rattled hard dust against the flank of the Land Rover. He knew, despite the seductive attractions of panic and flight, that he must stay. He had to hide the vehicle and find a vantage point, and force himself to wait. Not for long . . . they'd be desperate to find what the Dakota contained. And he had to know who came looking for it. High technology disguised as televisions and microwaves. Deliberation and forethought. Disguise. A KGB officer in Namibia, dead in the cockpit of an old Dakota—

He breathed deeply.

The pale sky seemed to tremble with heat, like a piece of cloth moving in the breeze. Wipe out the tracks of the vehicle and his own footprints, and then hide. No, first go back and replace the axe in its clips, wipe the edge of the blade free of wood chippings. Make the damage to the boxes and crates—so much of

it and unnecessary, it seemed now—look as if it was
the result of the impact. After *that*, hide.

"Sit down, Godwin."

The view from Sir Clive Orrell's spacious offices
as Director General of SIS looked out over the river,
and always seemed, once he had begun a conversation in his habitual, blunt, authoritarian way, to
deliberately face in the other direction from the
Palace of Westminster. The offices were aerielike.
Christ, I'm beginning to sound like Duncan Campbell
or *The Guardian*, he realized. On the other hand,
Hyde had once called this place Berchtesgarten-over-
Thames, though only after Orrell had taken up residence as DG.

Orrell gestured to a chair drawn up in front of his
massive mahogany desk, then wandered briefly to the
window. A pigeon looked, in the hot morning light,
more than usually supplicatory. Perhaps it was used to
Orrell's lack of open-handedness. Know how you feel,
son. Aubrey had handed them back to SIS and Orrell's
control when he went off ill; but Aubrey had resigned
all real interest in the investigation when they'd been
unable to find anything suspicious in February, when
they'd gone through Reid Group like bloodhounds.
Orrell, too, was about to renege on any interest he'd
ever shown. Pilate-soap, the scent of the season.

"Thank you, sir," he murmured obsequiously.
Orrell never wearied of deference.

Godwin glimpsed his report to Orrell on the desk,
together with one headed Grosvenor Square and with
the CIA symbol in the corner. Not a promising sight.

He placed his crutches behind the chair and
lumped himself down into its squeaky protest. Leather,
like the furniture of the entire office, as if Orrell had
once seen some televised drama of Whitchall life and

specifically noted only the appointments and furniture the sets had displayed.

"You wanted to see me, sir?"

Orrell, apparently irritated by the importunate pigeon, turned from the window and walked to his desk.

"Yes, Godwin—simply to tell you that I have"—he tapped at the sheaf of papers on his desk—"a full report from Grosvenor Square regarding the suicide of that man Shapiro, and on the basis of this report, I'm . . . about to stand down your unit." Without even looking at Godwin, he held up his hand for continued silence as he patrolled the wall behind his desk where the obligatory portrait of the monarch looked rather glumly at the print to its right, apparently disapproving of the arrangement of dead pheasants and fruit, though that was as improbable as Orrell's taste in art. "It is my decision, Godwin, and not taken lightly"—or inadvisedly, sir, like marriage with the CIA?—"indeed, taken after the most careful consideration and advice." He paused at the window once more. The pigeon was persistent in its puzzlement and pecked at the glass, slightly startling Orrell in his dark suit and ample bulk, outlined against the hot blue sky. "I think you have— with the utmost care and diligence, of course—taken this matter as far as is possible."

Godwin thought of Shelley, to whom Aubrey had originally handed him and Hyde and Chambers. Shelley had been immediately sidelined on some high-sounding European security service amalgamation in Berlin. Orrell, recognizing Shelley as Aubrey's acolyte, had, he thought, avoided being stabbed by posting Shelley back into Europe. After that, it was evident that the wind of skepticism—or the limp breeze of all-eyes-on-the-pension and the GCMG—was blowing through SIS.

Orrell was a caretaker—or care-avoider, depending on how you looked at it—a gentleman-in-waiting until the Cabinet Secretary got round to deciding the future shape and purpose of the service. Still, pompous old sod, the Yanks liked him. He was even more stupid than *their* Director.

"I see, sir. You've, er, read my report on the death of Mr. Kellett, the man we had inside—"

"The employee you suborned—to no good purpose, as it turns out." Orrell glowered. "A drug addict with a ridiculously expensive lifestyle! You have wasted thousands of the service's funds on that worthless little man, just to have him overdose on you!"

"Yes, sir." It was hopeless, as he knew it would be. Orrell wouldn't feel the shock of the new or unexpected if it hit him between the eyes, like a garden rake he'd absentmindedly stepped on. He removed the beginnings of the smirk from his face.

"You must admit, Godwin, that this pernicious and wrongheaded crusade of yours against the Reid Electronics Group and its associated companies has now come to a halt. That it has run out of fuel. This man Shapiro has evidently been hounded to the point of suicide by the heavy-handed methods of the Americans, which you seem so much to admire. Thus, the service is left with one suicide, one drug overdose, and your unwarranted suspicions that the Russians must be up to something big because they're murdering half the population of the capital!" The rhetorical flourish was evidently one he had rehearsed, he seemed so delighted with it.

"No, sir—"

Orrell turned to face him.

"The CIA is admitting they are at a dead end, Godwin—*you* are not. Why, pray?"

Surprising Orrell and himself, Godwin yawned. "Sorry, sir—sleeping badly."

Orrell nodded his acceptance of the fiction.

"I have talked with the Foreign Office and with the DS, and I have come to the conclusion that I have no choice but to desist from wasting the service's funding on this operation. It is stood down from this moment in time."

"Sir—!" Godwin pleaded.

It was the tone that Orrell seemed to have been awaiting, and he burst out righteously: "You exhausted Kenneth Aubrey's patience and probably his health, and now you seem determined to exhaust mine! Godwin, this business is becoming an obsession with you. The Malan group of companies has withdrawn from Reid, entirely. There is no, repeat *no*, connection even hinted at between the Russians and the Reid Group. Your own theories become more bizarre the moment they are confronted by any facts. Now we have two so-called murders on the same day to support your continuing this farce! It will not do, Godwin—it simply will no longer *do*." He waved a hand in Godwin's vague direction. "That's all I have to say. You would appear to have a few days' leave due—I suggest you take them and report to your section head at the beginning of next week. I commend your diligence, and deplore your lack of rationality. Goodbye, Godwin."

"Goodbye, sir."

He collected his crutches and stumped across the acres of carpet to the door. The pigeon had already departed. Presumably, it had witnessed Orrell rehearsing his outrage before Godwin's arrival. Godwin heard Orrell squeak into his leather chair and then the rustle of papers and their deposition in one of the desk's drawers. End of story. His last six months' work. Christ, was it really *easier* to believe that the KGB had suddenly become neater and cleaner than the Mormons?

He avoided all eye-contact with Orrell's secretary

and the young aide who leaned over her desk, long hair
flopping, rugby club tie bristling. More prop forwards
in SIS than a British Lions touring party, Hyde claimed.
Adding that all rugby players were closet faggots, just
by way of a variation of prejudice. Lady Orrell evidently hadn't yet inspected the new secretary, who was
good-looking, a class act. Dumb as a Swiss finishing
school could make her, of course.

He reached the corridor and even the lift before his
face collapsed into anger. He realized he was sweating.
His tie seemed about to throttle him, his shirt as enclos-
ing as armour.

Give it up? Sod *you*, sir!

2

THE ISLE IS FULL
OF NOISES

The sun was high now, no longer dust-tinged a nightmarish red as it had been at dawn when he had discovered the DC–3. The dust hung in the distance, like a horizon, solid-seeming as a range of distant, hazy hills. In the nearer distance, zebra and gazelle and wildebeest were no more than moving specks; much less real than the crashed aircraft and the tiny figures moving around it.

Anderson looked down from the branches of an acacia tree, once more refining the focus of the binoculars. He was already certain of their leader's identity, but just to make sure—

The man's face jumped into clarity, half-shadowed by the port wing. A strong, square face, clean shaven; a man of about forty. Dark glasses hid his eyes, but he had seen their remote, hard paleness on previous occasions. A thick neck, broad shoulders. An unquestioning, confident set to the body, even though it was relaxed and unmoving. The mouth and jaw were marked with a similar confidence, and it was not too fanciful to recognize them as the stigmata of a violent past.

It was Blantyre. Colonel Robin Blantyre, ex-Rhodesian Selous Scout, ex-South African Reconnaissance Commando—now, what was he? An employee of Malan-Labuschagne, who controlled the Walvis Bay area and its trade and minerals, or simply an ex-soldier who had stayed on in independent Namibia because he loved the peace of the Bush and leading an anti-poaching unit made up of identical veterans? Blantyre had been—was still?—both. He was also the veteran of two dozen raids into Angola, Mozambique, Zimbabwe and Zambia; the glamorous, fêted, bemedaled, dangerous Robin Blantyre.

Recognition had shaken Anderson in his perch high in the acacia like a sudden wind buffeting through the branches and the concealing leaves. Blantyre's presence there was charged with meaning—and danger. No mere accident had brought him to the crash site in answer to the scout plane's signal as it had buzzed over less than half an hour after he had concealed the Land Rover. It was in a dry waterhole amid sparse, stiff grass taller than himself. The crate he had broken open lay on the sand, where they had thrown it from the hold, together with the damaged boxes from which he had also removed evidence. Of what? Novgorod, 1989, and a KGB pass . . .

Anderson shivered. Blantyre knew him, probably knew who he had once been. They wouldn't believe he was a . . . naturalist, he had decided. Watching the game from the acacia. Slightly eccentric, well-meaning, harmless. He lifted the binoculars quickly and Blantyre seemed to be looking across the sand and the small teats of the dunes toward the tree and him. His growing unease during the hours he had been alone in the Bush, waiting, was now usurped by a chilly fear.

Blantyre had killed more people, in all likelihood, than he himself had; and Blantyre's killing was more recent. Suddenly, it was as if a leopard dozed at the foot of the acacia, cutting off all escape.

The two American XR 311 scout cars, the barrels of their machine guns pointing skyward like salutes, were parked close to the wreck's cold shadow. Blantyre was addressing the four men of his unit, his arm sweeping, pausing, pointing, making a grid of the landscape. They'd already searched the area of the wreck for tracks and signs. Blantyre knew—he was certain of it—that someone had visited the wreck, and broken open the crate and the boxes. His only problem would be deciding the damage was either happenstance or design. They had reacted quickly and expertly not to the wreck itself, but to the intrusion into the cargo. Theirs were the instincts of wild animals.

He leaned back against the bole of the tree, his feet planted firmly on two thick branches. He could not be seen, could not . . . He inhaled and exhaled slowly, rhythmically. The small breeze rustled the dark leaves. The five men who had arrived fifteen minutes earlier were, doubtless, South African Defense Force commandos in the thinnest of guises. He sipped water from a plastic bottle. Warm. The telephoto lens of his camera rested in the crook of his arm, the body of the camera against his hip. Despite the scream that seemed to louden and deafen in the back of his mind as he had worked, he had still photographed the interior of the Dakota, before wiping out his tracks and those of the vehicle.

To leave a darker stirring of the red sand. No detail, but nevertheless the certainty of some kind of instrusion. An armful of contents from the crate and boxes were stowed in the back of the Land Rover, and now he had Blantyre and the others on film. He had the Russian's snapshot and ID card. There was nothing else. He could leave.

He looked down at the foot of the tree. The grass and sand there had the dappled coat of a leopard or a cheetah, and he felt unnerved. He could climb down now, walk back to the vehicle, start the engine, head north back toward Etosha. Home. Contact someone . . . anyone.

The unit spread out with the suddenness of stones setting off an avalanche. The four men, two to a vehicle, started engines, manned the machine guns, spread out in a billowing cloud of dust, accelerating away from the epicentre of the Dakota. Now, he must stay. He felt cold, then hot. The two scout cars moved away from the wreckage, riding the terrain like insects skittering, throwing up clouds of dust. If he tried to use the Land Rover now, they would find him. He raised the binoculars with reluctance. A zebra dashed ahead of one of the scout cars as it circled toward the water hole where he had hidden the vehicle. Gazelle were distantly startled into motion by the other scout car.

He forced his attention back to the DC–3, picking up Blantyre sitting beneath the shade offered by the port wing. Cigarette smoke hung in the air. Blantyre had instructed them to discover any sign of the intruder. The dry water hole was a convenient focus. And, heightened as his senses were by tension, Anderson caught the distant, insect drone of aircraft engines, from the west. Events had long overtaken him, he realized, cursing the stupidity of that younger, reckless self that had prompted him to linger as if he could *do* anything! The dust rose above the dry water hole from the swinging curve in which the animallike scout car approached it. The flash of an elephant's gray bulk lumbering through the tall, dry grass.

Through the glasses, he ensured that the scout car halted and its crew of two descended from it. The still-invisible aircraft droned slowly closer. He was moving more quickly than any of them now, as he slid and tumbled through the branches of the tree like a small monkey. Then he dropped the last few feet to the ground from the lowest branch, scored by leopard's claws. His breath vanished for a moment, and he stood like a half-started sprinter, on fingers and toes, recovering it. The binoculars and camera dangled from their straps around his neck.

Then he cautiously stood upright. The Dakota was out of sight in a small fold in the land. The water hole was closest, and he should, in all innocence, return to his vehicle rather than head toward the wreckage. He began walking.

Naturalist, naturalist, naturalist—to explain the camera and the glasses. Blantyre knew him, thought him eccentric, all but despised him as a *royneek,* English. And living with—*married* to—a half-caste, a Namibian *Colored.*

Perhaps the sum of all those little contempts and dislikes would render him harmless in Blantyre's eyes. He reached the crest of the dune that sheltered the dry water hole, and found them inspecting the Land Rover, looking in the glove compartment, the door pockets, one of them unfolding a map as if to shake sand from it, then inspecting it for marks, incriminations, intent.

He stood on the crest for a moment, watching them, calming his body, sensing and measuring the perspiration beneath his arms, across his brow, timing his breathing. Then he began to move carefully down the slope, a lizard sliding out of his path across the tiny avalanche of disturbed sand. One of the two, a corporal by the uniform bush shirt he still wore, whirled round, hearing him.

He was squinted at by both men, neither of whom had produced a pistol, then the corporal removed his stained bush hat, revealing a line of white skin like a bandage between his ruddy tan and his dark hair. His face abandoned alertness, inquisitiveness. Just a middle-aged white bloke, a lot of them in the Bush. It was as if he had spoken. Then he did say: "You saw us coming? Heard us, man?" The accent was Afrikaans. Undeniably the corporal had been SADF—might still be, for all Anderson knew. Who knew what the South Africans were up to in Namibia? Certainly, Malan-Labuschagne Consolidated, still operating in that Exclusion Zone along the coast from Walvis Bay to Oranjemund, used none but ex- or current SADF personnel for security duty. "Eh, man? What you doing out here? You see the crash?"

He shook his head. "It must have happened before dawn. I've seen the wreck, though—through the glasses." He patted the binoculars on his chest. "I was about to—"

It was as if they had heard nothing of his careful alibi, his tone of voice, his innocence.

"You been over to that crash, man? Take a look around, maybe?" the corporal enquired, scratching his beard, his eyes alert amid their tiny lines and wrinkles. There was a quick, experienced cunning in his expression. "Why're you out here, man, and not on the road—uh?"

"Anti-poaching patrol?" Anderson asked as casually as he could, stilling a small tremor that had begun in his left leg.

"Maybe. You?"

"As you see, watching the local wildlife—" He patted his camera, still slung across his chest. "Taking a few photographs. You seem to have scattered most of the game, however." He was conscious of the Englishness of his voice and syntax; another mask.

"Did we? A pity that, man," the second soldier commented. The corporal grinned, shading his eyes with his bush hat.

The second soldier had climbed back into the scout car, and his fingers were tapping a disbelieving rhythm on the steering wheel. Or perhaps simple, dismissive impatience. A small group of zebra shuffled and browsed beneath trees some hundreds of yards away. Anderson attempted to concentrate upon them, slowly raising the glasses. The aircraft was visible now, moving in a wide circle. He tossed his head and asked: "Looking for you?"

"Interested? What are you doing way out here, man? Apart from taking pictures? Where are you from, Englishman?"

"Okaukuejo—in the Etosha. The game lodge. I run it."

"What's your name?"

"Anderson—Richard Anderson."

The corporal was silent for a moment, then nodded.

"Heard the name. You're from Jo'burg—a few years back?"

A breeze chilled against Anderson's drying shirt.

"That's right. And you're from the Transvaal, too, by the sound of your voice?"

"Maybe. Our colonel—he's back at the crash— would like to talk to you. Anyone we find, he said."

"You have authority? From whom?" The effort at normality, at being *white* as much as innocent, was wearing; to think himself back into South-West Africa, to forget the recent independence of Namibia. These men didn't have the minds to admit change. And they believed—since he was all they had found— he must have visited the crash site. "Doesn't matter. I have the time. I'll talk to your colonel, even though I didn't see what happened—and I haven't been near the wreck. Saw it through the glasses only some minutes ago—"

"Ag, man, the colonel isn't going to bite you!" the corporal said roughly. The suspicion in his eyes had been damped down by Anderson's innocuousness, his comfortable middle-age; hard though the latter was to admit. "Come on, then."

The corporal glanced up at the circling, dropping aircraft, a smallish two-engine passenger plane. Anderson watched it, too, as it levelled and seemed on its final approach. Smoke rose, presumably a flare to indicate the direction of the breeze, from where the Dakota must lie. It bent like the beginning of a question mark. Then the corporal climbed up beside the driver of the scout car, indicating that Anderson should start up the Land Rover. The aircraft dropped behind low dunes, out of sight. Come to collect the cargo and the two bodies. He started his engine, feeling the perspiration of relief and anticipated tension cover his body. Dark stains on his shirt. His forearms quivered as he gripped the steering wheel and followed the scout car slowly, lurchingly out of the hollow of the water hole. Over the lip, he fell into convoy behind the XR 311, to its left to avoid the dust its fat, low tires churned up. The machine gun mounted on the vehicle was hypnotic, despite its being pointed at the empty sky.

The acacia rose over the Bush like an accusation. He should never have stayed. They hadn't, it appeared, searched the Land Rover—but what he had taken was hidden in the tool box and the film in his camera was betraying. . . . They can't *develop* it out here, you bloody fool! he told himself. The corporal was none too bright, taken in by appearances. Knew only what he was and had recently been, not his more distant past.

The Land Rover bumped down the shallow rise toward the Dakota. The two bodies were lying near Blantyre's feet, in the shade, tidily and like a premonition. The small aircraft had come to a halt, the dust of its touchdown settling slowly. It bore civilian markings. Along its flank, disturbingly, Anderson read the acronym, MLC. The aircraft was from Walvis Bay. He attempted to prepare his features with an expression of confusion, mystification. The small plane sat innocently on a flat stretch of sand. Blantyre had risen to his feet and was standing with his hands on his hips, intently watching the approaching Land Rover. He was beside the open cargo door of the DC-3, as if indicating the evidence of a crime to its perpetrator. Anderson drew to a halt beside the Rhodesian.

"What's this, Corporal Uys? Where did you find this man?" His voice was clipped and precise, quiet.

Uys nodded behind him as he climbed from the scout car.

"Dry waterhole over there, Colonel." Uys moved close to Blantyre and began speaking rapidly in Afrikaans. Anderson assumed a look of incomprehension, of attentive bemusement, under Blantyre's casual scrutiny. He felt hotter, the Bush seemed no larger than a box, a cell, the midwinter heat oppressive and confining.

When Uys had finished speaking, Blantyre nodded and approached the Land Rover, holding out a large hand, a smile disarmingly exhibited, his dark glasses removed. His eyes were crinkled against the sunlight with skeptical intensity.

"Good morning, Colonel," Anderson greeted him, taking the man's firm grip. Where his hand had rested on his shorts, there was a faint smudge of nervous perspiration.

"Mr. Anderson. You're a long way from Etosha— a long way south." Blantyre put his hands back on his hips, continuing to squint much as a bird of prey might have done into shadows and thin cover.

"Back from a trip to Windhoek. I left early this—I presume this happened before dawn. I saw no sign, heard nothing. Sorry I can't be of more help."

"Watching the game, Uys says?"

"Yes."

"I'd heard it preoccupied you, Mr. Anderson. Lately. You don't like people or something?"

He shrugged. There was the faintest scent of contempt in Blantyre's voice, like the afterodor of a meal he had eaten; a halitosis of arrogance and invulnerability. It assisted his heartbeat to calm, his sweat to dry.

"No, not many of them. Perhaps I've been unfortunate in those I've had to deal with."

The small aircraft was one of the Riley adaptations of a Cessna model that the South African Defence Forces had favored for years when engaged in border surveillance, or crossborder intrusions against Frelimo and SWAPO. Twin Avro Lycoming engines, advanced avionics. Something in him continued to compile the report, despite his tension—no, his fear, at being confronted with Blantyre.

"What brought it down? Who were they?"

"One of our regular supply flights spotted the wreckage from the air. They must have—as you said— come down before dawn. No emergency call, nothing." He nodded at the bodies. "They were killed in the crash. Must have been making for Windhoek. It'll have been established by now." He looked at his watch. "Public relations, Mr. Anderson. It looks good for us if MLC flies the bodies out."

"You work for MLC at Walvis Bay now, Colonel? A little tame for you, I should have—"

"Sometimes." Blantyre was suspicious but not dismissive of the vague obsequiousness of his tone. The man liked being thought of as a hero; thought of himself that way, too, perhaps. A tinge of contempt in Anderson's mouth, strangely exhilarating. "You must know what it's like, Mr. Anderson, even after wars like yours, I mean?"

He smiled, shaking his head. "That was too long ago. I've forgotten—"

"Why don't you get down, Mr. Anderson? I'm getting a pain in the neck looking up at you." He heard Uys laughing as he climbed slowly out of the Land Rover. "That's better."

They were almost of the same height. It was, he admitted, like looking at an old photograph of himself. Blantyre seemed to recognize something latent in him. He hoped not.

Blantyre's touch on the skin of his arm was cool, light. He guided him away from where the pilot of the Cessna and two other men, working silently and methodically and without instruction, had begun unloading the cargo from the Dakota. Blantyre was smiling, relaxed. Uys began talking in Afrikaans behind them and Anderson was careful not to tense at the sound of his name and the disparaging description from the corporal. *Old royeek fart, married to a Bantu, living up north like a fucking hermit.* The obligatory expectoration by way of emphasis and dismissal.

"You know me, Mr. Anderson, and I know you. You were still practicing law in Jo'burg until a few years ago. You were out here before the—elections, and stayed on, or came back. Married, I heard?"

"I am. She's half German, half Herero, and her name is Margarethe. I'm very lucky. Of course, I could even live in the Republic with her now, but I don't have any desire to go back."

"Why not? Smoke?" Anderson shook his head. A battered American cigarette lighter appeared, its cap clicked open noisily, its flame smelling of lighter fuel, not butane. A beer advertised dimly on its scratched, dulled side as Blantyre showed it to him, smiling. "I found it years ago. Its previous owner didn't have any further use for it. Why don't you go back, then?"

"People. I prefer it here, as you surmised."

"Don't your liberal friends miss you? Not to mention all the Bantus who used to be on your list of clients—eh, man?"

"They could all pay, Colonel." He turned from Blantyre's scrutiny toward the XR 311 which, loaded with crates and boxes, was dragging a curtain of dust behind it out to the Cessna. Blantyre's cigarette smoke was acrid around him. Distant zebra. The glare of the sun on salt pans, insubstantial undulations in the far distance, beyond which lay the Namib and the coast—and Walvis Bay and MLC; South Africa's private enclave sealed off from the remainder of Namibia; the naval base and the factories and the secrets. "They could all pay."

"A lot of your liberal friends—they liked humping the black dollies, I hear? You defended a few of them."

"Yes. Before they scrapped those stupid laws and the Immorality Act."

"You defended white women who had the hots for what the kaffirs keep in their ragged-assed trousers, too?"

"Yes. One or two."

Blantyre laughed, loudly, slapping him across the shoulders. "No wonder you left, man! Who needs friends like that, eh?" He continued laughing, then said quickly: "And you ended up marrying a Bantu yourself?"

He nodded slowly. "Yes. I'm happy to be able to report that I did."

"No offense, man. But when pressure from people like you got rid of the pass laws and the immorality laws—uh, the end of civilization! A lot of people didn't like you, back home."

"I was aware of the fact." He realized that the slightly formal, rather prissy image of an English solicitor was good cover; his liberal ideals concealing him within Blantyre's bigotry.

"No offense, man."

They stood together at the top of the rise. The bodies had been zipped into long plastic bags. He shivered. He'd seen so many. SWAPO guerillas went into them, ivory poachers, black miners killed underground on the Reef because of carelessness or lack of safety precautions. He shook his head, then said: "I'd better be going. I shan't make Okaukuejo until midnight or later if I don't get off. You don't want me for anything, Colonel? I'm sorry I couldn't help."

"No, man. You get off. There's . . . no need to report this, yourself that is. It'll all have been done at the Bay, the paperwork. OK?"

"Thanks. A bother, having to give evidence to any investigation. Especially when one didn't see anything, anyway."

"Sure. Any tourists staying at the lodge right now?"

"One or two."

"I might drop by for a beer one of these days."

"I'll keep some cool, pending your arrival."

"You watch out for me, then, man—I'll be seeing you."

"Fine."

They had returned to his Land Rover. Anderson climbed in. Blantyre ground out his cigarette, shook Anderson's hand. By the dust that was approaching, it was obvious that the second scout car had been summoned back. Uys watched him with dim contempt. Blantyre's suspicions were allayed, if not dismissed.

He started the engine, waved, put the vehicle into gear and pulled away from the wrecked Dakota in a wide circle, raising as little dust as possible. He bumped up the rise and over it, dropping immediately out of sight of the wreck. He rounded a clump of thornbush and suddenly the shaking began; his mouth filled with sweet saliva. It was like some malarial attack. MLC was involved, through Blantyre, with a

KGB officer and with stolen technology from the UK. It was incredible, but Blantyre had forged the link, some kind of chain of conspiracy. Paulus Malan, he knew, had Russian links—gold and diamonds. Everyone in the Republic knew that. But this? What did it mean?

Damn stumbling on the wreck and damn even more the stupidity of old, unpracticed instincts that had made him hang around, just so that he might encounter Blantyre—who threatened to visit the game lodge. He must *do* something—

—and that something was to inform Aubrey. There was nothing for it but to fulfill those old instincts and contact the man who had helped him escape to South Africa in the first place. Why did he so willingly drift into memory? Aubrey was old now, but still empowered. Aubrey, who had accepted, even assisted, in Anderson's killing of a senior intelligence officer of his own service—his own superior. That had been after he had got back from East Germany, his fingernails pulled out by the KGB, his body exhausted and mind inflamed, having escaped from the imprisonment and torture his superior's betrayal of his network had visited on him. 1966. He had been a young man. Aubrey's man loaned to someone else, a double-agent. He had never been able to decide whether that had been Aubrey's purpose, to expose the double through him. He'd thrown the man from the third-floor window of his own flat, one dark night in November—and Aubrey had helped him flee.

Aubrey. Had to be. He must send him evidence of the things he had taken from the wrecked Dakota.

The Bush spread out silent and vast around him, devoid of life, it seemed. Isolated, he was a speck to be glimpsed by an eagle. He had to pass the information to Aubrey, then he could forget his past and return to the present.

*   *   *

"Look, there isn't going to be any sound of bugles!" Godwin snapped. "Pass the hoisin sauce—ta." His mouth full, he continued. "Look, Terry, I tried my *best!* No one wants to listen anymore—and Patrick's subject to a disciplinary inquiry over what happened in that pub. *If* we go any further, then we're on our own. It's definitely *unofficial.* It's a right fucking mess!"

Hyde opened another can of lager. Godwin's cat, Dubcek, was seated on his lap and he occasionally slipped it fragments of Szechuan beef. The cat seemed to appreciate its spiciness.

"I don't doubt you were rude to Orrell on top of everything else," Terry Chambers observed.

"Who could resist it?" Hyde replied, spooning more fried rice from its foil container onto his plate. "Have you had *all* that roast duck, Chambers?"

Godwin's kitchen table was littered with containers from the Chinese takeout in the next street, his small, untidy, unrenovated kitchen filled with the scents of the meal. Hyde looked up at Godwin.

"Well?" he asked. "What are we going to do? You've got a few days' leave, I could skip off, Chambers could go to his granny's funeral . . . " He smiled, as if taunting Godwin.

Godwin looked down at the table. Half a dozen cans of lager, emptied and on their sides, another dozen or more waiting. For most of the meal, nothing but the sound of their eating and, from Hyde's lap, the cat's purring. Their mutual resentment was almost comfortable, reassuring, characterizing them as victims, and therefore blameless. Godwin opened another can of lager for himself, then motioned it toward Chambers, who shook his head and swallowed from the can in front of him; and belched.

"Pig," Hyde murmured without malice or irritation.

"Are you going to get off this inquiry?" Godwin asked.

Hyde shrugged. "God knows. Depends who has it in for me at the moment and whether they're on the inquiry—or whether Orrell thinks it's fun to screw some of Aubrey's old workhands. Who knows? I'm not staying awake worrying about it."

"It's all been such a bloody waste of time," Chambers muttered.

"So you said—many, many times, sport," said Hyde. Then he looked up at Godwin and asked: "Why haven't you called Darren off the surveillance he's on?"

Godwin flushed and snapped back: "How do you know what he's doing?"

"He'd be here, otherwise—wouldn't he? Who's he watching—Malan?" Reluctantly, Godwin nodded. "Thought so."

"You'll drop a real ballock, Tony, if anyone finds out."

"I know that, Terry. Look, perhaps I didn't make out the best case to Orrell—"

"Who ever does?" Hyde asked. He thought a moment. "What's Malan been doing today, while we've been in the shit?"

"Business as usual. Just like yesterday and the day before," answered Godwin. He wiped his hands on his shirt and lumbered up from his seat. He passed Hyde a large buff envelope from the draining board of the sink. It was smeared with cat food. Empty tins and dirty dishes littered the draining board. "Have a look."

Enlargements, taken from a distance with a telescopic lens. Monochrome, paled by brilliant sunlight. Malan had been in London for the past two days, attending to the concerns of Malan-Labuschagne Consolidated and its European subsidiaries. He had been nowhere near any Reid Group company, nowhere near . . . oh, but he had been naughty, hadn't he!

Godwin was grinning as Hyde looked up, then passed the enlargements to Chambers.

"Where's Darren now?"

"Outside some theater in the West End. Malan's taking in a show. Remember when we first saw those snaps of him at the Bolshoi with the head of the Narodny bank years ago?" His voice sounded as if he were indulging some puntlike drift into sunlit memory.

"Why did he see Priabin? Where?" Chambers asked.

"Darren's scribbled on the back—what does it say?"

"Kensington Palace Gardens," Hyde said. Then he looked up at Godwin, a sliver of beef speared on his fork, his mouth filled with rice. "What's on your mind, Godwin?"

"I rang the limousine service Malan uses, this evening. Just to check, on Mr. Malan's behalf, what time it was booked for tomorrow, were they sure of the address. Tomorrow, at eleven, he's going to see MacPherson, CEO of Reid Group."

"And—?"

"Don't you see? If we had a bug in Reid, or we still had—"

"Kellett? He wouldn't have been invited to the meeting, would he?"

"Are you *really* thinking of an unofficial surveillance op?" Chambers asked dubiously, his eyes searching the littered kitchen as if for a bolthole.

"You've worried our Terence already," Hyde sneered. Then added: "And me. We're deep enough in the shit as it is, Godwin. You're getting paranoid about Malan and Priabin."

"I *know* something's going on, and we have to find out what it is!"

"Who's this *we?*" Hyde snorted. "Your bloody living room is littered with stuff. Any trick-cyclist given five minutes in there would have enough to have you put away. This business is eating you up, mate!"

"Doesn't the fact that the girl was there as well as Priabin even interest you—just a bit?"

"I can't do anything about that tart, Godwin. Look, we've been pissing about being SIS, DS, Special Branch, DTI inspectors, Customs and Excise—we don't even know who we are anymore or what we're really supposed to be doing!" Hyde chewed on a piece of dry-looking duck, crunching the peanuts that came as its dressing. He waved his fork in emphasis as Chambers nodded his agreement. "No one's bloody interested—I don't think *I* am anymore. This has been stuffed up a dead possum's bum for too long. It's a waste of bloody time. Why don't we just say sorry to Orrell and behave ourselves?"

"Look, just one surveillance, on the Reid offices in the NatWest Tower. There's an empty office across the street. We can use a van and the laser eavesdropper." He was red with desperation. "Look, if it doesn't work, and we come up empty, then we'll forget the whole thing—I'll just shut up about it. OK?"

The cat climbed from Hyde's lap onto the table and began sniffing Godwin's fingers, then his plate. Godwin absentmindedly stroked its back as it began eating his remaining prawns.

Hyde burst out laughing. "You're so involved with this, you can't see what's happening in front of your nose!"

"What? Oh." He shrugged and allowed the cat to continue its quiet, methodical assault. Then he once more looked up exasperated. "Well?" He pointed his fork like an angry baton. "Your bloody cynicism gets up my nose, Patrick—it really does! We're not talking about bags of bloody marbles or toffees here! These transputers and the WSI chips can go into *anything*—supercomputers the size of a vanity case, missile guidance systems, bomb detonators, satellites—it's *important!*" He ended almost apologetically, his features red again.

Chambers said: "Look, if we're caught, we'll really be in it—"

Hyde interrupted, studying his plate. "All right. Just tomorrow." He looked up and grinned. "Since it means so much to you. Darren's just about clever enough to keep his mouth shut—are you, Chambers?"

"Look, I might just have a career left in the service, unlike you two mad buggers. Tell me why I should risk it, if no one wants to know, anyway?"

Hyde clenched his fist slowly, but Godwin burst out: "It's supposed to be our *job,* Terry! Whether we're SIS, DS, or the Avon ladies, we're supposed to concern ourselves with the operations of foreign intelligence services on British soil. This *is,* in case you hadn't noticed, a foreign intelligence service operation."

Hyde pretended applause. "See?" he said to Chambers. "It's just somewhere to go in the morning, instead of staying in bed and growing your toenails." Godwin grinned in complicity. Hyde was hooked. A *mad bugger,* as Chambers had observed.

"After all, Terry," Godwin murmured. "We are assisting in the investigation of two murders. Can't get much more moral or patriotic than that, can you?"

Chambers snorted derisively.

"You'll get rice up your nose, doing that," Hyde remarked. Then he snapped at Godwin: "Can you get the stuff early tomorrow morning—on the q.v.?" Godwin nodded. "Right, let's do it, then." He paused. "Any more of that stir-fry veg left in the oven?"

A hundred yards from the main lodge, something moved through the Bush and unsettled him, though he guessed it must be a lion rather than a trained man. Stars pricked out softly and quickly, hanging like lamps against the velvet evening. The voices from the bar behind him seemed distant, his attention entirely focused on the darkness and what might emerge from it at any moment.

Only in Africa, peace. He'd read that line in a volume of third-rate poetry in a second-hand bookshop in Jo'burg years before, written by a Lutheran missionary a century ago, before the Bush had finally driven him mad. He had found that peaceful feeling out here, in Etosha with his wife, having sought its promise for years.

Blantyre and the DC–3's wreckage shook his thoughts like a rough hand waking him from a dreaming, satisfying sleep. Nerves jumped along his forearms, and he resented the sense of an old excitement that unsettled his stomach and made his whole frame itch with its new insistence. It was as if he had brought some ailment back with him from the crash site, something contagious. He had given up his legal practice for this place, this peace, picturing himself as a man able to grow old with diminishing regrets. A privileged hermit, Margarethe had called him. Or, ruthless in his enjoyment of peace.

Margarethe . . .

Anderson half-turned, sensing his wife reach his side, and put his arm around her shoulder. She held on to his body with her arms, resting her head against his shoulder.

"What is it, Richard?" she asked at once, as she registered his tension. She looked up at him, but he could not see the vivid blue eyes in the darkness, just the arrangement of facial bones beneath smooth skin that indicated her mixed parentage.

"I'm . . . going to have to find somewhere to hide . . . what I brought with me, yesterday." He squeezed her shoulders. Tenderness with her was always easy; he had grown used to it.

"But it is hidden—"

"Somewhere better. Blantyre is no fool, and he's dangerous."

"Couldn't you have left it there, then? Where you found it?" There was blame in her voice, but she did not release her grip on him. Her hands were cool through his shirt.

He shook his head. "No. It's important. To people I used to know in London. I'm sure it is. The Russian, especially."

"Important to you, too."

He shook his head with a vehemence composed of desire and denial. She moved away from him, then reached out and touched his beard, his mouth.

"I didn't think," he said. "I wish I had left it, I'm sorry."

"Richard, you are not the man you were—that was a long time ago. You must be careful, if he comes."

"He'll come. At least the letter's gone to London."

He reached out and stroked her hair, which she wore in long, tight ringlets, beaded and woven like rope. She held tightly to him.

"It happened," he murmured against her head. "I wasn't looking for it, didn't want—"

"It doesn't matter." Margarethe shivered, moving away from him again, rubbing her arms. "I will be glad when he has come, and gone." There was a trace of her father's German accent, amid the high, birdlike clicking of the Herero language she had inherited from her mother. There was hardly anything, when they spoke together, of the Anglicized, professional voice she employed as a visiting nurse. She waved her hand, as if warding off insects. "You are certain he will come, aren't you?"

"I don't think he really believed me. I wasn't practiced enough to fool him." He sighed. Her small, light frame seemed enlarged by his responsibility for her. "Look, it'll be all right, if we just keep up appearances." His hands took hold of her bare arms, which were chilly, goose-fleshed in the warm night. "Help me hide this stuff now."

"Where?"

"Down by the dam somewhere—maybe under the water?" he suggested. The urgency in his voice was a passable imitation of a former confidence. Margarethe, catching his tone, stared at him as if he had become a stranger. She shook her head.

"Be *careful*, Richard."

"Mm."

"Very well, down at the dam. I'll tell Joseph to attend to the bar, and check on the cook." Then she smiled vividly. "Would this Colonel Blantyre be expecting to see me wearing a goatskin frill on my head and smeared from head to foot in butter and ochre? Would that deceive him?"

Anderson laughed softly. "You're not afraid of him, are you?"

She shook her head. "Only for you." The braids of her hair moved across her face and shoulders. "Go and fetch the things you must hide. I'll speak to Joseph— hurry!"

There was a renewed outburst of laughter from the group of guests near the bar, and the noise struck against them as if in derision. He nodded to her, squeezing her upper arms, then she moved away as he released her. Anderson descended the three steps from the veranda that surrounded the main lodge, skirting the warmly lit restaurant and bar. Moonlight showed already on the thatched roofs of the line of guest huts down by the water hole, raised on stilts and platformed to support large tents. Night-lights glowed like faint planets through the canvas of the three closest tents. He heard the grumble of a lion some distance off, and farther still the muted bellow of an elephant; both noises startled him like sudden intruders. The Bush had constricted around his urgency, bringing everything, even Blantyre, closer.

He opened the door of the storeroom and groped for the heavy canvas bag without switching on the light. As he bent, he heard his muscles creak and the noise of his breathing. Blantyre was almost fifteen years his junior, and he was a killer.

He hefted the lumpy, murmurous bag onto his shoulder and relocked the storeroom, pausing in the darkness but hearing nothing but the laughter from the bar and the gabble of conversations mingling with the smell of cooking from the kitchen of a springbok he had shot earlier in the day. He walked slowly back toward the light from the restaurant as Margarethe came running lightly out of the glow. He called softly to her. She clutched his hand the moment she joined him.

"OK?" he asked.

"Yes."

They hurried down the moonlit path toward the faint sheen of placid water and the fuzzy globes of light shining through the canvas.

"What equipment is it—do you know? Won't the water damage it?"

"It's wrapped in polyethylene—I don't really know. Electrical equipment from a British company. But it's the Russian who was with it—who must have flown from Walvis Bay. That's what's wrong with it all. I don't think it should be here *or* in the Republic."

They reached the water. The evening exhilarated, the stars enlarged to soft blue, white and red globes, looming overhead. There was gentle, secret movement on the other side of the dam. Anderson breathed in deeply, as if he had come to the last moment of some extended holiday and was on the point of departure.

"Where?" Margarethe asked him.

They patrolled the edge of the water. Tall reeds, trampled, open stretches of sandy earth, stunted acacias.

"Here." He paused and unslung the canvas bag from his shoulder.

"What if the water should damage it?"

"The look of it will be enough—it doesn't have to work." He did feel elated, it was true, at the ease with which he could make himself and Margarethe innocent, above suspicion.

He gathered up some heavy stones, then knelt with the bag at the edge of the water. He submerged it gently, the bag disappearing in a bouquet of bubbles. Carefully, he lowered each of the stones on top of it. Disguise and anchor. The water was above his elbows. Reeds rubbed against his arms and shoulders. It would do—he flashed his flashlight. The settling sand masked the canvas bag. The stones appeared to be naturally there. The reeds hung over the water. It would do very well.

He looked up, startled as a drinking animal, at the noise of a vehicle approaching the game lodge, grinding and heaving up the rutted track. Headlights flared on the evening as if against a dark screen, bucking with the ground's undulations. Then the lights halted and the engine died, somewhere in the general glow from the lodge.

"Him?" Margarethe asked, gripping his arm with wet fingers. She had carefully, delicately rearranged two of the stones, then stirred up more sand that would settle on them and the bag.

"Quite likely. We're not expecting any other guests. Seems he's alone—only one vehicle."

"Then we should get back—"

He grabbed her arm in restraint.

"No," he warned. "We don't want to burst in on him like a couple of kids who've been caught at the jam. We'll circle around the lodge and come in from the opposite direction." He felt a quivering in her arm and pulled her against him, stroking her braided hair, his lips on her forehead. Her whole body was trembling. "It's all right, sweetheart," he soothed. "It's all right." He pressed her closer, kissing her. "Come on, all we need is a bit of nerve to get us through."

She swallowed and nodded vigorously. "Yes."

He dropped one arm and held her shoulders in the crook of the other, walking slowly as he clutched her against him. He wasn't afraid of Blantyre, not here, not now. Only afraid for her and already angry at the contempt Blantyre would display toward her. Yet there was, too, an old, familiar prickle of pleasure on his cheeks and lips, a recognized dryness at the back of his throat.

"I love you," he said. She pressed against him.

"This is just a game to you—I know that."

"I love you."

They climbed the slope, heading away from the lodge. He strained to hear but did not catch Blantyre's voice amid the renewed babble from the bar. Then, as they came to the head of the slope, he saw Blantyre standing at the bar, a glass of beer in one hand, his head moving slowly, methodically as he assessed each of the handful of guests—and seeming to look for him and Margarethe. She shivered against him, but only momentarily.

"That's him," he said unnecessarily, as they skirted the lodge in the darkness beyond its glow. "Leave the talking to me—and, remember that to him you're half-Bantu." He squeezed her against him as they turned back toward the lodge. "He'll be curious, he'll envy me your bed, but you won't be real." They separated as they climbed the steps to the long curve of the veranda. Blantyre saw them immediately.

Anderson ducked his head to avoid the low, thatched eaves. A bird rustled above him like a whispered caution. Blantyre was already coming toward him, hand extended, a smile on his large, square face. He studied Margarethe admiringly, much as he might have surveyed a prizewinning dog or farm animal. Anderson stilled his resentment. Yet she seemed exposed and vulnerable as she moved behind the bar—entirely his fault.

"Mr. Anderson. I told you I'd look you up . . . and the beer is cold. Thanks." He was at ease, grinning. "Nice billet you have here, man." His arm indicated the lodge before coming to rest on Anderson's shoulder; who steeled himself not to shrug instinctively against its pressure. Blantyre raised his glass and swallowed an ironic toast.

The other guests were evidently aware of his identity and reputation. There was an almost instant camaraderie with fame; they were obsequious and titillated.

"I'm glad you could come. Margarethe, this is Colonel Robin Blantyre. We're honored, my darling." Blantyre's eyes twitched as if to pounce upon sarcasm, but Anderson knew his expression was carefully arranged. "You must have heard of the colonel's reputation, darling." Again, suspicion was fended off by his practiced, legal blandness. Blantyre's esteem had impressed all of the guests, with the possible exception of the two elderly American ladies. The party up from Windhoek and the wildlife photographer from Port Elizabeth made Blantyre the center of gravity of the room, or the still, deep center of a small whirlpool.

Blantyre held out his hand and took Margarethe's fingers in his large grip. "Your husband told you how we met?"

She nodded, her strange blue eyes alert, the sharp angles of her face stretching the skin, masklike.

Blantyre turned. "Been out for an evening walk without a gun, Mr. Anderson?"

"A short step. There's not much out there likely to attack a man, Colonel. You know that."

Blantyre grinned, looking out into the darkness for a moment. "Maybe."

Conversation stuttered into life at the occupied tables as people settled for the evening meal and assumed that their host would monopolize the conversation of the dangerously glamorous Robin Blantyre. The two elderly Americans were listening as the wildlife photographer explained the newcomer's identity. Fascination spread like a pale, fungoid growth on each face as he spoke.

"Mm, that cooking smells good—you really do have something special here. I'm not surprised you left the law for it. Though how a man like you could have become a bloody solicitor beats me, eh, man?" He slapped Anderson's shoulder as if exposing some professional cover which had now been penetrated. Then he called to Margarethe: "You got a spare tent or room for tonight, Mrs. Anderson?"

"Just for one?" she asked coolly, exciting his admiration, reaching for the register.

"Just for one."

"One of the tents down at the water's edge, Colonel?" Anderson asked nonchalantly. It was like a remembered role in a renowned drama, not difficult to recapture. Careful—

"Fine."

Margarethe offered him the register and a pen, and he scrawled his name with an expected flourish, though the letters were surprisingly neat. She said, "You're attached to Walvis Bay, I gather from my husband, Colonel?"

"That's true, Mrs. Anderson, that's true. Then there's the ivory poaching patrols. We get called out on

those occasionally. Knowing the Bush as we do."
William the cook appeared from the kitchen and
caught her attention.

"Excuse me, Colonel."

"Of course." His courtesy was mocking.

As she walked away, Anderson announced to
Blantyre so that she could hear his voice, "My wife was
classified as Colored before such terms lost their meaning. I could have, through contacts in Pretoria, changed
that. She didn't want me to. We met when I came out
here on holiday."

"And stayed."

"Not at once. She came back to Jo'burg with me,
but she . . . " he smiled sardonically, "she didn't like
city life, not even in our liberal suburb. So we came
back here—to do this, in my advancing years."

"You're not that old, man." Blantyre seemed non-
plussed by intimacy.

Anderson could smell the barbecueing springbok
meat, and he looked toward the spit turning above the
fire. The scent of paraffin, too, and William and
Joseph's faces lit like those of hunted animals.
Margarethe was there, too, and he suddenly disliked
the imagery of hunt and pursuit and danger. His peace
waved like the distant flag of a lost cause in the sensu-
ous impression of the place at that moment.

The old past was breaking in: Blantyre was still
wearing his fixed and conditioned look of contempt for
Margarethe. Kaffir, black dolly, et cetera. Like the
neighbors in Jo'burg, on the hot, dry lawns moving in
their print frocks among their gardeners and maids,
struggling to forget that her hair was braided and her
face and arms were dark. They'd had to come back to
the Bush to avoid that, however apologetically handled
or avoided they were in the white suburb.

He gestured Blantyre to a table, then sat down
opposite him. William and Joseph, another cook, chat-

tered like nightbirds around the roasting meat. Margarethe consulted the orders for wine and beer at the bar, her face tightened in concentration, almost as if she were flinching against a premonition knocking at some invisible door. He smiled at Blantyre, who finished the last of his beer. This man is bad. Thoroughly bad, he reminded himself. Be careful . . .

"Well, well, look who's here!" Chambers announced breathlessly. "Right on time and right outside the NatWest Tower. Mr. Malan in his hired Roller—shit, here comes Michael Aspel with 'This Is Your Life!'" Chambers laughed at his own joke while Godwin shook his head.

"He's here, Patrick—are you ready yet?"

"Look, you'll have to be patient, the traffic down here is bloody awful!" Hyde's voice emerged from the transmitter sitting heavy and black on the folding table. "BMWs and Golf GTIs up to your eyeballs!"

The excitement was infectious—like a bloody school outing, Godwin observed. The morning sun glared beyond the tinted windows, against which a fly buzzed, as if decorating or weaving something around the barrel of the laser eavesdropper angled down toward the windows of the Reid Group offices. No one was alert to surveillance at that kind of oblique angle. The eavesdropper would have to be moved now that the window they had selected as their dry run had proved the equipment's veracity. *He took me to a wine bar—and then tried to climb into bed with me...a bloody wine bar!* And where Fiona and Sally were going for their holidays, and who with, and where they were meeting tonight and with whom, and that dishy man in sales. . . . Sleep-inducing, with hardly a prick of interest because they were unaware of being overheard. MacPherson's secretary and some other Sloaney girl.

The fly buzzed irritatingly on the windowsill. The windows were spotted and dusty on the outside. The office had been empty for some months, and he had been lucky to find it. Who would pay the bill for the month's rental, he could not imagine, and cared even less.

The venetian blinds on the focus window hung threateningly, as if they might collapse at any moment. If they did, then the eavesdropper couldn't pick up the infinitesimal vibrations of voices against the window's glass. *A wine bar dinner, and he even showed me the packet of condoms, to prove he was taking it seriously!* Godwin tossed his head. Chambers, peering down into their office, had admired the speaker's legs.

Which was the problem, though neither he nor Hyde had mentioned it—how close to the windows of MacPherson's office would Malan and whoever was with him be seated? They would need the group to be sitting as close to the windows as possible for the video and stills cameras to operate successfully. Most of MacPherson's smooth, rosewood desk was visible. He checked once more.

There was a breathing like ether from the transmitter, and the grunt of gears being changed. Godwin did not bother to peer out over the precipice of the windowsill to watch Hyde in the van that wore the necessary POLICE labeling, shuffling back and forth within its row of orange-and-white cones marking off its parking spot in Copthall Street below him. The van had to be precisely placed if the eavesdropper was to be exactly aligned with the receiver in the van, picking up the bounced laser signal and its collected aural vibrations.

"—think Mr. Kellett in Exports had AIDS?" he heard over the speaker.

A glimpse of printed cotton as a woman moved round MacPherson's desk.

"That's it, Patrick!" he shouted, flicking down the

transmit switch after lumbering across the room, intercepting Chambers. God, it was hot in this bloody office, the sun streaming in through windows that looked as if they were coated with nicotine.

"You don't drop dead from it," came the answer from the speaker, relaying someone's reply from the office via the van.

"Hold it there!"

"Are you sure?" Hyde asked.

"Hang on . . . "

"What about selling your flat, then? Any offers?"

"Yah, just one. But I think they're serious—people from the Midlands wanting a London base. Cheek—nothing *fancy,* they said, this will do! God, who are these people, no mortgage or anything?"

Silly cow.

"Patrick, that's fine. You can come up now—Darren can look after the equipment."

"Anyone want any lunch from round the corner—the yuppies' sandwich bar?"

"A Ploughman's with a French roll round it," Chambers called out. "Bring some beer, too."

"I'll have salad in a French stick," Godwin mumbled. The sense of company, of identity, was suspicious, and he disregarded it.

"I'll just write all that down, sir," he heard Hyde reply, then murmur something to Darren in the back of the van.

"Thank you, Sally," he heard the speaker linked to the equipment in the van blurt out. The movement-responsive camera clicked and the film wound on. He pressed the start button on the camcorder. A babbled murmur of greetings, assurances, welcomes, some laughter as trousered legs and MacPherson came into view through the lens of the still camera. Malan, presumably, someone else, and a woman's legs that didn't belong to the secretary. Even he'd taken that much notice, despite the monkishness induced—or suffered—because of his useless limbs. He watched the other legs walking and shuffling, then—

Malan, then another man—oh, yes—and then Patrick's nasty little female acquaintance from the pub. They'd managed to identify her as Valentina Malenkova, assistant Trade Attaché at the Soviet Embassy. What the bloody hell was she doing in the Reid offices? What fucking *nerve*.

Godwin checked the calibrating lights on the eaves-dropper's control box, made tiny adjustments, then switched on the backup tape recorder. Outside, the financial towers jutted out of an oily haze. MacPherson's Glasgow accent resonated, and then he distinguished Malan's accent. The second man was van Vuuren, CEO of MLC's EuroConstruct subsidiary, the company that built the Bucharest TravelLodge and dozens of other hotels and factories and sports centers and blocks of flats in Eastern Europe. Even undercutting the Japs with their quotes, so the story went.

It was proof, if proof were needed except for idiots, he thought, as MacPherson gestured his guests to a group of armchairs near the windows. Valentina—what the hell is a KGB agent doing with the CEO of Reid Electronics? *Oh, probably making the tea, Godwin,* no doubt would have been Sir Clive's reply!

From the speaker, pleasantries, mutual congratulation, expansion plans, common business concerns, the pace of orders and dates of supply. Then MacPherson coming bluntly to the point.

"Paulus—I know how hard you've been lobbying the board members you've been approaching, and I know they think you're right—*I* think you're right, for Christ's sake. But, I just have to tell you that we have to stay whiter than white—" A burst of laughter from Malan. "Sorry . . . but you know how careful David had to be in disposing of his own shares. We can't appear to be entering any joint ventures with MLC, and that's the end of it. Everyone's watching us—" Godwin smirked. "—just to catch us getting back into bed with you. I just can't do it."

The door opened behind Godwin. Then Hyde was beside him.

"What's Priabin's tart doing in there?" Hyde's curiosity was feral, angry. "Is MacPherson crooked, then?"

"I doubt it. He even refused to join the Masons twenty years ago, though his father was one. She's there as Malan's personal assistant, according to the introductions. They don't half give them good diction at the KGB school these days. She's even got a notebook on her lap."

"Talk about two fingers." Godwin heard the sound of a can being opened, then it was thrust into his grip. Then two other popping noises. Hyde flicked the pull tab against the window.

"Don't disturb the bloody machinery!" Godwin growled.

"Sorry, darling."

"Not that MacPherson won't do business with Malan if he can—he's doing plenty now—but he wants to keep his nose clean. Too many defense contracts won't come his way if he's seen to be sliding down the crocodile's throat."

Below, they laughed and the girl scribbled something in her notebook. Polished as a Swiss finishing school, these days, that KGB academy outside Moscow.

Malan: "I just want to help both Reid and MLC. Interest rates are high, you won't borrow heavily. You're jogging behind the rest of the wagons in the gold rush."

MacPherson was holding up his hand. Godwin, Hyde and Chambers were all crowded against the tinted window.

"I know it's in the company's interests, Paulus, you don't have to convince me on that point. But they went through this group of companies like exterminators after rats. I'm not having that again, not ever. It would do more damage to profits than any deals with you I have to turn down."

"It's a pity you have to sit on your expansion schemes, Mac."

"Don't I know it. But you haven't had the trouble we've had just hanging on to the few subsidiaries we still have in common. On the other hand, Paulus, I see no harm in cooperating in as many areas as possible—that aren't sensitive."

"Good. That's why Piet's here, to talk about that very subject."

"God, this is really fascinating," Hyde remarked snidely. He wandered away to a corner of the office and squatted on the floor. Chambers glanced at Godwin and smirked, tossing his head.

Van Vuuren was speaking now, his laptop computer on his knees, his fingers tapping. Something struck Godwin, but it vanished almost at once as he realized that the camcorder videotape had slowed to a halt.

"I told you to check the bloody tape in this!" he roared at Chambers. "Oh, shit!" The idea that had glanced across his imagination had returned, whole and visible, tangible enough to grasp. "Get another fucking tape in there, *now!* Oh, *no!*" he wailed as the noise of the movement-activated camera ceased. He slapped another cassette of film against it. It began clicking comfortingly once more. Van Vuuren was still tapping at his computer.

" . . . discussed this in outline before, Gordon," van Vuuren was saying as he typed into the laptop. "I'll just call up the outstanding orders." Christ, he was into MLC's mainframe computer in Johannesburg, connected to it by MacPherson's telephone line. God, have we *missed* anything? They'd be able to read the unfolded screen of his laptop, in enlargement. What had they bloody missed?

He glared at Chambers, who shrugged apologetically, as the camcorder began whirring once more. Again, there was that idea in his mind—not clear anymore, and not necessarily the one he thought he'd entertained, but something.

"Labor costs in Namibia are eleven percent below those in South Africa, and in the eastern bloc they're twenty percent below, even with our generosity." He could see van Vuuren smiling.

"Oh, you've found yourselves some new niggers, have you, son?" MacPherson observed drily. Malan laughed.

"As you say," he replied. "This is why you'd be mad not to come in."

MacPherson was shaking his head.

"It's not a moral objection," he assured them.

"In which case, we want you working at full stretch," Malan remarked. "We have a huge order for consumer electronics—"

"Oh, is that the one the Koreans can't meet, Paulus?"

"I—I'm afraid so. We need you—I'll be open about that."

"You want the stuff in a hurry, do you, son? It'll cost you, you realize that?"

"We'll have to pay what you ask—within reason."

"Oh, I'm reasonable, don't you worry. How long?"

"Three, four weeks, for the bulk of the order."

"Christ, you wouldn't like just to buy us out, would you? Hotels, leisure centers, factories, homes—almost every project you have under way at the moment. Is that right?"

Malan nodded. His face appeared severe and cornered—was it imagination to believe he was satisfied, even pleased? There was something fishy about the whole conversation. As if it was an elaborate pretense . . . no, not quite that. As if *Malan* were pretending. Pretending that he no longer had any influence over the Reid Group, that he came to them merely as a customer. Almost as if he could hear the South African purring like a cat. Was he still somehow in control of Reid, had hooks in the group, despite his public and publicized withdrawal? There was something about his face—he'd have to look at it in closeup.

"Christ," Chambers murmured. "Talk about winning the pools—that order's huge, I mean *vast*. How did Malan get let down by those little yellow buggers in Korea?"

"I don't know, do I?"

"We thought we'd have the component factories up and running over there," van Vuuren was saying. "But we haven't. They can't even work like blacks." He giggled. The girl appeared to be smiling, too.

"Then you'll be wanting supervisory personnel, computer programs—the whole works, eh?"

"I'm afraid so. Look, Gordon, can you be in a position to talk fully with Piet here tomorrow?" MacPherson nodded. "Good, then I'll leave you and him alone together to break this thing down, then you two meet again tomorrow, OK?"

"Fine by me, son."

"Jesus Christ," Godwin murmured. "Did you hear that?" He sighed orgasmically. "An order so big they'll need a fleet of planes to get it out—all bound for Eastern Europe."

"Bloody hell, you think we've—?" Chambers began.

"Oh, yes, I really think we have found something." He felt hot, flushed with some as yet unidentified success.

Malan wanted to increase the pace of supplies from the Reid Group companies to his own Eastern European subsidiaries. Soon, *now*. After spending yesterday afternoon with Priabin, and now having that woman alongside him. It had to be—just had to be—a KGB operation that also happened to suit Malan's book! He gripped Chambers' arm, who grinned, then winked.

"Go on," they heard Hyde call out, "tell Uncle Tony how clever he is. He likes that."

"Well, aren't I?" Godwin asked, turning around.

Hyde raised his beer can ironically. "Oh, you are mate, you are. Did I ever say otherwise?"

The door of the office opened. A young man in the uniform of an office cleaning company poked his head and chest round it, opened his mouth to speak, then evidently saw the range of equipment beside which Godwin and Chambers were posed. Then saw Hyde squatting malevolently in the corner.

"I—this office is being rented. I—"

The vacuum cleaner stood beside his slim form, as if he were anchored to it. His eyes moved robotically, but with quickening intensity and recognition from them to the equipment, back to them, then to the cameras, to the amplifier from which voices still came, to Hyde—

—who was on his feet quickly, in his crumpled police uniform, murmuring: "Listen, my son," and pulling the cleaner back out the door. "Yes, before you ask, we're the coppers, but you can't see the warrant card because we're not supposed to be here...mm?" He propelled the young man down the corridor with a firm grip on his elbow. The vacuum cleaner squeaked along behind them like a dragged child's toy. "We'll be gone in a half hour or so—OK? You just go and empty someone else's waste baskets and forget what you saw."

"Look, I don't want any—"

"This is official, but then I'm not telling you how or why." They reached the lift and Hyde punched the button. "You've suddenly come over all dizzy, sport, and will have to go home for a nap. OK?"

The cleaner nodded. The doors of the lift soughed open. Hyde pushed the man in ahead of him and kicked the vacuum cleaner away. He pressed Ground Floor/Reception. The lift moved with American swiftness and silence. The man was nervous, still bemused, the afterimages of what he had seen all but visible on his dilated pupils. Hyde remained silent, gripping the man's elbow, which had adopted a slight tremor. The doors opened.

"What about—?"

"You just go home and forget. That's what you do." The foyer was cramped, and empty. "There," said Hyde as they reached the revolving glass doors where the street already appeared goldenly hot. "Off you go, sport." He propelled the cleaner through the doors, following him, standing with him for a moment on the steps.

"Sorry," the young man offered, a belated excitement now appearing on his features. "I—right, I'll go and have a drink. Can I come back later? I—new on the job, see, I don't want to risk—"

"Yes. Half an hour." Hyde was squinting against the slant of the sun, looking toward the parked van. The final jigsaw piece of conviction slipped into place when the cleaner saw the van and glanced back at Hyde's unbuttoned police uniform with a new acceptance of its pretense.

"Cheers." He went down the building's steps to the sidewalk.

Hyde shaded his eyes and looked up toward the windows of MacPherson's office. Godwin might even be right; something was certainly happening. And soon.

He rubbed his hands through his tightly curled hair, then stretched luxuriously. Better check on Darren-the-Wonder-Dog while I'm—

On the steps of the NatWest building, directly opposite him, stood Malan and the woman from the KGB. They were both looking at him, the woman bending close to Malan, then looking at the van with POLICE on the side and shaking her head vigorously. She was talking rapidly, her hand making small, definite chopping motions. She'd seen him, and recognized him. The surveillance was blown.

Oh, shit—

Too late, he turned away.

3

AFRICA AND
GOLDEN JOYS

Blantyre pushed aside the heavy, round stones and then lifted the waterlogged canvas bag clear of the reeds, which rattled stiffly against his forearms as he disturbed them. The water was cool on his hands and wrists. He turned to Uys and grinned.

"Easy," he said, shaking the dripping bag so that its contents slithered against one another in their polyethylene wrappings like woken snakes. "Now, let's just make sure." He wrestled with the straps and buckles and freed them, then settled on his haunches. The other members of his unit stood idly, like spectators or automatons. Except for Uys, who said in a hoarse whisper:

"I thought you said this bloke used to be an agent, sir."

"A long time ago—not long after you were born in that shed on that Christ-knows-where farm, Uys. He's obviously forgotten his training." As if he had tickled a great fish onto the bank, he held up a sodden card-board box, then a miniature keypad, then a water-filled bag containing small, still shapes. He remembered carrying a goldfish thus home from a fair, or was it after that circling of the wagons at the Boer Memorial, during his childhood?

"Transputers," he explained. "Don't hurt your brains worrying about what they're for." The bag was dripping over the small selection of items he'd arranged on the wet sand like runes. He put it down. "He's for-gotten everything he ever learned, by the look of it, man." He checked the articles, rubbing his chin, the light of Uys' flashlight remaining steady. A lion snorted and grumbled on the far side of the dam. "It must be all here," Blantyre decided. "Just waiting to be found."

"Has he told anyone?" Uys asked.

"Who's to tell, out here?" He sighed and shook his head. "Bloody *amateur!* I don't even begin to know why he took the bloody stuff, uh?" He got to his feet, holding the empty canvas bag like something he had severed from a body.

"What do we do now?" Uys asked. He was the only one of the unit facing Blantyre. Its other three members, armed, now faced outward to give protecting fire into the night; scanning the lodge, the dam, the raised line of thatched platforms and their closed tents, the paths lead-ing to and from the artificial water hole. "Sir?"

Blantyre smiled, and he saw Uys' white teeth answer his expression in the darkness. The stars hung heavily, as if poorly suspended in the velvet darkness, and something slight and innocent slid through the water near them.

"How many of them, sir?" Uys asked.

"Eight guests, Anderson and the black dolly, maybe as many as six kaffirs. They all sleep away behind the lodge. Easy to just set fire to the place, or put a rocket into it."

"Just about the right number to make it an atrocity, Colonel," Uys observed.

"Ah, well, so many of these kaffirs are still running round Namibia with guns and grudges. Who can tell what they might get up to, in the dark?"

"Then we'll—?"

"We have to, Corporal. We can't leave Anderson alive to talk about what he found, can we? And therefore we can't leave any witnesses."

"No, sir. When?"

"Just before dawn."

"Then we just happen to arrive, just after daylight, having seen the smoke?"

"Exactly, Uys. Christ, what we might find—the mutilations and everything. Horrible!"

"Should never have let the South-West go independent, sir. Just proves the point."

Blantyre said, "He might last a week in the headlines, poor bastard. The atrocity at Okaukuejo Lodge . . . " He sighed. "Right, change the ammunition to Russian-issue, black faces for you blokes, use knives wherever and whenever you can. Make sure the bloody place *burns!*"

The others in the unit had turned round and drawn closer to him, as if he held out a bowl of food to hungry cats.

"OK, Pelzer," Uys said, "you collect up the evidence."

Blantyre looked at his watch. "It's just after one now. I want the raid mounted and over by six-thirty, so let's get moving."

The long signal from Priabin was—satisfactory. Babbington spread his fingers on it as he stood beside his desk, the cool early morning light falling on the decoded pages instead of the lamplight which he had switched off as he came to the last, unrelated item in the report. Turned it off as quickly as shutting a door against a gale. He'd stood up, too, quite suddenly and strode about the room. His fingers drummed on the pages now, but even then he felt obligated to snatch them away.

Once more, he walked to the high window overlooking the Arsenal. The morning was fine, almost cloudless. Below, he watched the falconers, two of them carrying goshawks on their gauntleted wrists and looking up toward the roofs of the Council of Ministers building, which contained his office. His head slightly to one side, he heard the cawing of a flock of hooded crows on the roof above his window, as if they mocked the two young KGB guards and their birds. He watched as the hood of one of the young birds was removed, then its jesses loosened. The falconer's arm flung wide and the bird rose into the morning sun, becoming black, then almost ghostly white, finally golden. It moved purposefully, as if aimed directly at his window, then it disappeared above him into the raucous, already fading laughter of the crows. The hawks hardly ever caught or killed any of them as they moved from roof to roof around the Kremlin. It was a sport without purpose or result. The young falconer near the row of Napoleon's captured cannon was already beginning to whirl the lure to summon the futile hawk back to his wrist.

Without purpose or successful result. It was not an omen, that vain pursuit, but it did, somehow, force Babbington to recall the final paragraph of Priabin's report. His wife had fallen from a horse, some miles from her home, and had suffered brain damage. The information had been gleaned from a report in *The Times*. Doubtless, that Murdoch rag that had once been a newspaper had gloatingly recollected what they deemed his "treachery." She, Elizabeth, was in a coma and not expected to come out of it, and no doubt his son, the unamiable Richard, would soon switch off the life-support and inherit her money.

He did not understand why Priabin had included the information, or why it niggled at the corner of his awareness like grit in a mental eye. He cordially hated her, as she did him, though she would not be aware that she hated him now, he imagined. Had he wanted to return, to be at her bedside, even switch off the machinery himself—he could not have done so. Nor did he wish that it be done. Richard could not lay hold of his money anyway; only the house and what she had retained of her family's poor resources and the money he had deposited in her accounts and the shares in her name were available to him. He'd drink and roister it away in a year, probably.

Babbington rubbed his beard and moved from the window with a slight smile as the goshawk returned to the falconer's wrist. It looked grumpily dissatisfied. Perhaps his son would not even wait a decent interval before ending his mother's unconscious existence. His daughter, who hated him with all the venom of her mother, would not restrain him, though out of pain rather than cupidity or indifference. No, Priabin should not have sent that item of information. It belonged, like so much else, to a past life, a former self.

But, the remainder of his signal was—satisfactory. Aubrey, as they knew, was still on sick leave. Orrell was a clod. Godwin a technician who had no inkling of what might in reality be happening, merely that someone had their hand in the petty cash! Malan had hurried the schedule competently. If the Reid Group had to be abandoned, then so be it. It would be stripped of everything that wasn't nailed down before the UK operation was abandoned. He ground his teeth. Kapustin had, he was forced to admit, been right. No smoke without fire, the finger of suspicion, mud sticks,

et cetera! The symmetry and secrecy of the Reid operation was compromised. It was wisest to abandon the
UK, for the moment—once they could replicate the
transputer and wafer scale integration technology successfully. However, he should signal Priabin and
instruct him to obtain whatever information he
thought Godwin and the damnable Hyde had obtained
by eavesdropping. Though it must be done under deep
cover; it could not be *their* interest that was revealed.
Orrell was a clown, but then Godwin might run to
Aubrey with his sniveling little tale and that perfidious
old man might, just might, be well enough to take
note. It was, of course, easily containable. A surprising
piece of enterprise by Godwin. But then, suspension
could not be any farther than around the very next corner, if the matter of obtaining the material was handled
subtly.

Priabin was clever enough for the business. He
was—satisfactory. It was, simply, a pity that Reid and
especially Inmost and its advanced microchip and
transputer research program would be lost to them—
temporarily. They would have to go back to America
in a big way when the dust of the Shapiro business had
settled.

Then he shivered, unexpectedly. For some unfath-
omable reason he recalled waking, as a young bride-
groom-to-be, at four in the morning, horrified that he
had forgotten to write his damned speech of thanks for
the wedding reception. He had scribbled feverishly in
the dawn light, and it had gone well. Elizabeth had
looked charming that day, yet already complacent and
resentful, knowing she had been bought and sold; his
family's money for her family's ancestry. An exchange
surely, rather than a sordid bargain? He remembered
now. She had looked charming for others, merely
sullen for him, even on their wedding day.

He breathed deeply. Perhaps her paintings would

increase in value with her death. It would help keep
Richard in the style to which he had early determined
to remain accustomed.

He reached the window again. The falconers had
gone and the crows were back, scrabbling and cawing
and sharpening their beaks on the tiles and guttering
above his head. The sky outside was clear and blue
with every prospect of a fine day. He turned over the
last page of Priabin's report, then picked up the telephone.

"Yes, I want to dictate a signal for Codes, to be
transmitted immediately to London. Come in now,
would you?"

As he slipped from the bed, he suddenly felt his whole
body bend beneath the freight of that other person in
the bedroom, Margarethe. He had endangered her. He
looked down at her tiny frame, apparently peacefully
asleep, the sheet and single blanket pulled up around
her, one arm exposed, its dark skin sheened by the yellow moon.

He had been unable to sleep. Blantyre meant him
and his wife harm; the fact was inescapable. He swallowed a hard lump in his throat as he looked at
Margarethe, then padded across the rugs scattered on
the wooden floor, pausing only to put on his shorts and
a thin sweatshirt, then his boots. The floor creaked,
Margarethe moved and murmured, then slipped back
into a deeper sleep, her arm now stretched across the
white space where he had been lying. He reluctantly
closed the bedroom door behind him, having taken the
old Browning GP–35 pistol from the chest of drawers
with little or no conscious thought. The butt was
already warming in his hand; he clenched it too tightly,
as if he had never before held a gun.

The predawn air was chilly after the bedroom and

living room, but not necessarily the cause of the shiver that enveloped him for whole seconds, until he shook it off as a dog might have done water. Then, head cocked to one side, he listened. Someone snoring loudly, the hum of an unseen insect. The fingertips of his left hand prickled with heat and gradually his body seemed to become more alert, thinner-skinned, its network of nerves closer to the surface. He went quietly down the steps and along the sloping track toward the tents silhouetted against the sheer of the water. He was pressed—compelled—to check the safety of the canvas bag and its contents, the proof that Blantyre and MLC were in collusion with at least one KGB officer who had spent a holiday—or came from, or had relatives living in—Novgorod the Great. There was little or nothing else. The cargo didn't mean anything to him; it might even be legal. Except that Blantyre was there. He walked with a swift, crouching lope.

Predawn was already beginning to pale into the day, making the eastern darkness royal blue, dimming the stars. The moon was almost at the horizon, tiredly jaundiced. A bird rustled in the thatch of the closest tourist tent. Creaking noises as someone turned over in bed.

For there was some kind of collusion, some illegality—he smiled at the prim, solicitor's tone of his thoughts—in the adjacence of a KGB ID card to British technology, in the shell of an old Dakota in the middle of the Namibian Bush. Otherwise . . .

Otherwise, he would have been dealing with some thick-necked, dim sergeant of police, even a black man. That, of course, was the confirmation. A whites-only recovery of goods from a wrecked aircraft. The stone had struck the water and the ripples had begun moving outwards—which made him thankful he had dispatched the airmail letter to Aubrey in London.

The relief in his breathing actually unnerved him

as he inspected the little sandy stretch beside the dam and found no footprints. Blantyre hadn't been here then—

—the canvas bag was gone, and the stones had been moved. The bag and its contents had been taken away. Anderson gasped with fear, uncertainty. He looked around wildly, his arms waving as if in protest. Blantyre's tent was lightless, and the scene around him was empty of people. It hadn't just happened, then. Distantly, he heard Joseph or William rattling pans or buckets. The royal blue of the day filled almost half of the sky now. The eastern horizon was paler. A kudu stepped innocently from the low trees on the other side of the dam, then paused, sensing a presence. Its horns were like silhouetted branches. Anderson could not avoid staring across the expanse of gray water toward the animal, recognizing its nervousness as his own, knowing that both he and the big gazelle were potential victims.

He stood up, wiping the water from his arms and hands with hard, rubbing strokes. The kudu crashed back into the cover of the stunted trees. Anderson ran wildly, then, dragging the pistol from the belt of his shorts, toward Blantyre's tent. He clattered up the steps, disregarding the noise, and tugged open the flap and the mosquito netting, plunging into the darkness—

—to find his bed empty. Slept-in, but now empty and cool. Fear seized his chest with a chill implosive force, making resolve smaller, allowing hesitation to hurry against him. He had not even thought of the consequences of bursting in on Blantyre, had the man been there and roused from sleep. His instincts were uncertain and unpracticed. He was no longer the jeweled and cogged piece of machinery he had once been. He was something rusted, abandoned in long grass and weeds, and no match for Blantyre.

Where was he? He had the evidence, obviously—he

knew. Anderson whirled around in the narrow tent. Insects had already entered. He lit the oil-lamp because he needed to perform a small sequence of physical actions to calm the shiver he felt mounting through his frame. At once, in the smoky lick of the flame, he saw thick-bodied insects as large as toffees throw themselves against the glass of the lamp. The tent was as tidy as a soldier's abandoned billet. As if Blantyre had merely left without paying his bill—

The first explosion shook him like thunder; realization was almost immediate. Fear flooded his present self, but there was a resurgence of that former self, already moving and assuming control of him. He dragged aside the tent flap. From the house, a gout of flame burst out of part of the thatched roof.

The tent's platform clattered beneath his hurrying boots as the house erupted again in a second explosion—a rocket, he realized, remembering the puzzling fizz of noise just before the crump of the explosion and the surge of flame.

He careered down the few steps, then ran wildly up the long slope toward the house, his hands and chest already bathed in the orange light of the fire as he raced against its progress along the roof. He was aware of every passing second, every millimeter of the fire's advance, aware of where the rocket had been directed, toward the house itself, toward the bedroom where he—she...the fire would be inspecting then swallowing each piece of furniture, each rug, each door, entering the bedroom, reaching the *bed*. Their primary target was himself—his room, his wife. A third explosion terrified him into halting for a moment, stunning him with the certainty that he was already too late.

He whimpered with terror and anticipated, certain loss, cursed his body for being too slow to get to the house. The thatch over the veranda caught, rustled like living grass for a moment, then roared upwards.

People behind him were waking, calling out to one another like dolphins separated and hunted; small, chirruping cries of alarm and incomprehension. There were others in the main house too. Would they kill them all? Or only those who were dangerous to them? Margarethe! He was forty yards, then thirty, then twenty from the raging thatch. Something staggered across the veranda as he reached it and rolled down the steps, burning, at his feet. It might have been one of the elderly American women. He coughed on the smoke that the dawn breeze thrust toward him. William was dead on the veranda, his throat slashed. Burning gobbets of thatch rained down on him as he crossed the restaurant, flinching against the noise of the flames and the falling thatch. He flung open the first door. Another explosion, near the dam—no time for them now.

He was calling out, screaming her name, his eyes watering, his throat raw and lungs filled with the acrid smoke. Behind him, bottles in the bar exploded. The narrow corridor of unpainted concrete was as smoke-filled as a railway tunnel. He shouted, yelled, pleaded for a reply.

A dark figure, a blackened rather than black face, the strange-familiar outline of a rifle, something stubby and foreign. The menace, the immediate threat, absorbed all his subliminal concentration. He killed the unidentified figure at once, with two shots, as he might a mamba he found in the house. His concentration was so finely focused that he saw the shots rip the shirt like the fingers of an angry mob, saw the white flesh before the red gouted. The body fell back behind a bloom of red fire that erupted from the floorboards at an open door toward the end of the corridor. He stepped over the flames and the body.

Joseph's bedroom door. Joseph lay half on his bed, destroyed by the frenzy of a long knife. Wild, disappointed men from the Bush, ex-SWAPO or some other extreme remnant; it happened still. Here it would appear the convincing lie of an atrocity carried out by local blacks against whites. He rushed on down the corridor, the smell of burning flesh too close to belong to anyone but himself. He dared not look down at his clothing, his exposed skin.

The bedroom door was as he had left it, closed. What remained of it. Flame licked at the dark wood and slid along the door's panels. He kicked at it, thankful he had put on the heavy boots. It sagged inward. The walls of their bedroom were orange with leaping fire. It was difficult to see the bed; smoke filled the room, flame shimmering through its rolling cloud. The whole bedroom seemed on the point of a single, massive combustion.

Coughing, he crawled toward where the bed must be . . . gun jerking forward at each movement of his right hand, the weight on his raw hands and knees hurting, splinters dragging into his skin, the heat scorching. He inched on, his chest tightening, his awareness concentrating more and more narrowly on the certainty of choking in the smoke if he stayed in the bedroom even moments longer.

He touched what he immediately knew was her hand and which did not touch his but merely rested there on the floor. The absence of any pulse in the wrist he held in his fingers prompted the terror of certainty. His whole stomach heaved and he fought the desire to vomit, swallowing again and again, concentrating solely on it.

Slowly, fragmentedly, he realized that the smoke was no thicker than when he had entered the room and that the flames were dancing sinuously in the breeze that was coming through a great gap torn in the bedroom wall. Her hand did not move, her wrist did not pucker with a pulse, her body did not stir. His hand climbed her arm like the touch of a blind man, then felt her small, delicate features, her cheekbones, lips, nose. The back of her head was slippery with blood. She would not move again, ever. He remained on his knees, doubled up by the scorching of his skin and the effects of the smoke; immobile with grief. She had been killed by one of the rockets impacting with the wall near the bed, flinging her across the room with the force of the explosion. He realized that he had not been making for the bed, but had been drawn to this spot in the far corner of the room where her body had been flung.

Smoke billowed. His throat was raw and his eyes streamed. His mind was quiescent, in traumatic rest, his limbs felt weaker and heavier. Slowly, he collapsed onto his side, near her, his hand holding hers. He could not see her body and could not bear to imagine the destruction that had been worked on it.

Nagging like a sore, like the pain of his scorched flesh . . . survival. His fingers were numb, gripping her hand. His mind was numb . . . survival. Blantyre. Strangely, the letter he had sent to Aubrey. The Dakota. Survival . . . Blantyre, who had done this to Margarethe. Blantyre, who had intended it . . .

. . . revenge, the illness of which he thought himself cured forever. *Blantyre*. Out there, somewhere, the architect and designer of this—her murder.

Part of him cried out as he began crawling, wanting not to leave her, protesting at his desertion. But the other self found the shattered door and the corridor and its rough floorboards, found the restaurant after the signpost of the South African he had shot. The smoke seemed to lessen, then increase once more. The thatch above the restaurant had collapsed into a dozen small fires. Bottles continued to explode like guns. A line of flames down by the water. No survivors. The fires were the exact, mocking shapes of the guest tents.

He hopped, staggered, jumped across the small distance from the veranda to the ground and fell. He rolled down the long, shallow slope, feeling as if he had not survived, that his real self was dead, burning beside her body. And yet he knew some other self lived more violently and truly than he had thought possible. He was already beginning to ignore the last of the screaming, the noise of explosions and killing. He was concerned only with concealment, escape. Until he could seize his opportunity and take the chance he knew would come.

Water. Stop the pain with water. But his pain was increasing and his grief was seeping back, the horror of knowledge and the touch of his fingers on her slippery, wet skin and her broken head. Hatred of Blantyre, whom he saw as clearly as if the man stood over him holding a pistol, drove him on hands and knees down toward the water. Dawn impressed itself even on his blurred, wet vision. Otherwise, his awareness became blank except for the palpable form of the man who had murdered Margarethe.

Renewed gunfire prompted him like a cattle prod. Things rattled agonisingly against his raw skin, then he was drowning. A terrified bout of coughing and vomiting, the noise in his ears of water being thrashed by desperate arms. The water seeming to further inflame his skin. He wanted to scream with infinite pain and rage.

Slowly, stroke by clumsy stroke, he swam out from the bank, his mind already unconscious, even her face distant, then gone. Blantyre's face, too—small and indistinct, then absent. Then her face coming back, as he tried to swim . . .

. . . unconscious, he opened his mouth, not sensing the water that rushed to fill his lungs.

Hyde was staring down at the Charing Cross Road and the early morning crowds at the junction with Oxford

Street. The slumped, dozing shapes of young and ancient had removed themselves from the doorways of the sex shop and the pub. The city looked normally untidy now, not desperate or abandoned as it sometimes did just before dawn.

Godwin was, as if a voice on an interminable tape loop, arguing with Chambers.

"It can be done, Terry. It's all in *there!*" They were sitting in front of the huge television screen, quarrelsome and yet as unmoving as two old people in a residential home. Less active than the bag lady down there, near the traffic lights, intent on a crumbling lump of something in one dirty hand which she kept pressing to her mouth. A stale, abandoned pasty or pie, probably. "And we can get in there, if we can gather the whole access code from the stills and the videotape."

"We'd have to get *everything* right—every single letter and number," Chambers warned. "And we had to change the films at one point—look, I'm not saying it's impossible, just that we'll be bloody lucky. And there's the fact that it's bound to be a secure laptop. There'll be an ID signal sent from his machine to the mainframe, to identify it, even if we knew the access codes. We couldn't use another machine—"

"No, we could bloody well use his, though!"

"How the hell could we do that?"

"Never mind, for the moment. Let's hurry up those enlargements of the stills and start picking the bones out of this tape with the help of the freeze-frame."

"Do you two want anything as mundane as breakfast?" Hyde enquired.

"What? Oh, yes. I'll tell Jim—"

"*I'll* get it. Jim stays on duty downstairs. Priabin knows about us. Ten to one, he knows what equipment we used and what we might have found out from Malan—which is nothing at all, but he won't see it like that. I'll get breakfast."

"Suit yourself."

"Lock the doors and keep your eyes on the security camera."

"We're safe up here," Godwin remarked breezily.

And perhaps they were. He'd check for surveillance when he got downstairs. The special lift could only be operated with a key, the two floors were sealed off from the rest of Centre Point, there were alarms, security cameras. And it was the middle of London and broad daylight. Perhaps Godwin was right.

He turned to look back at the television screen. A frame had been frozen. He recognized MacPherson's desk, the telephone attached to van Vuuren's laptop computer, the man's slim fingers poised over its keypad, about to insert himself into the MLC mainframe in Johannesburg. God alone knew how Godwin thought he was going to do the same.

He closed the door behind him. The corridor was glowing with dusty light coming through the fire-door window. Twenty floors up, a sealed unit within the building, in effect.

But the silence from Priabin was deafening.

"There," Godwin sighed in the darkness. "Perfect." He held up the last of the enlargements, close to his face, then added: "OK, turn on the lights."

The darkroom lights sprang out against the beige walls and the lowered black blinds, glanced off the enlarger, the liquids in the trays and the rows of prints that gleamed like washing lines arranged for some detergent advertisement. The room seemed suddenly warmer, almost fetid, with their efforts, and Godwin turned to grin at Chambers, who hurried forward between the festooned outer garments and lingerie of the lines of prints.

There were hands suspended everywhere in the

room, dangling from the clips and pegs along the cat's cradle of cords; hands poised, hands working, hands at rest. Fingers extended like those of a pianist, fingers clawlike or drawn back as if to pounce again. Van Vuuren's hands and fingers, van Vuuren's keypad, his screen folded open on his lap. Everything was—potentially—there. Godwin glanced at his watch. Four-thirty in the afternoon. Van Vuuren was back at the InterContinental Hotel. He had booked a table for dinner in the hotel restaurant with a high-class call girl who was mulatto, as beautiful and desirable as something gleaming from an ad for coffee or rum. Van Vuuren's suite would be unoccupied for perhaps as long as two hours, from eight until ten. And he would be certain to leave his laptop in his suite.

Godwin rubbed his hands like a miser or someone moving closer to a fire. Once they had solved the sequence of the still enlargements, he had power over van Vuuren, and thus power over Malan—and the satisfaction of a solution beckoning.

"OK," he announced, "let's start taking them down."

They were as eager as two children raiding an orchard, reaching up, pulling prints out of the grasp of their clips, gathering them into ordered sequences. Chambers hesitated. "We're not going to get enough detail off these." He inspected the enlargement he had plucked from its clip, as if nearsighted. "His hands were moving too fast—"

"I know that," Godwin replied sarcastically. "But look at the screen he's using, the VDU—clear as a bell. Try getting that quality from a freeze-frame on the video. Besides which, we had to change the bloody cassette halfway through. There'll be stuff missing—so don't get anything out of sequence."

"OK," Chambers muttered, pulling down the last of the enlargements, then holding them against his chest. "Set, then?"

Godwin grinned. "Set." He looked at his watch. "Four-forty. Let's get to it."

As they left the darkroom, the distant sighing of lifts was audible above the hum of computers and amplifiers. Late afternoon, home time, Godwin thought, but then the image of his unkempt flat and the sole company of the thin black cat appeared, and the noise of the lifts faded. Chambers lowered the blinds and closed them. The afternoon light was smoky at the edges of the windows. He was whistling softly as he tugged the huge television screen into the center of the room, inspected the video cassette and slid it into the VCR. Godwin busied himself arranging the sheafs of enlargements on a long table, as if he were laying places for an important dinner party. Van Vuuren was dining at eight. Perhaps he'd climb on the call girl before dinner, perhaps not. He looked up. Chambers was fast-forwarding through the arrival of Malan, van Vuuren and Priabin's woman in MacPherson's office. Trust Hyde to blow it all, appearing on the steps just as Malan left!

"OK?" Chambers inquired.

"OK . . . bit more—oh, ah, just there. He's dragged the laptop onto his knees—right." There was a hard, bright light pooling down on the long table, gleaming off the prints. The image on the screen was clear, detailed. Chambers, waving the remote control like a flag, seated himself in front of the screen and switched on a tiny pocket recorder. Settled with a pad on his crossed leg, pen poised.

"Ready for dictation, Miss Chambers?" Godwin asked.

"Not sitting on your knee though, Mr. Godwin."

"OK, let's watch this video nasty." He settled himself to comfort, leaned against the thrust of his crutches, the table neatly laid with enlargements, in their proper sequence. Outside, he heard a distant church clock thinly chime the hour. Five. The lifts sighed downward with gratitude. They had their own private lift, key-operated like the fire doors at the end of the corridor. They were isolated within the huge office block. "Right . . . Open Sesame."

On the screen, van Vuuren's hands opened the laptop computer. Chambers flicked a switch, and the conversation recorded by the laser eavesdropper filled the darkened room. Van Vuuren and Malan attempting to prove to MacPherson that Reid Electronics needed their business. They'd already listened to it so many times, it was becoming subliminal. Van Vuuren's fingers were poised, like some tricky shot of the bent arms and legs of a row of sprinters waiting for the starting pistol. Chambers stirred on his chair and Godwin felt tense, ludicrously on his mark, ready to move. Chambers held the tiny recorder to his lips, poised.

Van Vuuren's right hand attached MacPherson's telephone extension to the computer, then his fingers began jabbing at the buttons.

" . . . South Africa . . . that's Jo'burg, MLC's main building," Chambers murmured as Godwin shuffled along the table, touching and arranging the enlargements. "Now we're into the mainframe."

The room was oppressively silent behind the thin murmur of electricity and machines, behind Chambers' whisper and the scribble of his pen and even the tiny whirr of his pocket recorder. The still photographs caught most of the numbers—especially on the screen. Godwin was watching van Vuuren's fingers on the VDU screen, repeating everything like a prompter in a theater.

The screen recognized van Vuuren—at least, the fingerprint of his personal computer—in the photograph under Godwin's splayed fingers, which were white and coarse like anemic sausages under the light. ACCESS CONFIRMATION REQUIRED, spilled the VDU.

"Kruger," Chambers muttered, snorting. "Christ, how bloody original. They might have made it Krugerrand, I suppose," he added derisively.

"Kruger it is," Godwin confirmed. The photographs and the video were even better than he had hoped. Piece of cake, as they used to say—remembering ominously the panicky moment when he and Chambers had changed the video cassette in the recorder *and* the roll of film in the camera . . . there had been an overlap of whole seconds. He tried not to think of it, attending to Chambers and the sequence he was following, piece by piece. "Then these words—Afrikaans, Terry?"

"First one is . . . B-o-e-t-"

"-e . . . new word." Godwin skipped a number of enlargements. "Yes, here we are. Boete Erazmus. Who was he? Friend of Paul Kruger?"

"Doesn't matter, does it? Next?" Chambers continued muttering.

Godwin, elated and anxious in the same moment, was halfway along the table now, approaching what he knew to be a blank place setting. He skipped heavily on his crutches and announced: "E-l-l-i-s . . . Park. Ellis Park."

"Agreed. Why am I the straight man again?"

"Because, Ernie, you don't look as comical as I do," Godwin muttered. "What have you got next?"

Chambers pressed the play button of the remote control, then said, "Where's Ellis Park?"

"Who knows?" Godwin thudded around the end of the table, his fingers measuring the display on the photographed VDU as it changed letter by letter by—

"Shit," Chambers murmured. "End of tape."

Godwin had reached the gap he superstitiously hadn't left empty. He even crowded the prints there, as if to compensate.

"N-e-w-l-a . . . " Chambers recited, pressing the

slow-motion button each time, inspecting each frame, leaning forward on his chair, straining at the screen. "Then the new bloody tape says . . . what?"

Godwin was watching the jerk of the images on the TV screen, mesmerized.

"-s-v-e-l-d . . . Shit!" Chambers rounded on Godwin, his chair bucking like that which might have contained an angry child refusing to eat. "What have you bloody got?"

"Newla, like you, then I don't even have the end of the next word, or words. Was that being eaten as you got back?"

Chambers flicked on two frames. "Yes, the next one's -e-l-d . . . it's being gobbled. Then he's in. MENU'S the next thing to appear. You?"

"Menu," Godwin announced heavily, his fingers stirring on the print, as if to conjure something more from it. "Oh, balls." He waggled his crutches in exasperation, while Chambers sat gloomily with his chin on his arms, which were folded along the back of his chair.

The building around, above, below them was silent now, but the room was no longer cleverly secretive, comfortably engaged in exposure.

"Have we got the rest of it?" Godwin snapped. The names had not even begun to niggle or suggest. English and Afrikaans—they speak both, he reminded himself. Van Vuuren's access code—probably common to all MLC executives, at least the senior ones who would have been issued with fingerprinted laptops and allowed to access the mainframe's voluminous files—had a hole in it. If they couldn't decipher—really guess—what it was, then they couldn't access the computer in Johannesburg, down the telephone line in van Vuuren's hotel suite—that evening, or ever. Van Vuuren was leaving for South Africa the following morning. "Oh, bugger."

"Just number sequences," Chambers commented, having relayed them to his tiny recorder. "Then we get into the business. After the numbers—he only used the ones to access the project and shipment files, didn't he? We could have anything we wanted. The mainframe asks, you tell it in simple words—"

"Afrikaans?"

"No, English."

"So, we've got it all, except for—what? One word, two, three?"

"God knows. I don't. Oh, there's one joke, did you spot it?"

Godwin scanned the prints. "Yes—to confirm the menu, keep it on the screen—must be a fail-safe device. The trick answer—Mandela."

"Cheeky bastards."

"Everything—almost. God, we've got MLC's mainframe lying down with its legs open, and we can't get a hard-on!" Then Godwin looked toward a corner of the silent room as the alarm sounded. The security man's features appeared on the small close-circuit screen, intercepting the usual images of Centre Point's foyer or the emergency staircase in an unceasing, secure and discounted sequence. Godwin heard the distant wailing of a siren from beyond the lowered blinds. Chambers had risen from his chair and was approaching the screen. The room seemed isolated beyond the point of comfort.

"Mr. Godwin, there's been a bomb alert—might I suggest you evacuate, like the rest of the building?"

"I thought they'd gone home," Godwin said. Five-forty now.

"Mr. Godwin, most of the building was empty—a few people were left. They've gone now, I've checked. The bomb squad has been summoned—telephone tip-off. Looks like some Middle East connection. Can you come down now in the lift? I'm being evacuated like everyone else." There was a police uniform half in the picture behind their security man.

"Bloody hell!" Chambers yelled.

"Yes, Jim, we'll be down at once."

"Very well, Mr. Godwin." The screen went blank, then reasserted the images of the foyer and the staircase. A couple of people were hurrying through the foyer; the stairs were blank.

"Well?" Chambers asked.

"Well? Let's collect the stuff we need—just in case."

"They saw Hyde on the steps yesterday. Do you think . . . ?"

"Don't ask—just collect the gear, the videotape, the recorder."

"Right."

Godwin began to gather up the stills, shuffling them expertly into a heap, struggling along the table, while Chambers expelled the cassette, collected sheafs of computer printout, their notes, other papers. Christ, Godwin thought, let's get a move on, there's so much bloody stuff here. He glanced round at Chambers once more, his arms filled with still-tacky photographs, Chambers' embrace filled to overflowing—two pediatric nurses saving babies from a ward.

"Have we got everything—well, enough?" he burst out.

Chambers was stuffing sheafs of material into a loose bag, then kneeling to fill another, glancing wildly toward littered tables, shelves of videotape.

"Another couple of minutes!" he blurted.

The evening sun struck hotly at the edges of the lowered blinds. Suddenly, the room was menacing. A bomb scare. There was no way it could be counteractivity, no way it was simply a ruse. It was a real device: rush hour, crowded streets, corner of Oxford Street. Whoever it was, they were really in business. Godwin scooped videotapes into the open mouth of a sports bag, sweeping his arm along metal shelving as if he were engaged in some lunatic supermarket competition. "Ready?" he shouted in a high voice that didn't seem to be his.

"Ready!" Chambers called back in a voice similarly distorted.

"Then let's bloody well go. Let's get moving before they cut off the power to the lift!"

On the screen in the corner, an empty foyer, empty corridors, empty staircase. In another minute, they'd be isolated up here, with the bomb likely to go off. They hadn't burned the codebooks or collected them; there was a hundred thousand quids' worth of equipment in the rooms as well as all the secrets, lying around like dandruff now.

Godwin scuttled after Chambers, through the doors and into the corridor toward the lift.

Hyde paused at the corner of Oxford Street and the Charing Cross Road, the plastic bag of jazz records banging against his knee. He knew that Ros would want to add up the little sticky labels that betrayed Hyde's extravagance, and then berate him with the total before he could peel them from each record sleeve. Jesus, the traffic was glutinously still as he came out of the side street, a few horns tooting impotently, already more than half accustomed to an emergency. Red-and-white tape fluttered in the early evening breeze, clots of frocks and shirts and suits had collected on the pavements as the shops emptied and their cargoes stilled into observation. Oxford Street was taped to a standstill, as was the Charing Cross Road. Clutters of black taxis amid the queues of cars, all collected in front of the dias on which the real dignitaries of the occasion would be seated.

Centre Point. Suddenly, police everywhere, TV cameras, the first of the fire engines almost discreetly parked, the ambulances . . .

And the crowd began to move against him, backward, as the police swept at them like a stiff, new broom, brushing them away from the steps of the office building. He began struggling forward, no one looking at him, no one staring toward him, all of them gravitationally tugged in their concentration toward Centre Point, their heads craning upwards, waiting for the movielike shattering of glass and the spill of rubble from a damaged tower. He elbowed two women aside, then a man in a fawn suit with sweatstained armpits, then an old man—righted him, apologized, pushed forward—then more shoppers, more bags colliding with his own, which he dropped on the tarmac and managed to ignore after an initial pang.

A police uniform, a hand aimed at his chest deterringly.

"I'm sorry, sir, but—"

Crowds milling—the last of them, really—on the steps, people in ordered flight. He glimpsed Godwin and then Chambers, stooped with the weight of bags, papers protruding, a bulky laptop computer in Chambers' right hand; as if they had looted a shop. It couldn't be a bomb scare, not with those two carrying out their luggage. Too accidental to be real; it was arranged. He glanced up more than twenty floors. The blinds were down all along that secure floor. He waved his ID card.

"Just let me through. You've seen one before?"

The policeman winced, became angry, then nodded him through, tight-lipped with disdain. He sensed the crowd's sudden interest in him as he began mounting the steps, waving his ID now like a flag at anyone who moved toward him. Top of the steps, and Godwin almost bumping into him as he balanced himself for the short descent to the long-shadowed street and the expectant crowd.

"Where's Jim?" Hyde asked.

"You're bloody *late!*" Chambers snapped, sweating under the effort of his bags and computer.

"Where's Jim, Godwin? Why isn't he with you?"

"What?" Godwin's head turned toward the smoked glass doors and the dim foyer beyond them. "He—I assumed—"

"He'd be *here,* waiting for you, you pair of pillocks! What's happened to him?"

"I forgot Jim—"

"Oh, *shit!*" He glared at Godwin, then added: "This is no bomb scare, sport—or didn't you realize that?" He hurried toward the glass doors and the policeman nervously posted there. He flashed his ID card, then thrust the doors open. A police inspector moved to intercept him, his reflection sun-dimmed and slanted by the movement of the door. The constable shook his head at the inspector, who slowed, then turned to Godwin. Hyde pushed into the empty, silent foyer of Centre Point.

He glanced back toward the crowds, being shunted like retreating waves by a tidemark of blue uniforms. There were more ambulances now, the first fire engine had become a small flock, and he heard the wail of nearing sirens. No one would enter the building now, because his ID had told them that he, and whoever he sought, did not officially exist and wouldn't need to be explained away. Silence and emptiness in the vast foyer; deserted security desks, boards filled with engraved nameplates signifying emptied offices.

He began to run, because of Jim, the security man who should have been outside with Godwin and Chambers—Jim *would* have been, ex-Special Branch sergeant. Jim and his bank of screens monitoring the rest of the building, the lifts, the emergency stairs—

—because of yesterday, because Malan and Priabin's clever bitch had seen him opposite the NatWest Tower. He wriggled the key in the closed door, found it unlocked, opened it. His face brushed against the swing of a jacket hung up behind the door. On the console's desk, *The Sun* lay open like a cliché at the racing pages, pencil-marked. The chair was empty—

—no monochrome images of the stairs, the lift doors closed, the foyer and the secure floor. Jim's hand open like a flower, his face bland in death, eyes staring at the ceiling. A small leak of blood from the back of his neck, near the hairline. The collar was damp with it, hardly wet, really. A cigarette still smoldering in a tin ashtray. The screens had been switched off, but they'd been in a hurry. There was no pulse, no heartbeat; Jim's stubble against Hyde's temple as he listened to the body's chest. He perched on the edge of the chair and flicked at the console's switches. Screens enlivened, suddenly filled with empty corridors, blank walls, lift doors, the silence of the secure floor, some scraps and sheets of paper littering the corridor, dropped as Chambers and Godwin scuttled for the lift. The emergency stairs—fifth floor, sixth, seventh—secure lift doors closed. . . . Where was it, up or down? Should be down—

—inside the SIS offices. Three of them, blurting onto the screen, scuttling in their black outfits and ski masks, fingering papers, machines, collecting with furious, controlled haste. They'd been inside when the fake bomb scare alert began, waited until they could kill Jim—Hyde glanced down at the pale expression and the blank, open eyes—then gone up in the secure lift almost immediately. In five minutes, they'd be out the same way.

Priabin's people, armed with Uzis, dressed like the SAS at the Iranian Embassy siege . . . neat, all of it . . .

fingering whatever Godwin and Chambers hadn't had time to snatch up. And that was, undoubtedly, a lot. Clues to exactly what they were doing, how far they were into the maze.

"Stupid bastards," he murmured, slipping from the chair and closing the office door behind him. Locking it. Then he ran to the bank of lifts in the foyer. They'd hear the SIS lift going down and coming back up, they'd be waiting if he used that.

The floor below—no, above them, two floors to be safer. The lift soughed upwards, seeming noisier to his nerves. Priabin's people, had to be, not Malan's; he wouldn't get his fingers dirty handling rubbish like himself and Godwin and Chambers. Priabin had to follow after Malan's pet dislikes with the pooper scooper.

Two floors above the SIS offices, the lift stopped and the doors opened.

Christ, why did Godwin and Chambers have to believe *The Independent* and the Yanks when they were told the Cold War was over? He stepped out into the corridor, gingerly as a cat. Sirens from below, distant and unreal. Godwin and Chambers no longer believed that people meant them *real* harm, for Christ's sake! People would still come through doors, waving guns, even if their reasons had changed. Three men with Uzis—he took the Heckler & Koch out of his waistband and pulled the slide back, jerking a round into readiness. They had begun stuffing material, machines, computer printouts and tapes into soft canvas bags as he had left Jim's office and Jim's body. Not long now. They wouldn't hang about.

He went through the fire doors and down the staircase. He looked from a window down toward the diminished and shadowy street, to the army vehicles and purposeful movement of uniforms away from them. The crowd was welded by the hot glow of the evening sun into a variegated mass of shabby, faded colors, cordoned by a thin, dark line of policemen. He reached the SIS floor and its silence, his fingers touching out at full stretch of his arm at the fire doors. He pushed at the door, trying to remember if it squeaked. Silence as it opened, then the clicks and bumps like an old, damaged record amplified as he heard their noises. He held the gun with both hands, vertically in front of his face, elbows bent, as he shuffled silently along the corridor, back sliding along the wall.

The storeroom door was unlocked—fortunate sloppiness by Jim or someone else. He slipped into the darkness, closing the door behind him, hearing his breathing at once, magnified above their noises from the two main rooms of the floor. He flicked on the light. Dust, metal shelving dulled with it, a litter of old files, papers, tapes stacked like wheels, bins of tape waste and shredded printouts. Unspooled tape and confetti-like shreds of paper scattered over the floor. They'd searched the storeroom already, and abandoned it as an unyielding mine. He moved across the floor, listening, sidling by a trolley on which an old TV monitor rested. His hand fondled the shredded paper as if he were dipping into a tub of grain. He patted his pockets for the lighter—

—the lid of which clanged noisily, imitating old American lighters. He shoveled armfuls of tape spool and paper into the waste bin, then lifted it onto the trolley. Removed the TV, hearing every tiny noise louder than their noises from beyond the door. What if it's locked? Can't be, they opened it. He flicked at the igniter, flame spurted. He dropped the lighter as the flame adjusted into a tall, willowy column in the bin. Flare—

He heaved at the trolley and it moved with weak, squeaking protest toward the door.

"What was that?" he heard in Russian.

Door—

—open. Trolley . . . Christ! Through into the
room, dim with closed blinds, one man near the windows, another very close, the third swinging around,
the Uzi coming—

—*alarm*. The high-pitched, sinister threat of an
alarm wail. The flame and smoke belched out of the
bin. He slammed the storeroom door behind him. The
woodwork nippled near his face, then split and tore
from the impact of the bullets. He opened the door
into the corridor—empty. Twenty seconds. Flame glaring from an open door, reflected on the walls more
orange than the sunlight. They might guess, when there
were no sprinklers in operation, that it was a computer
room, no water allowed, that it would flood with an
inert gas in a matter of seconds, after the doors locked.

One of them had. Hyde was kneeling, hand flung
behind him as if in protest or remonstrance, pistol
extended stiffly. Two shots. The black-garbed man
bucked backwards, flinging up his hands, then fell
back into the room—popping out into view again like
some huge, comic puppet as the force of another man's
rush expelled him. Already the air-conditioning would
have shut off and there were only seconds before the
security doors and the lift doors all locked shut and the
room was pumped full of the inert gas.

Hyde blundered through the fire doors onto the
staircase, stumbled and rolled, scraping his hands and
knees, the gun hurting his hand as he collided with the
wall. He caught a lurching view of the street below,
then shook his head and turned, waiting for them to
come.

The doors must be locked. He could hear faint
banging, like distant central-heating pipes rumbling
with intruding air. No air in there, not now. No one
was coming out.

Then, no further banging. Silence. He went down
the stairs slowly, replacing the gun in his waistband in

the small of his back, adjusting his loose tie, straightening and brushing his jacket in small, obsessive movements. They were dead by now; asphyxiated. Choked to death, if you prefer, he admitted to himself. Murdered.

He pushed open the fire door on the floor below the sealed SIS offices and walked toward the lift doors. There'd be a captain or major somewhere and a chief inspector who could be told it was a hoax, a false alarm. Then, when SIS's forensic team went in, they'd find IRA or Lebanese or Iraqi papers on the bodies—Priabin would have covered all the angles. He felt tired, a little dizzy, as if with a summer cold.

"Yes, that's exactly what I mean, Valentina! He set off the fire alarm in a secure computer room and activated the safety system. It pumped the air out and left them to asphyxiate—you wonder why I do not underestimate these people!" Priabin banged his desk with his fist and all but rose out of his chair. Then he rubbed his face as if washing and settled back into the chair.

The evening paper was blazoned with a photograph of Centre Point and fuddled and hysterical with rumors—SAS HAD BEEN SENT IN, down to IT WAS ALL A HOAX. The television screen in a corner of the room, sound turned down, was jogging its images through crowds around Centre Point—he'd heard it already on the commercial channel news, then at six. The official version was that it was a hoax. Their final position would probably be—to counter the telephone claims of responsibility from his invented Iraqi vengeance squad—that the intruders, who may or may not have been from the Middle East, must have set off the security system. Committed suicide, as it were; an accident. Without the telephone calls to the news media which had been necessary to clear the building, they'd deny anything at all ever happened!

Dear God in Heaven, what an unholy bloody mess! Three good men—as important as their skills, men who could pass for Arabs—were dead and he knew no more now than he had before he'd sent them in. Christ, he'd even glimpsed on one news item Godwin and Chambers standing on the steps, arms filled with bags and files and cassettes, like two shoppers on the first day of Harrods sale! He glowered suspiciously at Valentina, who was watching the television screen intently. She appeared as shocked as he. She was, of course, wholly ambitious—she even suspected how bored and adrift he really was. She might, at some point, consider how this might be used to her advantage. She couldn't hope for his posting, but she could hope for a higher rung of the ladder.

Priabin shuffled through the reports on his desk; the woman's ears pricked like those of a cat. Sir Clive Orrell had rushed to the Cabinet Office to see Longmead, together with the ministers and their advisers who formed the antiterrorism Cabinet committee. They were still in session, judging by the comings and the absence of departures. The emergency at Centre Point was being wound down, returned to normal. Heavy police presence. The bodies had been smuggled out of the basement garage in an unmarked van. No doubt, any film of Hyde's presence had already been requested from the broadcasting authorities. At least they'll buy the deception that it was some Iraqi retaliation for the Gulf War, and they'd be left having to explain why the security services had offices in Centre Point. Then both his people and theirs could go back into hiding—a draw. Nil–nil, after extra time! Hyde would be debriefed—they'd probably be grateful he did it in such a low-publicity manner!

"Where's Hyde now?" he blurted. The girl twitched as if awoken, then turned to him.

"Vanished—for the moment. Being debriefed, I presume, sir."

"I doubt it. Godwin and Chambers?"

"They've been debriefed. They're at Godwin's flat in Kentish Town."

"They're being watched?" Priabin asked.

She nodded. "Then double-up the teams. Godwin and Chambers won't go far without their minder, Hyde. They'll lead us to him."

He banged his fist on the desk again. "Listen to me, Valentina! I'm not interested in revenge. I may indeed feel guilty we lost three men today, and I may appear to be overreacting as a consequence, but believe me, I'm not. We have to know what they know. To do that, we must isolate Godwin and Chambers, and it must be done carefully—accidentally." She was nodding in agreement, plucking her lower lip between a long finger and her thumb, red-nailed. "But Hyde has to be out of the way first—he *is* dangerous."

He turned to the window. Outside, the evening was heavy with retained light over the city, and the trees were dark beneath the warm sky, entertaining a twilight of their own. He scrabbled on his desk and lit a cigarette, the woman refusing his offer. He blew smoke at the ceiling.

Perhaps he needed to be this angry to be sufficiently decisive and ruthless. Center wanted people eliminated, or at least rendered harmless. He was—always had been—squeamish of gripping the cobras and milking their fangs. Not only was it messy, it was dangerous. They usually bit back. But now, the old deadly game was back, with a vengeance. The gentle city evening, to which he had long become accustomed, settled as lightly as birds on the embassy lawns. Dmitri, he instructed himself, move on to the cruder, simpler decisions that made you successful for so long. You cannot afford to be seduced by London and *glasnost*. He turned to

Valentina, smiling.

"I'm putting you in command—not because I think there's a can to be carried, but because it's urgent. I'll think, you decide."

"I . . . yes." She rubbed her forehead. Priabin remembered that there was one, just one, female Rezident in the service, and she was fifty-five and in Guatemala because not too many officers with aspirations spoke Spanish, because any future postings were limited to the outer circles of the inferno, Latin America. Valentina intended to improve the ratio, and probably before she was forty; that much had been evident within a week of her being posted to London.

And she was quick, alert and ruthless, and this was her kind of operation. He'd organized Kellett's death, of course, to keep him quiet, but Valentina had played Shapiro's whore for all it was worth—then overdosed him after sleeping with him. That she had shrugged off, finding his oblique and hesitant questioning little more than ludicrous. So she could be put in command of the removal of Hyde, to open up Godwin and whatever he possessed or knew.

"We're fighting over different bones, it seems to me, General, but we're the same dogs. Or we are expected to be the same. This man Hyde certainly is."

He nodded, and turned again to the window. The orange sky was like the glow from some huge, beneficent conflagration.

"Very well. Let's locate him and take him out of the game, Valentina. But foxhunt rules apply. Since we must retain secure cover, the death must be perceived as an accident. Other than those strictures, you have a free hand in getting rid of Hyde."

4

GENTLEMEN OF
THE SHADE

"Right, van Vuuren's in the restaurant, with the girl. He hasn't got the laptop with him. It's in the suite."

Hyde slipped into the seat beside Godwin. The coffee shop was all but empty. Chambers was visibly excited, like a kid—the bouquet of flowers was on the chair beside him. Godwin's briefcase, bulging and shabby, was beside Hyde's foot. The table was littered with printout paper and Godwin's sheets and notebooks, scrawled in his big, untidy handwriting.

"I haven't got the answer, not yet," he offered.

"Oh, for Christ's sake, Godwin! Van Vuuren's having dinner before he has a bonk, not on holiday for a bloody fortnight!" He leaned forward and, in a glaring whisper, addressed Chambers. "Have you ordered the champagne at the desk?"

"Yes. And fruit." Chambers was inordinately pleased with himself.

"Is that in case van Vuuren overdoes it and has to

go to hospital?" Hyde ground his fist into the woven table mat. "Look, when I bumped off the three Marx brothers this afternoon, I didn't expect Priabin not to notice. Orrell's trousers are on fire because he can't find me—I checked with Ros. I *have* to report in tomorrow morning, so let's get it right tonight, shall we? We haven't a lot of time to spare before they send someone round checking that all their doors are locked—and that means tipping off van Vuuren. And by the look of the tart he's with, he'll be rushing his dinner just to get back upstairs with her! Understand me?"

"Yes!" Chambers snapped.

"Right. Now, what's the access code?"

"There are five words, or groups of words, no group longer than two. Some English, some Afrikaans. The numbers we've got—look." Scribbled in the notebook, like some old, simple addition sum from his primary school.

"But the *words?*"

"Darren and I can't make head or tail of what might be missing. Dictionaries, guide books, maps, newspapers—I'm bloody knackered, the effort we've put in since—"

"Since three hours ago. Oh, shit."

"Darren's still using the computer, to try to come up with the answer. He'll call if—"

"Look, why not just pinch his bloody laptop? I'll bring it back later—or make it look like a break-in. You can't use it yet. So let's keep it until you can."

"As soon as he sees it's missing, there goes everything. Jo'burg will change all the codes, immediately."

"All right, Chambers, stop smirking." Hyde glanced at his watch. "You—get yourself into the suite, then let Godwin in. I'll watch van Vuuren. And you've got until nine, at the latest. It's eight-ten now. If you haven't cracked it by nine, then bring the bloody machine out with you. And that's *my* decision as case officer."

"Very well," Godwin agreed.

Chambers scowled, but Hyde merely tossed his head, indicating the door of the coffee shop.

"Right. Give me ten minutes, then follow me up." He made an attempt to ignore Hyde which, to Chambers' increasing irritation, produced no more than a sarcastic smile from the Australian.

He stood up, collecting the bouquet. To his back, he heard Hyde remark: "Don't forget to go down on one knee when you give her the flowers."

Piss off! he thought violently. The foyer of the InterContinental was crowded with guests; one or two fur coats, even in midsummer, the occasional drift of Arab robes. Luggage and movement. Hyde claimed there was no one keeping van Vuuren under surveillance except himself. Chambers began feeling hot as soon as he paused outside the doors of the lift, the flowers now as foolish as Hyde had made them sound, the adrenalin unfamiliar and coarse, like some powerful, cheap foreign drink. Piss off, Hyde, I'm going to get this right, he thought.

The doors opened. A Chinese girl, too much make-up, a bloated European or American with her, his neck boiling over the collar of his shirt, his stomach draped by his jacket like curtains at some ugly, convex window. Chambers shivered as he entered the empty lift. Then a porter held the door and a luggage trolley was thrust in beside him.

"What floor, sir?" in some barely decipherable accent. Chambers mumbled the answer.

The lift stopped at the third floor and the porter departed, then stopped at the fifth. A woman in late middle-age with too much heady, expensive perfume and stretched skin around her mouth and along her jaw. She got out at the sixth. From along the corridor, the noise of a television and a bellowing American voice. Chambers sighed, rubbing at his forehead. The doors opened again at van Vuuren's floor. Chambers blurted into the corridor.

Empty. Trays littered with the debris of afternoon snacks outside some of the doors, notices warning off staff already on some of the doorknobs. It would have been easier with keys, but the InterContinental used those bloody plastic things programmed to the lock of a single door, *for your security, sir.* He moved rapidly down the corridor toward the fire doors, hesitantly passing van Vuuren's suite as if it were the location of an ambush. Godwin and he had it, surely, but the words wouldn't come out right; like a drunk's lips moving loosely, they couldn't pronounce the access codes! With the bouquet in its cellophane and bearing the inimitable label of Moyses Stevens, he scuttled gratefully behind the fire doors, peering back through the wired glass at the empty corridor. How long did it take them to provide a bottle of champagne, for God's sake, when most of the guests were rushing out to four hundred quid restaurants to meet million-dollar deals?

Squeak, just as he was remembering the gaps in the access codes: Kruger, to begin, then Boete Erazmus, then *Ellis Park*—what did that mean, where was it? Then, oh, then, N-e-w-l-a- and nothing else except s-v-e-l-d, except for the joke word, Mandela. He agreed with Godwin, there was time for only two more letter groupings, the end of one word, the beginning or first word for the second. *Squeak*—

The trolley dragging the slow, huddled room-service waiter down the corridor from the service lift toward the door of van Vuuren's suite. The neck of the champagne bottle thrusting from the ice bucket, the bowl of fruit wrapped in cellophane, like the bouquet that rustled against his cheek as he began to breathe more quickly. Then a door opened and an open-necked shirt and bulging flannels appeared, at once berating the waiter, who shrugged expressively and doubtless struggled with English.

"What kind of craphouse *is* this hotel, anyway?" Chambers heard in a muffled roar through the glass.

A door slammed, taking the striped shirt out of view, and the waiter struggled on behind his trolley. Napkins, some wrapped cheese, an erect carnation in a thin vase. The waiter knocked at the door of van Vuuren's suite, waited, then knocked again. Cursed silently, the bent head and moving lips eloquent. Knocked, rang the bell . . . come on, *come on!* The bouquet rubbed against his stubble. The door opened to the program of the waiter's master card, and the trolley dragged him into the suite. Chambers swallowed, but there was no moisture at the back of his mouth, then stepped through the fire door, releasing it with exaggerated caution. Hurried the two intervening doors to van Vuuren's suite—door still open, thank God! The waiter fussing around the trolley, transforming it into a table near the window.

Chambers held the bouquet of orchids and carnations in front of him as he stepped into the room. The waiter looked up over the parapet of paper and cellophane at him, surprised.

"Ah, thank you, yes," Chambers mumbled. *Don't forget the tip*, Hyde had said. *It makes you legit.* How much, he had wanted to ask but had not dared, confronted with Hyde's anticipated contempt. He thrust the two pound coins into the waiter's hand, scribbled awkwardly van something scrawl at the bottom of the receipt, stared at the window and the first prickling lights of the city beyond it until—

—he whirled round. The door had shut behind the waiter. He was inside. He flung the bouquet into the bathroom, where it slithered down the side of the bath, spilling leaves and petals inside its wrapping.

He looked at his watch. Eight-twenty, Jesus . . .

The suite had all the warm-lit emptiness of temporary accommodation, the scents of carpet and polish rather than lives. Table lamps, standard lamps, subdued downlighters and wall lights. Yet the room was little more than the small hillocks and valleys of furniture. Two three-piece suites in the main lounge, two king-size beds in the bedroom. Christ, a second bedroom, two bathrooms, it was a bloody house, not a hotel room. Fruit in bowls and cellophane were strewn across the various tables and chests. Chambers opened a sliding cupboard door and saw van Vuuren's suitcases and bags, his clothes. Began to open drawers, discovering ties, handkerchiefs, drawer after drawer—a packet of condoms, taking no chances, even with a high-class working girl—his whole behavior like that of an obsessive, endlessly checking that things were tidied, drawers were shut.

The telephone rang. He stood rigidly still. Twice, three, four . . . seven, eight. Christ! He was sweating freely, caught as in a spotlight in the middle of the lounge, the low edge of a coffee table pressing against his calf. Thirteen, fourteen . . .

Silence. He collapsed into an easy chair. *Don't sit anywhere unless you plump up the bloody cushions!* Hyde shouted in his head. He jumped to his feet, unsteadily, almost dizzy. His hands—God, his hands were shaking!

Doorbell—

Oh, no! Godwin, must be. He squinted into the little convex hole in the door. Godwin's features, distorted as in the back of a shiny spoon, glowered at him. He opened the door. "Well?"

Godwin shook his head glumly.

"Oh, no—"

"Don't start, Gladys!" Godwin snapped. "Darren hasn't got a clue, neither have I. What's the bloody time?"

"Eight twenty-three, sod it."

"So, we'll just make ourselves comfortable, shall we, and wait until nine o' clock? Then we can lift that"—he nodded toward the opened wardrobe, where the laptop computer stood on its edge beside a suitcase—"and bugger off. Because, Terry, I don't have the bloody answer and that's a fact that can't be avoided."

There was a huge African moon looming like a bland, puzzled face just beyond the open slats of the blind. The smell of ether, of ointments, and the immediate pain, as if awoken by the scents, in his hands and on his stretched, stiff cheeks. He was lying down on a hard bed, near the window through which the moon rose and glowed. He gingerly flexed his fingers. They remembered heat, pain, and the long time before the relief of cool water. Then the images came—and the constriction in his throat, and the choking sensation, the smoke in his lungs and the smell of burning flesh that might or might not have been his own. Then he began to hear his own cries as they gripped his scorched and raw skin as he was dragged from the waterhole, to collapse on the bank and immediately discover the country of unconsciousness. He hardly sensed the present hold of his bandages and the ease of salves.

. . . *very lucky, Mr. Anderson,* he heard the Indian doctor saying once more, though the moonlit room was empty, and quiet except for his own strained breathing. *Superficial burns . . . no lung-damage, I am pleased to say . . . you might well have suffocated, even drowned, Mr. Anderson . . . very lucky indeed, sir. . . .* And then the doctor had drifted away from the edge of eyesight, and he had remembered Margarethe was dead. It was inescapable; he had not asked for tranquilizers or sleeping pills, just stared into that storm until it abated a little, out of weariness, perhaps. He felt he was poised at the eye of the hurricane, in a pool of calm that was too shallow.

Very lucky, Mr. Anderson. . . . The doctor's voice had faltered at that point, understanding that he was conscious, and remembered. Or perhaps the doctor had reacted to his glaring eyes, staring out of what he knew must be a blackened face. The doctor had turned away with a movement of delicacy, and removed and wiped his glasses. In so doing, he had released Anderson's weak hold on consciousness. *Very lucky . . .*

Christ, she was dead. Blantyre had burned her to death, had others killed or shot them himself. *Lucky . . .* the word blew away like a scrap of burnt paper down a long tunnel which had become his perspective on events. People had survived the attack and the fire; they had dragged him from the water hole where he must have been floundering like something half dead. But no one who had become important to his limited sympathies had survived, merely a few customers of the company that managed that area of the reserve for which he was responsible. *She* was dead. To his first, uxorious wife's painful, agonized death from cancer, he had been remarkably indifferent. Nature and disease could not be regarded as things to be opposed, and the woman had long ceased to have any meaning other than humiliation for him. But Margarethe was dead now, his second wife, his black dolly, as Blantyre had called her.

Someone had said, as he had drifted back toward unconsciousness, as the quick African dusk had striped the room because of the blinds, that *Blantyre hadn't been able to get there in time, they'd seen the smoke, his patrol . . . disgruntled ex-SWAPO people, Communists or something like . . .* He might have groaned aloud then, because they had come rushing to the bedside, assuming pain rather than protest.

Most of the day, he had lain in the back of the truck because the medical aircraft was grounded and he had had to be driven the hundred and thirty miles to the clinic at Otjiwarongo. He remembered only the jolting and lolling of his head, as if he had become some kind of idiot—and as if all thought of her was being shaken loose, allowed to drift like the cloud of dust behind the truck. Even his screams had been vengeful, occupied with losing thought of her, and the clinging image of Blantyre.

His body was numb with bruising and sedatives, constricted by plasters and bandaging. The moonlight filled the room, imaging the blind on the far wall. An IV bag glinted beside his bed, there was the faint noise of a fan, the occasional howl of a night animal from outside, which made him jerk and shudder as if it voiced his pain. He remembered the pressure of one of the guests' mouths against his own, attempting to revive him, but that was too imitative, too easily evocative of his dead wife's mouth, and he blotted it out. He did not know whether or not Blantyre knew he had survived the attack. Blantyre had apparently re-arrived, in all pretended innocence, two hours after dawn. By then, he had been on his way. Probably one of the survivors had explained that he had been taken to the clinic. A guest had accompanied him and the woman who had died beside him during the journey. He shook his head feebly, and the pain returned. Blantyre would know, somehow, in some way . . .

He felt the night and the out-there pressing against the window, against the flimsy walls of the room in which he had been left. He could remember nurses, attention, the relief of pain, but mostly now he was aware of the weakness of his body and the death of his wife. He felt shrunken, as if the fire had shriveled him like a fruit, so that she and he and the past few years were no bigger than seeds, waiting . . .

. . . for nothing to come back out of the tunnel into which she had been blown like a scrap of paper. His cheeks felt wet. The image persisted, of her as a scorched, brown scrap of paper, nothing more . . . a still, tiny body in the corner of the shattered, burning bedroom. His bandages now felt tight. Grief welled through him like a huge wave.

Eventually, his cheeks stung as the tears dried. He felt emptied, like a spilled vessel, retaining only the knowledge that Blantyre undoubtedly knew he had survived and where he had been taken. She had been swallowed by silence and darkness for the moment. Blantyre would come to Otjiwarongo soon. He must conserve what energy he possessed, to be ready. He flexed his fingers painfully, sensed his bruises and burns. How could he kill Blantyre, a wounded man like him? How could he? If Blantyre walked into the moonlit room now, it would be over in less than a minute with nothing more deadly than a pillow. He squirmed with mounting rage. Even his grief disabled him like another physical injury; the ink from some frightened squid, surrounding and enveloping him. Repellent, immobilizing. Blantyre could appear at any moment—at that moment—and he was helpless.

"Look, I can't touch the bloody thing—you know that!" Godwin protested as he stumped about the room. Chambers was reduced to following him, scuffing over the indentations made by his heavy crutches, having plumped up the cushions for Christ's sake! Godwin turned at the windows overlooking the Wellington Arch and continued. "Patrick's right. We'll have to take the thing with us and hope for the best!"

Eight-forty. Chambers gathered up Godwin's scattered notes, formulations—guesses, really—then straightened with a start as the telephone rang. Two, three . . . no more. Then it began again. Chambers snatched up the receiver, knowing it was Hyde and resenting Hyde's realization that their game was going down the tubes.

"Yes?" he snapped.

"Have you two buggers got anywhere, for Christ's sake?" Hyde whispered. "The girl's just picking at the meal because she wants to get it over as soon as possible with that little shit and he's already ordering his pudding because he can't wait to get her up to the room. He's bloody *drooling!* What have you got?"

"Nothing, bugger it—nothing! Satisfied?"

"Look, I wouldn't work with you again on pain of excommunication, Chambers. Pull yourself together. If you can't get into the mainframe, then bring the laptop out with you—but get on with it, either way!"

Chambers listened to the purr of the disconnected call, then replaced the receiver, which was filmed with perspiration. "It's got to be two other names—places or people!" he all but wailed.

"We've been through the Boer Wars, both of them, we've been through the map of South Africa again and again, the guide books—it's like bloody Mastermind. But there's no logic to it!" He stumped past Chambers toward the opened wardrobe from which they had not even bothered to remove the laptop computer. Godwin stared at it, as if willing it to confess and threatening it with pain if it remained uncommunicative. He poked at it with one of his crutches, poked at van Vuuren's Louis Vuitton luggage, the South African Airways labels still attached, the flying springbok gold against blue. Still flying the long way, via the Cape Verde islands, but that was being renegotiated. Soon, they'd be able to land at Nairobi, Harare, wherever they wanted. Why am I wasting my time thinking about it? he reprimanded himself, knowing precisely the virtue of distraction. They couldn't solve the riddle; they'd have to risk exposure by taking the laptop and hoping they could get into the mainframe in Jo'burg before van Vuuren or Malan had all the access codes changed. Hence the focus on the labels, the luggage . . . the springbok . . . the labels . . . the springbok? They were even talking about the England rugby team touring South—

Christ, the bloody Springboks! No one had been to South Africa for years, no wonder he—!

"Give me the phone—quick!" He lurched across the room and collapsed into an armchair, dabbing furiously at the numbers. "Yes—sports department!" he snapped. He was grinning weakly, feverishly at Chambers, who seemed afraid of him, as at lunacy. "*Evening Standard*," he muttered in a breathless voice. "Bloke I was in Uni with, writes on rug—Yes, Gareth Jones, please! Yes, it's very urgent. Tell him it's Tony Godwin—*Tony God-win*." He clicked his finger at Chambers, whispering, "Give me those names—quick! Come on—*there!*" Chambers handed him the list of names: Ellis Park, that's the one that rang a bell—well, now it did! After recollecting the springbok badge on a green jersey. The bloody South African rugby team! "What. Where is he? What? What's the number of the bloody pub, then? No, I'm not his wife, you cheeky sod. It's a matter of life and death, so it couldn't be about his wife, could it? What? Yes, got that. Thanks."

He cut off the call, redialed, looked up at Chambers and winked. His heart was thudding in his chest. Chambers held out his arm, pointing at his watch. Eight forty-five. Enough time, just enough, as long as the girl downstairs wanted a brandy before facing up to van Vuuren! "Yes—is that Boswell's Wine Bar? Good. One of your customers, he's there at the moment. . . . Bugger that, love. Police, OK? Now, will you get Mr. Gareth Jones to the telephone, please? Thank you."

He began to drum on the arm of the chair with his

broad fingers, as if already typing out the access codes on the laptop's keyboard. Chambers shrugged a request for an explanation, but Godwin waved postponement. He could hear his own breathing hoarsely loud in the earpiece. "Gareth? Tony Godwin. . . . Yes, and you? How's, er, is it still Tracey? Oh, sorry to hear that. Look, can you do me a favor? Just a couple of quick questions. . . . Yes, now. Look, you were on the last British Lions tour to South Africa for one of the newspapers, weren't you? No, it's not official, just a stupid bet. Well, doesn't matter if you do, just answer the questions, Gareth. If I read out these names, can you tell me the two that are missing, and spell them out? Yes, crossword, that's it. Yes, half the winnings. I've got Ellis Park, Boete Erazmus, and part of a word, New . . . what is it? Newlands . . . " Godwin scribbled, gesticulating with the pencil at Chambers as if to ward him off. "And the other word . . . yes, the four Test grounds of the Springboks, must be!" He felt the perspiration of relief dampen his forehead. "And the fourth . . . L-o-f-tus . . . what's that? V-e-r-s-veld—yes! Thanks, Gareth, I owe you a pint. See you!"

He sat back in his chair, exhausted. Chambers remained motionless, as if in shock, in the middle of the room.

"How?" he managed eventually.

"The labels on his luggage—a springbok. Badge of the South—oh, never mind now, get the bloody machine and attach it to the phone. We're in bloody business! Kruger—Mandela—the four Test grounds, four bloody rugby venues—and we're in to MLC's mainframe!"

Eight forty-seven . . .

The woman shook her head, refusing an after-dinner drink. Van Vuuren evidently didn't mind; there'd be booze in the room, even without Chambers' champagne. His head was already swiveling for sight of a waiter, his hand poised to wave. Eight-fifty, no, almost fifty-one. Christ, why do people have to rush their bloody dinners in expensive restaurants? Looking at the woman, on the other hand, Hyde thought, rubbing his chin, who could blame van Vuuren, even if he was paying for it?

The waiter arrived with the bill. Hyde was leaning back in his chair, craning to see into Le Soufflé restaurant from the hotel's cocktail bar. Van Vuuren signed it with a flourish. Does she take Amex? he wondered. That'll do nicely.

Hyde finished his lager and stood up, moving quickly to the telephone at the door of the cocktail bar. He dialed van Vuuren's suite. Waited . . . engaged. Engaged? He held on. Were they in? Or was Godwin ringing up pimply Darren for the answer! He dialed the number once more. Still engaged. The waiter had been satisfied with a twenty-pound note. Van Vuuren's impatience was evident.

Hyde hurried to the lifts.

"Bloody hell! Captain Flint's buried treasure, map and all!" Godwin breathed deeply. Behind him, Chambers photographed the laptop's screen while the printer they had coupled to the machine continued to grumble and cough out the information. Eight fifty-five. "Look at it. God, with a couple of hours and a bit of luck, we'd be able to open everything up on computer-predicted number sequences. Namibia—that's interesting. France—jackpot time. Terry Chambers, come on down!"

Fifty-seven . . . Patrick would just have to wait, it can't be choked off now. He dabbed at the keypad, drawing the number sequence from the notes balanced on his knee.

"What are you after?"

"UK companies whose pass-through trade had doubled, even trebled in the last few months, export companies, shippers."

"Why that area?" Chambers murmured, absorbed now in checking the printout, having tidied Godwin's papers back into his briefcase.

"It has to be leaving the country somehow. Who's sending it out, and where to."

"Could be useful to—" There was a loud, insistent banging on the door of the suite. "Oh, no!"

"You buggers—get moving! He's on his way up with the tart, for God's sake!"

"Hyde—"

Chambers hurried to the door and Hyde burst into the lounge, waving his arms.

"Come on, you stupid buggers—let's go!" He unplugged the printer and Godwin scowled in protest. Then he snatched the telephone receiver off the laptop and replaced it. "Come on, he's on his way!" He snapped the lid of the laptop shut. "Where does this go?"

"Patrick, another minute, for Christ's sake!"

"No! Get moving."

Chambers took the laptop and replaced it in the wardrobe, closing the louvred door on it. Hyde was plumping up cushions while Godwin was staring at his bulging briefcase and the printout as if he had walked into his own home to discover it burgled by strangers. Then he gathered his crutches to his sides and Chambers collected the case. Hyde was smoothing the carpet with hands and feet, moving disturbed furniture back onto its indentations in the thick pile.

"That'll have to do—wait!" He passed Chambers and eased open the door. The corridor was empty. "OK, through the fire exit. We'll wait until he's shut himself in. Bring the bloody flowers, Chambers! No, not the bloody champagne—that could have been left by the hotel. Just the flowers!"

Hyde closed the door behind them, then the fire door. Looked back through the wired glass. The corridor was no longer empty. Van Vuuren, shorter than the long-legged woman, coming down the corridor beside her, she holding his arm. They paused outside the door of the suite and then van Vuuren let them in. The door clicked shut. Chambers and Godwin, redfaced, were sweating; Hyde wiped his sleeve across his brow.

"Don't bloody do that to me again!"

"Christ, we did it." Chambers patted the briefcase and the printout under his arm, smirking. Then he threw the bouquet down the emergency stairs. Petals flew, stems snapped. "We bloody did it!" he announced.

Hyde came up the noisome staircase because, once again, the lifts were inoperable. The cozy officialese disguised his guilt. In reality, some little bastards had sabotaged the lifts yet again, isolating dozens of pensioners and Asians and children in their fortresslike block of flats. He passed a black man who was wriggling and grunting his way to sexual climax at a turning of the stair. The girl behind the man's shoulders was all but invisible. Her spread and braced legs indicated custom and acceptance. As he rounded a turn of the staircase, he heard a quick gasp and a few quickdrawn breaths.

But ninety-year-old Aunt Vi wouldn't move out to sheltered accommodation or even a nice little bungalow somewhere, would she? Not bloody likely. *Lived here all my life, I have, in this street.* Street? It had disappeared in the sixties under the tons of concrete and landfill required to raise these monstrosities, at the behest, he always felt, of developers and architects who either never set foot in the country again or lived in Georgian mansions just outside Bath.

He tossed his head. *Here I stand*, said Aunt Vi, who was one of the two middle-aged aunts in their mothball-smelling overcoats who'd come out to Woollongong to see him and his mother, and the one who'd come to Southampton to collect him from the boat, a ten-year-old orphan in a strange country.

Guilt drove him to see Vi once a week. Ros, he suspected, came quite often, though she never mentioned her visits. But chocolate fingers and Jaffa cakes were often about the place, in their opened packets—and Vi didn't spend her pension on luxuries. Gladys was dead and Vi was alone, marooned sixteen floors up in this dump. *Gött strafe England*—but this had been erected just where the bloody Germans had helped to clear the slums!

He reached the long, dark concrete corridor with its low balcony on one side and the disfigured row of doors on the other, where she lived. The cries of yobs, black and white, like the calls of wild animals, echoed around the four sides of the block and across the littered courtyard with its two burned-out cars and other rubbish. FORT APACHE—STEPNEY had been spray-painted on the wall at the turning of the corridor, though he could hardly read the letters now. That movie was years old, anyway. No one had touched up or repainted the joke. Mindless fucks and ballocks and a lot of swastikas were more in tune with the times and the vandalism and the educational level. Around here, the graffiti should be at ankle height if its distance up the wall was any measure of the level of intelligence. Youths called like lost souls as he reached her door; no, more as if they were locating other members of a pack prior to the hunt. FORT fucking APACHE! He knocked loudly on the door, calling out at once: "Vi—

it's me, Patrick. Open the door."

He could hear the television blaring vainly at her deafness from inside the flat; a wall of sound, like those erected in at least six of the flats along this landing, fending off the noises from outside. "Vi—open the door, it's Patrick!" he shouted through the letterbox.

In the moments that followed, he heard the television, the calls, high laughter, even some more covert noises from the courtyard—robbery or crack retailing. Eventually, her shadow loomed behind the reinforced, frosted glass and he heard the drawing back of the bolts and the opening of the security lock he had had fitted. In the hierarchy of the block, she was safer than most. There were black yobs, brown ones, and enough whites to find her some kind of deaf, dotty object of amusement rather than persecution. In simple terms, the shit went through the Asian letterboxes. And, of course, he had broken one yob's arm, two years ago, *pour encourager les autres.* He pecked at Vi's raspy, leathery cheek as she presented it to him, then locked the door behind him and followed her into the minuscule lounge. Good decorative order, Mayfair estate agents would claim, had they dared take a Stepney flat onto their august books. He'd wallpapered the place last year. The furniture revealed the geological layers of Vi's life and that of her sister, who had married better than Vi: comfortably solid Victorian, interwar utility, postwar appalling and some bits and pieces of the sixties. The television, herded into a corner by the massed furniture, thundered out some inane game show.

She sat down like a slowly collapsing sack filled with bones and little else. Her eyes were rheumily bright, and her lips were still becoming accustomed, it seemed to the dentures she had had for as long as he'd known her. His entire family, she was, since Glad had died. Her eyes wore their cataracts like acquired wisdom.

"You all right?" she shouted, leaning toward him, the familiar amalgam of foster mother and schoolmistress in her cracked old voice. Something survived of the stranger who had met him off the boat from Sydney almost thirty years ago. She watched the bottle in his pocket as if it were a pistol. Shaking his head, he tugged it from his jacket and placed it on the scarred Victorian dresser that dominated one entire wall of the lounge.

"*Yours,*" he emphasized. "Your nightcap." She shook her head, but he noticed that the other bottle, the last he had brought, was almost empty.

She had been his first memory of England, the mothball smell of her cardigan as she crushed him against her ample bosom, comforting but strange. The leaning, skeletal spires of the port cranes had risen insect-headed behind her. He remembered the chill of the port, the grayness of the sky. Remembered, too, that she had smiled continually during the train journey across the snowbound countryside between Southampton and London, her mouth even in those days filled with the dentures that seemed to move independently of her lips and will. He patted her hand and sat opposite her after reducing the volume of the television; settling into the comparative peace of the next hour, punctuated more by noise from outside than it would ever be by their conversation. Vi watched the television absorbedly, no longer able to hear the contestants or the quizmaster. It would make the game no less comprehensible for her.

He looked at her. Her brightness of eye was an illusion of comfort. Normally, she berated him about the neighbors—*those blackies and darkies*—or his unshaven appearance; she had blossomed during the time when he couldn't control his drinking, seizing upon him like a raptor upon a carcass, reinvading his life, refostering him, he supposed.

"I wonder what he wants?" Vi inquired, as if addressing someone else in the room. Not the cat. The yobs had thrown that from the balcony one day, turning it into a shapeless little lump that leaked down in the courtyard. That had been when he had broken the arm of one of them, after threatening him with joining the cat from the same altitude. Eventually, the cat's body had been kicked somewhere out of sight and Vi had had no pets since then. "Always bringing me something. I don't want *things* at my time of life!" she continued, apparently to the television.

The yobs drowned her words, running past, banging against doors like ball bearings. Black and white loiterers, off to mug their neighbors who didn't dare use their garages after dark. He detested Stepney with a deep loathing, probably because he had once lived in this flat with Vi, before he had gone into the army. Then into *that special regiment, what did they call it— SAS? Now, he's got a proper office job, in Whitehall.* That was how Vi explained it loudly to the Asian grocer. *Quite respectable, for a darkie, him.* She was sometimes suspicious that Patrick hardly ever appeared in a suit, of course, having a proper office job and all that. SAS probably, like garlic on the door, kept at least some of the vampires that roamed the corridors and staircases of the block at bay, so he didn't mind her broadcasts.

Someone rattled the letterbox. Vi hadn't heard, of course. Hyde tossed his head and watched the near-silent screen with her. She'd get up and drag herself across the room soon, to turn up the volume—when the next set of contestants smirked and posed. The letterbox rattled again. He got up to look along the passage. A shadow loomed beyond the reinforced glass. The letterbox rattled again. Perhaps they did bother her, but she didn't hear so how could she inform him? Rattle, rattle, a more persistent rhythm. A light flared outside, making the shadow more bulky and solid.

Jesus! The letterbox. Vi's head turned slowly as he clattered his chair back against a tea trolley wedged between the dresser and a Victorian table with a potted plant on it.

A piece of lighted cloth or paper was pushed through the letterbox and flared on the doormat. He ran down the passage as the shadow disappeared and stamped on the tiny fire, grinding it out. The smell of petrol and smoke and the singed doormat. Nothing really damaged. Oh, yes, just kids. They're bored, you know, unemployed. Fuck them!

"Vi!" he shouted. "Come and lock the door behind me."

He was forcibly reminded of how old she really was as she struggled into the passage, muttering: "Little buggers . . . not for months . . . " The keys rattled softly in her hand.

He opened the door and looked out, then kissed her cheek, shut the door behind him and heard it lock. Heard the bolts. The corridor appeared empty. Rap music blared up from the courtyard. Distant voices and raucous laughter echoed amid the concrete canyons like the neighing of horses. Beyond that, he heard something smash with the quick sound of breaking glass. He'd have to fit a fireproof letter box behind the door some time, if this was the new game. He heard nothing for some seconds except the usual noises of the block and the smell of overcooked vegetables and dog or human urine close by.

Then, from opposite ends of the long, sixteenth-floor alleyway, shadows. Two whites at one end, perhaps three blacks at the other, both groups intent upon convergence. He listened to Vi retreat and the volume of the television increase, then thrust his hands into his pockets and began walking along the concrete corridor, past door after door, toward the two whites. One of the blacks behind him was carrying a ghetto blaster that boomed tinnily off the concrete. "I Shot the Sheriff." Laughter, tinged with anticipation? He wasn't sure, but some electricity in his spine made him shiver. There was something about the burning cloth through the letterbox, something about the silent emptiness of the corridor by the time he had opened the door, and about this pincer movement now. Something about faces on the Tube. Bob Marley's amplified, distorted voice trailed Hyde along the corridor and the two whites slowed. Faces on the Tube, shadows in the dim streets, footsteps behind him on the staircase. Hoods? The two whites were ten yards away now, and had stopped, apparently outside a door. Then one of them began urinating through a letterbox while the other laughed and pulled open a can of lager. Bob Marley's voice had halted, too, bellowing some twenty yards behind him. Hoods? Organized, with a specific target? He touched at the pistol in the small of his back, then slouched forward toward the two whites, adopting the vague weave of a drunk—plenty of practice there, my son—and at once the urinating youth turned to face him, zipping his jeans. White faces, white designer sneakers, white hands. A mindless giggle from one of them. Specific target—himself. The fire—he could faintly smell petrol on one of them—had been specific too, to draw him out.

He felt the dryness of his mouth and sucked saliva from his cheeks. Why? *Who?* Priabin? Bob Marley had begun moving closer, stealthy footsteps shunting him forward. Five of them. He reached out a tentative hand, leaning against the rough-finished concrete that was the place's *texture,* for Christ's sake, a bloody *visual amenity,* shaking his head and laughing to himself—

—disconcerting them. The blacks had paused. Then he kicked the closest white just below the kneecap, hard, doubling him up with a cry of pain. Hyde brought both hands, linked into one fist, down on the back of his neck. Then the second white—gleam of a blade? The youth was watching his feet, trying to watch his hands at the same time, and was about to open his mouth to call out to the blacks. Hyde brought his forearm down hard just above the gleam and something tinkled metallically on the concrete, then drove his elbow into the youth's stomach and his extended knuckles into his face in a short jabbing movement. He felt bone break.

"Aw, fucking *Christ!*" the youth screamed, holding his nose. As he doubled over in his stunned pain, Hyde punched him on the side of the head, kicked the knife along the corridor, then turned to study the three blacks, one carrying the ghetto blaster and the others perhaps pickax handles. Guns? he wondered, feeling the cold electricity shiver through his frame again. He touched his own gun for reassurance, then shouted, "Whatever it is, you three—fuck off! Unless you want what these two got, piss off!"

He paused, then moved to turn away, not needing to hurry until he heard them move. Groans rumbled from the two white youths, curses and aggressive breathing. No, they wouldn't move, not for the moment, not until he reached the head of the staircase. Sixteen floors up.

Then he heard a whistle's peremptory summons from one of the blacks, and knew that it was no longer a confrontation, a swatting of violent, mindless flies. It was a pursuit. The whistle sounded for a second time, more urgently. He began running for the stairs.

The half-kaffir woman was kneeling on the bed like a bitch so that he could enter her, doglike. White garter belt, white stockings, smooth brown buttocks. Van

Vuuren allowed her hand to guide his penetration. He was sweating as his movements accelerated, as the litany of crudities hurried through his mind toward the climax. Kaffir bitch, kaffir bitch, kaffir—the telephone.

"Christ!" He shuddered as he withdrew, splashing the girl's buttocks with semen. He snatched up the telephone, angry at the evidence of his humiliation which had not quite become hers. The woman turned lazily, then smoothed her buttocks dry on the bed linen. Then she rolled across the bed and pulled the top sheet around her, waiting with the patience and impassivity of machinery. "*Yes?* What? No, no, you weren't interrupting me, Paulus." He studied the woman's fine-boned face for some reaction to his accent and to his subservience. There was none. "Yes . . . good. Oh, you've spoken to him. No, the shipment's cleared for tomorrow night, yes. The money's been deposited as usual." He replaced his glasses. The girl's breasts beneath the thin sheet. He picked up the champagne flute from the bedside table and sipped at it. "No, there are no problems . . . no? What? Oh, I see . . . yes, I understand. *Their* suggestion? No, yours, sure, Paulus. Yes, I'll give it some thought, begin making arrangements, yes . . . goodnight."

He put down the receiver and, as at a signal, the woman peeled back the sheet with a mechanical absence of sexuality, down past her garter belt to her thighs. He walked away from the bed and lit a cigarette, standing at the window as he watched the traffic clotting around the Wellington Arch, brake lights shining out in protest and rebuff. The shipment was organized, almost on its way. There had been the usual division of the spoils—on to France, then to Namibia. Yes, things would change now, obviously, since the bloody Russians wanted their stuff to go direct, more or less, in the planned build-up to the VIATE climax.

He heard the woman rubbing her arms as if she were cold. He knew that he could ignore her until he was ready. She would remain until she was paid, whatever the humiliations along the way. He picked a shred of tobacco from his tongue.

That guy Babbington waltzed with Paulus, and Paulus let him do it—that was the real pisser in this whole setup! Reid Electronics was too valuable to lose, that was the real point at issue. And it was coitus interruptus so that Paulus could relay his orders from Moscow, from that English bastard who'd gone over to them!

The French company. Now, that *was* too good to lose. But it was close to Reid. Malan was playing dangerous games, risking exposing Reid, but trying to protect the French company. If he opened the can, everyone would see the whole box of sardines in there. He puffed angrily at his cigarette. Panic, that's what it was, because they had to stay in Europe now that South Africa might—God help it—end up in the hands of the kaffirs, and that woolly headed old bastard Mandela might one day step up on the President's podium in Pretoria! Christ, he'd kill some black buggers the day that appeared on the bloody television news.

Coitus interruptus . . . that phrase? Oh, yes . . . he remembered masturbating to Havelock Ellis' dry, analytical, unerotic prose as a boy on the farm. His sexual education.

Kaffirs. He turned suddenly to the girl, angry, desiring only her humiliation. She rose mechanically onto all fours on the bed, with suitable subservience. Van Vuuren moved toward her.

He could hear Blantyre's voice and that of the nurse at the door of the room, heightened whispers magnified by the silence of the night as the moon declined.

" . . . under sedation, Colonel, two sleeping pills. You can talk to him in the morning, not before."

"Yes. A pity. He could help me . . . sleeping, you said?"

Anderson lay in an icy perspiration of terror. He was someone that Blantyre could despatch with consummate ease and without the slightest hesitation. The perspiration seemed to be soaking the pillows and the sheet beneath him. He stared at the ceiling, where the declining moon rendered the blades of the fan as big and dangerous as the rotor blades of a helicopter. Light seemed to stream in as Blantyre opened the door, but it retreated into a wide vertical band as his eyes adjusted. Sweat ran down his temples, as if the sense of his own scent were betraying him to the hunting animal who blocked out the band of light at the door. Blantyre seemed to inspect him minutely, for whole minutes, before—

"That's enough, Colonel. He's obviously sleeping."

"Yes. Obviously." The door closed and the moonlight slowly became stronger and cooler.

He was shivering now, his whole body shuddering with relaxed effort, and the anticipation of terror and terror experienced. Blantyre would wait, patient as a hungry lion, until morning. Then he would come in, check, assess, and decide that he must be eliminated. The shivering would not subside. It pained him with a violent disgust beyond the vivid sensation of helplessness. Once he might have broken Blantyre like an insect on a wheel. Now Blantyre was his nemesis. Anderson's violent past had simply bided its time, until he was unable to resist his enemies—then it betrayed him to them.

In the morning, doubtless with the appropriate papers, Blantyre would remove him from the clinic, take him gently away as if he were leading a friend, and then kill him out in the Bush.

And there was nothing he would be able to do to prevent it.

5

NOT FOR THE FASHION OF THESE TIMES

Surreal. The assault upon the senses of the noisome staircase of the block of flats, and the familiar-alien scratch of a walkie-talkie and the pounding of heavy footsteps. It was bloody Stepney, for Christ's sake, and totally alien. He cannoned off a turning of the stairs— fourth floor?—and skittered quick as a stone down the next flight to the half-landing. His own breathing was loud, and he quelled it for a moment, pausing against the wall, shuddering like the black man who had been fornicating against the wall as he had arrived at Vi's landing. Distantly he heard their voices, the calls of animals reasserting the identity of the pack. The walkie-talkie? He heard the call of the whistle again— answered, this time. He felt weak with exertion and the aftershock of the violence he had inflicted. Four floors—

He launched himself with calculated incaution down the next flight. The smell of curry and urine and vomit assailed him. His foot slipped in something and he righted himself, scraping his cheek against rough-cast concrete—the bastards who designed and built this are sunning themselves in the Bahamas, he told himself, encouraging the light delirium of movement and adrenalin. Second floor. He was near the bottom, he snatched the pistol from his belt and brandished it, scraping his knuckles against the wall as he careered downwards—

—bullied a body out of his path at another turn of the staircase, hearing the quick grunt of exhaled breath as he turned the corner. No one, not dangerous, but he had hit the soft, dark body anyway—where were they?

He floundered out into the courtyard and at once a car's headlights glared on in the dusk, sweeping across the concrete and rubble and litter and the burned-out wreckage, brightening eyes and bodies. He stood in the headlights, frozen like a rabbit. A walkie-talkie crackled, but the car's engine merely idled expectantly. Then a second car appeared—to a whoop of anticipation from one of the landings where the four sides of the building gloomed up out of eyesight all around him. Grass, thrusting through cracked flagstones near his feet, was made white and dead-looking by the light. A line of wash jerking in the wind like a row of hanged matchstick men.

The place was as bleak as anywhere in Eastern Europe, only a mile from the Bank of England. He was totally isolated and their numbers were unknown. Urgency from a walkie-talkie in shadow quite close to him. Then, the two cars facing each other with horns of light stretched out, moved, bucking forward across the concrete toward him.

The line of grubby, optimistic wash draped itself as if in protest, leaping onto the hood and windshield of the nearer car. Hyde rolled away from the light, across splintered glass and dog excrement and polystyrene rubbish that cracked under his movement.

The cars had halted as if pawing the ground with hooves, only yards from each other, their headlights out. But it was too late, they would already have temporarily blinded each other. A car door banged, but he did not pause to look, he was already scuttling away, almost on all fours while flashlights flashed weakly down from the landings and balconies and more and more lights went on around the amphitheater of the building. The sky above the flats seemed to lose the last pale wash of daylight. If he broke out, then the city would become alien like the courtyard, more dangerous to him than most other cities. He collided with a motorbike, sending it sprawling, handlebars like flailing arms.

Voices, calls, responses. Location. One of the cars sprayed light toward the direction of the noise he had made. It was a vulgar, conspicuous consumption of manpower and effort. Oh, yes, it was Priabin, and probably the woman—intent to make matters even after the fiasco of Centre Point.

He was standing upright behind a pillar with its small tiles long since peeled away to expose the stained, gummy concrete. He pressed his gun against his nose and lips like a holy relic. They'd want an accident, wouldn't they? Someone had to be in touch with Priabin direct—he was on the end of some cellular phone line, prodding, dissuading, agreeing.

He heard a cry of despair from somewhere a long way up. An old, cracked voice. "Why can't you bugger *off?*" Oh, yes, why can't you?

The cars' engines stilled into silence. No lights. A black shadow slipped down the alley near him and he whirled on it. A terrified Asian face stared back, eyes wide, hands raised, palms outward, almost white. Then the face and its body disappeared as Hyde shivered himself back into concentration—madness of a controllable kind. Silence and lightlessness invested the courtyard, except for the scratching of walkie-talkies and the whisper of voices. The sudden, curious lights in the block had vanished, taking with them all the other windows. No one wanted to know now, certain it was dangerous. Gradually, he heard his own stertorous breathing again, and realized that they might, too.

Shadows began to flit, like bats at dusk, small and quick and fluttery—three, four. The slap of sneakers on concrete, the whisper of their sudden halts and movements. He calmed his breathing, listened beyond the adrenalin and pounding blood, heard them scrabble and slither like rats. Closer.

Then he heard the blurt of noise, very close, from a telephone or radio, a voice questioning excitedly. He lowered the gun toward the deep shadow and almost squeezed the trigger, as if it were Priabin hiding there.

"Valentina?"

She heard Priabin's whisper mount in excitement. Their mutual elation was as intimate as congress in the darkness where she pressed against the wall.

"Yes?" she snapped back hoarsely, knowing how close she was to Hyde. "It's all right." Ridiculous, their conversation, as if they were two commodity brokers or estate agents fixing some obscure movement of money or property, not quite real. Only Hyde was real, over there, behind one of those pillars, visible in the last grubby exhalation of a lamp's light from the street. Had it been winter, she would have been able to see his breath palely clouding and to fix the target. She shivered with excitement. "Leave it in my hands," she added and cut the connection. Sorry immediately. If Hyde heard the ringing of the cellular phone in her pocket, he'd fire at once.

Hyde's weekly visit to his aunt's flat. Tonight's the night, she had said, almost smirking across the desk at Priabin. Let him go into that Afghanistan on parliament's doorstep, but don't let him come out. And their people and the louts they'd used before and the other louts those louts had recruited would have made it as simple as a fall from a high ledge. Except that Hyde had been quick and clever and brutal, and no one had gotten to the upper landings before he had made the courtyard. She'd let him come down because the real numbers, and the real expertise, were down here.

Which pillar? She raised the small nightsight binocular viewer to her eyes again, sensing her bodyguard shift his weight on his haunches beside her. The courtyard became gray and white, and ghostly shadows slipped through it as insubstantial as net curtains, her people closing in on the direction they knew Hyde had taken. Her gaze slid across the upturned motorcycle toward the pillars. Nothing. He would glow in a thermal imager, but there was no whisk of movement in the viewer. Her people were in control now, keeping the louts and hoods away from the smell of the quarry because they were too noisy, too clumsy. Another shadow moved, then another. It was like those scenes in old Western films, the Indians creeping up on the wagon train or the fort.

A shadow loomed against the pillar she suspected; arm held out, it fired a single shot. One of the net curtains in the binocular viewer blew more violently in the breeze of the gunshot, then fell. Immediately, Hyde's shadow was moving, away down the colonnade of cheap, scarred pillars toward the alleyway to the street.

She snatched the walkie-talkie from her bodyguard's hand. "Target is on the move. He must be making for the Tube station. All units, all units—follow." She spoke in English. Some of the louts had wanted walkie-talkies, and she had supplied them. It was all useful adrenalin and power.

She rose from her crouch, shrugging off the bodyguard's hand and his subsequent apology with equal indifference. Then she, too, was running, ghostly as the last glimpses she had had of her people in pursuit of Hyde. No caution now, only the hunt and its exhilaration. Hyde—

He turned once, at the corner of a street mean as anything in Prague or Berlin and now more dangerous. The Wall was down there, rebuilt here. Acres of concrete, the great bulk of the block of flats, the few working streetlamps, the few parked cars—one of them already up on bricks, wheels missing. Two figures flitted from shade to shade, through grubby light into shadow again. Mile End tube station. No police cars round here. Even if there were, they'd never stop for someone flagging them down, they'd just report it to the station. He pushed the gun into his waistband, against his stomach, then gripped the doorhandle of an old Ford, rattling it until the whole body of the Cortina moved and rust pattered into the gutter from the nearside sill. Locked. A single shot, then the high, distant cry of orders over a walkie-talkie.

People waiting, then. He was coldly certain of that as he ran down the shadowy side street, his shadow looming out ahead, then diminishing suddenly, guillotined by his passing beneath the streetlamp. Two more streets, then the tube station.

He heard the blurting of a car at speed, loudening as it turned the corner and the lights glared down the mean houses toward him. A television's blare from a strengthened glass window close to his face was lost in the roar of the car's engine. A BMW. He ducked into a doorway, then abandoned the idea of cat and mouse. He couldn't let them get ahead of him—not more of them than there were already. His shadow again, fleeing with the hopelessness of increasing size and lack of substance as the car closed on him. The cracked pavement treacherous as ice. Then the car slowed, as if scenting the ground. Another corner, the shabby lights of shabbier shops, the curl of spicy food and sitar music from an upstairs window, pots, pans, clothing racks, apples and strange, bulbous fruit ranged along a shop's reinforced window. Other shops already barred against the night. A dog snapping at his ankles, its owner half amused, half restraining. Black youths on the opposite pavement, shouting louder than their ghetto blaster.

The tube station. Evening traffic on the Mile End Road. Normality. The BMW and the other car queueing behind it now at the crossroads. Stuck. He wiped his forehead and his hand was wet as he rubbed it on his thighs. Jesus . . . Shops open, a McDonald's, a video store, the boozer. Cars parked, cars moving, light. He dashed across the road at the first glimpse of green from the pedestrian traffic signal.

In the entrance, just beyond the portico of the tube station, he saw a lout clutching a walkie-talkie against his cheek, as if struggling with some alien life form which had battened to his skin. Was he an amateur, or had he turned away in professional discretion? Did it matter? The BMW had turned onto the Mile End Road and was already drawing to a halt at the curb, twenty yards from the station entrance. A drunk lying in vomit on the footstepped tiles, a black rifling his pockets while others laughed and the drunk grinned solemnly. A legless beggar with a dog, a cap at the feet of his crutches into which someone had thrown a crushed lager can, at which the cripple stared. Crowd—a claret-and-blue scarf, then another. Rowdy louts, young couples, pimply and washed-out, girls in shapeless black. Someone jangling on a guitar somewhere nearer the platform, the thin noise coming up out of the stairwell of the escalator. His heightened senses welcomed the assault of impressions even as he glanced at the Underground chart on one tiled, urinallike wall, then watched the hunched man—professional, he decided.

Luckily. The blacks completed their asset-stripping of
the amiable drunk and jived toward the escalator
beyond the ticket barrier, grinning and raucous.

The man with the walkie-talkie turned as if surprised in some covert, impeachable act and found himself confronted by Hyde, who opened his cotton jacket
to display the pistol's grip, then smiled. A young couple
passed him, then an elderly, hesitant man, then five or
six youths. Hyde moved on, knowing the man could
and would do nothing, since the Transport Police constable and his sergeant were directly behind the group
of roaring youths, as if shepherding them with a long,
invisible cattle prod. He glanced back as his ticket spat
out of the machine. The man's face was angry. Hyde
passed through the barrier and descended the escalator.
The men from the BMW had been passing beneath the
portico of the station entrance as he lost sight of the
Transport Police. One of the yelling youths ahead of
him vomited theatrically across the division between
the two escalators, and ascending passengers flinched
away in disgust, and were intimidated by hard laughter
and rhythmically waved gestures. He watched the escalator behind him. How many of the amateurs could
they get to the station before the next eastbound train?
He could take the westbound Central Line, direct to
Earl's Court . . . but he wouldn't.

He saw the man with the walkie-talkie and the two
from the BMW; all three casually dressed, indistinguishable from other users of the station. He shivered
as he imagined himself being thrust off the platform
and falling against the live rail or in front of a train.
Crowds, he reminded himself. His pursuers no longer
possessed the advantage of the neat, discreet, anarchic
darkness of the block of flats where they would not
have been noticed, never suspected. Where was the
woman? He paused at the bottom of the escalator's
slatted movement, looking back. There she was. He

waved and turned away, apparently heading down the westbound tunnel of the Central Line. They'd not know this station, even though they'd had it covered. Embassy and Trade Mission professionals didn't frequent Mile End and Stepney. He doubled through a tiled archway, retracing his steps, and descended the short escalator flight to the District Line, eastbound platform . . . north-east, actually, old chap. Upminster at the end of the line, Hornchurch before that. Quite nice in parts, truly . . .

. And then he was afraid again, because the platform was all but deserted. Quiet, so that he could hear the distant guitar and the plaintive, almost tuneless voice of the busker. How old was he, for Christ's sake? "Blowin' in the Wind"? God, the innocence. Two people, kissing as if their appetites, if not their lives, depended on it; silent, gobbling desperation. Fifteen yards away. Adverts for underwear and a tedious intellectual comedy Ros had made him take her to. Further ads for mineral water and lager. The Underground map. Someone slumped in sleep on a bench below a hideously masked, grinning image of some unknown pop singer on a poster. A youth with a walkman standing close enough to the edge of the platform to be tipped onto the rails with minimal effort. Otherwise, emptiness. NEXT TRAIN, the overhead display admitted. Upminster. How long? The tunnel was silent—

—the girl, at once delighted with the stage onto which she had hurried, finding it all but deserted. Two men with her, one of them the man he had passed in the station foyer, stepping over the drunk and the beggar with exaggerated care. The girl waved at him mockingly and one of the men grinned, then bent his head to his walkie-talkie, talking quickly. Hyde pressed his back against the curved wall behind him, against a poster advertising Andrew Lloyd Webber's genius. Hyde tossed his head. Chuck me off from in front of a Proms poster, at least!

His head swiveled like one of the loose, bulbous eyes of a chameleon, back and forth along the platform. If they could get the louts here in time, why wait? There was no one watching.

The young couple devoured each other with silent, undiminished intensity and the drunk on the bench snored and smelt in his filthy clothing, emitting wind noisily. The woman looked disdainful but the second man giggled with excitement.

Then the woman was on the cellular phone—would it work down here? Christ knew. The tunnel was silent. His hands pressed damply behind him on the dryness of the poster. His temperature soared. They'd be armed, for certain. But they wouldn't want that kind of noise, would they? They were Soviet embassy people; he had the high-card hand, surely, on a London Underground platform?

At a gesture from the woman, the two men moved closer, sidling gently as rising water along the platform toward him. He rested one hand on the gun in his waistband. He glanced along the platform. Two others. Pincer movement. If he fired, they'd kill him at once.

The platform and the tunnel remained silent.

You know this place—don't be afraid, you *know* this place. Its name is Otjiwarongo—you know it well. He repeated it to himself over and over, as the huge moon slipped sideways beyond the window and its zebra-striped image moved across the wall opposite his bed, tiredly declining. He had discovered a simple, complete thought, and clung to it. He had gripped at the moonlight at first, then began measuring its progress, like a man under sentence, his nostrils widened for the first scent of the breakfast they would bring . . . the prisoner ate a hearty breakfast, wasn't that what they once reported? Clinging to the passage of time had weakened him, absorbed much of his diminished energies. Then he had imagined the town, because of the barking of a dog or some other animal, the snatch of a drunk's song, the engine of a vehicle.

Clung to Otjiwarongo, to knowledge of it, tracing it on some mental map, rebuilding a ghost town in his imagination; peopling it, too. People he knew, people who might help. The dog must have gotten loose from somewhere, for it nuzzled close to the wall outside, he had even heard it relieve itself against the wood. It barked occasionally, reminding him, prompting, nudging.

He had accepted the dog's admonitions as the late night grew toward the brief cool of dawn. So he was seated on the edge of the bed, in his T-shirt and shorts, weakened and sweaty with the efforts of discovering his clothes and remaining silent, repeating to himself again and again, *you know this place.* You knew it when its white area and black matchbox township were entirely distinct, before they began to melt together. You know where there are vehicles, food, supplies, weapons. But he could not avoid, or resist, remembering the place as it had been before independence, however partial and cosmetic that process had been. It was as if he were black, and hunted by the old power, by Blantyre, who would be coming back.

Anderson watched his arms shivering as his hands gripped the edge of the bed and he pressed the soles of his feet against the linoleum to still the tremors of fear that seemed to possess his whole frame. His breathing became louder. *Otjiwarongo.* In the township, the scrubby, dusty place . . . Joe Tsumis, who had a 4WD, more than one, and who had been a tourist guide up to Ovamboland . . . you *know* him, for Christ's sake, so get on with it and stop thinking of Blantyre!

He pushed himself weakly to his feet, fumbling cotton shorts out of the bedside locker, hovering uncertainly and almost with desperation on one leg, then the other, breaking out into a sweat that the night's cool could not allay. Then his shirt over an already sticky chest and shoulders, then his boots, breathing puffing and snorting in his ears, as if he were having some kind of attack, for God's sake! Trying to calm himself as he tied his bootlaces.

Afterwards, things were easier, as if he had recuperated in his anger. Bandages, the painkillers, his papers—because he wouldn't be allowed where he intended going without the papers that proved he was really a white man under his pale skin—and his wallet. Joe Tsumis wouldn't take credit cards, but others would.

Then he stood looking at the square of the window as the sky began to lighten. Distinct pinpricks of lights in the dawn from the town. He was then horrified at the thought that Joe Tsumis might have left or been killed in the three years since he had last seen him.

Slowly, deliberately, he wiped his forehead, then wiped his palm on the shorts. He hurried to the window, gripping the fine mesh screen with his fingertips. The air, already tired at the prospect of the day's heat, was only slightly cooler against his forehead as it leaked through the open window. He rattled the mesh softly. It did not yield. Pull, push? He inspected its fixings, the screws rusty in the chipped, peeling wood. Push—

A squeak like that of a small animal caught in a trap came from the screen. The quiet ripping of loosening screws. His sweating increased. The noises were unnervingly loud. Then, as he began shivering with indecision, the dog barked again, the noise peremptory, and he pushed at the rusty screen and it fell outwards. He clung to it with his fingertips, bending out over the sill and lowering it quietly against the wall. Breathing noisily but regularly. Carefully, he climbed through the open window and onto the ground.

No one. He began walking stiffly toward the few scattered lights of Otjiwarongo, along the dusty street lined with wooden, two-story houses, a few shops, a small hotel. The mission church's spire black against the first, quick grayness of the dawn. It was an image of a frontier town, like so many towns and villages and settlements in Namibia, frozen in the last century. Small aloes, patches of dessicated lawn, the tidy, packed earth of white-owned frontages and yards. A few lights were on behind still-drawn curtains or mesh screens—the lights of servants. Anderson passed the hotel furtively, on the other side of the wide, empty street. Blantyre must be staying there, there was nowhere else.

Then the township, half kraal, half battered petrol-can assemblage of sheds and huts. Leaking light as if the original contents of the cans were seeping into the town itself. Sheds in the back gardens of the last of the colonial houses, tents erected in the street. The boundary of black and white gradually blurring. Trees and plants and scrubby lawns became dirt patches growing vegetables. Independence and suffrage. But the invasion of the suburb that was so out of place on the high plateau scattered with native kraals was under way, like grass growing up through paving stones; irresistible.

But the township failed to distract him from the idea that Joe Tsumis was no longer in Otjiwarongo, or from the creeping sensation that, voyeurlike, he could sense Blantyre waking, stirring in his bed, getting up in order to cross the few hundred yards to the clinic, to find him gone and raise the alarm. Joe had driven him when he had first come to discover Namibia, to find somewhere to settle and escape; driven him northward with enthusiasm perhaps half a dozen times, because a white man had been the perfect cover for his gunrunning to SWAPO units in the Bush. Then Anderson had found Etosha, place of dry water, and the wardenship vacant, and had not seen Joe more than two or three times since.

Black men and women, mostly Damara and Nama, headscarved, language clicking in the suddenly lighter air as the sun was about to lift itself above the horizon ahead of him. The men soberly black-trilbied, white-shirted. There were only domestic jobs, but they were slightly better paid now. The dawn flared up, and the sky was deep blue directly overhead. He must hurry now, through the servants drifting toward the white suburb. Joe Tsumis—*be there*.

Tethered goats, chickens scrabbling in the dust. Children in dim doorways with huge eyes, curious and perhaps no longer afraid. He hurried on, down another nameless, shapeless street, then turned past a garage littered with old tires—Joe's?—and with a single old-fashioned pump. He was unsure. Squinting, he could see no 4WDs in the interior of the dilapidated barn beyond the pump. He spun around, dizzily studying the place, vainly orienting himself.

Then he saw it. Pink in the early sun, its chrome blazing, an ancient American Cadillac, convertible, palely upholstered. It was parked next to the garage, outside a more substantial, all-wooden hut of one story, but extended at the back, curtains at the windows. He was hot and sticky with gratitude, turning on his heel to study the street behind him. One ancient truck, bicycles, no white man's vehicle. He hurried past the Cadillac, past the vegetable plot and the three tethered goats—it was Joe's place. Grinning, he banged on the door, calling at once:

"Joe! Joe Tsumis! It's Richard! Richard Anderson." He banged again. "Open up, Joe!" A boy on a rickety bicycle stopped in the street to watch him, and he realized his knocking was like a visitation from the past: white, demanding, official. "Joe, sorry to disturb you . . . "

It was at that gesture to equality that the door opened. A young woman, Himba by her features, a cotton frock draped over her slim body, a baby at one exposed breast. A new wife? She appeared unsurprised, and unwilling. Then Joe appeared behind her, one hand behind his back, his beard grayer, his eyes suspicious, quick—then softening as he recognized Anderson. He pushed the young woman back into the house and the long-barrelled pistol appeared harmlessly from behind his back. Pots rattled somewhere at the rear of the hut, which was dirt-floored, but with bright Himba rugs and perhaps Herero weaves, too, in the matting. Tsumis watched him now, detached but curious.

"Joe—" Anderson began.

"What is it—Richard Anderson? What do you want from me?" Anderson rubbed his beard and shrugged, disarming Tsumis, making himself nothing more than a harmless white man who hardly noticed the pistol hanging slackly in Tsumis' hand. "What is it, so early, too?" Tsumis assessed him; dress, sallowness, bandaging.

"I—want . . . can pay—for your help, Joe."

The old, habitual glance either way along the dirt street, then: "Come in, man—come in."

He ducked his head to enter. Table lamps, rugs, a low table, a dining table and chairs; beginnings of substance. Voices sounded from a back room and the noise of people leaving. Empty bottles, cards on the low table.

"Sit down, Richard, man." Tsumis gestured to a chair, which creaked and tilted as Anderson lowered himself into it. His hands gripped the wooden arms as he understood change in the place, furtiveness and power crowding the corners of the room. Tsumis saw

his disconcertedness and said: "Times have changed."
He put the gun on the low table amid the playing
cards. Quick as thrown water, sunlight splashed in
through the open window, making the dirt floor rich
and the rugs vivid. "You want a laugh, Richard?"
Anderson shook his head bemusedly. "You want to
shake hands with the local MP?" Tsumis held out his
hand, then roared with laughter which possessed a cynical top register. He slapped his thighs. "Yes, man—got
elected at Independence." He leaned forward. "Got the
job, got as corrupt as hell straight away—got power,
Richard."

"Congratulations."

"Ah, the voice of the public schoolboy—I recognize
it. From the advisers they send us. Still, man, better
than that accent that says *keffir*—eh?" He studied
Anderson, then asked in a former voice he might have
specifically summoned, "What happened to you?"

Anderson shook his head, but was betrayed by
weariness, and murmured, "She's dead, Joe—murdered." The shock on Tsumis' face was real, sufficiently so to turn the leaking tap. Anderson sat, chin resting
on his sunken chest, and told Tsumis how, why,
when—everything except the motive for Blantyre's
enmity.

"Why?" Tsumis asked, eventually.

"I—something from the past, something old, that
happened in Jo'burg, a long time ago."

Tsumis shrugged dismissively. "And now—what
for you? I'm sorry, by the way—"

"Thank you."

"I know Blantyre. A pity you do." Tsumis spat. "A
bastard—a real bastard. I saw him once . . . "
Anderson hardly listened to the atrocity Tsumis had
witnessed in the Bush, years before. He banked the
pain of his emotions and waited for Tsumis to finish
speaking. The sunlight hardened, drying like paint on

the wall, and the low, long room was filled with slow motes. Tsumis, he guessed, would turn him in if it suited him—he'd always been capable of it—or he might help him, sell him what he needed. "So, he wants you?"

"Yes. I need to get away. A vehicle, supplies. I can pay."

"I don't take American Express—money will do nicely."

It was his shrunken, defeated condition, he decided, despising himself, that would make Tsumis help him. A harmless, bemused man, not worth much to Blantyre. And Blantyre was unpredictable, hated blacks, liked killing them. He controlled his sigh of relief at the realization, gripping the arms of the old chair.

"I can pay you, Joe—no favors, just business. A 4WD, some supplies—food and water."

"For how long?"

"Just for long enough to drive a long way away from here."

Tsumis nodded. Anderson heard a timid knocking at what must be the back door. The Himba girl appeared, tossing her head in the direction of the noises. Tsumis got up.

"Excuse me—business."

He watched the motes dance to Tsumis' movements in the slabs of sunlight crossing the room, hardly listening to the altercation over the installment of bribery or extortion at the rear door. Tsumis entered the room again, angrily waving a small wad of bright Namibian currency.

"See?" Tsumis challenged. "Corruption's damn inefficient round here since the whites handed over!" Then he laughed, and announced: "This is a dirt place, it always will be. Expect no better. There's nothing here but a bit of money. I'm collecting it, as much as I can—then we go to Windhoek or Swakopmund, and buy more power—I'm a Marxist who's corrupt as hell! Maybe one day, I'll be President, who knows? Then I'll do the right thing. Meantime, Richard man, I got to get connections." He waved the money.

Confident he could not offend Tsumis or lose his help, Anderson said, "You're not a Marxist, or anything else, come to that, Joe. You never were." Tsumis looked angry for a moment, then a past self grinned from behind the recently acquired actor's mask. "At least you're consistent, still being in it for the money."

Tsumis flung the notes across the room in assumed disdain. They fluttered to the packed floor like feathers from a bird.

"OK, I'll send one of the boys for supplies—three days, no more—don't want to arouse suspicion. They'll tell you how much. You want to see the Land Rover now?" The sun warned, climbing the wall opposite the window.

"How old is it?"

"No more than twenty years—think I'd cheat you?"

He slapped Anderson's shoulder, making him wince against the pain. They walked through the sprawling untidiness of the kitchen, Anderson hardly remarking the Himba girl. The children were scuttling like puppies, the gradations of age careful as calculation or the replacement of the other woman. Tsumis' hand remained on his shoulder even as they entered the yard and the morning sun struck him like a blow on the side of his face as they trod amongst the chickens and goats toward the garage. The sun unnerved him more than Tsumis' words.

"That Blantyre, he's a deep bastard, the worst. You watch out for him. I don't wish you dead, Richard." Anderson watched his shadow stride more confidently ahead of him, acting casual indifference far better than did his facial expression. "Let's get you out of here. More comfortable for both of us, uh?"

The inky blindness of the garage shed was claustrophobic after the brightness of the yard. He had thought of obtaining a vehicle and supplies as a complex, difficult task. Joe had made it easy—and thrust him toward his future with a large hand on his shoulder.

The Land Rover, emerging from the gloom, seemed drab, forlorn. Don Quixote's old nag. He clenched his fists, remembering the burning; squeezed his fists tightly, hurting himself. What could he do? How could he even begin to imagine he could survive, never mind succeed against Blantyre?

Silence from the hole of the tunnel. Hyde dragged his cotton jacket open so that the gun would be evident. They hesitated, so that he knew they would not close in further, but merely wait, shepherding him like dogs to some quiet, final place. The woman—that bloody imitation Sloanc!—was utterly confident. A nerve jumped in his wrist, potent as a hand across his face.

He calmed his breathing. NEXT TRAIN, where the bloody hell are you? He surreptitiously glanced at his watch. What time did the boozers turn out—eleven, eleven-thirty? It was ten fifty-eight. A bag lady wandered into view, two supermarket bags in each frail hand. She arranged herself on a bench—

—train, sighing like an ugly voice out of the tunnel's mouth, rushing toward him. The bloody cavalry almost missing the final reel! The bag lady ceremoniously arranged her plastic sheet and her newspapers: dozens of copies of the *Christian Science Monitor,* she must have lifted them from a Reading Room. She bore no resemblance to Vi; nevertheless she reminded him of his aunt. The train, as it slowed, was disappointingly empty. Eleven o'clock. They'd keep him on the streets until dawn, be in every pub, café, bus shelter and alley with him, always pressing close. The train came to a stop and he hesitated because any sudden movement might panic them, make them use a quick, small knife.

He boarded the train. Two more now. The woman and her two minders got into the same car, the others into the one behind. Up-bloody-minster. If he went all the way, it would be goodbye in the suburban dark. The bag lady, reposing like the carved effigy of some baron's lady on a medieval tomb, was whisked out of sight and the tunnel walls pressed against the glass, then vanished in the reflection of his own face as he strap-hung near the end door of the car. He watched his face, watched them, one lolling, the other man more tense, the woman reveling in the mounting tension. She'd been there before and liked the sensations.

Slowing—Bow Road. Blacks, a tramp, a Transport copper looking along the platform. No one left, two people got on. Signal from one of them? No, he didn't think so. But she must have told them where he was going, what he was doing, before she got into the uncommunicative tube. The train lurched out of the station. Posters and graffiti mocked, then the tunnel. Almost at once, Bromley-by-Bow, and still no more bloody people than before—shit. A few stragglers got off, a handful joined the train. Eleven-five. For Christ's sake, what time did the bloody boozers turn out in this part of London? The woman was watching him proprietorially while the men watched her and himself in turn, heads nipping back and forth mechanically. His legs felt shaky.

West Ham station. Transport Police in twos—a good sign. He clung to the station name as the trickle of boarding passengers attempted to fill the car by spreading themselves along the seats. Two high-voiced, raucous, harmless blacks, two old ladies, a couple of young scrubbers. The woman flinched from their taste-less mock-leather and studs and earrings and stiff hair. He smiled at her, shaking his head; attempting to regain control, confidence. The woman glared back.

Plaistow. The train stopped. A busker's saxophone from somewhere, the blacks in the carriage swinging their loose hips to its rhythm, then roaring with laugh-ter. No one suspicious boarded. If he could just get off the bloody train! He staggered against the restraint of the strap to which he clung as the train surged into the tunnel. One more station, just one more, and then the move would be entirely his, and probably fatal. It would be without distraction. Eleven-ten. The boozers, oh the boozers emptying, *please!* One minute, then two . . . the train rushed on, swinging around a slow curve of the track, then the lights and the first of the signs, Upton Park. *Please—*

—yes. As the train slowed once more, the plat-form's muddle became a crowd. Claret-and-blue scarves everywhere, around almost every neck. Drunks, the merely happy—a *crowd.* Hyde felt weak with relief, then he bunched and stiffened with tension as the train slowed and the crowd pressed to the edge of the platform, a landscape of grinning, hot faces and moving arms. West Ham had been playing a summer friendly against some Spanish club at Upton Park. This mob was on its way back to Dagenham or Barking or wherever.

The two men were distracted by the crowded plat-form as the train came to a stop, and were disarmed by the crowd's pressure against the unopened doors. Hyde was imprisoned. The woman seemed doubtful, watch-ing him from beneath a furrowed brow.

The door began sliding open and he thrust at the blocked escape route with a panic of adrenalin as they realized he was attempting to use the crowd. He was buffeted backwards, one foot still on the floor of the car, then he lowered his head and burrowed at them like a boxer with a shorter reach, lighter but more determined. Complaints, a struggling leg aimed in his vague direction, the bellowing of *I'm forever blowing bubbles,* and then he was five yards, then six, from the open door and turned, pressed against the curving station wall, to see one of the men swept back into the car and the woman's face pressed against the window like that of a furiously disappointed child. Even as the press of football supporters dragged him like a tide's undertow, off balance, he waved at her, then elbowed and swam through the remainder of the crowd toward the exit sign. Way Out—oh, yes . . .

The platform was now empty, except for the Transport Police, looking relieved—six, eight of them—and one of the two men who had boarded the car behind his. And who weighed the situation as he hovered near two of the policemen. The woman's face, caricaturing anger and disappointment, slid past him into the tunnel as the train gathered speed.

He ran up the steps. The lone KGB man wouldn't move without backup or new orders. He'd probably claim Hyde had identified himself to the police, rendering him powerless to accomplish the mission.

Hyde ran blithely up the escalator, a grin in command of his mouth. Centre Point, he thought. They'd try to head him off at the pass, any way they could. So, he couldn't go back to Centre Point. And they'd put a team in Philbeach Gardens, to wait for him. There wasn't anything to smile about, really. Still, he couldn't help the immediate sensations. Good old Hammers—

Van Vuuren watched the limousine chauffeur carrying his bags across the foyer of the InterContinental toward the bright heat beyond the glass doors, and put his laptop computer down at his feet as he glanced at his bill. He smirked to himself—flowers, champagne, yes . . . breakfast. The call-girl was not on the bill— Paulus drew the line at that. OK. Telephone calls, room service. He made to pass the bill to his assistant, who was already fishing his company Amex card from his Filofax. Then he snatched it back and said to the Chinese girl behind the glass of her kiosk, "I didn't make that telephone call—the one to Johannesburg. Will you check on it, please. These, yes, but not this one. When was this?" His voice, he realized, was already slightly shrill with suspicion. The girl assumed it was directed at the hotel. "Please be accurate. Find out what time the call was made."

"Anything wrong, sir?" his assistant asked. One of those more-English-than-the-English voices from Natal. A disparagement of his own heavy Afrikaaner accent in every syllable, even in his height and longish fair hair. Bright, though.

"No. I—this girl's checking something. I want to— may want Paulus on the line. Get hold of a telephone in one of the offices. Do what you must—get it."

His assistant moved along the reception counter, thrusting himself in front of two Arabs, and bent to murmur to the frock-coated desk manager, who at once began shaking his head. But the movement slowed like the coming to rest of one of those Russian dolls as the young man touched a breast pocket and van Vuuren was indicated with a gesture of his head.

The Chinese girl. The number was too familiar— and too secure—not to be recognized immediately.

"—call was made a' eight-fifty, sir. Sorry to—"

"I didn't make it. Who used the phone in my room?" he snapped. The tremor of suspicion now had its epicenter somewhere in his stomach.

"Sir, you must ha' used the telephone. Staff are—"

"Who *used* it?" he snarled.

But, at once, it no longer mattered. He glared at

the laptop at his feet as at an animal that had bitten him, after kindness. Someone had got into his suite and used it, linked it via the telephone line to MLC's mainframe in Jo'burg, asked it for information—

—bastards, those bastards who'd had MacPherson's office under surveillance. The British bastards.

His assistant was gesturing success.

"Pay my bill!" he snapped. "And look after *this!*" He held out the computer as if it had betrayed him. "Where?" he snapped at the frock-coated manager, and was shown into a cubbyhole brimming with a small desk, a telephone and an old filing cabinet. "Get out!" he shouted and shut the door. The airless, windowless cupboard of a room was hot—*he* was hot, for Christ's sake! Hot and terrified by the certainty that they had the codes and they had got into MLC's mainframe.

His finger paused in stabbing out Malan's number. God, Paulus would . . . He wiped his forehead with his fingertips and they came away damp. He inspected them with repulsion, inspected the receiver with an identical dislike. Then, reluctantly, he continued dialing the Johannesburg number, glancing at his watch. Malan would already be at work, in his office in the mansion. Jesus—it was too bloody awful to contemplate! Priabin and his jokers should have got hold of anything and everything. Instead, that mad bastard Australian had killed them, *three* of them! They had the bloody codes, they must have ripped the guts out of the mainframe! He ought to call the mainframe, access what it had been asked, what it had given away . . .

He moved the receiver away from his ear, but then heard the connection made and Malan's voice.

"Paulus, it's me."

"Piet, what is it?" Paulus already knew something was wrong. Like a lion scenting a flesh wound a mile away, he was so bloody sensitive to tones of voice, or just to the possible urgency of an international call from himself at that time in the morning. "Is anything wrong?"

There was no easy way to—

"Paulus, someone's—someone's been into the mainframe, using my—"

"Wait!" Malan snapped. Then van Vuuren heard another line being used, and Malan's demand for a check on requests made by van Vuuren's computer. "When was this?"

"Last night, just before nine—"

Malan relayed the time, then asked, "What happened?"

"They must have broken into my room—no sign of forced entry—I don't understand how they—"

"Photographic equipment, Piet. Surveillance by camera. You've heard of it? They must have photographed the screen as you tapped in in MacPherson's office. We were told these people would be stopped, and they haven't been! Wait—" A telephone was ringing distantly, and he heard Malan on the other line, repeating: "Yes, yes . . . yes . . . *yes*," then, "Stop all new shipments, Piet—stop them *now*."

"Paulus, what did they get?"

"They accessed anything and everything you opened up for them in MacPherson's office, Piet! Do I need to explain? From what they have, they could pinpoint the company and the airport. As with everything, it was only clever while it was secure. Get it stopped or changed, then call me."

The receiver hummed in his ear. The relief that shivered through him was unavoidable. Just because Malan had not panicked—as he had, in this shitty little room, preparing to grovel! His hands were clammy. The noise in his head was thunderlike. *Think!*

Stop tonight's shipment, that was the first thing.

They'd had no time to respond while he slept. They might have arranged surveillance in Birmingham—no, couldn't have, because Priabin assured him they were working unofficially, they had no backup, few resources. Just sufficient to get them into MLC's mainframe, that was all! Stop the shipment, then, get it changed for something harmless, something it was *supposed* to be on the Customs forms and the manifest. If that could be done, then those people could do what they wanted, go ahead as stupidly as they wished, and it would blow up in their faces. The more fuss they made, the more they'd be borne down on. Hauled off, like a dog from a child it was savaging. All the sympathy with the child, whatever it had been doing to annoy the dog.

He grinned, inspected his idea as carefully as he might have done a contract worth billions of rands, then nodded to himself. A knock at the door. Gert, the assistant. He waved him away and the door closed again.

Ring their man—make him, in turn, sweat as freely as he had done. Grab the bastard's balls and wrench on them. Then call Priabin. Consult him, get his people moving in on these bastards who'd made him sweat. Priabin should have taken—what was his name? Hyde. Should have taken him out!

He was sweating again. These people had to be removed—fucking Communists, couldn't organize a bloody thing!

He dialed a Birmingham number—021? 021 . . . the ringing tone, twice, three—then the answering machine. " . . . not able to come to the phone. Please leave . . . "

Where was he? He glanced furtively at his watch, as if he were being observed.

Then he remembered, the man was on a flight from somewhere, still on his way home. Christ, who did he ring *now*?

*   *   *

Godwin opened the curtains—he must have dozed for half an hour, perhaps longer, since daylight first surprised him—then he glanced around his littered lounge; cramped, in need of decoration, the old furniture. Chambers was lying on the lumpy sofa, soundly asleep. The Centre Point offices were strictly out of bounds to them, they'd had to bring everything back—home? Peculiar word, it seemed, at that time of the morning and with someone asleep in the room he occupied, often for weeks or even months, alone. Chambers looked like a yuppie fallen into a drunken doze rather than an exhausted sleep. Dubcek was lying against Chambers' stomach, legs extended over his waist as he lay on his side. The cat had already snagged threads from the fat, paisley-patterned tie that hung loosely around Chambers' neck. Godwin tossed his head, disturbed by company; pained by it, too, for some indefinable reason.

He inspected the street below the window: a milkman, a few early pedestrians, the first cars nudging or sidling out of their cramped residents' parking slots, and houses still blinded by curtains, the thinner material letting grubby light soak into them.

He turned to face the room, rubbing his stomach because of the indigestion of hunger. The previous evening they'd had only sandwiches of stale bread and corned beef because, by the time they had realized their late evening hunger, the takeouts had closed. After that, with the regularity of beer and the occasions of scotch, they had worked until three. Flipcharts still sat propped on a ladderback chair, and the mass of hard copy printout lay dismembered and seemingly flung about the room by a wind. There were also the reference books and the sheafs of paper scribbled on or screwed up and discarded without being tidied. He rubbed his temples. It had been strangely mindless, some intellectual equivalent of an acid house party or disco, where the throb of the work had been like emptying music, so that nothing else mattered. They had never been outside the experience even for a moment—except to find the takeouts closed and a lack of TV dinners in the freezer.

But on the displayed sheet of the flipchart folder propped on the chair, they had it, the letters dim in the subdued light that sidled around the too-close buildings opposite. The place, the company. Birmingham airport. SwiftEx, bulk shippers to Europe, including Eastern Europe. Simple as that. Both of them chasing through the mass of detail extracted from the MLC mainframe, making sense of it, cross-referencing with months of other material, sensing the acceleration and the pattern of shipments to meet a recent, unexpected increase in orders. And the orders coming more and more from verifiable MLC subsidiaries or associated companies. TVs by the thousands, microwaves, cookers, cellular telephones, air-conditioning—anything and *everything* manufactured by the Reid Group subsidiary, Reid Davies, in Birmingham. And the stuff went out from Brum airport, via a Brum shipper. They'd cheered, laughed, almost cried, had a large whisky each and crashed out. Knackered.

Worth it.

Godwin, grinning, lit a cigarette. Chambers' nose twitched, he growled his throat clear, and opened his eyes, stirring helpless as a baby for a moment before blinking at Godwin's shadow outlined against the window.

"God, what time is it?"

"Seven."

Dubcek stirred, clung on for a moment, making Chambers wince at the claws in his skin, then slowly and reluctantly abandoned his human pillow. "God, my mouth! Like a lion tamer's armpit!"

"Coffee?"

"Uh? Oh, right. Even if I do begin to slop noisily when I walk—" Then his head turned to the flipchart, as if he felt he might have dreamed the effort and the success. He grinned at Godwin, rubbing his eyes. "We did do it, then?"

"Yes, I really think we did!" Godwin returned Chambers' grin, rubbing his hair and brushing cigarette ash from his grubby shirt front. He pointed toward his own computer, resting on the littered, scratched surface of the dining table. "And it's all in there. The whole beautiful arrangement!"

"That can't be all of it—can it?"

Godwin shook his head. "Just *our* bit—the UK pipeline."

"And only where the stuff comes from, not where it goes. Well, except that French company."

"Dumas Electroniques. The mouse that swallowed the elephant."

"They don't own Reid Group, they're just the largest single shareholder since they bought David Reid's personal shares."

"But who owns Dumas?"

"God knows—the bloke who wrote *The Three Musketeers*?"

"But if we find out," Godwin pressed, "we might have the next length of the pipeline, then the one after that, all the way to—wherever. Malan's being used by the KGB, obviously."

"Why obviously?" Chambers called from the kitchen. Godwin could hear the gradual boiling of the kettle.

"He can't be getting the major share—so he's being used."

"Why?"

"Why would he agree?" Godwin repeated

Chambers' question. The kettle boiled and clicked off. Dubcek had followed Chambers. Godwin heard the scraping of a fork round a tin of cat food. "Because of the *concessions* in Eastern Europe and Russia. He's worked with them for years over gold and diamonds. They trust him, insofar as they trust anyone. Who else would they work with?"

Chambers brought out the mugs and handed him one. Then Chambers stared, unimpressed, out of the window. On the other hand, Chambers had an unsaleable flat in Docklands, a lot tidier and a lot more expensive to run. Kentish Town could become fashionable before Docklands emerged from its slump.

Godwin tossed his head. He just wasn't used to company.

"OK," Chambers said, "but what do we do now? No one who's afraid of Orrell is going to listen to us. Anyway, most of them are too thick to understand this." Then he added: "I can't see any suspicious vehicles out there—did you notice anything?"

"Wishing Patrick was here?"

Chambers looked scornful but uncertain.

"No, I didn't see anything. Anyway, from what he said over the phone, they want him removed first, then they'll come for us."

Chambers shivered. "He's a pillock."

"He's a dangerous animal."

"Why don't we talk to Aubrey?" Chambers was holding his mug in both hands, as if warming himself, looking somehow shrunken.

"The old man's ill. He's not even back at work yet. If he ever comes back. He might listen, but what could he do, with Orrell's nose so far up the Cabinet's collective backside?" Godwin shook his head. "I *want* to talk to Aubrey, but I don't think there's anything he could do, not at this stage."

"So, what do we do? That acceleration in there,"

he waved toward the flipcharts. "It'll break the bloody sound barrier if it gets any faster!"

It was true. The volume of goods passing through Reid Davies, the orders they were fulfilling, the shipping done by SwiftEx—it was all like a boil coming to a head. It had to be soon. Malan had just piled new, even bigger orders onto Reid Group. It was like that runaway merry-go-round in the Hitchcock film, spinning out of control, blurring into a rush and whirl.

And Patrick . . . they wanted him dead, and quickly. There was no doubt things were about to jump.

"You say it isn't Davies?"

Godwin shook his head. "Doubt it. He used to work for us, courier, sideliner, people-carrier. Aubrey wouldn't believe it was him—I don't."

"Then there are a lot of people he's employed who are in it. Have to be, to bring it off—sending the high-tech stuff out disguised as TVs and microwaves!" Chambers put down his mug and thrust his hands into his pockets. "What do we do then?"

"I'm going to ring Customs, and pretend we have Sir Clive's authority for surveillance on SwiftEx at Brum airport." Chambers nodded and smirked approval. "Meanwhile, you and I are going to drive up to Brum and sit outside Reid Davies' gates and wait for the latest order for an MLC company to roll out on its way to the shippers. Today, tomorrow—couldn't be later, could it? Then we'll send Customs in to open the boxes. Like it?"

"A bit. Orrell will have a heart attack—Christ, that sod Bannister, our glorious deputy DG, was pretty rough last night!"

"Bannister's as thick as only a confidant of Clive Orrell's could be—don't worry about him. As long as we kept saying we knew nothing and we were sorry for any inconvenience caused."

"This will be different. We're supposed to be on

leave, pending investigation."

"Do you want to do this, or not?" Godwin snapped.

"Yes, yes!" Chambers protested too violently.

"Look, don't chicken out now, after all the bloody work we've put in," Godwin raged, crossing to the telephone with an admonishingly loud noise from his crutches. He picked up the receiver and brandished it in Chambers' direction. "If Orrell and Bannister don't give a stuff, then I *do*! Look, it's going to take weeks, maybe months, as it is—with what we've got—to get inside Reid Davies and clean it out. Don't give me any lily-livered worries about your fucking pension now, Terry—just *don't*!"

He began dabbing out the number, feeling hot but pleased with his outburst. They needed to catch a shipment; that was *all* they needed to open up the whole can of worms.

The Special Branch man inspected Hyde's unshaven, weary features, and his antagonism became contempt. The morning was hot, even though it was only just after seven. Already, the shrill of a child exploded from the gardens, followed by the splutter of birds as they accelerated into the morning like small vehicles. He'd trailed around London, mostly on foot—one early taxi, a bus filled with people heading for work and resenting their impending separation from the bright day. There was a smell of petrol everywhere in the windless air. No one had tailed him or picked him up, not even as he ate at a breakfast caravan parked beside a railway bridge. He belched. Indigestible sandwiches filled with bacon and fried egg, and the aftertaste of sweet tea. He glanced up at Ros' window. She wasn't there, but who was it she had already let in who occupied her attention?

Because Priabin's people weren't here. Special Branch had frightened them off, parking outside his door.

"Can I help, officer?" he asked insultingly, hands in his pockets.

"Hyde—has to be, doesn't it?" the Special Branch man commented. "People waiting to see you." He nodded toward the flat before he got out of the Granada. The policeman was taller than Hyde, bulky and confidently smirking. Agent of the civil power—unlike, his expression remarked, the small man who confronted him. Another of those spooks, as the Yanks called them, getting his comeuppance. "Would you care to accompany me, sir?" He warily offered his cupped hand toward Hyde's elbow.

"I wouldn't."

"Yours is about to drop on you," the SB officer observed, sniffing the air like a large dog.

"Was there anyone here, when you arrived?" Hyde asked impatiently.

"Look, there's no one hiding in the bushes, not even your bookie."

"Oh, those important files you keep in Curzon Street. Any people in cars—you know, ones who didn't drive straight off to work?"

The car's driver looked angry and leaned belligerently across the passenger seat.

"Take clever-dick upstairs, Dean," he said.

Hyde spluttered with laughter. "It's true—the policemen are getting younger."

"Just let me see you laughing upstairs."

"Why—who are my houseguests, constable?"

"Sir Clive Orrell and Aubrey, the—"

"—old fart, you were about to add? OK, we'll go inside—just get your mate in there to have a look around the gardens, will you? As a last favor for a dying man?"

Christ, *Aubrey?* He'd come off sick leave to his flat with Orrell? Serious was not the word.

There was sufficient latent professionalism even in their situation for the SB man to nod to the driver and murmur: "Just play up to him, will you, Jack? Have a look for Mata Hari in a parked car, would you?"

Hyde clicked his fingers. "Glad to see you covered yourself there, *Dean,*" and shrugged off the attempted grip and strode across the pavement to the three steps up to the front door. He glimpsed Ros' volume fill the window of her flat, even the warning round O of her mouth opening, before he passed under the porch.

The birds vied with the traffic from the main road and the periodic coughing of engines starting up in Philbeach Gardens. Then Ros was at the door, the habitual where-have-you-been expression on her face collapsing quickly into confusion, into what's-going-on? He kissed her cheek in passing, shrugging his ignorance. Even though he could no longer pretend, even to himself. Aubrey was prepared to arrive in tandem with Orrell . . . goodnight, ladies . . . it was all about to fall in on his head. He climbed the staircase to the first floor, then the second, with Ros behind him, silently shooing him up toward his suspension. She seemed impressed, angry and reluctant at the same moment concerning the two august civil servants who were waiting for him. That's what they were, and it's *your* pension that's on the line!

As he pushed open the door of his flat, Aubrey whirled round in front of the French clock on the mantelpiece. Hyde appraised him, like a surgeon does a patient. The old man leaned heavily on his stick, but he seemed fitter than the last time they'd met. His skin was less waxy, almost tinted with health. But there was no sense of Aubrey's support for him, merely irritation, suspicion, distance between them. The bellicose bad humor of an old man galvanized into reluctant energy

and purpose. Hyde felt his stomach sag. There'd be no
help from Aubrey, just the ballocking and the suspension—dismissal?—from Orrell.

Aubrey seemed almost contemptuous of Hyde's
own un-shaven, highly odorous self, and at once began
to pace the room, as if he had been waiting for some
theatrical cue, his stick jutting out just ahead of him at
each step, as if in control of him. Orrell watched with a
bluff kind of calculation. Neither of the two new cats
had gone near him. Both of them at least feigned sleep.
The Burmese stray stretched itself, its legs too long for
its body. It always walked as if it had a sore backside—
like Orrell, except that he rolled. The other cat, the tortoiseshell with the black mask, was asleep on the
windowsill outside the open window, one ear idly
attending to the birdsong from the few paltry trees in
the back garden. Even now, he tried not to be interested in them. Ros had brought them home from some
rescue shelter. Instead, he tried ever more violently to
remember Layla, six months' dead and buried in the
garden.

As if at some invisible tug from a string Orrell
held, Aubrey said: "Patrick, where the *devil* have you
been? I have been dragged—requested to come here—
because you could not be located on the express orders
of your own Director General!" The formality was
strange and awesome; pathetic, too. The last refuge of
an old man. He glanced at Orrell and saw nothing but
satisfaction on his large, uncharactered face. Then
Aubrey let fall, amid his dry officialese, something of
himself as he said: "Why Sir Clive required my presence, I have no idea. You are no longer attached to me
by anything, not even some imagined umbilical cord!"
He turned his back on Hyde immediately.

Orrell seemed to consider Aubrey's remarks as sufficiently reprimanding, for he said: "You were ordered
to report to Century House yesterday for a full debrief-

ing. DDG Bannister"—Hyde maintained a stony inexpression—"issued that order at—well, never mind. But, after an incident of the significance of that at Centre Point, you must surely have realized your report would be required at the most senior levels?"

Aubrey's shoulders were twitchy, uncertain within his lightweight suit. The Burmese, Hyde noticed, had stretched one paw out toward Aubrey's straw hat, lying on the sofa. Another few inches and she'd become animated and destructive. To some extent, Orrell was inhibited by Aubrey's presence—authority, rather. What should he do? Authority haunted the corridors of Orrell's labyrinthine mind. Empty labyrinth, though. No Minotaur in there. Get rid of Orrell, then. Signal Aubrey with—

"Sir, I'm sorry." Aubrey's head cocked like that of a bird. Orrell, too, seemed suspicious if not surprised. Apology was his due, after all. Hyde flicked his hands, then rubbed his unshaven face. "After that, sir, you know how it is for field agents, afterwards . . . " He collapsed into one of the armchairs. Ros, in the doorway, he realized for the first time, emanated a puzzlement that he gratefully accepted. If she was bemused, then Orrell had no chance.

"Hyde, what are you saying to me?" Aubrey snapped.

"Sir, I'm saying that I went in there, gung-ho if you like, because I thought . . . well, didn't think, really, but I *knew* the bomb scare was a hoax, I *knew* someone was in there. When I found the security guard dead, I—just went over the top, sir." No speech he had ever made had been so studied. Out of anger, really, coming face-to-face with Aubrey and the old man's irritation, and out of his contempt for Orrell, of course.

Orrell cleared his throat. His eyes cast about on the dark carpet. "I see, Hyde, but we need to know! No time to allow you to wind down, get it out of your system, you know that. Not in these circumstances."

"No, sir."

"Very well." The sofa squeaked and the Burmese muttered in its sleep as Orrell stood up. "All right, Hyde. Get yourself cleaned up and get along to my office by two this afternoon. The heat's off this business, as from now. Make sure you are on time." The sarcasm was heavy.

"Yes, sir."

"Thank you, Miss Woode, I'll see myself out— Kenneth?"

"No, Clive. I think you have been far too magnanimous. I think someone should explain *accountability* to Patrick; I believe that was why I was asked to come?"

"Yes, of course, yes."

Hyde looked up as he heard Orrell's heavy tread retreat down the first flight of stairs. His grin faded as he saw the look of outrage on Aubrey's face, the quick, unstudied movements of his body, the flicks of the cane beside him. There was infinite reproach in every minuscule gesture.

Strangely, however, Hyde's anger at Aubrey seemed to sputter out almost at once. There was something self-accusing, even guilty, about Aubrey's expression. Hyde said: "In case you're wondering, it was Priabin. Not a gang of murderous wogs, but the KGB in there. Understand?" His tone was sullen, and Aubrey all but glowered at him. Behind that, there was something else, the abstraction of someone looking at old, mildewed, sepia prints of his childhood or some early love affair. "What's the matter with you?" Hyde prompted.

Aubrey glanced around the room and then sat heavily on the sofa near his straw hat. "I was contacted by the Commander of Special Branch," he murmured, holding up his hand for silence but not looking at

Hyde. "My real day-to-day authority now appears so slight that the Branch feels no compunction about waking me at five-thirty in the morning to ask your whereabouts. At six, Clive Orrell was on the line, requesting in an unavoidable way that I accompany him here." He sighed. "The commander's request was, incidentally, as to the whereabouts of that *devious little bastard*." He looked up and essayed, almost successfully, a tired and wintry smile. Then he said: "I'm sorry, Patrick."

Eventually, Hyde murmured: "What?"

"I'm sorry—"

"I survived, you mean?"

"Don't be paranoid!" Aubrey snapped, so much in a caricature of his waspish, professional self that Hyde almost grinned again, rubbing his hands through his hair.

The tortoiseshell had vanished from the windowsill at the moment of Aubrey's snapping comment. Ros had slipped back into the room and seated herself in the armchair nearest the door. The Burmese had invaded her lap and at once began kneading her sleeve with its paws and sucking at the material of her voluminous frock. Her broad forehead was creased with puzzled confusion, her eyes in sympathy with the small, old man on the sofa. He sat upright, clasping his cane.

"Coffee, Sir Kenneth?" Ros asked. The silence seemed to swallow the words.

"What? Oh, no thank you, Ros. Very kind of you, but no." Then he fell to studying Hyde, who felt himself obscurely reprimanded and admired at the same moment. "What is going on, Patrick? What is happening?"

Hyde blundered immediately into a summary of the previous evening and night, glancing in sudden rushes on Godwin's theories, the surveillance on Reid Group. Malan's name worked like a cattle prod on the old, upright body.

Aubrey's pale blue eyes seemed to search Hyde's face for signs of deception or imagination. Then he murmured: "Malan's behind it, then. He's there, behind everything? You're quite certain?"

Hyde nodded. "He's holding hands with Priabin. He's in everything up to his neck."

"And Priabin's intention is to remove you and open up the way to Tony and Chambers? You're equally sure of that?" The tortoiseshell reappeared on the windowsill, regarding the old man with a mild, steady curiosity, its head to one side. Aubrey said: "I am expected to add to the official reprimand you just received. Which will precede your official suspension this afternoon." Hyde snorted, but Aubrey held up his hand. "It was evidently felt to be chastening, for both of us, if I were to be the one who administered six of the best to someone who they regard as a favored pupil of mine." Again, the sad, wise smile. It was an Aubrey that Hyde found difficult to comprehend, as if he were seeing both too much and too little of the man's nature. Aubrey looked up. "You two will understand me—my confusion and perhaps guiltiness. I am barely recovered, I think. It wore me out, like any obsession, any passion." He shook his head. "But it seems fated, does it not? It cannot be let alone, nor are we to be let alone by *it*, apparently."

"We?" Hyde mocked.

"Oh, yes—the plural. We—*us*."

"What can you do?"

"I don't know. I might be able to prevent you being suspended, who knows? At any rate, I must put my hand to the business. I agree with your assessment. They intend something very soon, something crucial to them, of huge proportion."

"Then get me out of *here*," Hyde insisted. "They'll have those two idiots parked outside to make certain I don't go anywhere except Century House this afternoon. Get them called off—talk to Godwin, let me talk to him."

"For the moment, do nothing. Stay here. I mean that. Do nothing in *addition* to invoke Sir Clive's mastodon dislike. Because he will tread you under if you go any further with this on your own." He stared at Hyde. "Do you understand me, Patrick?"

"Look, there may not be any time left to sit on our asses!"

"I realize that! But *you* must do nothing more to bring down Orrell's wrath. You will attend him this afternoon, you will be polite—you will *remain* polite, you will appear to accept your fate, whatever it is! No, Patrick, you will do as I say."

Hyde eventually slumped back into his chair, waving a dismissive hand. "Oh, bugger off to your club and have a couple of early scotches."

"Hyde," Ros warned, but Aubrey smiled.

"You make not only a virtue but a style of living out of truculence, Patrick. Conserve it, for the moment. It will be needed. Now, I must leave. There is much to do and, as you reminded me, little time in which to do it. Meanwhile, you are to do nothing on your own account—*nothing*."

6

THIS NIGHT'S GREAT BUSINESS

It was the old house, still little more than a bungalow, white-painted with a broad *stoep* and a deep shadowy veranda, which his great-grandfather had built. The house was surrounded by the imitation English parkland that his grandfather had brought back in his imagination from his public school and his weekends at friends' country houses. Malan stopped the Range Rover and, as the air-conditioning sighed into silence with the engine, the heat of noon seemed to clamp itself upon the vehicle, claiming and isolating it. For a moment, he sat, both hands still gripping the steering wheel, looking at the shadows on the veranda, at the dim mesh of the screen door and the vague landscape of the cluttered hall through the open inner door. Malan felt a habitual reluctance to leave the vehicle, cross the short, hot patch of sunlight, and go into the house. His father's house—retreat, nursing home; place of abode and imminent demise.

He half-opened the door and hesitated once more. Music, probably Beethoven . . . yes, coming from inside. He shook his head, but he was unsure of his disapprobation—the music, the anticipated encounter, or the midday news he had angrily switched off. A lengthy report of the progress—and success—of the constitutional talks between the de Villiers government and the kaffirs—Mandela and the other ANC leaders. The document of surrender was the joke, sourly repeated, in the Automobile Club and the half dozen boardrooms he had occupied during the past day or two. Within a year, Mandela would be mounting a dais in Pretoria with the Presidential ribbon around his neck. At least, that was what the pessimists claimed—along with the Conservatives and the AWB extremists.

The newspapers on the front passenger seat were full of the same stuff, and they had caught his eye as he hesitated to confront his father—then their headlines and photographs of smiling blacks and whites shaking hands seemed to thrust him out into the hard, hot sun. His shoulders hunched against its heat and force, then he was under the veranda roof, in its deep, humming shadows. Hanging baskets of flowers, two old rocking chairs, a white, wrought-iron table and chairs, the hammock at the far end of the *stoep*. This place, where he had always met men older than himself—great-grandfather, though he was difficult to recollect except in his white massiveness, grandfather, and now father. This place. It tugged, though; hurt, sometimes. He hated it. He hurried through the screen door and it banged behind him, startling footsteps at the other end of the hall, because it was, for an instant, as if his dead sister waited to pounce out of the *stoep*'s deep shadows. His wife hardly ever came back to him from the sailing accident that had drowned her and his sister, Diana. Nor did his sister as an adult, herself married, twice divorced. She only threatened to come back aged seven or eight, his little sister.

The footsteps had been those of the black nurse, and she clicked across the parquet flooring toward him now, a respectful suspicion and distance in her eyes. She was carrying a tray of medicine bottles, pill bottles, all of which were mere placebos now, with the disease so far advanced, its full invasion force moved out from his stomach, occupying much of his body.

"How is my father?" he asked awkwardly, as if not knowing her language.

"Resting, sir." It was all she ever said, that and what she now added. "Do not stay long, sir—you'll tire him." His father, he knew, spoke to her for hours, especially when her husband came to collect her, and the night nurse came on duty. Even spoke to her children. Malan was angry with that, as at a trick of charm possessed by another man which made his way with people smoother, easier.

"Very well." He nodded. Dusty footprints behind him on the gleaming wood of the floor. Great-grandfather's animal heads glared dimly down from the walls, grandfather's faded watercolors were there, too, and the dozens of photographs, even some of himself, growing older. Maps, books, old furniture, rugs. A littered and comfortable place, like the main house had been until he had rendered it newly antiseptic, office-like. "Very well," he repeated, but the nurse had disappeared, presumably into the kitchen.

Shrugging his shoulders, he knocked on the open bedroom door and heard his father murmur wordlessly. The music ceased at once. He went into the room that smelt of bed linen, old heat, his father's age and shrunkenness, and the oppressive scent of roses brought down by one of the gardeners, fresh every day. Books littered the bedspread, his father's spectacles were near his shriveled, narrow hand, liver-spotted and long-nailed, and the swivel stand on which his books

were piled was pushed aside from the wide bed. Jeppe
Malan was propped against big pillows, his hair tidied,
his features decoratively glazed or varnished with attention to his inward self. Then the eyes flickered wide,
recognizingly. Malan bent and kissed his father's forehead, which was cool, and his father's hand caught at
his wrist for an instant, lightly as a girl's touch. Malan
pulled a chair to the bedside and sat down, unrelaxed.

His father smiled with saintly, ascetic lips nar-
rowed and made bloodless by the progress of the disease. His face, once much like Malan's own, broad and
confident, was deeply lined, pale; beatific. He could
think of no other image that fitted the dying man or
explained the new, farther distance between them. It
described Jeppe's assumption of some kind of moral
superiority, for Jesus' sake.

"What are you reading?" he asked, clearing his
throat. The floor was untidy with newspapers in
English and Afrikaans. "Besides the papers?"

"Some poetry, Paulus. Some philosophy, some history . . . " His voice was extremely weary, detached;
again that bloody sainthood imposed by the cancer!
His father was bravely resigned, but it wasn't that
Malan disliked or resented. It was this suddenly con-
templative man—no, he'd been that for years. Ever
since the war? He'd come back, so the legend claimed,
reluctant to run MLC—there were no surviving
Labuschagne children—and taken up wealth and
power like a burden.

"I see. I heard—" again, he cleared his throat. "I
heard that Mandela was here, while I was in Europe?"
It was not an accusation, though it was more than conversation to occupy time and the gloom. "Did you discuss philosophy?"

Jeppe Malan nodded. "Not that we agreed," he
observed. "He was sorry for me. My illness—"

Malan watched his own hands, with the freedom

of independent agents, clenching on his thighs. That fucking kaffir! He felt *sorry?* Sorry he might be in a position to nationalize, break up or ruin MLC in the next year or so! "Did he apologize for his Marxist attitude toward us?" he asked involuntarily.

His father's hand seemed to float toward his own, and touch it carefully, as if exploring for a moment before wearying and withdrawing again. He said: "I didn't ask him to apologize. He might have done." The old man sighed. The bed seemed too big for him, like adult clothes on a child—Diana in her mother's frocks and high-heeled shoes and makeup, at six or seven. He shook his head as if plagued by flies. The fan whirred softly about them, old-fashioned, hardly stirring the thundery air of the room.

"He'll ruin us—that's the only outcome," Paulus said.

"Unless there's no MLC left in South Africa."

"What?"

"That's what Mandela fears. You don't think he came because I was dying, do you? Well, not entirely." His breathing was ragged, his eyes wide and staring at the ceiling, as if he were absorbed in the movement of the fan. He continued: "He's afraid you'll get out, take everything."

"It's ours to take, Pa. What does Mandela want to do with it, huh? Nationalize the bloody mines, the gold and diamonds, the Oranjemund operation, the car plant, the chemicals and pharmaceuticals—*everything.* You know he hasn't wavered from that since the bastard first went to Robben Island." He shook his head. "That bloke makes me sick. Coming here to see a dying man just to persuade . . . " He shrugged.

"Persuade what? Persuade you not to continue with your European operations?" His father was silent for a moment, then nodded gently. "Perhaps he did." He smiled. "Millie was impressed when she found him at the door. Father of South Africa, and all that. Since Mandela came, she has read the papers with greater enthusiasm than ever when I've felt too tired." His head moved slowly and his eyes focused on Malan. "What are you doing, son?" His hand fluttered, but Malan's wrist was out of reach. "MLC is an African company, whatever interests we have abroad, in the rest of the world. It is not European." His father's face was blotched with a trace of color, near the cheekbones. It seemed a further exhibition of his illness. Malan shook his head.

"I haven't kept things from you," he said sullenly. Perhaps his sister always threatened to appear in the shadows because he was always a child when he came to this place. "The company's my responsibility."

"Agreed. So is this country."

"Not the way it will be!" he burst out, then calmed himself, breathing deeply. "Not the way things will be . . . "

But his father was nodding with a strained attempt at vigor. "Whatever happens. Do you think this country will be *better* if the company leaves? Do you think that?" It was an entire and onerous disbelief rather than a challenge.

"Your paternalism's old-fashioned, Pa. They don't want it, the kaffirs—"

"They will *need* us. Don't you think Mandela and the others realize?" He was tiring, as if the house and its past bore down on him more heavily than upon Malan.

"My concern is the future of MLC."

"MLC—my company, yours now—*is* this country. What will you do to *our* country? Have you thought of that?" His frail white hand was patting the bedspread, plucking at it occasionally, as if a small, trained animal lay near him on the bed. His idea of the kaffirs, Malan thought. To be patted on the head, stroked, made a fuss of. He just doesn't understand. Too old. Dying. "This is *your* country—what are you doing to it, son? What?"

The movements of his hand had become dismissive, as if he were shooing away his weariness, or the future. Malan stood up, seeing his father's exhaustion. As he bent forward to kiss his cheek, the old man's eyes were alight and unforgiving. He stared like the portrait of his great-grandfather, Jeppe's grandfather, out in the hall. Patriarchal, certain, old. And out of date, out of touch, as the country changed out of all recognition around them. Yet he felt pained as he straightened up, looming over his father. It was difficult to come, painful to leave. Always.

His father lay there, surrounded by the family detritus of the bedroom, its dried proteas in bulky arrangements on the sideboard and a dark table, the flies at the mesh of the screen, the hot sunlight leaking around the closed blinds. Malan was suddenly aware of the strangeness of the room rather than its overpowering familiarity. His father belonged in that white man's African room, but he himself did not. No longer. The main house was like a series of offices, an agglomeration of hotel suites. European, international, stateless. He shook his head and announced softly: "I'll come this evening," but his father was apparently asleep. Slowly, he turned away, passing Millie in the hall without remarking her presence as she hurried into the bedroom to inspect—

What? Her prize? Her tame white man, fallen? No, perhaps not.

The sun struck down and the interior of the Range Rover was as claustrophobic as the distance between the *stoep* and the vehicle. He started the engine and turned up the air-conditioning. It blew coolly against his flushed cheeks. The wheel was hot under his palms. He glanced at the bungalow. It had taken three generations of Malans before himself to build MLC. It mustn't be lost. It couldn't remain just African and *not* be lost. *He* couldn't remain South African without surrendering the company, watching it decline, be split up . . .

Which was why Jeppe could watch with indifference while it happened. Death had already shrunk the world to the size of that bedroom, MLC was no longer important to him.

Malan revved the engine loudly and careered away from the bungalow, dust filling the driving mirror.

"No, it's Ros' phone. It isn't bugged. I checked. Mine is."

"Good. What's the old man got in mind?"

Hyde shook his head. Ros was out shopping. The branch of the tree bending toward the open window of her living room at the rear of the flat was moving as if to encourage the last cool air to enter the room.

"Something that'll take too long. Has he talked to you? Well, he will. I can't bloody move, anyway. They're sitting in a car outside."

The Burmese on the brocaded sofa appeared sublimely indifferent. Ros did not encourage them onto her furniture, but the suite was already plucked and puckered from the exercise of the cats' claws. She fussed at it then forgot.

"Look, Patrick, nobbling a shipment is the only way out for us, if we can't wait for the old man. I've contacted Customs—"

"Christ! I suppose you used Orrell's authority?"

"No, Bannister's name was sufficient."

"That unforgiving bastard." He sipped at the can of lager, which had already warmed to tastelessness.

"Come on, Patrick, we *need* you." Godwin had known to ring Ros' number. She'd summoned him from his flat down to hers.

"I just told you, I can't bloody well move! Those two outside, Mutt and Jeff, will just whisk me down to Curzon Street or Century House if I so much as put the empty milk bottles on the step." He glanced at his watch. "I have to be in Orrell's office at two—it's almost one now."

"Patrick! Terry and I can't do everything by ourselves, and I can't bring Customs in until we're sure a shipment's left Reid Davies for SwiftEx. I've just explained all that, for God's sake!" The line was hollow, crackly, occasionally fading as they presumably passed under a motorway bridge. "I've left Darren behind just for the purpose. Now, can't you climb out the back bloody window or something?"

Involuntarily, Hyde glanced at the open window and its partial mask of leaves. The tortoiseshell cat, itself masked as if to mock secrecy, appeared, head on one side.

"What if I did?" he asked.

"Darren can pick you up—where? Outside Earl's Court? Would that do?"

"Look, I should see Orrell. If I don't turn up, they'll be after all four of us. Aubrey warned me."

"Bugger Orrell! If we nobble Reid Davies, we're all in clover—" The call faded momentarily, then: "—don't you see?"

"Christ, I don't—"

"Look! If we get suspended for finding nothing, it'll all have been a right bloody waste of time, won't it? At least this way we might get the job done!"

"Oh, stop bloody shouting, Godwin! You're beginning to sound like my mother!" He lowered his voice. "Right, call Darren-the-Wonder-Dog and tell him to pick me up in fifteen minutes, outside Earl's Court—the exhibition building, not the Tube station!"

"Good. He'll drive you to Bickenhill. Terry's drop-

ping me off there before he goes on to Willenhall, to
Reid Davies. See you."

Hyde put down the receiver and stared at it, shaking his head. Godwin simply didn't want to listen to
anything. Aubrey's direct order was a fleabite. Godwin
had already been bitten by his bloody obsession with
Reid Group, Malan and all the other buggers in the
game. It was like an affair, it wouldn't let him go until
he'd seen the woman in bed with his best friend, or
she'd left taking all his money. He crossed to the window and looked out. Over the garden wall, nip down
past the church to the railway lines, bingo. Simple, son.
Except for when it turns out to be a wild-goose chase
and Orrell appears snorting like a bull and pawing the
bloody ground! And you'll have fucked up any chance
of Aubrey bailing you out.

He shrugged. What have you got to lose? Most of
it's already gone, mate. Where's the gun, your wallet?

Shit, it was like Butch Cassidy jumping off the cliff.
No, it bloody wasn't. It was Redford and Newman
dashing through that door into the final, frozen frame
of the film, with two thousand sharpshooters waiting—
that's what it was like!

Absently, he stroked the cat, who seemed offended
at the unwanted, intrusive act.

Richard Anderson stopped the grumbling, rusting Land
Rover in the patchy shade of a scrubby acacia,
switched off the engine and at once clamped his hands
beneath his armpits, cradling them gently against the
pain. Each burn and bruise tormented him. He slumped
over the steering wheel, exhausted. The early afternoon
heat clung around the tree solid as a horde of insects.
The engine of the Land Rover clicked and protested in
the heavy silence. The last of the dust along the tarred
highway settled. He heard the call of some hunting

bird, a half-hearted scream in the heat. He emptied his mind, letting the towns through which he had passed, or bypassed—Omaruru, Karibib, Usakos—settle like the dust on the road and disappear. Let the slowly descending road ahead disappear, too, and the narrow, gleaming strip of sky along the horizon that might be the sea. Behind him, the escarpment had retreated into the haze, brown and gray, indistinct.

Eventually, he sipped water from the flask and splashed a palmful of it onto his face. His hand came away brown from the dampened dust in his beard and skin. As he looked up, the Erongo mountains seemed insubstantial in the heat. Turning his head, the northern edge of the Namib nibbled at trees and plants ahead of him, promising low dunes and sand all the way to the coast. Swakopmund, then Walvis Bay, both within the enclave still controlled by South Africa.

The goal was illusory, he realized. A small, bright bird settled in the decayed branches of the acacia, seeking absent flowers. He stared at it, the back of his neck aching. Walvis Bay was where the DC–3 must have begun its flight, and MLC had operations in Walvis Bay. A lizard slipped through the few poor fronds of tough grass that had sprouted in the shade after the minimal winter rains. Illusory. What did he hope for? That his letter had reached Aubrey, that Aubrey would arrive with the night-light and the comfort blanket for his childish grief and incapacity? He lowered his head. Perhaps that was what he did really want: a way of escape, at least a sense of others, of not being alone.

Something wet his wrist. The water would have dried from his face moments earlier . . . again. A cold, metronomic ticking of damp spots on his wrist, continuing regular as a clock. She had come out of the dark behind his eyelids and surprised him, her face close so that he was able to catch her scent amid the sensations of heat and dust. He had stopped the 4WD, and collided with his grief. To halt movement, even for a moment, was too long.

He looked up, sharply, as her image retreated once more. No dust rose above the tarred road, not even in the distance toward the hills. An aircraft trailed its white signal across the high blue. Blantyre would be in pursuit, however slowly or carefully. Guessing where he would go, knowing his history too well to be mistaken about his dreams of justice—and revenge. When he arrived in Walvis Bay, Blantyre would either be there already or close behind. All schemes of mounting some kind of surveillance on MLC's private airstrip in Walvis Bay or sniffing out and around their factories and offices were—ridiculous. Prompted by the impotence of his insatiable revenge.

He breathed deeply, time and again. Gradually—so gradually— calming himself, becoming nothing more than a man parked at the side of a road which led to an airport and flights out of Namibia. The mountains maintained their distance, the phosphoric, burning strip of sky that was the Atlantic or the coastal dunes remained narrow, distanced. The birds in the acacia chirped with lulling regularity. He sniffed loudly. Survival was paramount, and that meant buying a ticket and boarding an SAA flight to Jo'burg or Cape Town or even Windhoek.

To demonstrate that he had given up, that he was no longer any threat to them. To simply get out. Blayre was intent upon his death. He would thwart that. However far he might be forced to travel, and however unmitigated the grief he might find when he once again halted, he would thwart Blantyre's necessity to kill him.

"OK, I'm just down the street from Reid Davies—are you sure this is the right place? It's just a poky factory site in a back street!"

"Terry, this is the West Midlands—welcome to the home of tin bashing."

"For God's sake, they can't be smuggling transputers and WSI from here!"

Chambers watched the narrow, sloping street. It was lined with closed or open wooden doors, some of which bore signs that explained the mysteries that occurred behind them. What he had expected, he had no idea—perhaps something on some industrial park that patronized the district into believing it was no longer in the last century . . . maybe. But somehow, not this wierdly quiet street with a jazz record shop, some fenced-in units, a canal bridge halfway along its length, and all those stablelike doors, on one of which it proclaimed the headquarters and factory space of Reid Davies, a subsidiary of the Reid Group, Plc. And it was peaceful, even with the window open, on a sunny late afternoon, as if the place was dozing in the warm light like a cat. Christ, were they all on strike or out of work, or something?

"Oh, yes, they can. That area's full of little firms that turn out just the nut and just the bolt—or just the transputer or just the WSI circuit you need. Reid Davies owns most of the companies in that street, or didn't you pay attention when I told you?"

"Sorry. How are you doing?"

Tower blocks disfigured the afternoon. There *was* a Porsche parked along the street—no, two, neither of them the cheaper models. Godwin might be right.

"I'm hovering by the railway bridge. I've walked up and down, sat down, pretended to be waiting for a bus. When the hell are Darren and Patrick going to arrive?"

"Anything doing?"

"Sod all. SwiftEx has had deliveries and shipments from lots of clients, but not from Reid Davies. I've checked the airport, without causing a fuss, but nothing. If we want to check—*later*—then we'll have to lean on them."

"What about Customs?"

"Reluctant and skeptical. What would you expect? They'll cooperate, but I don't want to put them on alert until the Reid Davies shipment leaves the factory. Any sign of it?"

"I hope to God they don't check with Bannister," Chambers observed sourly. "I'll go and have a look. Ring you."

Chambers opened the door of the car and thrust the cellular telephone into his trouser pocket. It bulked awkwardly. He locked the car door and stood with his hands on his hips. The side street traffic was light, pedestrians few unless overalled, or briefcased like reps. Grimy windows, some of them broken; old, warm brick sooted and crumbling; corrugated, tiled and slated roofs. He felt hesitant, undecided. He rubbed a hand through his hair and checked the parking meter, then his watch. He began walking along the uneven tarred pavement with its surviving cobbles outside many of the closed doors. Those that were open exposed narrow alleyways or cobbled courtyards. He shook his head. It was difficult to reconcile this setup with transputer manufacture. More like the setting for quick respray jobs on stolen cars. As for wafer scale integration technology, the next generation of chips and microcomputers—forget it.

Reid Davies, across the street. A single-decker bus in blue-cream livery slid past, exposing like a drawn curtain the glimpse of two large trucks, both emblazoned SwiftEx, one with its rear doors closed. The other was being fed by a forklift truck, lifting a stack of crates on a pallet into the shadowy mouth of the truck. He perspired with reaction and excitement and fumbled the cellular phone from his pocket, dabbing out Godwin's number.

"Here," he blurted out. "Two trucks, both SwiftEx." Another forklift trundled to the truck and fed it. "I think one of them's already been loaded." Cars obscured the courtyard. "The second one's almost stuffed to the roof—TVs, by the look of it— microwaves, VCRs—the usual stock-in-trade. What do you—?"

"Hang on there for the moment. Let me know when they leave. I'll get over to Customs in the meanwhile and get things set up. TVs and bloody microwaves! That's what they make in there, and another of the companies in that street is part of the WSI manufacturing for Reid Electronics, and a third idoes packaging work on the transputers." Godwin was gloating, but Chambers felt no resentment. "They switch the boxes, simple as that. Must be."

"Reid Group packages its stuff here?"

"I wonder how much? There's certainly some, from Darren's checks on those subsidiaries of Reid Davies. Christ, when we've opened the boxes at this end, we might be allowed to go all the way through that street like a dose of salts! OK, hang on until they leave, then tail them here. See you."

Chambers switched off and tucked the phone under his arm. He leaned against the crumbling brick of the grubby wall behind him. Transputers, WSI, packaging—the smell of a small foundry like burnt bread on the air. Christ, it was coming together, it really was. If enough Reid Group packaging and shipping was done from here, then it made it so bloody simple for them! He glanced furtively around him as if the grimy windows would betray their interiors, and he would see clues like flags. God, it could be a real bonus, this one—

Cars obscured his view of the courtyard of Reid Davies, then he saw the tailgate and the doors of the second truck being closed and noisily bolted and locked. A blue sedan passed slowly. The gates were opened to their widest extent and he felt his heart thud as the engine of one of the trucks was started up. A man in overalls strolled out into the street and the truck's reverse lights came on and its warning horn began sounding.

Chambers turned toward the car. The blue sedan had slowed to a halt beside it.

"For God's sake, what are they doing about it? What are *you* doing about it?"

Babbington had been on the point of leaving his office when his assistant had called him back—bawled down the corridor like a fishwife that Priabin was in secure telephone contact and was declaring an emergency. He had snatched the remote telephone from the young man's hand and slammed the door of the inner office behind him. The delays and grumbles of encoding-decoding by the encryption unit in the outer office further irritated him.

"I—suggest, General, that it may be too late to do anything but show our hand." Priabin was concerned, his confidence ebbed.

"Where is *Mortimer*? Why can't he be reached?"

"He's been out of the country on business. I'm not certain when he's expected. Van Vuuren claims he returns today, but he's vague about—"

"Forget *Mortimer* then. I expect it's too late to change the shipment in any case."

"It has been loaded."

"You've surveillance there?"

"Yes."

"Good. Then employ it. Chambers is there, you say, and Godwin at the airport? How far is Hyde from Birmingham? It must be where he is heading."

"An hour and a half, perhaps more. The traffic's

heavy on the M1, there are roadworks."

"Keep Hyde away. Stop the others—as *discreetly* as is possible in the circumstances. But stop them. Meanwhile, *I'll* speak to Malan. He must find a way to irritate MacPherson with the news that the consignment may be delayed. Someone, at least, must prompt Century House to wake up and notice what some of their finest are doing! As for you, there are no excuses for delay. Keep those damned people away from that shipment!"

"Look, we're stuck in a six-mile backup and there's sod all we can do about it!" Hyde snapped. "Listen to the bloody travel news, why don't you? Some truck jackknifed and overturned. Bloody French apples or something all over the northbound carriageway! Gloria Hunniford just told us!"

Darren Westfield grinned, then attempted to appear gravely concerned, like a poor actor's too-sudden change of mood. Hyde grimaced at him and banged the parcel shelf of the Escort. The fact that he suspected they had been tailed by a Renault all the way from Earl's Court was now irrelevant. The other car was stuck half a mile back as glutinously as they were themselves. A police car, siren wailing and blue light winking palely in the bright afternoon, passed them at speed on the hard shoulder. Hyde wiped his forehead.

"Watch your back, Godwin. We were tailed." He glared at Darren, who appeared more likely to break out in acne than perspiration. "Darren here didn't realize it—"

"Neither did you until we reached Watford," Darren observed quietly.

"If they're watching us, then they must be watching you and Chambers. If you move, they might too."

"OK, got you. I'll watch out. The consignment's

loaded and about to leave—Terry just called in with the news."

"Right. Let's hope to God the traffic clears and all the incriminating evidence is on that truck. Otherwise—" he glanced at the dashboard clock. Two-thirty. "Otherwise Orrell, who is probably chewing the office carpet by now, is going to have my balls deviled for tomorrow's breakfast." He heard Godwin chuckle.

"We'll save your virility, Patrick. I'll keep in touch."

Hyde lowered the cellular telephone to his lap and drummed his hands on his thighs.

"Got any good books?"

"No. Want the paper?" Then Darren's attempt at Hyde's mood vanished, and he asked naively: "Is this going to be all right?"

"I should think so. They're just watching us. I spy with my little eye something beginning with . . . "

Chambers reached the car and inserted the key in the lock. The blue sedan must be waiting for a parking meter to become free. Two men. He opened the door—one of the men was using the carphone—and put his own telephone on the passenger seat. He looked up. The first SwiftEx truck was backing out of the narrow archway of Reid Davies, reversing horn sounding continually like a burglar alarm.

Slamming of a door behind him as he bent to climb into the car. Hand on his shoulder, jerking him round. Men from the blue car—?

"What's the—?" he began.

"It's him," one of them, the taller, bulkier one, confirmed.

The flash of the knife and a searing sensation in his side as he attempted to wriggle free. The nerves becoming instantly numb against the anticipated pain, his hand grasping feebly at the knife blade, cutting itself across the palm, then the knife entering him again, somewhere in the area of his stomach. Difficult to tell, the pain of the first wound made him cry out, made their activities indistinct. As he slumped to the pavement, his back against the car and his legs spread out like an abandoned doll, he heard little more than the noise of the truck's continual horn as it reversed into the narrow street. Felt only their quick, rough search of his pockets, his jacket, which was then thrown down beside him. Saw a hand with his wallet . . .

Mugging. They didn't want his wallet, just the credibility it would give to this pretended street crime. His hand was red as he pressed it against his stomach, and he stared down, gaping, at the sight of his blood. Then he heard someone shouting, *after* the noise of their car. Feet on the tarred pavement, close to him, a shadow bending over him . . . minutes, by the clock-spread of his blood, after the car had gone. Overalls bending over him, the noise of the truck's horn silent now. Things becoming dim, all except the pain, which seemed to be everywhere, even behind his eyelids, which were red as he closed them, then dark, empty . . .

Van Vuuren listened, for perhaps the dozenth time, to the busy signal from *Mortimer*'s carphone. At first, it had been a surge of relief to hear that the phone was being used, that the man had returned, must be in his car driving from London or wherever. Now that he could talk to him, he could alter the consignment or get it stopped. But it was continually busy! Angrily, he slammed down the telephone. Three o'clock. He had been stuck in MLC's offices in the Strand, staring at the walls, at the river and Charing Cross station from the high windows of ShellMex House, since eight in the morning and he'd accomplished nothing—*nothing!*

Paulus had been on the line four times, pushing, carping, instructing, threatening—all to no bloody purpose. He couldn't get hold of the only man who could alter the damned consignment! Because they'd got into his suite, used his laptop, rifled the mainframe in Jo'burg, knew what they were looking for. Must know—they were in Birmingham, for God's sake!

He pushed the remnants of his lunch away from him across the borrowed desk. The telephone blurted and he snatched it up.

"Paulus—yes! No, I can't get—what? Oh *no*. Can't it be turned back?"

"Listen to me, Piet. Priabin's been given specific instructions regarding your new friends."

"But if Customs—"

"Customs won't. I've had Babbington on the line. I've made a call. Customs are satisfied."

Van Vuuren wiped his forehead with his crumpled handkerchief. Relief was immediate and made the image of the gray handkerchief, newly damp, something repellent and shameful.

"But what if—I mean, *how?*"

"Calls can be made that purport to be from Customs at Birmingham airport, Piet. To Special Branch, inquiring as to the legitimacy of their instructions from a Mr. Godwin, who seems to have the right credentials, sir, just checking. Do you understand now, Piet?"

Jesus, why didn't he think of this before? Or did he, and just left me to sweat it out?

"Then you don't want me to—"

"I want you on the evening flight home. Here, tomorrow. OK, Piet?"

"Yes, Paulus."

The telephone was replaced in Malan's study, or the office or wherever he was. Van Vuuren replaced his receiver and sat back in the leather chair, which was hot against his buttocks. The sun glittered on the river, a dead light because of the tinted windows. His hands were shaking. It had been close. He held up a trembling thumb and forefinger, almost touching each other. That close. Waterloo Bridge in the tiny gap of tinted air between his quivering fingers. Oh, Jesus. He slapped his hand down on the desk. Three blokes, or was it four? Didn't matter, they'd blundered against the whole bloody applecart, man! Almost tipped it over. One consignment that wasn't what was claimed on the manifest and the Customs and insurance forms, and they'd have had as much assistance and backup as they wanted and a new set of burrowing tools to go after the pipeline . . .

. . . and now, they couldn't. They'd be stood down, disciplined. Locked up for all he knew, which would be satisfying, for all the fucking sweat and nerves he'd used up over the last eight hours!

Paulus' cool cleverness—he envied. Usually, he could ignore it, he was autonomous in MLC, trusted and good. But now?

Paulus wouldn't harbor; he'd let it go. It wasn't really his fault. He recalled the half-kaffir girl, the restaurant meal, and felt queasy. Paulus would know why he'd left his laptop in the suite.

The river and the sky did not look cool through the tinted glass, but merely without vitality, despite the movement of trains and the craft on the water. From behind the windows, the weather appeared thundery, dully yellow, like clouded brass. He poured water from a jug with a nerveless movement of his wrist, and the water splashed on the leather surface of the desk.

But it was over, he reminded himself. They wouldn't be allowed to issue parking fines after this! Those English bastards were finished.

Gradually, his nerves settled. The plastic cup was empty of water, the traffic thickening up across the bridge. Over. Pity the Russians hadn't murdered the bastards and bugger the indiscretion!

Two of them, then eventually three—those he could identify, or had become suspicious of. He attempted to relearn old tricks, tried to think like Hyde, between the recurring, malarial bouts of terror which had begun the moment he had called Chambers' number. The phone had been answered, hollowly, from inside a vehicle— the ambulance in which Terry Chambers had just died, on his way to hospital. Two stab wounds. Dead. He was still quivering with shock, and fear. Unbelievable, but *true*. They'd killed Chambers, just like that.

It was five-thirty. Just so long as he patrolled the upper gallery or the ground floor of the terminal, alongside or beneath the biplane suspended from the ribbed roof, he might remain safe. He did not dare use the toilets, or one of the bars, or the bookshop or boutiques. Nor become too enmeshed in the milling herds of holidaymakers who had flooded the building in search of their charter flights and packaged familiarities. They'd taken Chambers out with the ruthless efficiency of machines. Neither Customs nor the police were of avail. *Please, sir, they might want to kill me, those men over there.* They'd just laugh. Anyway he was there against orders, and nobody had sympathy with that sort of behavior.

God, he was shaking like a leaf! They'd killed Terry, just snuffed him out. And they were here now, looking for the chance to do the same to him. Hyde had been right, too right! He swallowed saliva, almost choking on his fears, then tried to concentrate, pick them out—

One young man loitered for the umpteenth time against the garishness of book racks outside W. H. Smith's. The second man, middle-aged and conspicuously holidaymaking with a bright shirt and tugging his suitcase on a folding metal trolley. It went everywhere with him, up and down the escalators and round and about, like a large, awkward dog. The third man had taken him a long time to spot—but were the difficult ones dangerous, or was it the man you saw first and eventually discounted who did the bloody job in the end? Terry hadn't had the time to find out. The third man was impatient, clock-watching, stridently silent as he studied the arrivals board over and again. He drew attention to himself, but only as someone meeting a friend from one of the many delayed flights. Greek air traffic controllers or Spanish Customs on strike, it made little difference to the neat terminal suddenly becoming a doss house filled with truculent victims. He had no idea whether there were more than three—whether the man who had used the knife on Chambers—*Christ, a knife in the street to look like a mugging*—was in the terminal building. He could have entered it in the last hour, as the passengers for the evening flights flocked in, ambushing or assaulting each other with their luggage.

Five forty-five. He could at least avoid the toilets with some degree of comfort, as a trained, disciplined cripple.

He planted himself firmly on the escalator and descended from the gallery, watching the main floor of the building adjust itself to his balance, knowing that the man with the impatient glare at the arrivals board was behind him now, and seeing the man with the dog-like suitcase at the bottom of the flight of moving steps. He glanced wildly round. The third man was on the stairs, just starting down. The suitcase, tartan-lidded, seemed to crouch at the bottom, waiting to pounce at his ankles. Christ, they'd got fed up, they'd been told to move in.

The escalator was steep, smooth as an icy slope as

it moved him toward the man with his doglike trolley. Even he, with his lack of tradecraft, understood the eagerness on the face above the bright shirt. The man in the suit behind him no longer attended with the slightest pretense to the arrivals board. His eyes were attentive only to Godwin and the man with the trolley.

In one bound, he was free? With two fucking *crutches* in place of a confident stride? Why—why now? Had the bloody trucks arrived at last? When he had inquired earlier, Customs had pronounced there had been delays on the M6, holiday traffic. Three hours from bloody Willenhall!

"Passengers for Suntours flight to Malaga . . . served with sandwiches and other light refreshments in the . . . " floated past his head as he reached his conjunction with the inevitable and the dog-trolley was thrust under his crutches, tripping him. The Russian was immediately on him like a dog himself, apologizing with:

"—didn't see you, please, I'm so sorry," in good English. A woman watched and was reassured. "Let me help you—"

"Need any help?" The man in the suit. "Let's get him on his feet—saw the whole thing, accident—"

Godwin lay sprawled on his back, having turned so at least he was able to watch what they intended doing to him, his crutches spread out on either side of him like extra legs, as useless as his own. The two Russians bent over him; one of them reassured passersby, then the other did so, explaining his clumsiness. They held his arms all the time as they crouched beside him, one of them kneeling on the crutch still attached to his right hand and elbow. The other crutch was removed, then their hands reached under his armpits.

"—coffee, tea, something stronger, set you up, so sorry." They were both smiling solicitously, much like a vet and his nurse, one holding the animal, the other the final needle, they were that confident. Needles? Here, now, something to keep him quiet?

He was dragged to his feet and their proximity hemmed in the strength of his shoulders and upper torso. He gripped the crutches they thrust back under his elbows, disabling him anew. He was sweating violently, almost dizzy as if they had already sedated him, shaking his head like a wounded bull, their after-shave and cool skills both heady. Oh, shit, he was bloody *useless* at this, bloody hopeless! They'd caught Chambers in a quiet street and opened up his guts, now it was his turn—

—moving. They held him slightly off-balance, so that he teetered ahead of his crutches and his dragging, clumsy feet. Just quickly enough to control him, make him concerned not to stumble and entirely lose his balance, making him stare at the floor as they moved him toward the sunlight as the automatic doors of the terminal ushered in new crowds. Almost at the doors, colliding with a luggage trolley, hearing the Brummy apology fade behind him, the air outside a hot breath on his face.

Collision with another trolley, the apology, his stagger because the man with the bright shirt had released his arm—cried out? Apologies again. Christ, bloody apologies—*apologies!* Australian accent.

"Oh, sorry, mate, didn't mean to—"

A trolley, deft as a sword, shunted into the suited man's stomach and shins, then Hyde's hands under his right arm and around his waist and they were outside. Godwin whirled round clumsily, dizzily. The Russians were on the other side of the tinted, sliding glass doors, revealed and masked as trolleys towed brightly dressed groups into the terminal. Then Hyde was shaking him.

"You OK? Christ, you don't half need looking after, mate!"

He nodded, managing to adjust his weight on the

newly assured crutches and calm his breathing.

"All right," he puffed. "All right." Then, squinting at the tinted doors: "What will they do now?"

"Sod off if they've got any sense. There's three of us—" Darren's young features were pleasurably alarmed. "How many of them?"

"I saw three. Terry's *dead*! They killed him in the street," Godwin blurted. "I—couldn't tell you over the phone. They killed him—"

"Bastards," Hyde muttered, visibly shocked, running his hands through his hair. "Both of you—*watch* yourselves. Now, where's the bloody shipment, since they've told us it's not kosher. Bastards," he finished softly.

"It's not here yet. Held up on the M6 at Spaghetti Junction."

"Or waiting until you'd been scraped off the floor. What about Customs?"

Godwin felt a warm lassitude of shock now, with Hyde and Darren beside him and with his weight heavy on his crutches. "Oh—they haven't checked my authority. At least, they hadn't. They'll do the consignment as a spot-check. The SwiftEx plane's on the tarmac. They'll try to take it straight aboard, since the trucks are late." The two Russians had drifted out of sight into the slow, muddy crowd moving beyond the glass. "Where are they?"

"Probably calling Priabin to ask what to do next. If we wanted proof, you and Chambers are all the evidence we needed. Not even Russians kill for microwaves. Let's go and see Customs, Godwin. And *you*"—he glared at Darren—"keep your *eyes open*. What does the third one look like?"

"Young, five-ten, dark hair, yellow polo shirt, yellow slacks."

"Fag, is he?"

The Customs officer came through the doors the

moment before they reached them, recognizing
Godwin at once, his face suspicious and dismissive of
Hyde.

"The trucks have arrived from SwiftEx, Mr.
Godwin. However, there's been a—complication. Can
you come along now and sort things out?"

"What complication?" Hyde snapped.

The Customs officer looked to Godwin for illumination. There was an air of irritation, of having been
somehow deceived by callers at his door who mentioned their Mormon sympathies only after—

Hyde said, "What complication? You look as if
you've just been sold a timeshare."

"If you're all together," the Customs man murmured after Godwin had supplied their names, "then
would you all come with me." It was no longer a matter of request.

"What else has gone wrong?" Hyde hissed as they
entered the terminal.

Godwin shook his head, the tremor in his arms
only stilled by the movement and pressure of the
crutches. His legs, insofar as they responded to anything, felt weak. He was shivery. What *had* gone
wrong?

"Can't see anything. Yellow shirt and slacks? That
him?"

"That bloke's nearly fifty and the scrubber leaning
on the trolley's his daughter."

The corridor they entered was quiet, occupied by
occasional uniforms—airlines, police, Customs.

" . . . for Majorca, there has been a further delay . . . "
faded behind them.

"In here," the Customs officer indicated, holding
open a door. "My superior would like a word—yours,
too."

Godwin bundled himself into the office, aware of
the hum of the air-conditioning, then of the airport's

chief Customs officer, then, finally, aware of Deputy Director General Edward Bannister as he rose from a small sofa.

"Shit," he heard Hyde murmur behind him as the door closed.

"Godwin," Bannister acknowledged. "And Hyde . . . would you like to call Sir Clive now and apologize, or wait until you have a more formal opportunity?"

"I should think the DG's gone home by now, sir," Hyde replied.

"Westfield, I think you can leave. I shall, of course, require a statement from you in the not-too-distant future." He waved his hand in dismissal. The door closed behind Darren.

The Customs officer, Warren, appeared at once satisfied with Bannister's icy tone and his command of the situation. He smiled momentarily as Bannister said: "Don't sit down, gentlemen. Ah, Mr. Warren, might I prevail on you to loan us your office for a few moments?"

Warren stood up. "Certainly, Mr. Bannister. Good job we—" He glowered at Godwin with a new rage prompted by a sense of consequences avoided.

"Yes, indeed. Thank you, Mr. Warren."

"—serving an evening meal in the . . . " for a moment before the door closed once more.

The room shrank around Godwin now that Warren had departed and he burst out: "Sir, you've got to act now! Terry Chambers was killed this afternoon. The trucks are here now! You have to get Customs to—"

Bannister seemed baffled not so much by his words but by Hyde standing stiffly to attention at Godwin's side. It was pure mockery and Bannister knew it. Not now, Patrick, please not now.

"I have not journeyed here in the noisiest of helicopters to open crates of television sets, Godwin,"

Bannister said sarcastically. He was venomous, narrow-minded. A former civil servant in MoD . . . army intelligence. *Displays army levels of intelligence all the time,* had been Hyde's observation, months before. Above all, Bannister devoted himself to hierarchy and its expression throughout SIS. "And neither have either of you," he added.

"Sir?"

"Yes, Godwin?" Bannister regained his position on the sofa and studied them with the glance of a barrister assured of the jury's verdict.

The window behind Warren's desk was one-way glass and overlooked the tarmac. As Godwin watched, the SwiftEx aircraft, a small Boeing, was approached by the two trucks Chambers had seen leaving Reid Davies in Willenhall. There was a Customs van there, too, but it suggested laxity, even indifference, one man leaning against its roof. There was something overpoweringly unflurried about the scene that enraged Godwin.

"Sir, you have to order—request—Customs to inspect that consignment from Reid Davies—" Godwin sensed Hyde's silent, stiff tension beside him, strong as a charge of static. Bannister's features were a mirror of the calm, unhurried scene beyond the deadening effect of the window. "—they killed Chambers, sir!" Godwin blurted, attempting to bludgeon action. His own danger made his shiver in recollection.

"Muggers, so West Midlands police inform me." Bannister was untroubled, imperturbable. "They have, quite rightly of course, begun a murder inquiry."

"Sir, they killed him because he was on surveillance outside—"

Bannister held up his hand. "Unauthorized surveillance. Specifically *denied* surveillance. We are not dealing with impropriety here, gentlemen." The tone was housemasterly, ironic. "We are dealing with something that equates to paranoia—to persecution of legitimate businesses by members of the intelligence service."

He leaned forward as Hyde murmured, "This is a fucking waste of time."

Bannister's cheeks wore two spots of color for a moment, then he observed drily: "I'm sure you will regard this matter in a different light, Hyde, once I have finished what I came here to say." He sat back on the sofa once more. The back of one of the trucks was open, and the sole Customs man had entered its interior. "The effect this could have in the left-wing media, on television particularly, is something I would have expected you to make strenuous efforts to avoid." The Customs man, clipboard and a sheaf of documents in hand, re-emerged into the tobacco-colored light, scribbling on forms, then handing papers to, presumably, a member of the aircraft's crew.

All over.

"Oh, shit!" Godwin exclaimed.

"Ah, precisely what you will discover you have been standing in, Godwin." The Customs man got back into his small, white van and the vehicle turned and sped away from the Boeing. Oh, *shit*. "It is almost my pleasant—certainly my necessary—duty to inform you, gentlemen, that your careers in the intelligence service of your country . . . " The aircraft was being loaded now from a forklift that chugged out of the rear of the first truck toward the flank of the plane. Godwin stared at it as at some lost vision of contentment. " . . . are over. From this moment, I am not too sorry to say, you are no longer on the staff of the service." He cleared his throat. Hyde was wound tense as a spring beside him.

Then Hyde burst out, "Christ, Harrow has won the Wall Game, or is it Eton this year? Doesn't bloody matter a toss, though, does it—*sir*? *Your* lot has won, either way!"

It seemed all that Hyde wanted to say—or, perhaps, could say.

Bannister murmured, as if brushing a speck from his shoe, "Your class attitudes are nowhere near as fresh-minted as you seem to think, Hyde. Fortunately, this service is no longer to be run on such maverick and impeachable grounds." And with a spark of genuine outrage he said, "Do you have no understanding of how the world has changed?"

Hyde was still waving his arms, as if he vainly expected to fly out of the situation. Then, slowly, he moved them back to his sides.

"You will deliver to me now," Bannister intoned in a dignified, marmoreal voice, "your official passes and documents, and in your case, Hyde, I assume a weapon? And any and all other materials relating to your recent activities such as you may possess. We cannot have—*I* will not tolerate—maverick operations that are aimed at the fabric of society or that may undermine the state!" The man's anger was genuine, Godwin realized. Christ, *another* bloody idealist! "Therefore," Bannister added, recovering his sangfroid, "it is necessary that we dispense, entirely and for good, with your services. Both of you."

Beyond the window, the forklift raised its third or fourth load toward the cargo hold of the small Boeing without the slightest effort or hindrance. Godwin, removing his passes and other ID from his wallet as he leaned tiredly on his crutches, blinked back tears of disappointment, and rage.

P A R T   T W O

THE MERCHANDISE OF VENICE

*The world is too much with us; late
     and soon,
Getting and spending, we lay waste
     our powers:
Little we see in Nature that is ours;
We have given our hearts away ...*

—Wordsworth, Sonnet

7

FORMS AND
VISAGES OF DUTY

He allowed Mrs. Grey to serve the coffee—silver pot; her favorite bone china—while his head whirled with Chambers' death and the dismissal of Hyde and Godwin, who sat opposite him now, overawed by Mrs. Grey's silent ordering of the crockery. And there was that other matter, flying in his head, over *there*.

He glanced toward the Georgian tea table where he habitually left his opened letters until Mrs. Grey inquired as to their provenance and destination. The curled, opened edge of the Jiffybag lay there still, its small gape like a sifting mouth, as large as a whale's in the effect it had had upon his memory and his present concerns. FROM: R. ANDERSON it had claimed on its reverse side. On the obverse, the postmark had proclaimed NAMIBIA—a place he had promised to visit in a foolish, expansive moment. He had opened the slim package with a smile, in anticipation, to find—

A KGB identity card and a photograph of a woman

holding a child, on the reverse of which was scribbled NOVGOROD, 1989, and a note evidently written in haste and with hardly a mention of their mutual past. A Dakota aircraft . . . electronic goods on board labelled REID GROUP, PLC. . . . plunged into the Namibian sand. And MLC involvement—and Blantyre, who tried to kill Ros to cover up the affair of his murdered niece.

The past was like an animal, ignored or perhaps beaten into a corner, and which had all the time been waiting its chance to attack, seize him by the throat. It had allied itself with an equally violent present, the moment they had struck Chambers down in a quiet Midlands back street, pretending that robbery was their casual motive. And it infuriated him, creating a towering rage against Priabin, Bannister, Orrell, but most especially against Malan, whose hand was in this violence. Who had had Chambers murdered just as surely as he had been responsible for Kathryn's death. Damn them, they were *still* killing his people!

Hyde was noisy with his coffee, recalling Aubrey's attention, but he was unable to forbear rubbing his temples for an instant before clearing his throat and saying: "I . . . am sorry . . . and concerned . . . at the manner in which things have been done."

Hyde's eyes had already become glazed with indifference. Godwin seemed eager for a reprieve. Aubrey wondered if he might be offering no more than scraps to what one otherwise-sober journal had called *The Dogs of Yesterday*? He studied them both. In Godwin, the fire of obsession still flared, together with a sense of fear, now that Chambers had been summarily disposed of. Hyde, of course, was incapable of reconstruction, though he could as easily leave this business as remain within it. There was one further consideration—his own exhaustion. And his angina pectoris, which had elicited for an old man the professionally

wise sympathy of a specialist in his middle years and
good health. The unspoken *What do you expect at
your age?* He refrained, with a conscious effort, from
touching his chest above the heart. Kathryn's death had
worn him out; the impotence and rage of unsatisfied
vengeance against Malan had exhausted him. And
these two—one politely, the other without illusions—
knew as much. He glanced once more at the tea table
and the eloquent mouth of the Jiffybag. A temptation
and a goad; perhaps more of the lash than the induce-
ment in it, so accustomed had he become to his semi-
invalid condition and the ministrations of Mrs. Grey
over the past weeks. Nevertheless . . .

He had to admit the contents of the Jiffybag were
sufficient to rouse an old conscience. Namibia—
MLC—Malan and the KGB. Godwin's long-sought-
after pipeline, the connection, the *link*. He could not,
under any circumstances short of his demise, ignore the
contents and implications of the letter. Clearing his
throat, he announced: "I have received information
that convinces me not only that we must act, but that
our speculations were, in large part, accurate."

Godwin's head snapped up from the fingers he was
moving indecisively among the biscuits provided by
Mrs. Grey. A custard cream fell onto the carpet in
response to his surprise. "Sir? Information from where?
Who?"

"Totally unconnected with our inquiries. Pure happenstance. But which encourages me." At once, like a
conjuror certain of his audience's attention, he took the
ID card and the photograph, folded within the brief letter, from his breast pocket. He had donned a jacket as
he might have done chainmail when the doorbell had
sounded. "This is the confirmation."

Hyde snatched the letter. "Where's this from?" He
inspected the signature, then looked up. "Christ, isn't
he . . . ?"

Godwin, peering across at the pasteboard card, the photograph and then the letter, exclaimed: "Namibia? An old transport plane . . . MLC . . . Jesus Christ—sir!"

"Is this proof? Does it convince you?" Hyde snapped. "This Anderson—he is the bloke who got out of East Germany in '64, came back and killed a Deputy DG he claimed had betrayed him?" He hesitated. There was another aspect to the legend, one that no one ever voiced publicly. Certainly not in Aubrey's hearing.

Aubrey nodded. "The very same."

"Did you—" Hyde began, at once disappointed, as if he had encountered a passion already preoccupied by another.

"Off the record, that rumor might not be without foundation—there may have been an arrangement." He had helped Richard Anderson escape to South Africa and supplied him with sufficient funds to buy himself into a legal practice. Because the man he had killed had betrayed him, was a double agent. It was the simplest solution.

And the partial admission, he realized, finally closed the circle. He could do no less for Hyde and Godwin and for Chambers' memory, or for his dead niece. Richard had repaid his debt with a reminder of newer, more pressing obligations. So be it.

There was, however, the problem of Richard's whereabouts, even his continued health. He had rung the game lodge in Etosha. The line had been restored, but the voices had been distant and masked, yet clear enough to inform him that Anderson had been taken to the hospital, after an—*atrocity* was the word that recurred. Counteractivity was more accurate, he suspected. Just as they had killed Chambers, attempted Hyde's life, threatened Godwin—they had tried to kill Anderson. Had they succeeded?

"Where did this come from?" Hyde asked, waving the ID card.

"One of the bodies in the aircraft."

"It's that neat, then? What does Anderson say?"

"I can't contact him. There was an attack on the game lodge where he was warden. He was alive, afterwards. But I tried the hospital—he'd discharged himself, through a window at dawn, and hasn't been seen since. I don't know where to find him, I'm afraid."

"Too good to be true, then, isn't it?" Hyde scoffed.

"Or too bad."

"That bastard Blantyre. He's in it."

"Yes."

"So, Anderson encountered Blantyre, Blantyre's bright enough to be suspicious, he torches the game lodge. How many bystanders died?"

"Anderson's wife, for certain."

He glanced toward the door. Mrs. Grey would not come out of her kitchen unless summoned. He was glad for the absence of her narrow rectitude, her solicitous, mummifying care. Not that he was ungrateful; it was simply that he must do without it now.

"Then you'd better bloody well find Anderson—or give him up now," Hyde observed. "If Blantyre's after him, on Malan's orders, he's got the life-expectancy of a Para going over the top, sir. Christ, he's just something Blantyre wipes off his shoes!" Hyde was animated by venom. "I know Blantyre! He didn't get brutalized, he was born like it."

"I can do nothing—for the moment. I must wait until Richard gets in touch. He will, if he's alive."

"The pipeline went through Namibia, then," Godwin remarked.

"What? Oh, yes. Does that surprise you, Tony?"

"No. It's clever. Their old long-way round the Cape. Now, they're using their Suez Canal. The stuff had to be going direct via EuroConstruct and its subsidiaries—via Paris, and Dumas Electroniques."

"Why are they still using Namibia, since 1989 made things so much easier?"

"This has to be Malan's share of the proceeds, I assume."

Hyde whirled round from the tall window. "Look, we know they were using Namibia as of last week. It doesn't matter why. What matters is what we are going to do about it. Reid Group is being robbed blind and the stuff leaves Reid Davies in Willenhall disguised as tellies and microwaves. Anderson confirms that much. So, are we going for it, or just going down the pub for a pint and a sandwich?" He glowered at Aubrey. "Are we going to go on picking this like a spot, or are we going to *do* something?"

Softly, Aubrey announced, "We are going to do something about it."

Godwin sighed aloud. Hyde eventually relaxed his shoulders and his grim expression. He had searched Aubrey's face for confirmation, and at least found no contradiction in his studied lack of expression.

"What first, sir?" Godwin asked with perennial enthusiasm.

"All the material you have, Tony, stored in that computer of yours." He rubbed his hands as if at a fire. "I want everything you have on, or suspect of, Reid Davies. Meanwhile, more coffee, I think," he added briskly.

Hyde tossed his head, but more in recognition than derision. Aubrey smiled to himself.

"You old bugger," he heard Hyde murmur, his back to him.

The moment he left the air-conditioned foyer of the Mermaid Hotel, the sun struck down on him and it was as if his skin was immediately permeated with the nauseous smell of fish. It was impossible to assimilate or ignore, hanging over Walvis Bay like an invisible cloud, heavier than the sunlight. There were deep purple pools of shadow on the opposite side of 7th Street. His new clothes made him itch and the back of his neck, exposed by a haircut, crawled. He touched his shaved cheek gingerly, checking his new face and identity. Then he saw Blantyre, climbing out of a Mercedes, thirty yards further down the street, which was divided almost racially into sunlight and dark shadow.

Anderson wanted to flee back into the plant-ridden foyer, into the drifting whores and their pimps and the businessmen and middle-class blacks, just to get off the naked street, out of the sun.

Blantyre crossed the broad pavement and entered an office building. MLC had offices on some of the upper floors. He'd discovered that two days before, within hours of his arrival. There was no one else in the Mercedes. His body quivered, and he sweated inside the new bush jacket and the neat, pressed shorts. His face was hot and exposed, and he suddenly felt more recognizable. Then he uprooted himself from the moment and hurried back into the foyer.

He sat down in an armchair that faced the side windows, his back to the doors, and stared unseeingly at the mats and the half-filled ashtray on a low table, his hands blurred but visibly trembling at the edge of his eyesight. It had happened as he knew it would. While Blantyre was absent, he had engaged in half-hearted surveillance and a kind of recuperation, a brief remission, until Blantyre's tall, broad shape emerging from the long, pale car had proved that the disease had not been eradicated. It was stronger than before. He could do nothing, he realized. He had learned nothing since his arrival; the MLC warehouse complex to the north of the town, with its own small airstrip, hadn't revealed anything. No one—until

Blantyre—had arrived at the MLC offices other than the regular staff. He'd sat at a café table opposite the building for hours, pretending—yes, pretending. He was terrified of Blantyre, afraid for his life. Which is why he had not called Aubrey from Walvis Bay; had not checked whether his packet had arrived, or whether it had intrigued the old man in London. He didn't want Aubrey's interest now! Anything but that.

In this town—South Africa's last frontier they called it—he was forced to admit the fraudulent manner in which he had spent the past two days. Amid the coffee-colored or white whores and their pimps, the drug pushers, the businessmen, he was an alien. The place thronged against him like the passengers in a crowded bus, the kind of place he had fled for the emptiness and animals of Etosha. He was a bird of passage, less at home than the flamingoes on the lagoon to the south of the town. There was nothing he could will himself to accomplish.

He looked round at the reception desk. His packing would take mere minutes. He could leave the old 4WD in the parking lot and take a taxi out to the airport. Checking out would take moments, they weren't busy. His name was assumed, he would pay in cash drawn by credit card on his account in Windhoek. Blantyre would not know he had been here.

There was a flight to Windhoek at noon, another to Jo'burg that afternoon. He could take either one, if he hurried. While Blantyre was still in the MLC building. He stood up stiffly, and felt dizzy for a moment, before his head cleared.

When he stopped, it would be time for Margarethe to confront him accusingly. He hurried to the lifts. Getting away from Blantyre was all that really mattered.

* * *

Aubrey put down the telephone in the hall of the flat. Mrs. Grey seemed disapproving as she glanced from the open door of the kitchen where she was preparing lunch. The junior minister at the Foreign and Commonwealth Office had appeared disappointed at having his lunch appointment with Aubrey canceled at short notice—much as Mrs. Grey seemed to resent having to prepare cold salmon and salad for himself, Hyde and Godwin. Aubrey felt a mischievous pleasure in the sudden rearrangement of his day. He reentered the broad living room. Trees and Regent's Park lay beyond the net curtains at the tall windows. A faint breeze shifted the curtains carefully, like a frail hand.

"That young man needn't be too concerned at failing to attract my patronage," he announced. "He's a protégé of Geoffrey Longmead, and therefore bound to travel far."

The green carpet was littered, to Mrs. Grey's intense annoyance and silent deprecation, with printout sheets containing the information Godwin had extracted from his computer, via the laptop which was coupled to Aubrey's hardly employed electronic typewriter. The littered room, further untidied by the presence of Hyde and Godwin, pleased him. Somber, anxious, urgent, but yes, definitely pleasurable. A homecoming of sorts.

"Well, Tony?"

Godwin gestured at the carpet. Hyde, peculiarly posed in a chair near the window, sheets opened and untidy before him on Aubrey's occasional table, was studying the unfolding sheets and making notes on a pad.

"The stuff went to Dumas Electroniques. Dumas owns a large shareholding in Reid Group—thanks to David Reid selling them his shares. But there aren't any details on Dumas. It's still a small company. It's expanding, yes, but not as much as you might expect.

It's all wrong. Dumas shouldn't be behaving like a minor company any longer."

"Or receiving dodgy shipments from Reid Davies," Hyde remarked.

It was as if he had been given the task of minding two truculent, easily bored children while their mother, some vague relative, had taken herself off to the Harrods sale.

"What about Reid Davies?" Aubrey asked.

Godwin pointed to a hastily heaped collection of printouts and scribbled notes torn from a pad, lying on the floor. "Staff roll, recent contracts and shipments— as much as we have, sir."

Aubrey picked up the sheaf.

"Look," said Hyde, "it's obvious they must have been using Namibia when things were normal." He smiled involuntarily. "Malan took his share off the top, then no doubt shipped on the rest via Mozambique, even Ethiopia, to Moscow. Now, though, MLC has subsidiaries sprouting like bloody mushrooms all over Eastern Europe and in the USSR."

He scratched his temple with a pencil, looking much as a puzzled child might have done. Aubrey dismissed the thought. Hyde's survival instincts included intelligence. Others had discovered that an instant too late, on occasion.

"So?" Godwin muttered, leafing through a notebook, noisily flicking pages in frustration.

"So, it's easier now, that's all. That stuff went to Dumas, and Dumas must be sending it on. Both through Namibia and direct. So, whatever Dumas is or isn't, it's doing the KGB's job for them. Either they own it or Malan does—they at least have to control part of it. They couldn't do it any other way."

"And *did* that shipment go to Dumas?"

"It did, sir," Godwin replied. "I checked."

"Then what, in Heaven's name, *is* Dumas?"

"Naughty," Hyde remarked. "Very naughty."

Aubrey returned to his chair, skimming the material on Reid Davies, which was immediately intractable. There was nothing in Richard's letter regarding any French company. Willenhall in the West Midlands seemed unpropitious territory for any grandiose and covert scheme—

—except that Chambers had been murdered in that quiet back street, and the shipment from there had been whisked off to Dumas last Friday evening with Orrell's blessing!

He knew what he must do and that was to talk to Michael Davies, who part-owned and completely ran Reid Davies. Get in there and root out the method of the thing.

He pondered Anderson. He had fled the clinic rather than been discharged, and had disappeared. Much to the chagrin of Colonel Blantyre, he gathered from the administrator of the clinic, who had been most helpful. Where had Richard disappeared to? He felt chilly with the sense of Anderson's violent past reinvigorated. But he was twenty-five years older now, what could he do? Blantyre unnerved even Hyde.

Mrs. Grey appeared in the doorway and seemed at once appalled and unable to announce lunch. She reproved him for deliberate, self-induced overexcitement with a small, sharp glance.

"Wine, Sir Kenneth?"

"I think Mr. Hyde would prefer beer, Mrs. Grey. You did get some?" She nodded tightly as if she had been forced to admit to some demeaning act like shoplifting. "Some Chablis for myself and Mr. Godwin. Thank you, Mrs. Grey."

She retreated like the survivor of a defeated army, with enormous reluctance. Her gaze was firmly on Hyde and Godwin at the table in front of the window, shuffling papers, muttering together like children engaged in some complicated game.

Then Hyde burst out, "I bloody *told* you I recognized some of these names! There *are* old STB people on the boards of these companies that are MLC subsidiaries or associates in Czechoslovakia! Look, that bastard Novak, for example. How the hell Havel didn't have him buried alive I'll never know. See? There!" He tapped the sheet with his pencil, holding the continuous paper under Godwin's face.

He nodded. "And they've got contracts outstanding with Dumas. Christ, it's the bloody pipeline, isn't it, going through Czecho to Moscow, Dumas, these Czech subsidiaries, the KGB." Godwin turned to Aubrey with a beaming smile. "We've got them, sir—I really think we've got them!"

"I'll bet bloody Husak himself is on the boards of some of these companies. Oh, Jesus—all we have to do is tie everything up in one neat parcel."

"Can we?" Aubrey asked eagerly.

"We'll bloody well try!"

The Namib Desert stretched away southward and to the east, the monotony of the plateau nibbled at by the huge, reptilian mounds of the dunes, beyond which the sea glittered pale as the hazy sky. The tinted windows of the departure lounge seemed barely to reduce the glare and the openness that unnerved him. Anderson felt heated and drained, as if he had wandered in from that landscape.

His ticket was crumpled in his fingers and his one small bag rested beside his feet as he sat slumped forward, appearing to be preoccupied with the book in his other hand. Smudged print from his damp thumb at the bottom of each turned, unread page. The flight to Jo'burg was scheduled to take off in another hour. The plane had just landed, a small Boeing, and taxied toward the terminal building, whiter than the dunes against the dulled glare of the sea and sky. The plane and the place pressed against the windows of the lounge.

The handful of passengers who had disembarked and trooped like trained chimps across the hot tarmac drifted into the air-conditioning of the lounge, divided from himself and the waiting emigrants from Walvis Bay by a single barrier. Another handful waited for them, a few children in anticipation, one uniformed chauffeur holding a scribbled placard, a few women—

—Blantyre. Anderson shuddered. The pillar against which he was seated concealed him but seemed insubstantial as he flinched against the recognition. The man must have followed him—

—no, he could not have, he'd already raised his arm to attract the attention of one of the disembarking passengers. Which man? Blantyre, standing beside the uniformed chauffeur, was obviously meeting someone, and assumed his role in attracting the attention of . . . a small man, light glinting on spectacles, slightly balding, squat-figured, and carrying a briefcase, which he at once handed to the chauffeur, and shook hands with Blantyre. The figure of the man? The strut and arrogance of his stride, the turn of his head? Anderson struggled with an old, mental image, attempting to superimpose it and match it with the man's walk, and face. He shook his head. He knew—had known the man, but no longer. Years before, somewhere, Jo'burg probably.

A couple of days and he would sever himself from Africa and Blantyre. He would release the money still in the bank accounts, sell the few shares, then head for the UK, or some still-underdeveloped corner of Spain, up in the Pyrenees, perhaps. But he did know that man. . . . He bent forward gently, carefully, following Blantyre and his companion as remotely and curiously as a telescopic lens. He stood up, keeping close to the pillar, the book dropped unnoticed onto an adjoining seat, his bag stirred by his foot. Blantyre was an employee of—

Was it MLC, something to do with Malan? He couldn't remember, so why try? He realized he had moved out of the shadow of the pillar and past the first few rows of seats in the wake of Blantyre and the shorter man in the sleek suit and the glinting spectacles. He moved carefully, as if through a darkened room littered with furniture arranged to distress the unwary. Pillar to pillar, eyelines blocked by passengers, by the newspaper stand, by—

Shriek of a child beside him, startling him as if the girl had pointed him out. Blantyre and the other man were paused inside the doors while, presumably, the chauffeur brought the limousine to them. Desultory talk. As he hovered against a coffee machine, his passport pressed importunately against his left breast. His ticket was still in his left hand and he thrust it into his jacket pocket. He was hot again, tense yet less fearful. Especially as he moved among white faces and white security guards and the black faces were reduced to their former lot, bending above wide brushes or mops being squeezed in buckets. A big black woman was working behind the newsstand.

Anderson watched Blantyre and the other man from behind the newly arrived morning edition of *The Afrikaaner,* knowing the safety of reading without buying as the black woman studied him from the corner of her eyesight. He cracked open the broadsheet, shuffled it straight, appeared to read. Blantyre and the other man conversed easily, but with much the same distinction as might have been exhibited between the black woman and himself. Flashes of cloud rather than sun fled across Blantyre's face. Anderson began to feel he would not be recognized, even with a direct and angry glance. In the newspaper, history fleeted. Mandela and the South African president, de Villiers, shaking hands at yet another meeting. Proposals for some sort of proportional representation, more promises to control the rumbling township violence, and the ANC acceding to a lack of nationalization—Malan there suddenly, in the newspaper, flanked by lieutenants.

Flanked by the other man—he raised his head, then looked down again, then up again—yes. *That* man—van Vuuren? And the recognition tailing off like the fall of a firework from the night. Van Vuuren. MLC senior vice-president, the caption read. He repeated the name, again and again . . . and nothing. Certainty in one sense, but the past refused to come out of its locked, rusted box.

At least he knew his name. He cracked the newspaper together and folded it. Van Vuuren. An MLC Lieutenant. The connection. He put the paper down, and saw another flash of angry, thunderous cloud on Blantyre's face. Blantyre was being given distasteful orders. Anderson looked down at uncertain fingertips, resting on a South African propaganda magazine, government inspired in the old days. *Panorama,* or something. He flicked pages because Blantyre's head was beginning to move as he was unsettled by his subordination to van Vuuren. Plants, landscapes, proteas, jackals and leopards—anything but human realities . . . hospitals, black nurse and white child, ringlets, starched uniform, small figure within it—

Rage. The photograph of the hospital had brought back, as in a comet's orbit, the only bright thing in his night, Margarethe.

Van Vuuren moved toward the doors and the uniformed chauffeur beyond them as they slid open. Blantyre, the underling, servant, followed in his casual slacks and bush jacket. He knew van Vuuren belonged to his past, when he had crept through the Bush of the apartheid laws, the marriage forbiddings and the

Group Areas Act and the instances of rape and insult and attack by white upon black. He clenched his fists. He almost had hold of the man, almost knew him . . . then it vanished again, so firmly had he determined to put that life behind him, out of mind. Offices and ploys and information. The lot of a man, which he had first learned to become in Johannesburg, in a lawyers' office.

He shut the magazine with a jolt of his hand. Van Vuuren and Blantyre were climbing into the long, dark Mercedes beyond the tinted doors. How?

AVIS, the sign like a beacon. Avis. Car hire. A minute, two. He hurried to the doors and saw the Mercedes head toward the main road to Walvis Bay. A flock of pelicans turned gold in the light of early afternoon. If he hurried, he could pick them up, find out where they were heading.

Surprise and exhilaration ambushed him as he approached the Avis desk, but he did not even pause to consider the sensations.

"Well, what do you think? Back in the game, mate, and it's the old game, too!" Hyde's challenge was almost blithe, and strangely welcome. "There's Novak, and, besides him, a colonel in the STB, two captains and a couple of oiks as union conveners—Jesus! You know these names as well as I do."

Aubrey pursed his lips and plucked at the lower one, aware that the action loosened his half-dentures. The list was provocative precisely because it was so familiar. Hyde leaned over his shoulder, his breathing excited, his pencil tapping at each name in turn. All were staff of three Czechoslovak companies formerly owned and operated by the state and now cooperative ventures with two Western organizations, Malan-Labuschagne Consolidated of South Africa and

Dumas Electroniques of Paris. Both those companies had invested heavily, supplied managerial skills, improved efficiency, modernized, just as hundreds of Western companies had done with thousands of antiquated industries and companies in the former East. Except—

MLC and Dumas had, presumably, either encouraged or at least allowed former Czech intelligence personnel to work in, even control, the companies in question. Novak was brutal, but clever, an expert in industrial espionage—irony that—and once deputy rezident in their London embassy. Novak had disappeared, presumably to Russia to some safe KGB haven, soon after Havel and Dubcek had stood together on the balcony of the Hradcany Palace in 1989. Now he was back. Sanitized, trusted, powerful once more: Antonin Novak.

Aubrey looked up. Regent's Park lay golden and green under the late afternoon sun beyond the net curtains. Novak's presence as joint managing director of one company and senior director of the other one Hyde had located was neither happenstance nor coincidence. It was enemy action. "We anticipated this sort of thing in Rumania, possibly Bulgaria—not in Prague or Plsen."

"Christ, sir, where do you think all these people went when Havel brought his scooter and Frank Zappa into the Hradcany? Intelligence and security were their only growth industries over there—the Czechs' biggest employer! If you put them all out of work, it would be like closing down ICI and BP over here. They knew where all the bodies were buried; how could they have been gotten rid of, unless they'd agreed to go quietly? And Novak bloody didn't, that's obvious." Hyde was patrolling the room, hands waving above his head. "If you looked at Poland, Hungary—anywhere—I bet you'd find the same thing. The police *economy* after the police state!"

"I agree—jobs for the boys does not fully describe it, does it?" He smiled. There was an itch in his palms and a nervous excitement unsettling his stomach. His chest felt tight, but he no longer considered such intimations as those of mortality.

"Business as bloody usual," Godwin announced happily, with the grin of a man entirely, finally justified. "Except now it's real businesses they're into."

"We have neither the time nor resources to expand our field of inquiry—understand that, both of you." His hand indicated the litter of continuous paper, notepads the typewriter they had rigged to Godwin's laptop as a printer. "We have found sufficient indication that certain individuals and organizations are engaged—in collaboration with known operatives of a foreign intelligence service—in activities directed against this country. We are committed to the defense of the realm, and it is on that basis that we shall proceed." He smiled.

"We're no longer empowered to defend the fucking realm," Hyde announced sourly.

"Ah, yes. I shall have to see Geoffrey Longmead and have that little matter put right."

"How?"

"By worrying him. Dumas bought David Reid's shares, David Reid is the great white hope of the government. Geoffrey approved the laying-on of hands, the anointing of David Reid as eventual successor. Any breath of scandal that might touch David should be investigated."

"Kept quiet, you mean."

"Exactly, Patrick. So, Geoffrey will want me to look into this, very quietly, just in case. And I will need both of you. Indeed, it was what you were attempting to do all the time, against the most willful obstruction."

Hyde was smiling, shaking his head. "You crafty old bugger," he murmured.

"Precisely. Now, Tony, what *is* Dumas?"

"From one angle, little more than its Lichtenstein holding company and a couple of small factories producing consumer electronics, even electric can openers and toothbrushes. From another, it controls, works with, has joint ventures in common with, owns shares in, has bought out dozens of companies, here, there and just about everywhere." He shook his large head. "I doubt we can crack that nut in time, sir."

"Then we'd better concentrate on the other side of the coin and the Channel, hadn't we? The people who sent that shipment to Dumas: Reid Davies. Mike Davies in particular." He snapped his fingers. "One other thought—since Novak came back from Moscow, he presumably came back with KGB approval, even instruction. Correct?" Godwin nodded. "Then Malan's connections with the KGB are even more pronounced than we thought. These people are all tied together—Malan and the faithful van Vuuren, Priabin, Novak, Dumas, MLC, Reid Group wittingly or unwittingly." He smiled cunningly. "MLC and Dumas are deeply compromised by having people like Novak on the boards of companies with whom they do business or which they even part-own. Oh dear, Geoffrey Longmead will be delighted to have us hush this up with a quiet little investigation!" He sighed with a deep satisfaction, then felt his eyes prick. They'd killed Chambers—this was the way back at them.

There was a polite, perhaps even reluctant knocking at the door of the drawing room.

"Yes, Mrs. Grey?"

She moved like a blindfolded child in order to ignore the condition of the room.

"Sir Kenneth—while I was out, um, shopping for the things you requested"—Hyde's lager—"did the window cleaner call for his money? I'd like to make a note. He was next door when I went out and gone by the time I came back."

Hyde was standing beside her. She appeared a little agitated.

"How long does it take him, usually? Back and front?" Hyde asked. Aubrey sensed the tension and alarm beneath the calm, careful words.

Mrs. Grey nodded. "I insist on back and front being done. Perhaps forty minutes, what with moving his ladd—"

"How long did it take you to find and buy my beer, Mrs. Grey?" His eyes glinted. Mrs. Grey seemed embarrassed, yet disarmed by his manner. Aubrey began to suspect.

"No more than twenty minutes. Which is why I inquired whether—"

Aubrey made to rise and speak, but Hyde flapped him back into silence.

"And he'd gone by then. No other flats, houses in the block. How many does he do?"

"We're always last on his round. Once every two weeks."

"Van or bike?"

She seemed puzzled for a moment, then nodded.

"A small van."

"Think carefully, Mrs. Grey—no, look at me." He held her arms gently. "Did you see or even pass the van when you went out?"

The angry, determined concentration of the elderly. For a long time. Then, with certainty: "No, I didn't. Just the ladders and him at the top. I remember wishing him a good morning, but he often doesn't reply." Aubrey found the tension of suspicion increasingly unbearable, but Hyde seemed possessed of infinite patience.

"But, you recognized him?"

"Well, yes, he—I didn't look closely, of course. He

was wearing the usual overalls. Perhaps the van was parked beyond the corner?"

"Thanks, Mrs. Grey," Hyde murmured. "That's all, love." He went to the windows and tugged aside the net curtains. The sunlight on the Park reflected through dusty glass. Mrs. Grey glanced at Aubrey, who smiled reassuringly and nodded her toward the door. She moved like a supplicant.

When she had closed the door behind her, Aubrey said heavily, "Well? Damage?"

By way of reply, Hyde pointed toward the top corner of the left-hand window. Then he slid it upward and climbed onto the windowsill, balancing there for a moment as if on the point of some acrobatic, backward dive toward the street below, then he climbed back into the room. He held out his palm, in which lay a small metal button, across the lines of his hand. He nodded fiercely, his breathing loud. Godwin crowded against Aubrey and him. Then Hyde turned to the open window and flung the button toward the Park.

"Catch some married bugger fornicating in there after dark," he muttered.

"You mean—"

"Oh, everything. I mean *everything* we've said. This room's been bugged ever since we got here. They know the bloody *lot!*"

A collection of child's building blocks, scattered to some vestigial sense of order across the reddish sand. Anderson studied the Malan-Labuschagne Consolidated (Walvis Bay) factory site through his small binoculars, neat as those used at a racecourse to pretend interest in the event. Van Vuuren had been taken in the Mercedes to the Mermaid Hotel in the town, then, within a half hour, had been brought out to the factory complex that sat uninterestingly behind a high fence. The flat, low units cast lengthening black oblongs of shadow toward each other. Van Vuuren and Blantyre had disappeared into the bronze-glassed, six-story building that evidently formed the office accommodation. There were garages, fuel pumps, sheds, single-story factory units, and a large parking lot, almost full, presumably with staff vehicles. Any subsidized business park anywhere in the world and no longer out of place on the edge of the Namib, though this only nibbled unconvincingly at the desert. Unlike the leached, dug, transformed wilderness created by MLC and Anglo-American further down the coast at Luderitz and Oranjemund, the diamond coast. A man-made lunarscape, dead, bitter, gray. There was a small airstrip, too, on the far side of the complex, with a miniature control tower and two large hangars.

He scanned the place once more. The first few figures emerging beside their stretched shadows, heading for the parking lot. Almost five in the afternoon. The drift at once became a loose crowd, and the first cars turned out of the lot, bringing up dust from the gravel road toward Walvis Bay, behind him. The sea was already turning gold and the pelicans and other birds were almost bloodred or black-like scrawled, charcoal signs against the evening sky. A flight of seabirds, goitered pelicans, then something moving with less grace and more purpose; a small aircraft, coming in over the narrow peninsula across the lagoon from the town, dropping lower, the sunlight silver and glinting on its glass and metal. A fire truck had appeared from the mouth of one of the hangars. Anderson waited, content with his merely observing self. The camera lay beside him, its lens still capped. Nothing had happened and he was satisfied with the sensations of routine, of undemanding purpose.

The aircraft, a small jet transport, was audible now, gradually drowning the noise of the cars. The fire truck took up a position near the airstrip. The plane turned in the distance and seemed to hesitate, as if balancing itself on a sloping wire it would slip down toward the narrow runway. It then slid lower, tentatively at first, then with a seeming hurry, its flaps fully lowered, the clean lines of the wings broken into the geometry of deceleration. It touched the runway and the engines howled with reverse thrust. Then it slowed quickly, turning gently down the taxiway toward the larger of the two hangars. The fire truck slinked away in disappointment. The parking lot was all but emptied, presumably only security people remained, plus those who would unload the aircraft's cargo. Its flank turned toward the sun behind him. ST. MICHEL, PARIS. A flare of logo, some winged horse or something like. Paris. It slowed docilely at the mouth of the hangar, where overalled men gathered and the first forklift appeared, bright yellow and blue, blazoned with MLC.

And van Vuuren and Blantyre, getting out of an open 4WD, van Vuuren in shirtsleeves, Blantyre still like a film extra stranded by the financial collapse of a jungle epic on the fringes of some modern, suburban drama. It was easier, each time, to caricature the man—especially from the crest of this stray, small dune that had wandered off from the vast herd of them a few miles to the south. It was no more than a dozen meters high, a dozen in length. The sand had been firm enough to allow him to leave the gravel road and circle behind the dune, where he had parked the hired car. The cargo door of the aircraft was opened from inside, and steps were lowered. Blantyre followed van Vuuren into the cargo hold. The evening sky grew more vivid, with purple nibbling at the eastern horizon.

Photographs? The aircraft was proof of what? Nothing, at present. The pursuit of profit, the business of trade. He lifted his hand from the barrel of the lens and excised the thought that this was time-wasting, vacation from revenge and grief alike. Blantyre emerged from the black doorway, then van Vuuren. Anderson could still remember nothing about the latter man . . . some kind of professional dealing. But then, some of his partners had prepared tort and contract work for MLC companies. He had been the token liberal, and done the token liberal things in defending black men and women. Won just once, ruining the defendant's nervous sanity even as he achieved the demotion of a police lieutenant to corporal for a two-month disciplinary period. Rape.

Blantyre signaled the forklifts forward. A crate appeared in the doorway, to be speared through its pallet and hoisted away into the light. Anderson adjusted the focus of the small binoculars, straining to read the stenciled name on the crate, the imagery of the crashed DC-3 and its cargo suddenly stinging him alert, like the sand pattering against his shirt and exposed neck, lifted off the dune by a small, cool salt breeze. The dune's shadow stretched toward the wire-enclosed compound. The forklift turned into the sunlight and he attempted to identify the lettering. Hardly legible at this distance.

R . . . L, there, the smudge of LIMITED, presumably. R . . . E . . . I . . . the second word wasn't GROUP, it ends in an s, he thought, blinking away eye strain. Was it even REID? D and S, first and last letters—REID DAVIES? BIRM—INGHAM? The forklift passed into the hangar and then a second trundled away from the aircraft with a pallet of boxes. Indecipherable. Perhaps the size of box to contain a television set, something of that kind . . .

He placed the binoculars on the sand and took up the camera, uncapping the lens and focusing. The fork-lift—stupid not to have thought of it before—leapt closer than through the binoculars. Television sets. REID DAVIES LTD., BIRMINGHAM. In smaller letters, on each of the boxes, something—something. There seemed no distance now between himself and the aircraft, or the men's faces. He avoided aiming the telephoto lens at Blantyre. Van Vuuren was still a stranger, distant as the image in the newspaper. The other faces were anonymous. On the crate that now filled the cargo doorway, he read PART OF THE REID ELECTRONICS GROUP. He heard the camera click and the motor whirr on, as if someone else had depressed the button. Click. The crate would be sufficient, he decided, as the breeze against his neck and shirt awakened nerves, demonstrated his isolated exposure. REID DAVIES was clearly visible on the television sets, but he'd missed that with the camera. On the crate now he could make out both the name and its association with the Reid Group. The neat, gleaming aircraft *was* the DC-3, a second chance—

"What are you doing here, man?" The voice, behind and slightly below, startled him. He had heard no vehicle, no laborious ascent of the small dune, or slippage of sand. "Hey, man—I asked you a question. What are you doing here?"

"I recognized the bloody woman!" Hyde exclaimed. "Two men in a van—*not* the window cleaner's van— and her in a Golf GTI. She was off like a rat down a drain when she saw me." He slumped into an armchair, rubbing his face, then tugging at his hair with his fingers. "Oh, ballocks! We look such bloody *mugs!*"

"I—I agree we might have been more secure than we were," Aubrey murmured, "but it was not to be anticipated that they—"

"They've had the bloody jump on us all the way."

"I told you they were worried, sir," Godwin offered apologetically.

"Then what do you suggest we do?" Aubrey asked. "If there is anything to be done? I suggest we continue, now we are guaranteed a degree of privacy. You have an alternative, Patrick?"

Hyde merely glared, then shook his head. The room was somber with more than the early evening.

"Right. We'll have to move swiftly then," Aubrey remarked. "We must get into this business, break through on the narrow front we have: Reid Davies to Dumas, to—" He thought of Anderson. There was no help there, not until he could talk to Richard. Was he even still alive? "Tony, that material from your surveillance on Reid Group's offices?"

"Yes, sir?"

"You—what was it you said about this VIATE exposition in Venice?" He clicked his fingers impatiently.

"Wonderful cover story, I think, sir? Or was it wonderful opportunity?"

"Exactly. Either will do. Get hold of a list of exhibitors, and examine their connections with one another. If something very big is about to happen, and—Chambers' murder and the attempts on Patrick would confirm that—then volume and bulk increase in proportion. And VIATE is concerned with the most advanced high-technology, not microwave cookers. If *I* were Malan or the KGB, I would very much want to get my hands on a great deal that will be exhibited at the Venice International Advanced Technology Exposition. Wouldn't you?"

8

THE LADDER TO ALL
HIGH DESIGNS

He was wearily angry. No, he decided with a great effort, he was weary *and* angry. The long evening dipping into night had worn at him in successive, creeping waves of information, response and indecision. When he had finally rid the place of Hyde and Godwin, it had been close to one o' clock. Mrs. Grey had come out of her room in her dressing gown to ascertain his condition and digestive requirements, but he had shooed her off like a small, aged hen and gone to his bed, stubbed and extinguished like a smoked cigarette. He'd lain for most of the night in that semisleep that seemed, at his age, his moments of greatest clarity. Unaware of the time, he'd tottered into the drawing room now, the morning seemingly advanced across the grass of the Park. He paused to open the window because of the cheap cigar Godwin had required in his depression and one of those sweet, crumpled cigarettes Hyde continued to smoke, then he picked up the insistent telephone. The previous day's incursions by unmannered barbarians had evidently reduced Mrs. Grey to a fetal desire for sleep.

"Yes?" he snapped. "Yes, Kenneth Aubrey speaking . . . Richard, is that really you?" He seemed close, over one of those crystal intercontinental lines.

"Kenneth, you got my package?"

"Richard, I tried to get in touch—"

"Doesn't matter, had to keep moving." The breathless exchange of urgencies, the focusing of imagination and attention into his awakening thoughts. "You got the package, Kenneth? Make any sense?"

"Richard, your wife," he could not help blurting.

"Man called Blantyre. Not important, for the moment. You understand the package? I'm not sure I do, except that none of it should have—"

"One of our concerns, Richard, one of our concerns. You'd left the hospital, disappeared. Where are you?"

"Swakopmund, a boarding house. Cheap, out of season. I'm in the enclave. They're still flying British stuff in, Kenneth, I have photographs. Same company or companies. Reid. I know who he is—I don't know why the Russians are involved or why. They killed my wife. Do you?" The anger and the half-contemptuous demand stung.

Mrs. Grey appeared at the door, and he waved her innocuously out of the room.

"Richard, I'm not quite certain. There's some sort of pattern emerging at this end, into which your information instilled a great deal of clarity. But you, why Swakopmund? A holiday resort, is that right?"

"I've seen another flight, another cargo, Kenneth. Same people—at least, a subsidiary. MLC's plant in Walvis Bay took delivery last night—Paris air shipper flew it in. I had a bit of contact, not much."

Aubrey realized that he and Anderson used old jargon so precisely that the words were like signals of recognition between members of a clique.

"Which subsidiary?"

"Some company called Reid Davies."

It had to be part of the shipment that left Birmingham for Dumas, that Hyde and Godwin had failed to stop and which had been the cause of Chambers' death. His breath caught, then, almost unwillingly, Aubrey continued with the debriefing charade, which was easier and more convenient for both of them.

"What contact?"

"Patrol. I was on surveillance. Convinced them with an ornithologist routine. I *hate* the ease with which it works, Kenneth, my new harmlessness!"

"I do understand, Richard. Reid Davies—yes, we know them. We've had contacts here, too."

"Then it's real—I mean, not just local. It's widespread and important."

"Appears to be, Richard." He sat down with a surprising degree of gratitude, facing the net curtains and the day beyond them. Invigorated though, not tired. But he was dizzy with the unexpected exhilaration and the swirl and rush of conflicting priorities. Richard alive, Richard's proofs, his possible danger.

"This man Blantyre?" he blurted.

"Yes?" Anderson replied warily.

"What . . . imminent risk is he to your safety? To the safety of the agent-in-place," he added, an involuntary smile seeping onto his old, dry lips. "Are you all right, Richard?" he insisted when there was nothing to interrupt his reflections.

"Oh, I'm OK, Kenneth—just OK. As long as this isn't something of no importance. I haven't got the time or energy."

"No, I don't think it's that, Richard. Indeed, far from it. What happened?" And after Anderson's brief narrative, he asked anxiously, "This man van Vuuren. To us here he seems very significant. But you can't recall in what context—"

"No. I know who he is now, not who he was. Sorry. I don't think it's important to me. I want Blantyre, but it seems more complicated than that. So I'll work with you, Kenneth, now that I've foolishly aroused the guard dog. You tell me what it's about. Why the secrecy about these shipments? Who's robbing who blind now?"

"As far as we can make out, Richard, there's Russian involvement, together with MLC. Malan himself, this other man van Vuuren, Blantyre, of course . . . " He hesitated, sensing the silent rage at the other end of the connection. "It's high technology, as you suspected. We're nibbling at the edges of this thing, Richard, but I want Malan!" His anger seemed like an echo of the silent cry from Anderson. He thought of Kathryn, his dead niece.

"Why?" Anderson asked bluntly.

"I, like you, lost someone. Blantyre was not involved, but Malan was."

"Very well. What do you want me to do?"

"Will you go back for me, Richard, be my agent-in-place? Keep them under surveillance, discover what you can, report to me regularly. Stay out of contact for the moment. Just surveillance, arrivals and departures, goods and individuals. Will you do that?"

The silence was lengthy. Then he replied, "For the moment—couple of days, perhaps. Yes." He paused, then added, "I'll rack my brains about van Vuuren, perhaps there's some hold I might have if I did remember."

"He's important, Richard—very. It would help greatly."

"Then I'll try," Anderson replied heavily.

"Resources—money, Richard?"

"I can buy what I need. I'll get myself organized, Kenneth. I'll report this evening. Seven, your time." Again, he hesitated, then added fiercely, "I *want* them, Kenneth. I won't be sidetracked into something nebulous and long-term. I want"—there was something that choked in his voice—"bodies, Kenneth. At least one. Understand that. And if *I* can't do it, then you'd better send someone to do it for me. Do you agree, Kenneth?"

Heavily, Aubrey murmured. "Yes, Richard. Your fee. I understand."

"Then I'll get moving. This evening." And the connection was at once cut. Aubrey shivered and fumbled for a cigarette and lit it, his hand quivering. Somehow *too* close—the past *too* insistent with that casual pact between them that a man should be killed. He paced the carpet, tugging at his lip, failing to enjoy the cigarette. Perhaps he was unprepared for such a brutal rush back to those violent times.

He stubbed out the remainder of his cigarette and returned to the window, hands once more in his pockets. He thought of Priabin and the fact that he had bugged the flat—*his* flat—and knew all they now knew, as Babbington surely would. He realized then that their knowledge would precipitate action. He clicked his fingers in impatient summons of an idea. In his old age, ideas were reluctant, sullen servants at the best of times, but now, when he needed them—

Anderson was keeping MLC and van Vuuren under surveillance. Hyde and Godwin must get into Reid Davies today, tomorrow at the latest. And what was it he and Godwin had said about Venice—all canals lead to Venice? VIATE—Venice International Advanced Technology Exposition. *They'll all be there. It would be like pinching the takings at M & S, Marble Arch, on a summer Saturday, if Priabin and Babbington could have their pick of what'll be there.*

What a conduit, a *confluence*, Aubrey thought. All

those Reid and MLC and Dumas companies and associates and subsidiaries, flowing goods into that meeting of many waters. Oh, indeed, what pickings in that cash register!

He snapped his fingers with pleasure. He'd see Mike Davies. An idea began to gleam like uncovered gold. Venetian gold.

"*Think* about the implications, before you alert Babbington. Think about *him*." He sighed. "Aubrey is the most cunning and alert of old men. Put him in one of these private rest homes and he would be running the place—and making a larger profit—within a month. Because the man on the street, the field agent, has a peculiar accent and kills without compunction, don't assume that Aubrey—or even Hyde for that matter—functions by mere impulse or out of old habits. We've woken people who didn't want to sleep in the first place, and now they know we haven't slept either!"

"General?" she remarked sullenly. "They have a critical path direct to Reid Davies, and the VIATE buildup is happening there!"

Priabin rubbed his chin. "I can't alert SIS again, not by any route. Even they might think there was something wrong. We shall have to rely on *Mortimer*. There's no other way."

"I don't trust him!"

"Why? Because you don't know him, or because he isn't a believer, only a mercenary?" he snapped back, spreading his arms wide in a dismissive gesture. "Most of them—even we—are not believers, whatever ideology you choose as a yardstick. *Mortimer* is reliable. If not, his life is in ruins. He knows that. And Aubrey has no suspicion of him. Which is why he needs coaching and why he's flown down to London today. I shall brief him." Her flicker of doubt stung him, and he growled: "Listen to me, Valentina! Mark me well, young woman. Babbington is focusing everything on VIATE, risking the whole enterprise, when it is not really necessary. If Aubrey rolled up the entire Reid Group tomorrow, we would be back in the UK and in business within twelve months, through Dumas. General Babbington is jeopardizing the whole of European operations for the sake of a coup, one stroke of daring. Remember that if you are ever tempted to send any unauthorized signals to Moscow Center marked EYES ONLY—BABBINGTON. Now, Valentina, do you understand?" His fist banged the desk, only partially for theatrical effect. The girl flinched bodily in her chair.

Finally, she nodded.

"Good," he remarked. "The VIATE snatch is too greedy, there's too much. Like looting a jewelry shop. It's dazzled Babbington. He won't listen to reason anymore, not on that subject." He spread his hands on the desk. "Please understand that, Valentina. Babbington is as dogmatic, even fanatical, as Aubrey himself. Whatever the size or significance of the bone, they will fight to the death over it. That is their mutual past, present and future. I sometimes think if you scratch the surface of each of them, nothing really exists for either except the prospect of defeating the other." He grinned. "Meanwhile, our company, Dumas Electroniques, is gathering in the harvest Babbington ordained. We have to keep Aubrey's nose and Hyde's fists and boots out of the caviar for a week at the outside. Let's concentrate on that, shall we?"

The fog lay around the dune, damply chill, writhing like great, slow funnels of smoke, all but obscuring the MLC factory complex. To Anderson, perched on the dune's crest, it was like being in a small boat. In another hour, the mist would have lifted, exposing the complex and the dune. He heard the noises of vehicle engines, the putter of forklifts, the heavier throat-clearing of articulated trucks. He heard the occasional, illusory call of an invisible voice. There was no other cover except the dune, no other vantage point, despite the risk of discovery—*re*discovery.

From the sounds of activity, coming blindly out of the swirl and heave of the sea mist, he imagined that a shipment was being made ready to leave by road, presumably southward to the Republic. He glanced down at the folded map in its polyethylene sheath, then rubbed his bare arm with his free hand; it was too cold not to be warmly dressed. He hadn't expected fog.

They'd take the gravel trunk road east, then join the tarred road south to the border and eventually, Cape Town. He presumed it was the shipment of Reid Davies stuff the French transport plane had flown in the previous day. Yet it could be something else entirely. Whatever, it was a long trek. Perhaps that was what attracted the Boer, van Vuuren, to the overland route? He tossed his head. There had been no transport plane in either of the hangars. One of their aircraft was missing, he thought bitterly. And capable of claiming lives long after it had crashed in the Bush. The voices coming infrequently out of the mist, even though male, were ghostly hers. He shivered.

The mist, twitching rather than moving with the great, majestic indifference of the sea, rolled more quickly as it thinned and warmed. The dunes to the south thrust though it, ochre-colored now in the strike of the sun. The voices diminished, as did the mechanical noises and the putter of engines. Beyond the wire, as it emerged from the fog, four articulated trucks took on shape and bulk, together with their yellow, attendant forklifts. He raised the more powerful binoculars he had bought and focused them. So far as he could discern through the gray conjunctivitis of the failing mist, the crate was labeled REID DAVIES. His chest tightened and he dipped below the crest of the dune, lying on his stomach. A small, bright lizard slipped away from him in a miniature avalanche of damp sand. He raised his head and the binoculars. A set of doors slammed shut and were locked by an overalled driver. Each truck bore the logo MLC. He scanned the scene, but there was no sign of Blantyre among the scattered men. The cars emerged from the parking lot, the first windshield and strip of chrome catching the early sun. Heavy engines were being revved and the gates of the complex clanged hollowly as they were opened. The first of the huge Volvo trucks lumbered toward and through the gap.

He glanced back down the dune toward the hired 4WD. He should tail them, ensure their route south or perhaps east into South Africa. It was at least a thousand miles to Cape Town, more than twelve hundred fifty to Jo'burg. MLC had extensive manufacturing and distribution—and R & D—facilities in both cities. How long? Two drivers to each truck, he saw as the second Volvo lurched through the gates onto the gravel road and turned east. Dust billowed, yellow and thicker than the remaining mist. If they drove without stopping, he wouldn't be able to trail them successfully. He wouldn't be able to stop for supplies, water, rest—for two days.

He was not equipped, not in any way. The third and then the last of the trucks rumbled through the gates, which were shut and locked behind them. The column of dust hovered over the road, drifting eastward toward the checkpoint at the boundary of the Walvis Bay enclave. Anderson experienced an urgent, sharp disappointment. He lifted the binoculars reluctantly and scanned the complex. Van Vuuren emerged from the office building with a chauffeur, who carried his briefcase. Two other men accompanied van Vuuren, their postures suggestive of subordination— hunched shoulders, eager smiles, waving hands. Van Vuuren, short and bulky in the well-tailored light top-coat, was oblivious of their deference. He climbed into the waiting Mercedes limousine.

Anderson glanced toward the retreating column of dust, his pillar of cloud that should be going before him. He wrenched himself away from the convoy, from his angry disappointment, back to the Mercedes. Van Vuuren—that *something,* the *past.*

The Mercedes headed toward the gates, the two men watching it, one of them with his hand raised. The gates were opened.

He was sliding down the shallow dune toward the 4WD before he considered the purpose of the action, the map thrust into his shirt, the binoculars in his hand. He could hear the Mercedes, which had turned toward Walvis Bay, purring along the gravel road. It emerged from the bulk of the dune, retreating beneath its own pillar of dust. The sun struck down, making the concrete of distant buildings gleam like a Mediterranean village. The glass fingers of hotels and office blocks shone. He started the engine of the 4WD and drew out of the shadow of the dune onto the road, maintaining his distance behind the limousine. That *something* hurt like a flesh wound, a thorn under his skin. If only he could remember! He had shut out so much of his past that it was like an attempt to relocate his home in a drowned village beneath a new reservoir, years after the event. But it's *there,* he told himself, some hold on van Vuuren, something he is—or was— something he did, some connection with that bloody law practice that had wasted so many years of his life!

The outskirts of the town, his thoughts maddening him like insects around his head. Scrubby bungalow plots, a few scraggy bushes and flowerbeds, washing on a line. A garage, then the wooden buildings becoming concrete and brick and glass and climbing into the morning, the gravel road becoming a street. The drive-in cinema and then the sports stadium. Van Vuuren was not heading for the airport—the railway station? The MLC offices? The hotel?

He followed the Mercedes down Thirteenth Road, then turned after it onto Seventh Street. The perpetual stink of fish from the harbor oppressed him through the open window of the 4WD. The Mercedes drew up in front of the hotel, and the chauffeur opened the rear door for van Vuuren. A consultation of watches, then a nod from the driver. Anderson halted at a parking meter thirty yards behind the Mercedes and watched van Vuuren enter the Mermaid Hotel. Then he got out and walked toward the tinted glass of the foyer doors.

The doors sighed open upon palms and greenery and air-conditioning. He shivered at the drop in temperature, and located van Vuuren almost at once, collecting his room key at the desk. Anderson sat down on a long, curving bench seat behind a miniature rock garden bright with flowers and tiny shrubs. Van Vuuren consulted his watch once more. Anderson looked at his—nine-thirty. The foyer echoed to footsteps on the polished wooden blocks. A few businessmen, all but outnumbered by staff. Then the billowing noise of a vacuum cleaner from somewhere just out of sight. A tall woman came through the doors and removed her sunglasses. Dark-skinned, but not black. Half-caste, as they had called all of them—still did in private—or Coloreds, like Margarethe. He swallowed drily, his throat tight and dusty. The woman looked around with a casual, professional glance. Early for a whore, but then, perhaps he was wrong. Was he accepting stereotypes, the idea that she could not be as well-groomed and dressed and confident without having seen white men reduced to paunches and bulging erect penises, their socks still on, even their trousers ridiculously round their ankles? Couldn't she just be a business-woman?

She seemed to recognize a glance among glances and at once walked toward van Vuuren, who had ordered coffee and gestured her to a seat without him-self rising to his feet. The woman smiled—yes, profes-sionally, he decided with a recollected lawyer's eye. He'd dealt with them, with the futility of their com-plaints against white men who had abused them, refused to pay, beaten them. Glamorous black and Colored whores.

The woman accepted coffee, but the image was indistinct beneath the confusion of other images. Van Vuuren's face, the woman, other women, *one* other woman—her face against the light coming through his office window. Behind her permed-straight hair the crowded high buildings of Johannesburg, shadowing her features. She'd chosen the seat deliberately to hide her bruising and split lip and swollen eye from him as best she could. Rape. The girl wasn't a whore, and that had been important. Why? Van Vuuren's face, the light coming off his spectacles as he sat—sat *near the win-dow of Anderson's office,* glancing out occasionally as if bored and preoccupied, the same high Johannesburg buildings behind his profile.

Colored girl, bright, utterly beautiful beneath the bruising, he imagined . . . worked for—

Confusion of images, like a multiple exposure of the same frame of film. Van Vuuren, the girl, *this* girl now, the waiter, the girl in Johannesburg, accusing van Vuuren of raping her at . . . at—*his office,* late on a Friday afternoon as she was on the point of leaving to catch her train to whichever township . . . van Vuuren's lawyer smiling blandly, a man Anderson knew . . . his senior partners' faces, all leaning grotesquely toward him as into the lens of a camera . . . and—

—the case disappearing. The girl disappearing, contempt of her healing face, weeks after the assault. Vanishing into unemployment and the township. The case had never come to court. Van Vuuren had been in the Broederbond, van Vuuren had been important, he had been white and rich. And he liked a *touch of the tarbrush, so what? That's not a crime, Richard*—and laughter dismissed the event. But it *was* a crime, wasn't it? Back then it would have been—not against the person but against the law.

Van Vuuren finished his coffee and dabbed his lips with the handkerchief from his breast pocket. He stood up at once. The man had bluffed his way out of the accusation that he had raped the girl on his office sofa, and Anderson's law firm had assisted in keeping the matter quiet because the police might, just might, have wanted to talk to van Vuuren about his infringement of the Immorality Act. Even if he had wriggled out of any charge, it would have ruined him with the Bond. Hence the Anglicized law firm. Van Vuuren had chosen to discredit the girl or bribe her or whatever had happened after the senior partner had taken it out of Anderson's hands. Had it become public, the Afrikaaner community would never have tried him; they would merely have punished him with ostracism.

He felt queasy with recollected and now more vigorous guilt. And angry as the girl stood up, her purse tucked into the crook of her arm, and followed van Vuuren toward the lifts. Anderson shook his head and the images separated and then dimmed. He rubbed his hot, damp, forehead and pressed his fingers against his temples. Van Vuuren had raped—had had intercourse with—a black woman. Social and perhaps even business banishment. Malan—the son at least—would not have approved or remained supportive. A divorce would have been pressed upon the wife, and the case would have risen into the sunlight like a weed. The girl had had to be kept quiet, the case made to disappear like a thin stream in the dry season. The girl had been brave to consult a lawyer—and stupid. He had been guilty, handing her over to the senior partner and allowing him to dispose of the case.

Van Vuuren and the whore entered the lift.

Anderson sat back in hot relief at the feat of recollection and the sense that the pillar of cloud from the Mercedes had been real, the one from the Volvo trucks no more than an illusion. He breathed deeply.

Now what?

Imprecisely, and in another hot rush of images and scraps of thought, he saw Mandela's face, saw the President, de Villiers, shaking Mandela's hand, cosigning acts of repeal with Mandela and other ANC leaders. Van Vuuren's crime disappeared. No! Only his *immorality* disappeared. Now his *crime* became real. The rape of a colored girl, however long ago, by a prominent white South African businessman, was more than ever intolerable, scandalous. Anderson closed his hand into a holding fist. It could put van Vuuren there, just there.

"No, Tony. That is my decision and it will be adhered to. I am not requesting authority—or granting it—to examine Reid Davies from top to bottom. Not at the moment. It would scare too many people into flight. Any frontal assault, any direct approach—is likely not to be successful. Geoffrey Longmead has agreed—out of sheer panic—to your temporary reinstatement, to your working for and with me. Which means the greatest care on our part. We are in business, but our working capital is small—don't waste it, either of you. By the way, were either of you followed here?"

Aubrey stepped carefully across the pentaclelike outline of a human form still visible on the carpet tiles. The midday sunlight streamed down into the Centre Point office, into which Aubrey had let all three of them with his personal set of keycards. The walls were scorched as a result of the fire Hyde had started to operate the inert-gas fire-extinguishing system that had killed the three Russians. The offices had been casually tidied, superficially cleaned. Apparently, Century House had no immediate use for them. Electricity, the telephone and fax machines and the computer equipment remained functional.

"We could gut that place like a fish," Hyde observed.

"*Any* approach to Michael Davies must be oblique, unsuspicious. Patrick, do you see?"

"I suppose so." The response was sullen. "If we get much quieter, creeping about like this, they'll think we've died anyway." He shrugged. "What's the plan?"

"VIATE—the exposition. Tony, what do you have thus far?"

"At least fifteen of the exhibiting companies are Dumas subsidiaries or associates, or they're linked to them or Reid by large cooperative ventures, especially research and development work. There are a few others . . . " He was posed by a flipchart on an easel, and turned over one of the heavy, squeaking folds of paper. A lopsided piece of complex genealogy occupied the uncovered sheet. " . . . who've borrowed some very funny money from a couple of banks we're interested in. Or from connections with the dubious bank in California in the case of the Yank firms that are coming. That do you, sir? It's all I've had time to get round to."

"Fine, Tony, fine." Aubrey approached the flipchart, rubbing his smooth chin. His hand, moving like that of a casual magician, detailed the lines and boxes and company names, as if to make them disappear or enlarge. "I see. The core of our operation."

"What operation?" Hyde asked from his chair near the window.

"Ah. You and Tony are going to VIATE—as accredited members of the sales or scientific delegation of Reid Davies Ltd. You will be inside, fully entitled to be there, unsuspicious."

"And?"

"You move through the bloodstream of that exposition until you find what we need, evidence of disease."

"Wonderful! How do we get employed by Reid Davies in the next couple of days? I mean, I know Godwin and I are rare birds, but they might—just might—not want us on the payroll."

"That is what we must settle with Mike Davies. This evening. We're having dinner at his home near Birmingham, all three of us. You'll like it, Patrick. He has quite a good cellar *and* stocks Australian lager!"

Hyde slapped his thighs. "Look—you don't want to arouse suspicion, right? Now what bloody story have you told him? And how do you know he's one of the good guys?"

"He was one of ours—one of *mine*."

"People change."

"Not in this case."

"Then why don't we ask him to let us look inside his company on the q.v.?"

"Because someone in there may run to Priabin or Malan, and there might be telephone calls to others and the net result would be that the rumblings in the Cabinet Office become an eruption! Please understand the likelihood of that, Patrick, if you stamp around in your loudest, most inquisitive shoes."

Hyde shrugged once more. "Just testing you," he muttered.

"Good. Finally, a quorum. Excellent!"

"What's the cover story for Davies?"

Aubrey glanced at Godwin, who cleared his throat and said: "We've received information, from one of our sources on the other side of what-used-to-be—"somewhere over there"—that undesirables like Novak seem to have infiltrated some of the companies that have invested or set up in Eastern Europe. . . . Oh, make it up as you go along, then!" he burst out in response to Hyde's cynical grimace.

"Just so long," Aubrey said, "as we have the story straight in our minds before this evening, that former intelligence and security people in Eastern Europe are milking funds from companies in the UK. A sordid little financial scandal. It should have everyone patting us on the back and shouting their encouragement for us to continue."

"It sounds too much like the truth," Godwin commented.

"It would have to, would it not? To be convincing to those who know something of our activities. I have cleared this with Century House and with Longmead. Davies will no doubt check with Century House. Thus, the parallel with the truth." Aubrey turned from his contemplation of the traffic at the junction of the Charing Cross Road and Oxford Street. A shirtsleeved, frocked crowd, busy as lemmings, surged across the pedestrian crossing as the lights changed.

Longmead and Orrell, like most career politicians and administrators, enjoyed machinations, complexities, office politics. Such exercises had often seemed glutinous as mud to Aubrey, and with little reward to the spirit. Cleverness, mental agility, the arts of deception—for the purposes of probity, and good, of course—were truly pleasurable. His was not the deception of princes; rather, the jester's detached, vigorous, mocking intelligence.

"Clive Orrell will be rather unnerved, I imagine," he observed, preening, "when he realizes that all those reports and digests he's so assiduously ignored might have some foundation."

"Scared shitless," Hyde cackled.

"Unnerved at the prospect, since he's disregarded all these people and their new legitimacy for months. But he won't demur from our investigation. Longmead all but had the vapors. Filthy lucre always excites his disapprobation, probably because he married it unhappily. You agree, Patrick?"

Hyde grinned.

"Then let us extrapolate, add conviction to outline, shall we? *Before* lunch."

Anderson approached the boarding house, which huddled behind smarter, larger houses, some of them rest homes for the wealthy, others with pretensions to the status of hotels, all of them confronting the white sand of Swakopmund's North Beach. He had found a vacant parking space in the next street. Long shadows of the two-storey wooden houses lay across the street like heavy, velvet cloaks. It would take him little time to pack. He would be in easy time to catch the evening flight to Windhoek, then a connection—probably the following morning—to Jo'burg. Van Vuuren had flown out of Walvis Bay on the afternoon flight, direct to Johannesburg, so he had returned to the boarding house immediately.

He climbed the three steps to the porch and opened the screen door, walking through the open inner door into the cool of the small, dark hallway. The landlady, German by descent like so many in Swakopmund, was invisible, but there was a smell of onions and overcooked vegetables from the rear of the place. When he brought his bag down, he would call her and pay. He looked at his watch. Four. He should call Aubrey—from the airport if not earlier—and inform him of his change of tack, of the new, vigorous breeze at his back. Van Vuuren, who had raped a colored girl. In the present climate of the republic, even his membership of the Broederbond wouldn't save van Vuuren from scandal, ignominy and prison. Or exile from South Africa. It would be a very public way to demonstrate the best of intentions by the government and all prominent whites—to wash their hands of van Vuuren in public. Nor would it save him from Anderson's blackmail. Once the old evidence had been obtained, and even the woman found.

He reached the first floor landing and paused outside the door of his room. He touched the door with his fingertips, to find it unlocked. The key—he stared at it in accusing disbelief—was in his right hand. The landlady? The hair was rising on the back of his neck, and old itch flaring between his shoulderblades. He listened, knowing that hesitation betrayed his caution. Nothing. He glanced back down the staircase, which had creaked his presence at every step. The afternoon flooded through a stained glass window at the end of the corridor, haloing some early German missionary or explorer. He hesitated, then flung open the door to its full extent, flattening his body against it as he heard a screech of pain and the clatter of something heavy onto the floorboards. He wrenched the door back and slammed it hard against the man behind it a second time, then a third. A hand—white, fingers curled like a claw—appeared at the edge of the door, as if to resist his attack, then slid down toward the lock, then lower—

Anderson sprang behind the door. Above the mask of blood and the empty, unconscious eyes was the white band across the forehead against the deep tan. He recognized that, more than anything else. Uys, the corporal, from the Bush, one of the people who—

He knelt on the man, fingers at once at his throat, knees into his chest so that the breathing he wanted to stop became more jerky, coital in its surges and rough movements. He squeezed the throat, harder, the blood pounding in his ears as if he heard Uys' blood rather than his own, his vision confined to Uys' tightening, gagging face, slackening, head lolling as soon as he released his grip. Anderson lifted his head, himself gagging for air, breathing for the first time, it seemed, since he had flung back the door. He crawled away from the body on all fours, shaking, nauseous.

Then he dimly took in the room. It had been ransacked without noise but without care. Entry had been through the open window, from the side of the house. His few new possessions were scattered on the bed and the rug, linings were torn in his suit, trouser pockets turned out. Uys had found nothing because there was nothing to find. He had his passport and credit cards with him.

Shakily, he climbed upright, holding onto the edge of the bed. Then he sat down and listened to the rattle of pans from the kitchen, the noise of German from a radio or record, the creak of the house in the afternoon sun. Weary. Empty. Calm, too. Margarethe had hardly been present, except as a recollection thrusting him on to do what he had done to Uys. Now, she seemed absent altogether, as if having withdrawn her approval or consent. He did not know which—

—time-wasting. Stand up, get your things.

Suddenly, he was violently gathering his clothes and camera into the empty sports bag. The film had been exposed to the light by Uys—he glanced at the sick, bloody features that lolled above the stained bush shirt. Then he crossed to the window. Uys could not have been alone—

Blantyre?

Not now . . . please.

The 4WD could be reached from this alleyway below him, between two of the wooden houses, without reentering the street onto which the boarding house fronted. They would be watching from that street, must have alerted Uys, but no walkie-talkie or earpiece. He ran his hands over the body. Nothing, except the gun half tucked beneath the bedside rug by the twitching of Uys' foot as he had died. He snatched it up. Spare clip? No time. He hefted the bag, his hearing intent upon the betraying staircase. Nothing. Then the screen door slammed, as if to warn him.

He swung one leg over the windowsill, his shoulder looped through the sports bag's handles so that it swung across his back as he climbed out of the window and began lowering himself down the iron drainpipe. He was sweating profusely. He'd killed a man and Blantyre might already be climbing the staircase.

9

IN WHAT GLORY
ONCE HE WAS

The old man was reconstructing the past; that much would have been obvious to a child. Hyde sat in the bay of the drawing room, on a narrow, moiré-covered Edwardian settee beside the French windows. Aubrey was perched like a comfortable owl on a small sofa while Davies relaxed on a longer brocaded sofa to one side of the marble fireplace. In a moment of silence, Hyde could hear the French clock's tick from the mantel. Godwin hunched grumpily in an armchair, cuddling a small whisky tightly to his chest. Aubrey wove the fantasy of the room and his shared past with Davies—with all of them, really.

Outside, Davies' children ran and whooped across the broad lawn beneath the birds. The swallows neatly scissored the evening air as the rush of swifts cried about the Victorian house, calling through the open windows before they climbed vertically into the darkening blue. Hyde sensed himself lulled, and probably

excessively mistrustful of Davies. But Aubrey seemed
assured and confident, even though the man hesitated
and vacillated and failed to register quite the degree of
shock the old man's revelations deserved. Swifts pad-
dled violently through the air away from the house as a
small girl held onto a reluctant cat's tail and was
dragged behind a rosebed—the small cry of minor
injury occurred a moment later.

Hyde felt himself to be little more than a brooding
presence, a stilled machine awaiting implementation.
He stood up at the thought and wandered through the
French windows into the garden, standing beside the
sundial on the terrace as the children immediately
attended to him. Pink entered the evening sky, remarking the outline of more distant clouds, giving the
evening a shape, perspective. The swifts' hooliganism
seemed at once more urgent.

Davies was concerned—yes. He seemed to want to
assist. He'd worked as a valuable courier for the service
a number of times. Hyde began to wonder whether it
was not the peace of this place, its evident satisfaction,
that irritated him—which irritation he directed at
Davies. Maybe he was just slow on the uptake, confused, his first thoughts being of the problems caused
to his business. Davies had changed, though Aubrey
hadn't noticed. Perhaps he'd just grown a few years
older, his borrowing was too high, he just liked success
and didn't need Aubrey coming around like a death's
head. *Memento mori*. Pointing the finger and recreating
the old, Faustian bargain. Hyde sighed. Whatever,
nothing mattered until they got to Venice, he and
Godwin in suits and smarmed hair—salesmen.

The swifts were three hundred feet up now, calling
urgently to one another as they gorged. Black, sooty
fragments at one moment, then reformed and rushing
with undeniable purpose. Davies' wife had called the
two children in. In their stead, two pigeons bumped

across the lawn. Hyde glanced toward Aubrey—

—Aubrey looked through the French windows. Hyde seemed tensely angry, almost disappointed. Inwardly, Aubrey sighed, then turned to Michael Davies, who appeared suddenly ill at ease, as if discovered drinking his whisky too quickly for taste or sense. It was like trying to recall a swimmer well out of his depth, or one who had become adventurous and no longer required the certainties of the shore. Davies had been one of his best couriers and observers, but that had been in his youth, like prowess at games or with women; he was married now, and had given up women and cricket for the sake of his business. The change of times and circumstances jolted.

He leaned forward on the small sofa in his most confiding manner. "You see, Michael—and I know it's an imposition—but I'm concerned at these Old Guard people popping up at every hole in the box." He smiled disarmingly. The increase of dentures had meant, humiliatingly, practice before a mirror to perfect what had once come so easily! But, Davies was unsuspicious— reluctant, but unsuspicious. "If a couple of my people— Tony here and the more anthropoidal example on your terrace." Don't flinch, Tony, you should know my tricks by now. "If they could somehow slot into your operation at VIATE, feel their way around, it would be so helpful."

Davies nodded and sipped his whisky, attentive to the noises of his son and daughter, who seemed again to have invested the garden. Aubrey saw Hyde stroking one of the two cats and talking, on his haunches, to the children. Perhaps his was a lulling exercise, too? With Michael Davies, it was that strange and unexpected exercise of taking spies and couriers out from the warm, back to the cold. Davies might well consider Aubrey's proposal as an illegitimate intrusion.

"Unfortunately, Michael," he remarked, "my companions and myself remain the children of darkness, however changed the times. Ours is a traditional calling that hasn't yet lost it purpose."

"Kenneth? I don't understand."

"These rather distasteful people with their distasteful pasts, Michael. They come within my bailiwick, I'm afraid. To see such people gaining a new credence, perhaps new power—what with the rather naive governments elected in some of those countries—is of legitimate concern to the service. We must therefore explore the possible dangers. Many of these people will undoubtedly be at the VIATE exposition." He turned to Godwin, who rustled paper in his briefcase beside the armchair, nodding in vigorous support.

"There's a list here somewhere . . . " Aubrey began, but Davies interrupted with, "I believe you. I can't say I've come across anyone who stuck out like one of the old sore thumbs." He smiled engagingly. "But then I'm rusty and a lot of them look as if they might have been in their secret police at some time! Except for Havel and Dubcek and Walesa, one or two others." He sipped at his whisky. "Another, Kenneth?"

Aubrey shook his head and declined. Godwin held out his tumbler and, with a grin, Davies refilled it from a decanter on the Victorian sideboard.

"Thanks," Godwin muttered, reassuming his affable grin.

"Well, Michael? Can you see your way clear to assisting? Without too much disruption to your business in Venice, I mean. I shouldn't want to—"

"Kenneth, you always were irresistible!" Davies laughed. "There were plenty of courier jobs I really didn't want to do for you but did anyway. Tell me, does Hyde possess a suit? Otherwise, you'd better buy him a double-breasted example of the species. I take it you do, Tony?"

"One suit, interviews and weddings," Godwin returned.

"Good." Davies rubbed the hair at the back of his neck. "I'll have to think carefully about what role I cast Hyde in. He doesn't look too bright, does he? Au fait with the kind of stuff we make, I mean." Godwin's bland smile reassured Davies that he had not underestimated Hyde. "As for you, Tony, you shouldn't be any problem. I'll put you with someone on our computer-based exhibits, OK?"

"Fine with me."

"Thank you, Michael. I expect this little adventure to have a great many spinoffs—for the service and perhaps elsewhere." Aubrey smiled, then said innocuously: "And how is the business, Michael? Prospering, it would seem, since you're exhibiting at this VIATE thing?"

"Doing quite nicely, thanks, Kenneth. Not the same as running your own show, but Reid Group's about as comfortable a senior partner as you could get, so . . . " He shrugged. "Wolf from the door, that sort of thing. You know."

"Good, good. You fit nicely into their setup then?"

"A lot of subsidiary work comes our way, plus a lot more in the way of funds for R & D. It's OK."

"I was concerned at the time, when things looked so bad. What with that single MoD contract canceled and seeming to spell the end of so much of your hard work. You might so easily have gone to the wall."

"Things are OK now, thanks, Kenneth, so stop worrying about me." Davies' confidence was vigorous, even blasé. "It wasn't your responsibility, just because I'd worked part-time for you. You didn't owe me anything." Shade of resentment there? Aubrey wondered, but Davies' smile disarmed his curiosity. "Anyway, Reid Group came along at just the right moment and they didn't want to asset-strip the company, just help it expand. Great."

The door of the drawing room opened and Carole

Davies appeared, hot-faced from the tropicality of the kitchen.

"I'm just about to serve dinner, Mike—Sir Kenneth. I just hope the meat's still *pink!*" Aubrey did not demur at the employment of his title. Carole Davies seemed to derive such a genuine pleasure from its audible announcement. "Would you take our guests in, Mike?"

Davies was on his feet.

"I'll just get the kids in—"

"The au pair can do that, Mike. Take Sir Kenneth into the dining room. Must dash—"

Davies shrugged at her retreating form as they moved into the paneled hall.

"Ever been to Venice, Tony?"

Godwin had just had time to wink at Aubrey. Behind them, Hyde drifted through the open French windows, hands in his pockets.

"No, I haven't. Looking forward to it, Mike."

Aubrey's attitude had been dubious, hesitant and dismissive by turns, Anderson thought as the taxi took him, less reluctantly than might once have been its wont, along the Soweto Highway toward the township. The road elbowed its way between golf courses, sports complexes, neat, tree-lined suburbs and the omnipresent red-earth dunes of Johannesburg's history and wealth. White wooden, stuccoed, brick, even pillared houses attempted neatness and an assertion of values, which the vast barrows thrown up by the deep gold mines of the Reef, the Witwatersrand, diminished and even mocked. The neat, still-white suburbs huddled together amid the red-yellow, acid-looking mounds as if to suggest the alienness of the place that surrounded them.

Aubrey . . . Anderson tossed his head and glanced

into the driving mirror, then into the side-view mirror, shuffling on the hot plastic seat of the taxi like a schoolboy with a weak bladder. Nothing—no car had followed them from the city center. He had shaken off Blantyre, then. He'd been there, at Jan Smuts airport as Anderson had disembarked. Had seen Anderson as Anderson had seen him. Nothing in the newspapers during the two days since he had left Swakopmund— no dead bodies in boarding-house bedrooms, no white fugitive sought for questioning by the police. Only Blantyre, knowing he would come, or at least expecting him. Waiting patiently like a porter at the airport.

He shivered with recollection. Lurking, hiding, waiting for hours, until he had deemed it safe. Booking into a hotel under an assumed name, watching for surveillance even as he studied the office building that housed his former legal practice. Knowing that Blantyre knew he was in Jo'burg, fearing that he also knew why he was there.

The highway became dustier, the dust reddening the late afternoon light ahead of the taxi and glaring through the tinted windshield. The sun's great ball disfigured by pylons and electricity cables and the huddled outskirts of the township. Woolen-hatted youths, men wrapped in blankets and wearing trilbies, women in cardigans and wide skirts. The taxi passed the station waiting to accomplish its day with the return of hundreds of thousands of black faces. He shrank inwardly. It was Soweto. Even more than the Americanized, high-rise center of Johannesburg, it bluntly confirmed that Etosha and the game wardenship—and his dead wife— were elements of an illusion. Was that why he had left those things he had deliberately not wanted to take with him, wanted to abandon, with his old housekeeper, Mary M'tebisi? Somehow, he had not wanted to toss them into one of the dustbins they had filled with the detritus of the white suburb and the white life to which neither he nor Margarethe could successfully adapt. His dark suits he had given to Mary's husband, half his size, much of the furniture too, but he had made Mary keep, like some dangerous talisman, the office keys and some of his old papers and a handful of other things that typified what he so desired to leave—

—and yet had not left, and hadn't been able to throw away.

The taxi driver turned to him, asking the address once more. Yes, there was less reluctance, but not less disdain on his face than there might once have been.

His great escape. He tossed his head, angrily baffled by his own former actions, and his present luck, in leaving keys, cards, files with Mary. Had it been pretense when he had claimed that the amulets might protect her and told her that she could send for him if she or any belonging to her were in trouble with the police or the Bureau of State Security? Had he known he would, one undetermined day, be forced back? He directed the driver and attempted to settle back into his seat; alive with nerve endings, anticipations, the sense of having once more become a player rather than an observer. Aubrey evidently felt he had a stronger hand in Europe, better cards—for the moment. Aubrey might even be using technique, goading him into activity by a display of mild indifference. It was possible, though it hardly mattered. His own motives drove him, not any priority of Aubrey's. He shook his head, dismissing the idle speculation.

"You read about that explosion, man? In the papers?" the taxi driver asked, old contempt and enmity thick as his accent. "Bet those kaffir bastards are hiding out in here, someplace, huh?"

Anderson murmured something noncommittal. One of the more lurid newspapers lay on the hot plastic seat beside him. ATROCITY was the headline. A damaged bank near the MLC building. Extremist elements,

Communists within the ANC, even a Left-wing White connection . . . the usual witch-hunting, carried out these days even in Johannesburg and Pretoria in a reedy, plaintive and ineffectual voice. It was over, almost—and without a final bloodbath of white against black. There were murders in the townships, Zulu against Xhosa, there were terrorist outrages and dire warnings from the far right. But it *was* going to be done, and done without the chaos that had been predicted for twenty years.

A police patrol, unheckled and unstoned, passed them, traveling out of the township. White driver, black partner. No SADF vehicles or uniforms. Youths playing football on a scrubby patch of waste ground near a derelict petrol station, a single goalpost erected. Barefootedly assured, even brilliant. The contrast with the newspaper was strident, reassuring.

Eventually, narrower streets, after a crowded African market. Some large cars, but the place had been thick with cars, whether old or new. The place was . . . what . . . generally better-off than in the old days, when there were rich blacks, but small in number. There were taller buildings against the lowering sun, too, rather than just the pylons. There were businesses—white businesses—here now, factories and office buildings. Telephone wires crisscrossed the street and orange sky.

Then Mary's tiny breeze-block bungalow, with the vegetable strip in place of a parched front lawn, a goat bleating somewhere behind the house as he opened the taxi door, and a new, extended section attached to the house. An old woman was shelling peas into a colander beside the front door. He paid the driver and the cab turned unhurriedly round and moved away into the orange-glared dust. He stood, hands on hips, inhaling the dusty air and the scent of cooking as the old woman watched him before scuttling inside, leaving the colander of black peas beside the stool on which she had been hunched. In another moment, Mary's bulk was in the doorway, her eyes shaded by her hand as she attempted to make out his features. Then she seemed to wobble into a jelly of excitement and surprise, almost flinging her apron over her face, placing her hands there instead, as if he had come back from the dead for no benevolent purpose.

"Mary?" he said, moving forward to the curb of planted stones that marked the boundary of the property. Children squealed like wounded animals in some game at the back of the house.

"Mis'r *Richard!*" Her voice rose into a wail of welcome. She hurried forward and took his extended hand, holding it much as a fortune-teller might have done, turning it in her own pale-palmed hands. Then she looked sharply into his eyes and appeared to know everything. At least, that there had been trouble. She looked back at his palm, then his face. "You' welcome— *welcome!* In, in!" She shooed him forward, toward the door. He ducked his head on entering, his movements awkward since she still held onto his apparently revealing—and welcome—hand. The old woman might be her mother, her husband's mother, he did not know. She returned to the colander as soon as he entered, deferential as if nothing had changed. It probably hadn't in her mind, after a life of invisibility. The children he could see through the rear window of the living room, beyond the plain wooden table where the setting sun spilled on its cracked, scratched, deeply polished surface. Linoleum covered the earth of the floor. A door was opened onto a . . . he peered and Mary giggled like a child. A bathroom in lurid pink. Bath and washbasin and toilet bowl. Through the window, he could see that the tiny, decrepit shed that had been the outside privy had disappeared. Ritually burned no doubt, he thought with a smile. He went, respectfully, to peer into the bathroom. Soft white towels, soft toilet paper, new linoleum on the floor. Mary continued to giggle and he turned to face her.

"I'm glad, Mary, so glad." As she nodded agreement, her flesh wobbled. Her bulk made the living room seem tinier than it was. Two small faces appeared at the back door, curious, unrecognizing. He remembered the girl as a suckling baby, the boy as a sullen two-year-old. Mary gestured him to a chair and he nodded his thanks. The children drifted away. "Where's Thomas?" he asked lightly, as if trying to distract her now studious gaze. He remembered, Margarethe had once said *our passivity only* looks *like folk wisdom, Richard—remember that. It's really just the patience of dumb animals, waiting.* It had shocked his liberal pretensions. Watching Mary watching him, he was uncertain Margarethe had been right.

He had betrayed himself now, knowing his eyes glistened, seeing his barely hidden distress on Mary's mirroring features. But she, mercifully, did not inquire, and he asked quickly after her husband, then the children, then the old woman and the extensions of her family and her husband's family whose names he could recall. A litany of success, at least that was how she made it seem, as she bustled at the stove in the galley-sized kitchen and rattled saucepans and cutlery. As she had done when she and Thomas and the new children had lived in the largest wooden hut he could place on the grounds of his house without arousing the ire of the neighbors and the curiosity of the authorities. Not very brave, he thought sourly. One room and a toilet was not necessarily compensated by his pleasant manner when she served him breakfast, or the bonuses and occasional treats and clothes he had bought the children and herself. The fact that she retained a gratitude that might be described as eternal was a silent, poignant accusation.

He shook hands gravely with Thomas, who took off his black trilby as he saw Anderson rise from the chair at the table. Thomas, too, was indebted, reminded of small kindnesses by his presence; so that they were both like pet cats or dogs, their response out of all proportion to the attention given them. Yes, Thomas' job was in the township, a concierge at some new office building. There would be black executives, doubtless, but not Thomas among them: his lack of education.

He ate with them, accepting the offer of beer from Thomas. The children seemed incurious, as if he, a white man, was no more than an aspect of the landscape of their lives, to go largely unnoticed, as blacks had been in a former white landscape. Mary cleared the dishes and returned to the table. Thomas' voice could now be heard clicking and chuckling in Xhosa among the voices of neighbors, which Anderson snatched at imperfectly. He spread his hands on the table.

"I need what I left with you, Mary," he announced, at which she clutched his hands in her moist palms, her face distorted with concern.

"What trouble is it?" she asked.

He shook his head. "White trouble." He smiled bitterly. "White mischief."

She seemed both puzzled and anxious. "Why you come back here?" She sounded as if she were pleading. "Why?" Shaking his hands in hers.

"I had to. Things—things didn't work out, Mary."

"—so *tired*," she said. "Nothing here for—you mean harm." It was as if she had accused him of some crime; reluctantly but of necessity.

He began shaking his head, but then nodded. "It's something that has to be done—*I* have to do. For which I need my stuff. The keys and papers."

The quick dusk had gone and the vast township glared with neon and streetlighting through the windows. The rumble of vehicles was louder, more persistent than when he had last come to Soweto. They sat in the unlamped darkness, her eyes staring brightly at him, her round, double-chinned features worn at by his mood.

"Where's Missis?" she blurted, as if to dissipate the tension that was gathering like a storm in the room. She seemed planted on her chair, determined not to bring him the things he had asked for. "Where?"

"Dead," he announced. "It's why I've come back, Mary. That's all you need to know." He could see the snail tracks of tears on her black face, the glitter of her wet eyes. She might even mourn for Margarethe later, after he had gone. For the moment, she was restrained in subordination to white reticence. "Thank you," he murmured throatily, now shaking her hands gently. "Please, Mary, the papers and the keys. Bring me the box—I won't need to trouble you again."

She sniffed loudly and wiped her eyes and nose with a large handkerchief. She disappeared into the one bedroom, and he heard rummaging, scraping noises. Then she returned with a metal box such as a film cameraman might have carried. Thomas' and the other voices chuckled like a stream outside the door. The occasional insect cruised the room, as if searching vainly for a lamp against which to incinerate itself. She placed the box on the table, its locks and clips closed.

"Thank you, Mary," he said, patting the box with the nervousness he might have shown a strange, growling dog. "I—where's the nearest taxi driver, Mary?"

She nodded, understanding that his visit was completed and she was divorced from him now by the box placed between them. He had returned to his past and she had a fearful inkling of his dangerous purpose, of which she disapproved. But, he suspected, she also wished him gone, so that she might sit alone and mourn Margarethe.

Traffic sounded outside, drowning the conversa-

tion of the men on the front step. Their voices continued as the flicker and wash of headlights entered the
room through the door and windows. He glanced
round at the door as the conversation hurried and
became alarmed and Thomas' head appeared in what
might be accusation in the doorway. Mary was concerned, her hand on the box.

"What is it?" he asked, and was answered by the
noise of a siren outside and the screech of brakes, then
something bellowed through a megaphone in distorted
English.

"Terrorists . . . police . . . remain in your homes,"
he snatched from the bellow. The newspaper's image of
a bomb explosion, the cry of atrocity. ANC dis-
claimers, counteraccusations from the Conservatives, a
breakaway extremist group, white and black.
Satisfactory scapegoats or inventions—

"Stay in your houses. This is a security operation."
The megaphone was closer now, other vehicles were
coming to a hurrying stop and there were running footsteps and the bemused outcries of surprised innocence.
He heard the breaking of glass, the shattering of wood.
Cries, orders, the greatest of haste. Thomas reentered
the room, glaring at him. The other men had dispersed.
Thomas spat on the floor, to Mary's outrage. Feet
could be heard pounding toward the house. Mary
grabbed at Anderson's hand as he clenched the carrying
handle of the box, and she tugged him through the rear
door, her son at once appearing, to be gathered to her,
then whispered to.

"White man—have you seen?" he heard shouted.
"Terrorist! A white man, him we want!" Mary had
heard even before he had, and dragged him away,
understanding simply because of his wife's death and
his request for the box. Behind them, Thomas' voice
was raised in supplicatory protest and denial. Anderson
hoped to God Mary's neighbors wouldn't give him the

lie. Somehow, they knew! They'd traced his former life like a neat, clear path, the names and the people.

He turned to Mary and kissed her cheek clumsily. Then the boy took his hand reluctantly and dragged him toward the teetering fence at the end of their patch of dirt behind the house, clearly visible in the haze of lights from the front. If Mary and Thomas told the truth, they probably would not be hurt. They couldn't, any longer, simply disappear into the police cells and reappear falling from a high window—could they? Behind the lithe, small boy, he slipped through a gap in the rickety fence, dragging the box after him, its weight surprising in his panic. There were raised voices behind him, Mary's protests vigorous and loud. There seemed a sense of abashed pause, perhaps the running down of the impetus of the snatch operation.

"No white man here, no boss here—boss," he heard fade on the air. Their search would, perforce, be brief. They'd have a riot on their hands if they weren't careful.

He was sweating profusely, shivering with avoided danger. The boy led him on, turning gleaming eyes on him from time to time as they wound their way through huddled lanes of shops and drinking shibeens and open-doored brothels and gambling parlors. The smell of urine and drink and refuse assaulted him, the past kept alive. The boy's pale palms waved him on, despite his weariness and fear and the increasing weight of the box.

Under other circumstances, it might have been entirely amusing, this charade of inspecting Hyde and Godwin and their transformed appearance. *Washed behind the ears, clean fingernails?* It was on his lips to say the words aloud, just for a moment. Instead, he nodded and said: "Very well, sit down, both of you.

Your next-to-Godliness is intimidating me!"

Godwin grinned and Hyde at once tugged his tie loose and unbuttoned his collar. "Christ," he muttered.

It was, or promised to be, a hot, clear morning. Already the pecking birds and drifting first visitors were slightly masked by a haze in Regent's Park. He glanced at *The Times* folded neatly beside his plate at the window table. David Reid had announced in the House the previous evening—fortuitously in time for the *News at Ten*—an EC aid package to the Soviet Union which would, conservatively, amount to $10 billion, "to unfreeze the transport and distribution services" and avoid the shortages of previous winters. Another costly effort to keep Nikitin in power, assuage his unpopularity at home. Unless some of the people they had identified as having legitimized themselves—joining companies, banks, even PR companies—were very swift they would miss the gravy before it poured away like water in the desert!

Godwin, too, glanced at the headline.

"Bloody stupid move," he muttered. "It'll just disappear."

"Exactly my sentiments," Aubrey remarked. "Now, you have whatever you need in terms of secure communications." He handed Godwin a small, folded piece of paper. "The Italians have been very helpful. One line in your hotel, another at the Exposition itself, both entirely secure. Checked twice daily. My own telephones will be similarly checked. You've drawn whatever else you need, Tony?"

"Yes, sir."

"Don't fuss, sir," Hyde remarked with a kind of buoyant sourness.

Godwin looked at his watch. "We'd better be going, sir. The car's got to get us to Brum airport before ten-thirty. Any news from Anderson, sir?"

"He's shifted his operation to Johannesburg.

Something he thinks worth pursuing as far as our friend van Vuuren is concerned. He should have reported in last evening, but didn't. I'm sure there's nothing to worry about. Yes, yes, you two get off. And find something. Find out what they're moving or hoping to move. And remember our Italian colleagues will supply as much support as you need the moment you request it." He shook their hands. There was a small current of excitement running between them. Despite his somber thoughts during the night, of his dead niece and Malan's ultimate culpability, this had something of an adventure about it.

"We'll try, sir."

"If we can catch them with evidence in their sweaty grasp, then we can go through the whole of Reid Group, Reid Davies' peculiar packing operation, even get the French DST to go through Dumas like a fever in the blood." Godwin was openly grinning. "Which is what we all would wish. "But"—he raised his finger portentously, knowing that he must impress them with theatricality—"whatever grandiose visions we may entertain of foiling Babbington, or any sense of personal revenge of justice,"his voice faltered for an instant, then continued, "whatever the prizes would *seem* to be, there is only one real prize. I've looked very carefully at Reid Group's R & D program. WSI and transputer technology—both well down the line toward production. I have no inkling as to how much has already gone missing, but I want whatever is supposed to change hands in Venice *stopped*. I want it traced, halted, accounted for. If they are using the VIATE exposition to smuggle material, then those are the things they will be smuggling. Locating the next stages of their pipeline, even implicating Novak and people like him, come second to this. This is—no more and no less—an intelligence operation against the security service of a foreign power. Do I make myself absolutely clear? At no time and in no manner is the recovery of the smuggled technology to be jeopardized." It was so difficult to reconsign her to the back of his mind, out of mental sight! So difficult, too, to attempt to ignore Babbington and the everlasting enmity between them. But he must. "Not even in order to catch Babbington or Malan red-handed! Or to unearth Novak. Not at the moment. Understand?"

Eventually, and with marked reluctance, they sobered and nodded. Aubrey felt relieved. It was possible to operate within distinct boundaries.

"Good, then I'll keep my desk and diary as free as I can. Westfield will be assigned as my aide for the duration. Yes, yes, you must hurry!"

"Valentina, what the *hell* is going on? I find this request for more of these"—Priabin's hand wiped across the monochrome enlargements spread over his desk, his other hand knurled into a fist on his hip—"placed by *mistake* on my desk this morning. A request from Centre. Your secretary was trying to recover all this stuff when I walked in! What the hell is this?"

The noon sunlight thrust down through the trees along Kensington Palace Gardens as he turned to the window. His anger was mingled with dismay, even nerves, and he did not wish her to identify anything other than his rage and superior rank. But, dear God, what games was she playing?

He turned back to her before she could reply. She looked hunched and fearful on her chair, as if there was jam still around her mouth.

"You've been reporting, behind my back, to Centre—to Babbington! To the extent that you've kept this information from me. Godwin and that bloody animal Hyde leaving from Birmingham airport, with the Reid Davies party, on a flight to Venice." His anger was so genuine his voice did not even suggest falsetto. He banged his fist on the desk—a picture of Hyde slid onto the carpet, Hyde in a suit!—and the woman flinched gratifyingly. She wasn't yet nerved to duplicity, at least not against her rezident. "Well?"

She burst out with: "You know I disagreed with your decision not to inform the Centre!"

"You disagreed? I gave you an order! You want to play the old games, do you, you stupid arrogant bitch?" Her eyes flared, but Priabin had no wish to restrain his insults. "You want to play the old games of deceit with one hand, but you want it all to be above-board and respectable on the other! You can't hand me or yourself over to Babbington as you've done and expect to be promoted on merit at the same time!" He rubbed his hands through his hair. "Besides," he added, turning again to the window, "you don't play the game well enough. You've only learned it second-hand. You can't *play* with these people, you give nothing but hostages to fortune! Kapustin is an unreconstructed Stalinist and Babbington is paranoid about Aubrey and England. Did you expect sense from either of them?" He turned back to her. "My God, I'm so bloody *disappointed* in you. When Babbington sees these pictures and whatever piece of meaningful prose you attached to them, all he'll wonder is why you and I didn't get ahead of the game, why they were already leaving before we noticed. Ten black marks, Valentina!"

The woman's eyes glittered with angry, humiliated tears, but she snapped back defiantly: "We didn't know."

"Oh, grow up, Valentina. The world hasn't changed at all for us. Because *they* haven't changed, back at Centre. They're still running the KGB, which is really the MVD out of the NKVD—and the grandfather of these fine horses is the Cheka, for Christ's sake!

Leopards change spots a lot more easily." He slipped into his chair and leaned across the desk. "All that happens now is that we're held to be incompetent—me primarily—and your career will be blighted, you'll be used rather than employed. Is that what you wanted?"

"Of course it wasn't."

"My bloody job, then? You fool—Christ, I thought you were cleverer than this."

"Oh, for God's sake, don't keep playing the same bloody song!" she yelled, her cheeks pink. She swept her hair out of her face and glared at him, her hands quivering as if she were registering a minor earthquake. "Look, I did what I thought best. I thought you were wrong."

"Evidently." But he smiled shakily. "But why the hell haven't we heard from *Mortimer* about this? He's on the bloody spot, for God's sake! Why hasn't he told us that Hyde and Godwin are part of the Reid Davies team heading for the Expo?" He waved his arms in the air. "Dear Christ-in-Heaven, is the whole bloody thing going up like a flare?"

"You want me to talk to him?" she began, then added, penitently: "I can't, can I? He's on the plane, too."

"Maybe he's scared—or thinks he's too clever for them. Aubrey must have enveigled him into it. Davies, I mean. Old loyalties, old favors. But what is Aubrey after in Venice? He's within a touch of the whole scenario. Why is he bothering with Venice?"

"Proof. A way in?"

He nodded. "Probably. If he could expose the Expo operation, he would be given carte blanche, and then some . . . must be that." He looked up, and smiled. "But you have dropped us in the shit. We'll be lucky to climb out. Unless we can sew this up in a bag and drop it in the river. Think we can take Hyde and Godwin out before they do too much damage?"

Her eyes widened, then she nodded. "What about Babbington? He's due to—"

"He won't be able to stay away now, will he? Now you've told him who's at the party. Sorry. But, we'll have an audience." His features glowered. "If we don't secure the consignment's free passage, then we're finished, both of us. Me for not knowing, you for not acting on what you did know." He rubbed his cheek. It was, appallingly, like explaining something to a child, and a rather naive one at that. "If I hadn't found out, I'd have been for the chop. But you—you would have been regarded as little brighter than an idiot." He spread his hands. "You see, all the rumors you ever heard were true, after all. There are werewolves and vampires in the night!" He grinned. "So, now we both know what's going on, we're about to do what we should have done in the first place. Pull the rug from under Aubrey, who's always been our responsibility." He waved his hands toward her. "So let's get organized. I want to be in Venice tonight—tomorrow morning at the latest, with everything in place."

He had slept in the main railway station, his head nodding on his chest, his presence as unremarked as that of the handful of drunks or blacks or the few Boer farmers from the veldt waiting for the morning trains. Mary's boy had taken him to the Soweto station and at once abandoned him in the swirl and crush of disembarking passengers from the crowded trains from the city. The few police had not noticed him. There had been something almost . . . what? Polite? Something restrained, anyway, about the police raid, the care they had taken to isolate the object of their search as a white man, their calls for calm, their later politeness to Mary and Thomas—he had rung Thomas at his work. Mary's husband had been puzzled at the leniency, the immediate abandonment of the search. None of their neighbors had informed the police of his visit. Thomas' silences eloquently voiced the hope that he would not return.

His hotel was under surveillance, however. Hence his return to the Central Station, his bag at his feet, the metal box beside it. He had used the service lift to get to his hotel room, packed his few things, left the same way. He had recognized no faces, only gestures, postures. Perhaps they had not been looking for him, but it was wiser to assume they were. To have mobilized the police, even for a low-key incursion into Soweto, was unremarkable, but in it he sensed their evaluation of him as a threat.

He aimed the directional microphone through the thorny branches of the bush behind which he was crouched, then adjusted the volume of the sound. The buzz and chatter and deep male laughter from the *braaivleis* at the rear of van Vuuren's house seemed startlingly loud, and he reduced the volume. Snatches of conversation sounded in the earpiece he now plugged into the recorder. He raised the binoculars to his eyes. The African dusk flared in the neat, tree-enclosed garden with the two barbecue fires. Van Vuuren's face was reddened by the coals of one of them. He was nodding and grinning with a bearded man at some remark or joke. Bright print dresses drifted like clumps of moving flowers through the increasing soft gloom of the garden, or were grouped like small rock gardens. High chatter, the Boer accents almost de rigueur, like the presentation of credentials.

The surveillance equipment was easy to purchase, most of it at discount prices, even in closing-down sales heralded by signs of hope white-painted on shop windows in large letters, as if to declare the shutting down of a repressive state. Fifty percent off the apparatus of control. He smiled grimly. The place was changing.

Not down there, though. There were faces he recognized from the Conversative Party, even one or two of the thicker-necked compatriots who belonged openly to the AWB. Strangely, he was invigorated by the images in the lenses and the voices in the earpiece, as if he were inspecting specimens in glass bottles, museum artifacts. Buying the rifle and pistol had also been a simple matter. Gun sales were up. There were one or two boastful holsters down there, slung around paunches and astride bush jackets and khaki shorts or slacks. Polished, bearded faces, unabashed and still loud. One or two businessmen of the Broederbond variety, a sportsman or two. Van Vuuren was wearing a shirt that might, in the dusk, have passed for a Springbok jersey. Anderson remembered now that van Vuuren had once been a promising rugby player, until a knee injury. Not international material, but with enough kudos to begin his business career amid publicity and good wishes.

The large, white-painted wooden house at the far extent of the garden was located on a winding, tree-lined avenue littered with traffic impediments and discreet surveillance equipment in the suburb of Bryanston. It was close to the *Buiteklub,* the country club, whose grounds and golf course he had crossed, as if walking an invisible dog, to reach the knoll above van Vuuren's property. The carefully planted trees and bushes that marked the club's boundary provided excellent cover and the gently rolling ground placed him above the man and his guests and his house.

He realigned the microphone after a gentle, rhythmic sweep of the garden. Steaks and *boerewors* sizzled amid the soft explosions of beer cans, the heavy or high laughter, the certainty expressed in the small noises and movements of the guests. The evening darkened as van Vuuren's voice murmured like a point of focus amid the wash of noises, in reply to his bearded companion's remark.

"You leaving for Europe tomorrow, Piet, I hear."
Van Vuuren had confirmed the information. Anderson
swallowed, then dragged his fingers across his lips. The
exultant noises of golfers killing a snake at the side of
the fairway behind him struck against his back like a
mocking, urging hand. Then, in front of him, through
the binoculars, Blantyre's form drifted into the smoke
and glow of one of the barbecue fires, against a background of printed dresses and the occasional flicker of
a white-shirted black servant. Blantyre made directly
for van Vuuren, and the bearded man at once drifted
away. Anderson pressed the earpiece with his fingers,
but the conversation was like a distant broadcast interrupted by the renewed ether of the party.

" . . . sign of him, why are you worrying?"

"You leave tom . . . won't follow . . . "

" . . . interested in me, man?"

" . . . idea. Just be careful . . . "

Gusts of laughter and intoxication, and the barking
of a dog that was gamboling between the bunches of
dresses and pale shirts and the flames and smoke.
Rottweiler or something of the kind—remember that,
he instructed himself amid surges of disappointment.
Van Vuuren was leaving for Europe the following day.
Blantyre understood that he, Anderson, was interested
in the man, was cautioning him. They must, somehow,
have discovered he had followed van Vuuren to the airport in Walvis Bay. He looked at his hand as it shivered
just in front of his face. Behind him, the last golfers
climbed into their buggy—they must have been hunting
for lost golf balls or even for the snake, rather than
playing in the quick gloom. They turned their vehicle
around and climbed a slope toward the distant club-
house.

He felt isolated by their departure, rather than confirmed in his raptor's posture above the unsuspecting
braaivleis. He could no longer group or hold these peo-

ple in the palm of his contempt. Blantyre had suggested their retained power to control and hurt. Margarethe sprang up like the evening breeze, making him shudder.

Then Blantyre was leaving.

" . . . good flight, man."

"There's nothing is . . . "

"Don't worry, man—don't worry. It's taken care of," he heard in a burst of silence while the dog was rubbed fondly and the next helpings of steak and sausage came off the busy grills.

Blantyre walked up the garden toward the house, nodding to the round form in off-white that hung like a ghost near the patio: van Vuuren's large wife. The small, obnoxious son's tones had piped intrudingly in his ear since he arrived, demanding attention, food, more attention. Van Vuuren's daughter seemed as plump and uncertain as her mother. Then Blantyre disappeared around the side of the house and almost at once a car's engine sounded above the noise of the barbecue party. Anderson shivered, but he could not regard the involuntary spasm as one of relief. Blantyre occupied space with such utter certainty, even on a darkened lawn and lit only by the occasional spurts of barbecue fires.

He gathered up the recorder, pulling the earpiece from his head. He had much to do. It had to be that evening or night, there wouldn't be another opportunity. He realized now how hollow his stomach felt, how shrunkenly cheated his whole body felt. Van Vuuren was leaving for Europe in the morning. He had to break into his old offices that evening, had to get hold—physically hold—of van Vuuren that night. He had to know this place, the spread of the golf course, the streets leading to van Vuuren's front door. Whatever Blantyre knew or did, he must concentrate on van Vuuren.

He gathered the awkward bundle of the microphone, recorder and camera in his arms and galloped breathlessly down the slope, across the adjacent fairway, toward the nearest green and its limp flag.

The big stars had begun to emerge; he had to hurry.

The lagoon was being boiled in the sunset color of the water and the few buildings he could briefly glimpse and at once recognize were dyed with its agitated, surreal color before the aircraft dipped too low toward Marco Polo airport for him to take in any more. A few spires and towers half-submerged in an orange sea was his impression as the wheels touched. The engines produced reverse thrust and the airport buildings blurred from a string of lights then reemerged as dull, low shapes sprinkled with separate, weak lamps. The sky was pale and the few clouds deeply pinked like flower heads. Priabin glanced at Valentina in the business class seat next to him. The Rome resident should have flown up by now, so should the backup team from Milan. As many as a dozen people—another six in economy class behind the dragged-across curtain that had separated this compartment from the bulk of the passengers. Venice. The flight was two-thirds full, mostly with businessmen; some tourists in short-sleeved shirts and slacks or dresses appeared misplaced. The plane slowed and then turned onto the taxiway toward the terminal building. An announcement in Italian and English instructed them to remain in their seats, then that infuriating, rubbishy Muzak broke out again. He always hoped that, if ever trapped in a plane plunging toward a mountain or the winter ocean, the music would be more appropriate during his last conscious moments.

He tossed his head and grinned at her, loosening his seatbelt against instructions. Already, the insatiably businesslike were at their overhead lockers or clambering into their creased jackets.

It was quite simple, even ordinary. Babbington himself had been obliged to admit as much, to see the matter through Priabin's eyes. The shipments must be protected, inspected, approved, then sent onwards. Other than that, there were two matters, intimately connected. Siamese, really, in their oneness. The liquidation of Hyde and Godwin. The prevention of their learning, uncovering, reporting anything—anything at all—and their certain and permanent retirement from the scene of activity. Full stop. Period.

He looked at his watch. Eight. The flight was on time. Hyde and Godwin were already under surveillance by the first group he'd managed to get sent in from Milan—emergency activity, overriding priority. Babbington himself was due in Venice the following day. If he inspected the operation and found everything to be in order, then he'd let matters drop. His career and that of Valentina would be back on the rails. There had been a minor rant, defused in part by the flatness of tone induced by the encryption unit on the telephone. But in Babbington, too, there had been a little fever of excitement, a welcome for the familiarity of what was a small-scale, traditional, wet operation.

Valentina stood up as the aircraft came to a halt and the door at the front of the fuselage was opened by the stewardess. He slid into the aisle—she had not permitted herself to accept the window seat, of course. He grinned.

Full stop, dead stop—for Hyde and Godwin.

10

QUICK AND IN MY ARMS

Hyde moved with the casual hurry of the last tourists coming out from beneath the porticos of St. Mark's. He glanced up at the gilded images of greater dramas and meanings. But he was relieved, and challenged. It was the old game, however finessed and with altered priorities. It was still the old game—

—had been from the moment they had picked him up, two of them at first, then three. He had been watching Harry's Bar where Michael Davies was entertaining some prospective buyers from the united Germany, Czechoslovakia, France and even the most liquid African nations. A drinking session that had already begun to bore Hyde, sipping a small beer beside the Grand Canal where one of the day-trippers was wobbling into the first of the evening gondolas. Even the Italians hadn't seemed to be insulted by the leering grasps and mockery of the gondoliers. By leaning wearily on the table beneath the awning that welcomed the flies from the canal, he had been able to see the door of Harry's Bar. When Davies' cluster of employees, clients and prospective customers had emerged into the narrow *calle* that ran between the bar and the hotel up toward the Piazza San Marco, he had drifted behind them—only to find that they had moved, in a laughing, hand-to-shoulder group, into the cathedral. The pigeons had lifted like puffs of gray smoke in seeming protest of the flocks of tourists in brighter plumage. Hyde had followed them into St. Mark's—

—knowing that one of them was already behind him, because the man with the newspaper who had floated along the waterside near Harry's Bar was the man from the pub in London, before Kellett had been murdered. His newspaper reading was too avid, too deliberate. And he had been watching Hyde as well as the bar.

Someone in Davies' group was important to Priabin. The man with the newspaper had not been demoted to a cushy posting like Venice or Rome, he had been dispatched to this place like a plumber, plugging leaks, tidying up cracks in the supply.

He had known for certain as he had shuffled and weaved behind Davies' half-bored group, diminished beneath the ornate domes and alcoves and blocks of celebratory marble. There were two others, and one of them was the woman, Valentina, though at first he had not recognized her behind the huge sunglasses and the bright yellow false hair. Eventually she had defined herself by her walk, her posture, and the authority that peeped from beneath her assumed anonymity. One of Davies' group was to be protected then—from him.

When they had moved out from the sultry, gold-struck gloom of the cathedral into the piazza once more, Hyde became certain of their intent. Their entire concentration had turned to him. He shrugged his

shoulders into a slouch they would take for unaware-
ness, even boredom, and became more aware of his
surroundings. As he moved through the flocks of
pigeons and tourists, he was aware, too, of the gun
thrust into his waistband. The sky had darkened overhead and the shadows filled the piazza, so that the café
lights sprang out as if it were an earlier, winter's
evening. He slid between drifting and strolling sightseers, past the exhibited daubs of art students as the
public buildings and their archways gloomed about
him.

Shouldn't be there, of course. Should be at the
expo site with Godwin, checking the Reid Group subsidiaries, the exhibition stands, the warehouses. But
Mestre and the expo site were across the causeway and
Davies was here, entertaining in the dining room—
booked for half an hour's time—of the Gritti Palace.
And he wanted to see Davies when Davies wasn't
aware of him, when the man wasn't on guard. He
wasn't sure, but there was something . . .

He passed under the archway of the Ala
Napoleonica and into the Calle dell' Ascension, knowing they were drawn with him now as a comet by its
tail. The Davies group, pausing occasionally to glance
into shop windows, make conversation, slap shoulders,
was ahead of him, and he matched his pace to their
casual saunter. The narrow shoplit *calle* was crowded,
slow-moving as a snake in hot sunshine. He did not
look behind him, not even when he stopped to glance
blindly into shop windows, or hesitate as if deciding his
destination. They, too, were enclosed by the narrow
street's tall buildings and would be unwilling to make a
move without a clear escape route.

Davies, shepherding his group like a tour guide,
headed them toward the rear of the Gritti Palace. Hyde
turned after them. Suddenly, there were fewer people as
they drifted toward the narrow little hump of a bridge.

A church's high, stained wall was rough and cool against his palm, as he halted, watching the group. Laughing, they moved toward the lights from the hotel's foyer. Another small humped bridge, another church, gold-tipped by the last of the sun, and they had disappeared. He lounged against the wall of Santa Maria, hands in his pockets, indecisive and apparently bored. Casually, he scanned the tourists and one thin dog, two cats, a group of Japanese towed behind a guide with a wand, the flash from their cameras blinking out repeatedly. One flare caught the woman and she flinched, as if identified. One of the men was still with her, but the one from the pub—who might even have killed Kellett, for Hyde did not know the man's capacities yet—was on the opposite side of the narrow bridge, ahead of him.

The Japanese disappeared into the gloom of the evening toward St. Mark's Square. The crowd was diminished by their absence. He tossed his head, looked at his watch, then moved toward the foyer of the Gritti Palace, peering in, seeming satisfied. Then he turned and crossed the bridge—the man he knew inspected postcards in the gloom with sudden intensity as he passed him. Nerves began, the tickling of the hair on his neck and scalp, the itch in his palms—but it was controlled, even satisfying. The narrow streets and tiny, toylike bridges were sparse with people, quiet, until he reached the Campo San Stefano, knowing that they would guess he was heading for the Accademia bridge; pulling them away from the equilibrium of confidence and numbers, into quieter and quieter streets and squares. The sky showed the first stars. A scrubby, long *campo,* dotted with a few trees and washing thrust out from windows with drunken shutters. A man smoking in one window, in a vest, a woman leaning her huge, melonlike breasts on the windowsill of another apartment, hair straggling untidily around a

weary face. He came to the Grand Canal and ascended
the wooden bridge, pausing in the middle of it,
absorbed into the stretch of palazzos, churches and
darkening water. He glanced casually from side to side.

The woman was not yet on the bridge but her companion was, his yellow shirt identifying him. The man
from the pub, dressed in pale slacks and a loose blue
shirt, drifted past him to the other side of the bridge.
He signaled recognition and stillness to another man at
the far end of the bridge, beneath the shadows of the
Accademia Belle Arti, where pigeons minced and fussed
between the students and sightseers on its flight of
steps. Four of them now—

—split them, hurry the process. He turned his head
with deliberation and stared directly at the woman,
nerves jumping in his palms as he gripped the
balustrade of the wooden bridge. She halted as if
accused, then turned to look down at the canal. He
grinned and swallowed the unexpected excitement that
had risen into his throat. He felt lightheaded, slightly
dizzy. He hoped Godwin wasn't under the same
threat—should have thought of that earlier. As long as
Godwin stayed in lighted places where there were people erecting stands and moving machinery and electronics—too late to worry now.

He moved away from his apparently absorbed
stance in the middle of the bridge, and descended to the
campiello in front of the Accademia. And began to
walk more briskly down the broad, almost deserted
street beside the gallery. Away from the Grand Canal,
away from other people, always certain they were
behind him, waiting for them to close the gap.

Anderson turned off Commissioner Street and up the
ramp of a multistory parking deck, the old Ford rattling. He snatched out the ticket from the lips of the

machine and the barrier rose. The car climbed the slope as wheezily as an old man. The lowered window brought him the echoes of his own car's asthmatic, gargling exhaust and the occasional, distant screech of tires. He climbed floor after floor of the deck, until the vehicles had become no more than a scattered few dots overawed by the empty, muggy space of concrete. He pulled into a spot and turned off the engine. Silence, at once. The warmth of the evening came through the open window. He rested his head against the back of the driving seat, smelling petrol, the close atmosphere and the fried, queasy scent of frankfurters and onions from far below.

Anderson got out of the Ford and locked the door. Then he went to the trunk and brought out the metal box. The mike and recorder lay like unusable fishing tackle. He slammed the trunk shut. Enjoyable, the emptiness of the place. There was a retained blaze of light from the Marshall Hotel and the adjoining shopping mall and a patchwork of light and dark from the tower of the MLC building.

He knelt by the metal box and examined its contents once more, as he had done on the half-empty train from the township and in the station concourse, whenever woken from his drowse by a cleaner or a raised voice. Keys—he knew every one now and touched each of them like separate runes. He had not kept the file on the young black woman who had been raped; he had surrendered that to compromise and failure almost from the beginning—when the senior partner, Seaward, had informed him that such-and-such would be done for such-and-such reasons . . . *all right, Richard? I don't see a problem here. Could do us much good, indeed.* . . . Truth to tell, the litigation and conveyancing and tort had come in from MLC and he had, indeed, not seen any great problem.

If he could find the files, and find the girl—or anything he could bring to bear on van Vuuren, no excuse would be accepted. Match to straw, it would go up in fire. He held the keys in front of his face. There was nothing else in the box that was of any immediate help, just old combinations, telephone numbers, storeroom codes. He thrust the sheets into the inside pocket of his jacket, smelling the scent of dry, arid grass on his sleeve as he did so. Stood up, reopened the trunk and replaced the box. Ready?

Ready.

He checked that the car door was locked, window closed, then walked toward the lift at one corner of the acreage of concrete which seemed now scented with old oil-leaks and the omnipresent onions from the street vendor's stall ten floors below. He looked over the edge of the deck's concrete sill. Commissioner Street was a blur of light and neon and crowds. On the other side of the deck, where its fumes must not intrude, was the glow-through glass of the shopping mall under its huge expanse of toughened glass. The great greenhouse which cultivated rich white children and token middle-class blacks. Though even that might have already changed, he corrected himself. Changed a little, anyway. He descended in the lift to the concourse of the Marshall Centre.

The lift doors opened and closed swiftly, as if the shabby, metal interior regarded itself as unsuitable for display before the opulent garishness of the concourse's boutiques, stores, advertisements. He stepped out onto the intricate, immaculate tiles. Three terraces of expensive shops, discreet supermarkets, enveigling, seductive windows. A huge baobab tree arched upward from the ground floor toward the dark, sullen glass of the greenhouse roof, and exotic blooms and broad, glossy leaves sprouted everywhere; an ordered jungle, unlikely to reclaim the ground beneath the tiles. He crossed the crowded concourse, moving more purposefully than the drifting, relaxed crowds in bright shirts and dresses. The place was neither alien nor familiar, merely a landscape against which he moved. The entrance to the office building that contained his former law firm was diagonally opposite the lift doors from the parking deck, but he felt little familiarity in retracing old steps. The vast, tinted glass doors of the MLC building were two glittering boutiques closer to him. He bumped into a young couple, who were polite, but seemed amused at his urgency. He shrugged off the impression, and moved toward the doors—sighing open—and into the foyer of the building that contained the offices of Bright, Seaward & Seaward, et cetera. Their former junior partner, bought in by money Aubrey had supplied after he had fled England, was returning. He smiled grimly, clasping the keys in his pockets. The foyer was virtually empty. A large black woman was being dragged behind a huge, pincer-action broom. Lists of nameboards hung like scrolls of honor at some university between each set of lift doors. He glanced behind him. The world of the concourse seemed dimmed, was silent, beyond the nicotine shading of the doors.

There was a security man in the basement of the building, alarms, security locks, key-coded locks on the doors. If any combination had been changed, the location of any infrared sensor altered, he would be discovered. The alarms would trip, sounding in the nearest police station, three blocks away. Breathing deeply, he summoned the lift with a single, determined jab of his right forefinger.

The lift's silent, rapid ascent to the fifteenth floor dizzied him. He was sweating as it slowed quickly and the door opened onto—

A silent corridor; empty. He paused in the lift for an instant, then walked out and let the door close behind him. The corridor was familiarly strange; something of the past remained, but that was, in reality, only the reluctance with which he had come to it each morning. Driven to some sort of radicalism by mere boredom? He shrugged the idea aside.

The offices of Bright, Seaward & Seaward lay at the end of the short corridor, beyond the blackwood doors with their ornate, brass doorknobs. He faced the doors and the gleaming brass with an ironic smile, and jingled the keys in his pocket as he moved toward them. There were no security cameras on this floor, though the files he needed would be on the floor below, where cameras—

He flinched at the ease with which he had contemplated the burglary of his old offices. Once, it had been a momentary exercise to examine the layout of the cameras and the way in which they reported to their screens in the basement, supervised by one doltish, idle individual. He touched the brass doorknob of Bright, Seaward & Seaward, then pulled out the keys with his other hand. A passing amusement, to spot the blindspots, the angles, the inefficiency of the expensive security system his partners had been sold! Now, though, the idea unnerved him. He glanced toward a long slit of a window set in the angle of the corridor and saw the streetlamps far below him and the fuzzy, caterpillarlike running-together of car headlights on one of the motorways. He shivered.

Carefully, with a touch that seemed ineffectual, he inserted the key into the lock. He turned the key in his fingertips, sweating profusely. The lock gave in easy surrender, its slight click drowned by his exhalation. He pushed open the door, which protested slightly against the thick pile of the carpet inside. He was confronted by glass doors and a box on the wall with a code keypad. No card had to be inserted, just the number. He shut the outer door softly behind him. One wrong number and the alarm would sound in the basement and the idle Afrikaaner, kept on by his Anglophile partners as a kind of house white, would wake himself and struggle up to this floor in the lift, gun ready. His fingers hovered above the keypad. Two-nine-zero-three—why had he employed the anniversary of his first marriage, when he had been in the process of starting anew, forgetting and erasing the past?

Cancel! His other hand had been on the handle of the glass doors, pushing as he completed the number. Nothing—no yielding. Cancel. He redialed his number and listened. Silence outside. The alarm light remained dead. He was sweating again.

Bright's number—what was it? Not a date, part of a number, too complicated to remember. Seaward—the old man, not the son who was dead from the neck up and totally alive in the region of his loins. The old man, Dick Seaward. . . . He smiled, almost gently.

Death of someone, the strangest choice, as if he never wanted to forget. Death of his daughter in a car accident. Anderson flushed at the memory of the prematurely old man thrusting his photographs upon him, of the grave and the headstone and the girl's age, together with the immediately immaculate quality of the girl's life. The girl, who had come to him because she knew no one else who would help her—who had the expertise—to obtain her an abortion. The girl had not been particularly promiscuous, simply uncaring and unlike able. Unlikely sanctity visited on her after her death in a highway accident in Europe, on a day unimaginable for old Dick Seaward. Teeming, driving rain and a partial fog and the spray from forty-five ton trucks—and the car driver's head filled with the afterglow of cannabis. Outside Frankfurt. He knew the details so well because the Frankfurt police had been helpful and discreet and he had received the official and the unofficial mail, while Dick Seaward in the next office—that one there, at the end of the corridor—had been erecting his shrine.

He bit off all recollection, realizing its ability to evoke and threaten. Except for the date, on the police report, on Seaward's lips so often—the sixteenth of February. Seaward's entry code because he had discovered love in a blinding moment of guilt and loss, and would never let her slip his mind again. He dabbed the numbers out carefully on the keypad, holding his breath.

Pushed at the door—stiff—*open*. He stumbled inside, a prickle of perspiration along his forehead, closing the door behind him with a nerveless hand, remembering that the alarm would sound if the door did not relock. Leaned against the glass, surveying the surroundings. The rectangle of blue carpet and the receptionist's desk, the corridors leading off in three directions, like *points of our peculiar compass, one quadrant missing,* as the senior partner, Bright, had announced, to the obsequious smile of the receptionist, the day he had first seen these offices. And he had spent years in this place, accommodating to its peculiar compass. Until he had tired of it, one morning and for no apparent reason. It might have been the tie Seaward's son had been wearing, or a sick joke, or the polish gleaming on Bright's shoes. By that time, anything would have done it, however trivial.

He padded across the thick carpet. The window in this inner foyer looked down toward the gleaming city, its lights lying confidently and carelessly about like the first South African diamonds. He shook his head, passing the offices with the nameplates. He was here to render his account, and his ex-solicitor's fees were horrendous.

He thought of old Seaward and his daughter as he passed Seaward's office and imagined its disheveled appearance. Seaward might not be dead of drink or guilt; more like undead, but with no way for Bright to be rid of him. Seaward had enough money to remain in the firm as long as he chose, as equal partner. He followed a turn in the main corridor to its junction with a single door, blank of names or description—the door to the lower floor and the file room and security safes. He fished out a small bunch of keys, inspecting them almost lovingly, as if his memories of this place were all pleasant. He rattled them, then held out the remembered, correct key and jabbed it into the lock. There had been no alarms connected to this door. The cameras and the poorly sited infrared beams were at the bottom of the stairs, waiting for a moment's unwariness. A knitted cat's cradle of a trap which had its blind spots, gaps and weaknesses. He glanced back along the empty, pictureless corridor, but it was impossible to convince himself that anything would be found in Seaward's office, or even Bright's. Everything he would need—if it hadn't been shredded or thrown out—would be in the secure room. The decisions to do nothing, the statement by the girl, van Vuuren's account of the attempted rape in an office in that building over there.

He glanced behind him as if expecting a window to open in the blank walls of the corridor. Then, with a grunt as if weight lifting, he turned the key.

Open. Easy. Down there, silence and the near-dark. Smiling as he recalled old habits, he reached beyond the door and switched on the lights. Stepping onto the first tread of the stairs, then beginning to descend, carefully testing the steps, furiously remembering the angles and compass of the minimal number of infrared beams, and the blind spots of the cameras. Once he got beyond the first door, the bleak little foyer of checkered tiles on which an African rug had always seemed to have been spilled like paint, he wouldn't have to worry about the cameras or the beams—well done, Bright, you old bastard, saving money everywhere you could—

Christ—oh, sweet Jesus Christ! His head turned
and he looked back up the stairs at the light switch.
You bloody fool! The lights going on would have registered on the security cameras. The guard would know
someone was down here, his screens would be lit up
like a bloody Christmas tree.

There were six of them now, and he knew their faces—
would be able to identify each one of them. He had
been trailing them around, even down to the Quartiere
Santa Marta, where the tourists never went and the
whorehouses leaned against poor apartments—the first
bit, everyone hoped, that would slip into the lagoon, so
that La Serenissima could make a dignified exit.
Trailing them by the nose, to ensure that there were no
more.

He shivered even now, at the recollection of one of
Micheal Davies' group. Novak, Antonin Novak, former senior colonel in Czech Intelligence. Novak was
here, with Davies. He needed to call Aubrey but now
dare not risk it. Novak had been a name he knew
instantly, but a face he recalled only with difficulty.

The six men and the woman had him hemmed in
now on the Fondamenta delle Zettere, opposite the
island where the Venetians had put the Jews, La
Giudecca, with its dim lighting and few poor spires,
over which the lights from the Lido could hang like the
glow of stars.

He'd dragged them through the dock area, then
back along the *zettere,* as they began slipping through
deeper shadows and he had begun to hear, above
radios and television sets and raised voices, the noise of
walkie-talkies.

Hyde shivered. Time to get out of it. As he
crouched inside the small, enclosed, paved courtyard of
a neat old *palazzo* that had been converted into flats

and which blinked out modestly toward La Giudecca, he heard the shuffle and skid of a pair of sneakers beyond the wall. They were using the radios, coordinating their activities. Trouble was, his head was filled with recollections of Novak. He shivered again as a sneaker squeaked like a weasel out on the canalside promenade. The lights from the Lido's chock-full hotels, boarding houses and cafés glowed behind the Church of the Redeemer, outlining its dome and cross and the figure that slipped across the gap of waterlit moonlight, gun in hand.

He twitched as he heard a television set switched on in one of the flats, blaring out strident Italian voices. He settled himself down again onto his haunches, clutching his arms across his chest, chin resting on his forearm. The moonlight gilded the water in lines of pale-gold braid. A stunted tree grew out of a pot, like a rebellious houseplant amid the courtyard's paving. A cat had wandered incuriously past him ten minutes ago. Novak's features kept coming out of the evening, taunting him. What could he be doing here, in Venice, kissing bums with people like Davies and the Africans and Germans? He clutched his upper arms with his hands, squatting in the darkness, listening for—

Crackle of a walkie-talkie or cellular phone. He heard it, then another and a murmuring voice, sensing its location was betrayed by having to answer. The woman, undoubtedly. He slid his torso up the rough brick wall until he was standing pressed against it, his head cocked. He couldn't make out the words, only the urgency of the whispered reply. Gradually, as if teasing at a tiny knot in silk with numb, clumsy fingers, he sensed the location . . . just . . . there. He breathed shallowly. On the other side of the wall, in the next courtyard—

—sweat along his forehead. They'd search this one next. He was aware of the woman's higher-pitched voice coming through the walkie-talkie, the urgent whispering of the man, then a male voice at the other end of the channel, replacing the woman's. He heard the tone of authority, the voice somehow familiar, even though the words were indistinguishable. Then the noise of a *vaporetto* or water taxi's engine, heading out toward the Lido, drowned all other noise and his fingers twitched like a pianist's against the wall behind him. Damn. The darkness was hot, breathless, the moon had lumbered above the courtyard wall, spilling silver light into it, onto the tree that leaned drunkenly and on the gleam of the cat's eyes at the corner of the building. Slowly, the noise of the *vaporetto* diminished.

Out of the growing silence rose the murmur of voices from one of the flats, then the sharp, small cry of a baby. Then the absence of the crackles and spurts of static and the whispers from the other side of the wall. Hyde forced himself to slide noiselessly to its angle, then toward the entrance to the small, hot courtyard. Then, startling him, as the moonlight threw a shadow toward the tree, he heard the phone or transmitter spurt again.

Priabin's voice, had to be. That had been the familiar one. He swallowed carefully. Kept his moist palms pressed against the wall at his sides. Watched the shadow hunch into secretive reply. The man was still on the broad paving of the *zettere*. Hyde strained to hear the exchange in Russian.

" . . . here, I know it, General. I need backup."

"I'm calling this off," Hyde heard in reply. Why? "All units—" Where was Priabin? With the woman?

No. Her voice exploded in the stillness, almost as if she was beside the man throwing his shadow into the courtyard. " . . . must be *removed!*" he heard, then Priabin's reply: "You want to explain to *him?*"

"Five minutes!" the woman pleaded, enraged. "Just five minutes! Maxim, are you sure?"

"—saw him go into one of these courtyards—backup. Sir, we can—" Shit—Priabin was going to give in.

"Where exactly?" Priabin was teetering on the edge.

"About a couple of hundred yards from you, sir. Opposite the church—directly opposite."

A silence, then, "Very well—five minutes. He's arriving in an hour."

Another silence, then, "All units—" And something like "converge." Then the shadow, which clutched its transmitter against its head in a gesture of toothache, began whispering, and Hyde edged to the end of the wall, judging the length of the shadow, the distance of the whispering voice, listening beyond it, too, for the first quick footsteps of the backup.

Decision. Movement. The shadow became unwrapped, stretching in shock as Hyde moved the few paces, closing on the man, striking him across the face with his forearm, hitting him in the stomach with curled, hard knuckles. Chopping against the side of the falling man's neck, the transmitter rattling on the flagstones.

Footsteps. His head turned rapidly. Two men running toward him from the direction of the Old Customs House—

—and the *boat*. Suddenly, the *vaporetto* he had thought heading out toward the Lido was a small motorboat idling in the braided reflections of moonlight, thirty yards or so from the *zettere*'s edge. Its engine started up with a gunshot noise, then a growl as it sprang toward him like an animal. He saw the woman and Priabin, presumably, in the bow. There was a third man, marginally in profile, head slightly cocked. Hyde couldn't see the rifle. He ducked and wove toward the next courtyard entrance. The first bullets plucked dust from the wall above his head, then he was in darkness again, his breathing louder than the noise of running feet, themselves almost masked by the magnified insect-noise of the boat's engine. He threw himself toward the courtyard wall, clung to its top and then dragged himself onto the top of the wall, dropping at once down the other side. The narrow canal that linked the Giudecca and the Grand Canal became visible as moonlight occupied the darkness as dimly and hesitantly as a mist.

He paused, pressed back against the wall, two or three feet opposite the reflected square of a window from which a light burned. Something—a rat—scuttled near his feet, then moved into the narrow canal with a small swallowing noise. He shivered. Listening, he detected voices urgently moving about beyond the wall. He hesitated, then began walking quickly alongside the canal, past the occasional thin dog and narrow alleys, skirting a tiny bridge, moving carefully away from—

A blare of light from the searchlight on the bow of the boat. He saw the outline of a rotting, wide-waisted gondola in its gleam. It washed the walls of grubby buildings, then seemed to search him like fingers through his hair and clothes, spilling over him as loud as a cry of alarm. And the woman's voice, he was certain, through a distorting megaphone, all caution abandoned.

He ran on, scraping his hands and body against the wall as if trying to become part of it. Ahead of him, there were lights from the hotels and palazzos along the Grand Canal, but they seemed to retreat down the tunnel of the narrow canal and its buildings. The noise of gunfire crackled again.

His hand went from him and he staggered—an opening like a slit in the night, the narrowest of alleys. He lurched into it, off-balance, then continued as chips of stonework came from the wall close to him. The whistle of the bullet, nothing of the explosion. Priabin had ordered the marksman to fit a silencer. There were footsteps and shouts, too.

A church loomed mockingly in a weed-strewn little *campo*. Other spires and domes rose beyond it like mountains. The lights of Venice were brighter. The noise of the motorboat had stilled, but the footsteps were more urgent now. He drew the gun from his waistband, and sighted at the exit from the narrow alleyway, his shaking forearm stilled by the rough, grubby stone of the church wall. He fired immediately as a shadow-figure became visible—he did not consider which, until it rolled on the ground, screaming and clutching its thigh. A second shadow dodged back into deeper shadow.

Lights were coming on in upstairs windows with the stuttering regularity of people rising for work. But there was clearly alarm in the way curtains were drawn back. He could not have sent a clearer signal of distress than by wounding the man who thrashed about in the moonlight. Hyde grinned and fired two more shots at the open mouth of the alleyway but there was no returned fire. A woman screamed from one of the open windows. Then the first two unannounced shots from the sniper's rifle plucked out stonework, scarring the grubbiness with pale scuffs. Hyde ducked back. Waited. The woman went on screaming, even behind the shutters her husband had reclosed. The man on the ground still writhed and cursed.

Hyde listened to his own breathing. Any route he chose which did not attempt to double back on them would drive him away from the bridge across the Grand Canal and toward the narrowing spit of land that was the Old Custom House Point. They'd make an easy kill of it there.

The man on the ground was being encouraged to drag himself toward the shadows of the alleyway. White hands flapped into the light, urging him toward their batlike fluttering. Then hands grabbed him, there was a squeal as he was dragged upright and his cursing began to diminish rapidly, then became more strident, violently protesting against pain—

—and haste. They were going. He breathed with relief, leaning his head back against the angle of the wall. Hearing now, as they must have done, the siren from a police launch, rounding the point by the Customs House or already in the Giudecca canal. *I want to report shooting.* In Venice? Lucky they came at all, it might have been the Cosa Nostra, and then what would the cops have done? Someone was leaning furtively out of a nearby window, a thin man in a grubby T-shirt, who saw him and called out, pointing, only to be dragged away by a large woman in a tight, spotted dress—

—then Hyde had flitted across the square, into the moonlight and out of it again, into the shadows of the nearest *calle* which gave way suddenly to another *campo* and its inevitable church.

As he jogged toward the Salute landing to find a *vaporetto,* he wondered who was arriving within an hour who was important enough for them to pass up the chance of killing him. Christ, whoever it was had real pull, and had to be from Moscow Centre. Interesting. Was he flying in or coming on the train? Flying.

Marco Polo for you, then, my son—and those bastards will be there, too, though not necessarily expecting you.

He began shivering with the nausea of reaction as he reached the Salute landing and a *vaporetto* chugged and wheezed toward the side of the canal.

The last of the sunset was streaming across the net-curtained windows, as gauzy and sight-hampering as the nets themselves. Young Darren Westfield was made as comfortable as Mrs. Grey's immediately maternal attentions could render him. He was perched on the edge of an easy chair in the drawing room of the Chairman of the Joint Intelligence Committee. Aubrey would have smiled inwardly at the boy's discomfiture, had not his anxieties precluded it. There had been a wasp in the room early in the evening, and he had trapped it between a Spode cup and saucer and ushered it back through the open windows. A pity he could not do the same with his worries.

Aubrey looked down at the litter of notes and files around his feet. It did not seem to diminish his imperial significance as far as young Westfield was concerned, but to himself it made him an old man, comfortable in disarray. But there *was* something—

What possible kind of expertise did Novak have to offer MLC and Dumas that was not illegal? Novak was among the most cunning and brutal of the old school. He had ordered killings with ease, was a masterly interrogator in his brutish fashion, had controlled people with ruthlessness and consummate skill—

He tossed his head. Perhaps he qualified as a born-again capitalist, after that *vita!*

Rubbish. Either he retained covert power that Malan could still employ and exploit in partnership with Babbington, or . . . what?

The phone rang, startling him, and he snatched it up from his side.

"Patrick, yes."

"I haven't got long—someone's arriving in about an hour, someone important. I'm tailing Priabin—the gang's all here."

"What of Tony?"

"No idea. I'll check with him later. I thought you'd like to know. He's here. Former Senior Colonel Antonin Novak of the STB. Dressed in a business suit and taken out to dinner by Michael Davies. OK? Be in touch."

Aubrey hung up the receiver and stared in surprise and satisfaction at the ceiling. Novak. He smiled. A *business* expert! He had controlled liaisons between the IRA, Qaddafi, and the remainder of the terrorist groups in Europe. He'd even been photographed with Saddam Hussein once. He shook his head, as if to clear it. But, Novak—with Davies? In Venice on business?

He clicked his fingers, startling young Westfield.

"Darren, check those surveillance photographs that either you or poor Chambers took. The various contact ones, not the NatWest Tower surveillance." Westfield put them into his hands in a glossy sheaf, and he flicked through them. Eventually, Priabin and a man still recognizable despite new clothes, hairstyle, moustache—Antonin Novak. Priabin, the woman, Novak and van Vuuren. In a restaurant, out of doors, the woman squinting in the sunlight, having removed her huge, fashionable sunglasses. Aubrey all but purred.

"Curiouser and curiouser," he murmured. There was something, though, nagging at him. Something he had glimpsed, or with which memory had made some brief connection, causing a fitful spark. What was it? he demanded angrily of himself.

"Darren, where are the names of those companies Colonel Novak now serves with such capitalistic fervor? Find them for me."

"Companies connected with Dumas—companies with which Novak has a connection?" Darren murmured, shuffling through heaps of paper. He consulted his notes, checked through another pile.

Aubrey sighed with impatience, and his chest felt alarmingly tight, as if his angina were about to revisit him. He rubbed at it, his other hand tapping nervously at the arm of his chair. It was something to do with one of Novak's former areas of expertise, with Libya per-

haps, or the IRA—the connection was there somewhere, but it wasn't yet clear, dammit!

Then Darren handed him Hyde's scrawled note.
"Here, sir—sorry it took me so long."

He stared at the names, both of them, as if they
were crystals that only slowly sank in a thick fluid.
Diamonds sliding deeper into amber. Oh, my God, my
dear God . . .

One of the companies produced Semtex explosives
and had, in the past, supplied Libya who had, in turn,
supplied the IRA and the other dark angels of
European terrorism. The second company was a manufacturer of very modern, very effective small arms,
mortars, antitank weapons, rocket launchers. The circle closed with a loud, ringing snap. Malan, Reid
Group, Dumas, and now Novak. Shipping arms to—
white South Africa? Weapons and explosives—and
people in South Africa who would use them, and others against whom they would be used. *Plus ça change,*
et damned cetera!

"Darren—quickly! I want these two companies
examined, top to bottom—everything they produce
and have produced or even *might* be producing!"

My God, he recollected, then saw on the page he
still held in his hand—nerve gas. One of these
damnable companies had once been a producer of
nerve gas for the Warsaw Pact.

"Yes, both companies—the one outside Prague
and the one in Plsen. And get me Tony Godwin on the
line, I must talk to him and Patrick without delay!
Hurry, young man—*hurry!*"

11

IN SUCH A NIGHT AS THIS

Twenty-three minutes. He'd wasted that much time . . .

The guard had not been alerted by the light he had stupidly switched on, then clicked off again in his panic, having stumbled back up the stairs to the switch. He'd waited in the dimness at the top of the stairs for the door to open, for the noise of an alarm or the siren of a police car. He had heard one that had made his heart bump with a wooden, knocking sound in his chest, but the siren had faded away somewhere as he held his breath, a faint insect noise lost in the dull murmur of the traffic below.

Wasted, *wasted* . . .

His rage made him slipshod, careless. Files were already spilled on the cool, checkered tiles of the secure room, their contents lolling like white and pink tongues. Filing cabinet drawers gaped like jaws. He couldn't find what he wanted, even though no new filing system seemed to have been introduced—other things were in their old places, the partnership profits, shareholding details, tax returns, staff salaries and bonuses, all where he remembered them to be stored. And the old files—the sensitive, the erroneous, the political and the unscrupulous—were where they had always been. His keys had opened the cabinets, his fingers had riffled through the files, recognizing the names of plaintiffs, clients, masquerades and deceptions—but nothing on the girl or van Vuuren! Not in these cabinets, or in the Malan-Labuschagne files. He'd found stuff that would send Bright and old Seward to prison for years, and not so much as a traffic violation by van Vuuren!

Anderson paused, wiping his brow with the back of his hand. Then he gripped the edges of the open drawer, which was at chest height, as if needing sudden support. The lighting was subdued in the sterile, cool room. He had dodged the single security camera which focused on the foot of the stairs outside, and the two infrared beams that backed it up, sliding along the wall, then dropping into a crouch to scuttle like a large rodent to the inner door. Once inside the room itself, there was no security that the correct keys could not compromise, as his had done. For what, though? For bloody what? His fists banged the edges of the drawer in a fury of disappointment. Twenty-five minutes since he had first descended to the lower floor. He was in that bloody place where he had sworn he would never set foot again, shoved on by a clever scheme that mocked him now like hollow laughter. Like the cold sweat on his forehead and beneath his arms. He lowered his face until his forehead rested on the edge of the drawer, which creaked metallically with his weight.

Where, for God's sake? Had they shredded them? Not like Bright, that, though Seaward might have done it in one of the sudden fits of rectitude he had suffered ever since his daughter's death. A fitful, apologetic

morality which might have prompted him to sanitize
portions of these confidential files. He shook his head.
He didn't know. There might be other files missing. He
thought he remembered others, mostly involving abortion arrangements, liaisons between black and white
that had turned sour or possibly dangerous. There were
other cases like van Vuuren's—even the deaths of girls
or black servants, killed in sexual or authoritarian
rages. He could find some but perhaps not others. He
didn't know half of what had gone on in Bright's office
over the years, or out at his Parktown home, the
murkier side of the practice, or the things in which
Seaward had colluded before his daughter's death had
broken his world like an eggshell.

Breathing deeply, he unlocked other cabinets and
pulled out the drawers and desultorily flicked through
the files, aimless cross-checking, mere occupation of a
decent interval before admitting failure. Where,
dammit, where? Thirty minutes, thirty-five . . . the tiles
were littered with strewn files and sheets. It did not
matter. Who would guess it was him, anyway?

Forty minutes. Nothing. He had opened a hundred
confidential files, and found van Vuuren's name twice,
as a character witness. Character witness!

He slammed the drawer back in and turned away
from it, kicking aside papers and files as he made his
way to the door. Frustrated pride nipped at him like a
dog at his ankles. The anger of disappointment, of
impotence, was fiercer. Cautiously, he opened the door
of the secure room, studying the infrared boxes posi-
tioned on opposite walls, and the single camera; he saw
on the floor the imagined marks of his knees and hands
and back as he had outwitted the security system.
Bright's expensive, incompetent system. But mockery
was no palliative. He got to his hands and knees and
prepared to scuttle across the floor, looking up all the
time at the infrared sensor focused in his direction,

whose beam he must not break by movement, looking at the little blank eye that would flash if he—

Light on.

Temperature. Not just bloody movement, temperature. It had never functioned efficiently. To register the rise in temperature required a bloody gang to enter the place, not just one intruder—but he was hot, with rage and frustration. He burned, for God's sake!

He ducked beneath the camera's limited eyesight and tugged open the door. Was the alarm connected to the police, or just to the basement? He couldn't remember, so he slammed the door behind him and bolted up the stairs, fleeing down the deep carpet past his old office, past that of old Seaward. He'd have to take the stairs, the idle bastard in the basement would use the lift. The heat of his body mocked him.

He blundered against the glass doors, his hands leaving hot prints that shrank as the glass cooled again. Seaward's office, the guard, lift coming up, Seaward's office—the old man's bouts of guilt, of purging, the moral laxative of his daughter's death. The thoughts came quickly, out of the waves of fear and panic. Seaward drank himself stupid most afternoons, in his untidy office, behind the closed venetian blinds. Guilt, expanding like the effects of a pebble in a pool. *Seaward would end up feeling guilty about everything*—how many times had he said that? He glared round in his panic, and the distance to Seaward's office seemed immense. He could almost hear the lift sighing swiftly up to that floor. Seaward would have taken the files on cover-ups, on payoffs to injured or assaulted blacks, especially young women. Three of the files he knew of, besides the girl who had come to him, had been missing. Young black women either dead or abused or both. There could have been fifty more, for all he knew.

He blundered back along the corridor and

wrenched at the handle of Seaward's door. Then he glanced back toward the glass doors and the darkwood doors beyond them, still closed. Sirenless hum of traffic from below. Locked. He stepped back and kicked at the veneered door—kicked again, then a third time, and the lock burst. Another alarm would have sounded now—if Seaward had bothered or remembered to set it. Anderson staggered into the office, coughing with effort. Then he flicked on the lights, which exclaimed on the wreckage of the room. Untidiness, the smell of cigars and whisky in the sterile air. Blinds closed, desk littered with papers, cabinets open, drawers unlocked. He moved behind Seaward's desk, after closing and wedging the door, and opened the few drawers that were closed. Photograph of the dead daughter, looking sullen in sunlight, in an ornate silver frame. He shuffled the untidy heaps and mounds of papers, then hunched down behind the desk so that he would not immediately be seen by someone opening the door, forcing the wedge. Seaward's decline everywhere. Bottle in one drawer, glass in another, as if that minimal separation was all he could maintain. Nothing, nothing—

The faint buzz of the security lock sounded as someone punched in the correct code. He paused, waiting; looked down at his hand resting on a heap of files in the bottom, right-hand drawer. Silently, his nerves jumping, he fingered them one by one, reading the African names on the tabs. Three, four, five—that one he remembered, he'd found them—then the girl's, Veronica Mokesi. *The Mokesi girl is lying,* he heard van Vuuren reciting in his head, his lips contemptuous as they easily spilled the lie.

The door of Seaward's office was pushed an inch open and met the resistance of the wedge. Seaward hadn't needed the wedge for years, his door had always been uninvitingly closed against the world. Then the door was thrust awkwardly, hesitantly open and an Afrikaaner accent—same voice of Roets, the anthropoidal security man—called, "Is that you, Mr. Seaward? Set off the alarm again." Then the error was discovered as the door handle rattled loosely in Roets' grip and his breath exclaimed surprise and suspicion. His voice, a moment later. "All right, you bastard, come out where I can see you!" Roets' bulky, potbellied figure was posed as a heavy shadow in the doorway, then took on color and form as he entered the room. *Veronica Mokesi.* The file was under his damp fingertips.

Then Anderson stood up, his hands in the air, suddenly calm and decided. He smiled at Roets' surprise and the slow dawn of realization that the intruder was known to him.

"What—man, what the hell are you doing here, eh?" he scowled.

Anderson glanced down. The black girls in their files, the abused and the bribed and the seen-off-the-premises . . . and Veronica Mokesi. The picture in the file would be of a bruised face.

"Good evening, Roets. How unfortunate." His accent had always irritated Roets. The man's face twisted with contempt and the gun was hefted in his hand. "I came back for something. Just a few years late, that's all."

"You broke in, you mean! Well, we'll wait for the police now, man. The alarm goes through to the station, see. They'll be here in a minute. You can talk your way out of it with them." He laughed. "Sit in the chair," he ordered as Anderson was already lowering himself into the capacious leather swivel chair. It creaked in the hot, stale-scented silence of the room. Roets pushed his cap back on his head and heaved his belt higher around his stomach.

"Thank you, Roets. Some of Mr. Seaward's whisky? You don't mind if I do?"

"Hands on the desk!"

Anderson shrugged. There was a pleasure in his own calm lack of nerves. Contempt still came easily, a kind of emotional backup. He moved his fingers as if playing a piano on the edge of the desk, near the blotter and the heavy silver picture frame and the set of pens inscribed to commemorate some charity work. The file on Veronica Mokesi stared out of the pile as if the girl herself watched him.

"Christ, man—what are you doing here?" Roets asked, as if he felt compelled to break the heavy silence.

"Old business, Roets. Unfinished business."

"Seaward doesn't keep any money in his office, man."

"I know that, Roets." The dismissal in his voice angered the man. His head was cocked to one side, listening. Anderson tensed against the first distant whine of a police siren. Yet he was still calm, imperturbable. Roets was sweating. "It's not money, Roets. That would be too easy."

"Don't tell me, man—save it for the cops. I don't care. I just caught you breaking in here. Lucky I didn't shoot you!"

"Wrong color, Roets. There might have been questions." His hands continued to tap out some run of silent notes on the desk, as if miming to a recording. Picture frame, blotter, letter opener, pen set, paperweight.

Roets shrugged his shoulders by way of reply and glanced down at the pistol in his fist. Evidently, it bolstered his chronic sense of inferiority. Paperweight. Some rough-shaped rock that sparkled like fool's gold mounted on a small black base. It was beside the sullen, unsmiling girl's photograph. He would have to rise quickly and snatch it up in the same moment and—

Siren. Roets' smile confirmed it.

"Must be the taxi you ordered, *Mr.* Anderson." He laughed.

Concentrate . . . let him wind down from that little pitch first . . . concentrate. He would have to snatch it up, rise, throw. Roets was seated ten feet away. He couldn't miss. Veronica Mokesi's file watched him from the drawer and he felt prodded by the success of finding it, by the prospect of van Vuuren—

Siren louder now, descending through the scale like a recorded voice slowed down. Roets was still sweating. Rise and throw, rise and—

He threw the heavy paperweight at Roets, who ducked instinctively, and quickly for a big man, but whose bulk toppled the chair on which he was perched. He went down on one knee and remained there long enough for Anderson to rush from behind the desk, and kick out at Roets' head, catching the man on the temple with the toe of his heavy boot. Then he kicked again, more deliberately, his left foot clamped down on Roets' wrist so that the fingers loosened around the handle of the pistol. Roets' eyes whitened and his head flopped sideways. Anderson picked up the pistol and hesitated only for a moment. The file. He snatched it out of the drawer, clasping it tightly against his chest. A keepsake for van Vuuren.

Outside, the siren's note dwindled into silence. They'd use the lift, too, but they might block the stairs at the bottom. He caught sight of himself in the glass of the girl's framed photograph. White enough, clean enough. Walk with confidence, go with God. He smiled at Roets' unconscious chins and white eyeballs.

Then he hurried from the office, clutching the file, the pistol left harmlessly on the desk beside the framed picture.

"Yes, it's him all right. I'm not likely to mistake *him*, am I?"

Hyde's voice was masked and small, as if he were

whispering. The shock of his identification of Andrew
Babbington arriving in Venice failed to strike with any
clarity; it was distant and diminished like the effect of
the international telephone call. Aubrey continued to
stare at the most recent clutter around his feet, holding
the crystal tumbler and its second small whisky in his
right hand, the receiver feebly against his cheek.
Babbington, after all these years, was fixed in the past,
in embalming fluid, his image cold. Aubrey rubbed his
temple meditatively with the tumbler, at a loss really,
for any response. Darren Westfield's gloom seemed real
enough, but it might have been politeness and nothing
more. After all, there was no proof that Novak's connection was as sinister as Aubrey conceived it to be.
There was only circumstantial evidence, littered around
his chair. Mrs. Grey had retired to bed, her glance
reproving him for depriving young Westfield of his
sleep, *growing boy and all that*, he supposed. The sup-
per she had prepared had been substantial, on
Westfield's behalf.

"You don't seem very interested," Hyde remarked.
"I'm in this shitty little airport, wearing overalls and
trying to look like an Italian, and I see Babbington get
out of a Russian jet, and you're not gloating—sir." He
paused, then added: "They're all here for the divvy
up."

"What? Oh, apparently so," Aubrey murmured.
Circumstantial evidence. Giles Pyott's late-evening help
and curiosity over the telephone had only added to the
weight of Aubrey's intuition, not to the evidence. "Er—
well done, Patrick. Priabin is there, too, you say?"

"Three cars, out on the tarmac. Still sitting there.
Tinted windows, full security cover. The gang's all
here."

*It proved impossible to keep tabs on such stock-
piles, Kenneth*, Pyott had said. *In the end, we had to
take the word of Czech ministers, Russian assurances,*

Polish promises . . . you know the form. We never had any real figures, any real idea of the scale of the problem. If they say they've destroyed such and such a warhead or launch vehicle, we accept their word. No, Kenneth. There were factory inspections, records, of course. Whether they were accurate, who would know?

Pyott had, at long last, learned to refrain from questions of his own, however intrigued he might be. Aubrey had dismissed the possibility of such inquiries airily. *Bee in my bonnet—not important. Good night, Giles.*

But the bee had become a little swarm of anxieties and forebodings. He all but glared at Westfield, seated on the sofa, eating the last of the sandwiches Mrs. Grey had prepared for him, a glass of beer on the occasional table beside him. He knitted his brow defensively, even helpfully.

"I—something *else* has come up, Patrick. Something that might be—more difficult, dangerous perhaps. Something that is of concern to us, of *intrinsic* interest."

"What?" Hyde replied after a moment's silence. "Will you want me to tail Babbington?"

"Probably. Why? Are they leaving?"

"Not yet. He must be having his papers inspected out there. Customs van—the Fat Controller's put his top hat on for this. What's wrong?"

"Something has to be established—Novak's motive for attending the Exposition."

"Collecting his fee—supervising for Babbington? Who knows? Does it matter, except that it ties people neatly together?"

"It may well do. It's a matter of the companies— are they moving yet?"

"No. Get on with it though."

"Novak's companies, those with which he has a

recent and significant connection—among them are an arms manufacturing company and one of those nasty little businesses that produced nerve agents for the Warsaw Pact, back in the Dark Ages. I—"

"And you think . . . why? Who to?"

"Malan. South Africa. Even van Vuuren? The Middle East, Third World countries—I don't know, Patrick. In this case, possibly the far Right in South Africa. The white Right. Van Vuuren is a Bond member, has AWB associations—"

"Van Vuuren isn't here."

"But scheduled to arrive tomorrow."

"I can't swallow that lot."

"Then help me to dismiss my fears. The possible scenario is worst case. Nerve gas and arms supplied to the supremacists who loath the de Villiers government, the new constitution, Mandela—everything. Find out whether Novak brought anything with him apart from a change of clothing, Patrick. Indulge me—put my mind at rest."

Was it ridiculous? He looked down at the carpet. In the subdued lighting, the scanty evidence seemed insignificant. Or perhaps through the mellowness of two malt whiskies! Was there a heart of darkness here, something obscene, or was there merely the matter of KGB penetration of the Reid Group?

"That's what you want?" Hyde persisted. "You want me to concentrate on Novak—not Babbington or Davies or anyone else, just Novak?"

"For the moment, yes," Aubrey replied heavily. "I can't ignore it, Patrick! If there is anything, anything at all, to my fears, then it is that which must be stopped. At any cost."

"OK, you're the boss. I—wait, they're moving!"

Hyde slapped the receiver back onto its rest and skittered through the few remaining passengers near the luggage carousel. There'd been no familiar faces among the passengers. Babbington had come alone. Hyde thrust open the doors and the warmth of the night created immediate perspiration, wrapping itself around his face like a heavy towel. He hesistated in the shadows of the terminal building as the procession of three black limousines moved slowly past, their passengers invisible behind tinted glass. As they headed for the airport exit, Hyde ran to the hired car. If they were driving, then they weren't going directly into Venice.

They could be, he corrected himself, dragging open the door of the small Mercedes and thrusting the key into the ignition; the windshield fogged up with his excitement. Trust Aubrey to spoil that! Babbington arrives, tying the whole bundle into a lovely prezzie, and the old fart is dreaming about bloody nerve gas!

He reversed out of the parked line of cars, heaved the wheel round, then headed for the airport exit and the main road to Mestre and Marghera. There was little traffic, the occasional headlights bumping and swerving toward him in the other lane, the taillights of the three-limousine convoy nearing slowly, then settling as he maintained a steady distance behind them, then dropped back, then moved closer, dropped back again. One other car's headlights splashed on the road behind him. Out on the lagoon, Venice burned like a small, hilly island whose vegetation had caught fire in dry weather. Old fart . . .

They were all here, that was the point, surely? Even Babbington in his excited greed couldn't wait to open the parcels, he had to come and look for himself! And Davies and Malan and van Vuuren would be on their way. It was exactly as the old man had predicted, as Godwin had guessed. It was happening, like the movements of a precise, predictable mechanism. All he had had to do was to link them together and find, among the warehouses, the evidence, the proof, and stuff the bloody lot of them. Now, Aubrey was talking about nerve gas and the white nuts with the Nazi-style symbols and salutes in South Africa, for Christ's sake!

He slowed once more, dropping back from the convoy, which was moving at no more than fifty. Slow, bright ships moved across the lagoon. Nerve gas, arms? Novak was there on a jolly, had to be.

The cars turned north toward Mestre. Must be the Exposition site. He couldn't believe Babbington would be staying in a seedy, second-rate hotel in Mestre—not his bloody style, that. If they were heading for the Piazzale Roma, across the causeway, they'd have turned left. He slipped behind an old Fiat as he turned north. Babbington wouldn't have to worry about being spotted now. It wasn't risky to come out of the Centre and swan around Europe any longer, was it?

Mestre's grubby suburbs, the rubbish dump behind the gleaming billboard of La Serenissima. There was a rubbish dump, too . . . landfills they call them now. A parked bulldozer, some gulls still scratching and hovering and no doubt efficiently opening plastic rubbish bags in the dark. The town center glowed ahead. Then the little convoy turned left, toward the Exposition site. Hyde slowed and followed.

The occasional gleam of light from a gated villa, patches of poor housing, the twists of new roads and their pale concrete verges in the headlights. The warm air hurried into the car through the open window, Mestre glowing off to the right like something irradiated. Aubrey had no idea what he was talking about. The convoy turned again. The Exposition site, for certain. Dark trees dimly throwing back the headlights of the Mercedes. Aubrey *could* sense things while he sat in his drawing room, reading philosophy or Dickens. But, this?

But they had committed atrocities, the AWB. And there were other insects under the stones nastier than he was, now that the government and Mandela were holding hands.

Lights glaring from around a swimming pool, people cavorting and the snatch of loud Muzak. Then the car was past the open gates of the garish villa and the road ran through a few new stunted trees, before the darkness opened out. The low, hangarlike buildings of the exhibition center—the site of VIATE—were visible as they huddled against the big, warm stars. The convoy of limousines passed between two of the exhibition halls, nipped through an open red-and-white barrier, and made toward the warehousing complex. Hyde was aware of the quiet beyond the engine, and switched off his headlights after turning the car at right angles.

Gradually, night sight. The stars burnished, the sky was no longer black but glowing and patchily dark. A few loose, high clouds stretched thin as extinct striplights. He listened to the slow retreat of the three limousines, then the sudden silencing of their engines. A moment later, the slamming of a door. He could walk from where he was, the Mercedes slouched against the side of one of the smaller halls. The warehouse complex was a couple of hundred yards beyond it.

Voices from a group of people, men and women, crossing the concrete toward the exhibitors' parking lot. The noises of other cars, the slitted glow of lights from the halls containing the Exposition. Godwin would probably still be in there somewhere, winkling out facts like a chimp extracting termites from a nest with a thin reed. Hyde tossed his head, then wondered what Godwin would make of Aubrey's cloudy fantasy of nerve gas and arms to Terreblanche and the rest of the lunatics. He slipped along the side of the hall until he reached the angle of the building. There was a sliver of moon, low down, but the concrete was pale and betraying. He could see the tail lights of the three cars, drawn up neat as docked ships, near one of the warehouses. Warehouse 14. A row of parked vans, various emblems on their flanks, two forklifts. A small huddle of figures around the limousines, near where light spilled extravagantly from the open door of the building. Hyde raised the nightsight binoculars to his eyes and waited for the starlight to accumulate and the shifting curtains of gray and white to solidify into distinct ghosts.

Eventually, Babbington, Priabin and the smaller figure of the woman. The heavies—including those who had pursued him through the *calles* and *campos*— disposed themselves according to instinct or training or orders from Priabin . . .

. . . who was talking to—what a load of balls Aubrey was talking! There he was, shaking hands with Babbington, hardly nervous at all, dear heart. Davies. Michael bloody Davies. One of us, is he, you old fart? One of theirs. Forget nerve gas, he had Davies shaking hands with Andrew Babbington, and that would do as the underpinning for a successful operation. And Warehouse 14, which had nothing to do with the Reid Group or Reid Davies. Warehouse 14, and fucking Davies shaking hands with Babbington. Oh, you beaut.

The twisting, tree-shadowed street was quiet and deserted, except for one old lady walking a toy dog which seemed more arthritic and reluctant than she herself was. A bowed, slow figure moving through an element she remained certain of; not even the paving slabs were irregular or in need of repair here. Anderson jolted the car over another speed bump—perhaps they might even begin calling them sleeping policemen here, soon? He smiled away an onset of nerves, then slowed the car on the opposite side of the street from a house well set back behind a high hedge and drooping trees, its security light shining through slowly swaying branches. Van Vuuren's residence. One in the morning.

He backed the car quietly until he could see, through the wrought-iron high gate, that there were no interior lights still on. He listened. No noise or pad or snuffle of the dog. Was it inside, too? Had to be. He switched off the engine and the headlights as the silence settled lightly around him.

The night was cool, the large stars seeming close against the fly-speckled windshield. Big cars or fun cars drawn up in long drives or under carports. The occasional noise of dogs, the blurt of a cat across the silent street. The security firm's patrols were lax, and they still looked for black faces in old and garish cars. Lack of imagination assisted him, a white man. Just as it had as he had entered the foyer from the second floor stairs and passed the two policemen with a friendly nod and a slightly quizzical glance on his way out of the office building. By now, they might have related his departure to Roets' description, but it mattered little. Stories of revenge and a need of cash would be all too convincing to Bright, who they would have awoken by now. Seaward would be unwakeable before nine or ten in the morning, and unfocused before noon. Veronica Mokesi's file, in the boot of the car, would not be missed for a week, if ever.

Now, van Vuuren.

He got out of the car and crossed the street with studied casualness, touched the wrought-iron gate near a spider's web, then pushed it open, hesitating at the slow creak and waiting for the dog. After ten seconds, still nothing. As he walked up the flagged path beside the gravel drive, he could see the tiny shapes of moths and insects in the halo of the security light. The lawn was dark under the stars.

His fingertips tingled and his heart raced. He felt elated amid the wealthy normality of the street and the suburb. As he neared the house, the knoll from which he had watched the barbecue vanished. Then he was in the light and the insects circled him. The camera stared like a cyclops. He listened once more for the dog, but there was only silence. He stood on the single step, within the porch's arch, and pressed the bell.

Dog, loud enough to be outside, and he jolted back from the door before realizing it was barking inside the house. The smell of the watered lawn seemed fresher in his relief. A light had flicked on in the inner porch as he had rung the bell, and he looked up at the camera, knowing his expression would be distortedly benign, even respectful.

Van Vuuren's harsh voice.

"What is it, man? It's bloody one in the morning!" The dog continued to bark. "Shut up, you bloody dog!" van Vuuren shouted. A murmur that was more distant, presumably the plump wife.

Anderson leant close to the entryphone.

"Mr. van Vuuren? I have the right house?" The Afrikaaner accent was understated but unmistakable. "I have a packet here for you from a Mr. Malan. You are Mr. Piet van Vuuren? This is the address on the package."

"Yes, I'm van Vuuren. From *Paulus* Malan?" There was the soft grunt of someone bending to put on slippers or struggling into a dressing gown. So much the better, in pajamas or dressing gown, for what was to come. "Who are you? I don't recognize you."

"Secure Messenger Service, Mr. van Vuuren."

"Why didn't he use *our* people?"

"I'm sorry, Mr. van Vuuren, I don't understand. The office gave me this package to deliver here—is there a mistake or something? I only do as I'm—"

"Yes, yes!" van Vuuren snapped. "Wait a moment."

A form beyond the leaded glass, illuminated from behind, the dog's shape padding toward it. Anderson tensed involuntarily as van Vuuren's squat shadow enlarged and then shrank again as he reached the door. The noise of bolts being drawn, a secure lock being turned by a key. The dog's snuffling excitement around van Vuuren's legs. The door opened on a safety chain and van Vuuren peered blearily out without his spectacles. The Rottweiler's snout thrust through the gap at knee height.

"What package, man? It's one in the morning—you only work at night, or something?"

"I was told it was urgent, Mr. van Vuuren. The office told me to collect it—"

"Yes, yes! Do I sign for it?"

He was holding the Jiffybag out of reach of van Vuuren's first, exploratory grasp. The dog nudged at his wrist and, in his irritation, van Vuuren loosened the chain and snapped at the animal, which slunk away with a quiet, sullen whine. The door opened wide—

—as van Vuuren's bleary eyes cleared and focused on the pistol that Anderson thrust into his flinching, rotund stomach.

"Step through the door, Mr. van Vuuren—*quietly*," Anderson whispered. "At once."

Van Vuuren gargled: "What do you want, man? Who are you?" The pale, stunned face was as empty as a moon.

"It doesn't matter. You'll learn everything in time. This way, Mr. van Vuuren—please."

For a moment—just a moment—van Vuuren hesitated, his bulk almost protected by the door, his hand still gripping its edge. But the pistol was still thrust into his stomach so that he slumped into a smaller, deflated shape and came through the door. His stomach gingerly inhaled against the pressure of the gun as his hands flapped loosely above his shoulders. Only his eyes glared and resisted.

"Who the fuck are *you*, man?" he snarled.

"Nemesis." He was pleased at the portentousness

of his tone. "Richard Anderson—do you know the name?" He slipped behind van Vuuren, closed the door softly, and prodded the man forward with the gun. Van Vuuren flinched to one side, then steadied himself, hands still raised. "I think you'd better appear a little more casual. Hands down." They reached the gate. "That's my car over there. Please get in and drive where I tell you." Amusingly, he saw van Vuuren glance down at his soft leather slippers, then up again. "It will be all right. It's not far."

"What do you want, man? Money? What?"

Anderson shook his head. "Something more precious: information. Don't shake your head. You don't want to be the first, do you? Even before Blantyre?"

He pushed van Vuuren into the driving seat, then rounded the car and got in. The dog had begun barking again inside the house and lights had gone on upstairs.

"Who are you—*what* are you, man?" van Vuuren demanded, perspiring freely.

"Your jailer. Your interrogator." He grinned and handed van Vuuren the ignition key. "Start it and let's go. As we travel, I'll tell you about my wife's murder, shall I? I remember it—vividly." He nudged van Vuuren in the ribs, and the car jerked away from the curb, almost stalling. "Very vividly," he sighed.

Hyde all but slopped coffee from the plastic cup as he spread his hands.

"Babbington was taken to this villa, behind cypresses and high gates, on the Padua road, north of Mestre. Davies went with him, they must have had half a bottle of something, then Davies was driven back to the Piazzale Roma and caught a late water taxi back to the Gritti Palace. That's it. That's what they did, after they'd obviously gloated over whatever was in Warehouse 14." He shrugged again. "Now you know why *you're* not allowed to talk to the important customers—it isn't your image, it's Davies. He's up to here in it."

"Then I'd better tell the old man, hadn't I?" Godwin asked.

They were seated behind a fold of the washed-gray screen of the Reid Davies stand in the main hall of the Exposition. Hyde regarded his business suit with suspicion, while Godwin seemed about to erupt from his, the waistcoat riding up over his stomach as he slouched on his chair. The hall's constant noise of air-conditioning, talk, laughter, intruded.

Hyde scratched his nose. "What about this bloody nerve gas scare?" he asked. "The old fart sounds more and more like *The Sun* every day." He grinned. "*Our boys go in—and cover themselves with sores.* I can see the headline now in the Brighter, Bonkaway JIC Digest." He shrugged. "I don't see that, do you?"

A tall blonde whisked past them, draped as elegantly and efficiently as a matador's cloak in front of two French businessmen heading for the upper level of the stand and the champagne. It was ten-thirty in the morning. Hyde squinted after them, then shook his head.

"I don't suppose temporary, forced-on-him staff get privileges, do they?" he inquired of the plastic cup. "Unfair, really, having her first, when we're going to stuff him, wouldn't you say?"

"Am I to tell the old man, or not?"

"Why bother at the moment? I'm going to have a look in Warehouse 14, just to make sure. Then we'll tell Aubrey his nerve-gas scare is just that. OK?"

"What if Davies wants to know where you are?"

"Tell him you saw me wandering off with one of the tarts on the Yamaha stand. He'll like that. It'll suitably demean me and convince him. Not that I wouldn't mind . . . " He finished his coffee. "Anything else you want me to look at?"

Godwin shook his head. "There's a lot of warehouse space—much too much, if what they're supposed to be showing is anything to go by." Godwin flicked through a notebook. "You can have a go at some of this stuff if you come up empty." He grinned, looking up again, then added: "I don't like the old man's dark hints about nerve gas and this bugger Novak, though. I can't discount it as easily as you do."

"All right, then, *you* watch Novak. You suck up to Aubrey while I solve the mystery. I don't really care."

"You obviously didn't get much sleep last night."

"You know me so well, darling."

"Not that well!"

"Watch out," Hyde cautioned, still smiling as he squinted through a gap in the folded screen. "Here's Sonny Jim with a gang of Japs, waving his hands about. I'll fuck off before he sees me."

"OK. See you. Have a nice day."

"Do your tie up. Anyone would think you weren't a proper salesman!"

Hyde smiled, then slipped behind the screen, out into the main hall, a structured, designed maze of stands and exhibits. Huge computer mockups in plastics or polystyrene, the subtle gaudiness of every known and many unknown electronics companies in the consuming world. Hostesses and salespersons glinting and winking like silver fish in a great pool. The ubiquitous business suits cramming the aisles. The smell of used electricity sharp as saltpeter. The assault of noise.

Everything faded in the stark Venetian sunlight outside the hall. The lagoon shone like a mirror along the horizon and the churches of Venice nudged incompletely, sketchlike through the midmorning haze. The interior of the Mercedes was hot, plastic-scented. He threw his jacket into the rear and undid his tie. A group of businessmen emerged from a long black limousine outside the hall and patted and laughed each other inside.

Warehouse 14, then. Hyde rubbed his face. Davies, eh? He allowed the thought to repeat itself for perhaps the fiftieth time, and bring the same smile to his face. Gotcha. Davies must have been caught in the same expansive, ruble-filled net that had caught Reid Group and Dumas. Just another fish hauled up. No wonder the Russians had a hard currency problem and a supply of some of the best high-tech in the West. He ran his left hand through his hair. Snapping Davies like a stick would be fun.

He started the engine, pausing for a moment at a thought of Richard Anderson. Not much left for *him,* was there? He put the car into gear and pulled away from the illusory shadow of the main hall out into the glaring sunlight. A coach from the Piazzale Roma decanted thirty or forty suited men and women into the sun's blows. Hyde watched the rituals of laughter and back-patting and initial salesmanship in the driver's mirror. And, almost in the moment they disappeared, the warehouse was ahead of him. He drew against the side of the hall where he had masked the car the previous night, got out and opened the trunk. Quickly he tugged overalls up over his trousers, snapping the clips on his chest, throwing his tie into the well of the trunk, then changing his shoes for rubber-soled boots. He collected the loose, oily-looking workman's tool bag which contained the camera and the spare film and the pistol, and strolled across the aching sunlight. He slouched effectively. There were transport vans drawn up in front of the warehouse, and two men lounging in one of them. They disregarded his small-framed, overalled lack of threat. Jesus, I don't even need to get myself tattooed to complete the disguise.

A radio playing old hits, clear enough to make him skip to remembered lyrics and rhythm for a moment, the sunlight heavy on his shoulders. Then he was innocently round the angle of the building and hidden from

the men in the van. Shale, pebbles, weeds, cracked concrete, the occasional discarded beer or Coke can,
cigarette stubs. He continued to the next corner, and
found the ladder to the angled roof, complex enough in
slopes and gulleys to have belonged to a Gothic cathedral. Checking his isolation, he began to climb. The
building's steel was warm even on this shaded side, the
corrugated metal of the roof hot on his palms as he
grasped its edge. He looked down. No one. Venice
floated offshore like a gaudy, phantasmagorical oil
platform.

Skylights, oh, *sky*lights. He scuttled, his hands and
feet making crablike, bony noises on the corrugated
roof. He ran doubled up along a gulley, startling
pigeons into the air. Swallows moved like needles
weaving an intricate piece of embroidery close to the
roof, then up into the air, plucking out the thread.
Discarded cans indicated sunbathers. He looked at his
watch. Still not eleven. He imagined Godwin awkwardly explaining his absence, and grinned. Venice seemed
to have moved in the haze, like a great ship drifting
with the tide, the masts of churches, the foc'sles and
poops of palazzos and cathedrals and museums merg-
ing into one another. Beyond the city, the Lido was lost
in the sun's consumption of the water.

Skylight. He dropped to his haunches and peered
through the bird-specked, grimy glass. Any warehouse
on any new industrial park anywhere. Dusty, sunlit
concrete, the movement of a forklift, the drift of two
shirtsleeved men. He rubbed at the glass
gently his hand wetted with perspiration from his forehead. The sun was angrily heavy on his neck and back,
like an animal that had pounced only half in play.

He looked up again, not toward the illusory city,
but more immediately down at the acres of concrete
and other warehouses and exhibition halls. He was
invisible, except to the returning pigeons and the flick-

ing swallows. Good. He settled back and, using the binoculars through the smudge of half-cleared glass, glimpsed Reid Group on two of the crates down there, beneath the skylight.

He stood up, hardly curious, and saw Novak. Well, he sensed it was him and swung up the glasses and was certain. Getting out of a big BMW with two evident bodyguards from one of the very old schools. Novak, coming toward Warehouse 14.

His disappointment was momentary, but sharp as a child's, as Novak disappeared through the opened doorway of an adjacent, smaller warehouse, followed by the two bodyguards. The door closed behind them and the noise of it arrived a moment later, small as a touch. Hyde, hands on his hips knotted into fists, stared at the glinting BMW, at the closed door and the small warehouse and its low roof.

All in a day's work, but I don't—I really don't—believe there's nerve gas.

The aircraft seemed to wobble slightly, as if adjusting its livery to make the best impression when it landed at Marco Polo. Malan looked down, even as he picked up the telephone from beside his deep seat, and pushed aside the remains of his cooked breakfast. Venice, a city he found attractive for only the briefest stopovers, seemed to be slowly boiling in a silvery, saucepanlike lagoon, so that it threatened at any minute to disappear into the gleam and haze of light.

"Malan," he announced, picking a shred of bacon from between his teeth. "Yes?"

It was Blantyre. "Sorry, Paulus. It's van Vuuren."

"Yes?"

The city passed beneath the belly of the jet. Mestre's ugliness seemed less well concealed by the heat. Then he glimpsed the airport ahead and below.

"He—he's disappeared. Someone came to his house last night—a messenger that stupid wife of his claims—and van Vuuren went off with him."

"Someone who?"

"The wife saw a white man's face, she says, on the entryphone screen in the bedroom. Says she watched. Saw nothing, though."

"A white man?"

"I think it might be Anderson."

"What does he *want,* Robin?"

"To get even?"

"With whom, man? With MLC, for Christ's sake? Robin, you didn't do that well. He even killed Uys— don't ask how I know, I just know." The runway was distinguishable now, a narrow strip of concrete savored by the water on either side of it. The aircraft straightened, its nose down. Then it seemed to plunge at the airport.

"He wants blood, Paulus—or maybe information. He was connected with Aubrey."

"Twenty-five years ago!"

"Nevertheless, Piet knows everything. I would have said Anderson would have been looking for me, not Piet."

"You'd better find him, Robin. Quickly. Use all the influence you must, but find him."

He put down the receiver and stood up, to be assisted into his jacket by the black manservant. Then his seatbelt was deferentially fastened. He attempted to relax, but the moment in which the wheels encountered the runway was unsettling, as if a shiver of apprehension ran through the aircraft and his body. He clenched his right hand as the terminal building emerged from the oillike slide of deceleration. Anderson had van Vuuren. Why? For Aubrey?

He began to dismiss the idea, then remembered Aubrey's niece, Kathryn. *He* was blamed—

That bloody old man! He clung to things like his father clung to the last scraps of his life. Clung to memories and revenges. His hand continued to clench and unclench.

Anderson looked out of the grimy, cobwebbed window to the derelict forecourt, weed-strewn, and the listing, tired old petrol pumps that remained. The roof of the forecourt sagged wearily. The owner of the petrol station had abandoned the place two years before, heading for Australia and away from the dread of a black majority government. The forlorn, mistaken little site was on the edge of Diepkloof, where the suburb straggled away toward the great-backed mounds of spoil from the mines. A distant dam's white concrete gleamed in the noon haze. He swallowed Evian water from a big plastic bottle. Behind him, van Vuuren shuffled in his restraints, the legs of his upright chair squeaking on the linoleum that lay cracked and contoured on the floor. A rack still half-filled with nibbled, moldy paperbacks, a few empty shelves, the smell of disuse. Behind the one room was a tiny kitchen, but the water, electricity and gas had long been disconnected. It was a sad, meaningless place which slowed down, even stopped, the passage of time.

It was perfect.

"Do you want some water, Piet?" he asked, turning to face the man tied on the chair. Van Vuuren scowled silently, wrestling with the rope that held his hands behind him and his feet to the legs of the chair. His thin strands of remaining hair were awry, his pajama shirt open and sweat-stained—the heat in the place was suffocating.

He was nowhere near collapse. Concerned, yes, especially with regard to his interrupted business life, his trip to Europe. But not unnerved.

"Suit yourself. It's hot for the time of year, I think. Cooler in the Bush."

"Why don't you fucking well go back there, then?" van Vuuren raged, struggling with the ropes and moving the chair with small protesting squeaks. "Why did you come here, man? What do you want with me? Why don't you tell me what you want?" His reddened face glared.

"You want to talk?" Anderson asked.

He had left van Vuuren alone, gagged and immobilized, while he had driven to a supermarket in Diepkloof for supplies. He'd taken his time, then driven around. He had been silent for the most part while they were together. But van Vuuren seemed incapable of working through his outrage, his snatched-away comforts of large house, money, family, and arriving at isolation. It was as if Anderson was still the outsider, the not quite real; the kaffir presence that was little more than a shadow or a dream. Even now, he remained defiant, glancing at the window each time a car passed with certainty rather than with fearful, desperate hope. There was only the occasional car. A new highway had taken most of the traffic years before. Perhaps the garage owner hadn't left merely out of bigotry and fear, after all.

"You want to talk, Piet?" he repeated.

"Don't you fucking call me Piet, man!" he shouted back. "*Mister* van Vuuren to you!" His accent grated as he raged, straining against the ropes and his circumstances.

"OK, Piet. You don't want to talk. Not yet."

"*Mister* van Vuuren, you bastard!"

Anderson smiled and shook his head. "Mr. van Vuuren. You don't seem to think I'm in earnest. This"—he gestured at the decaying room—"isn't real to you, somehow. I assure you it is." His own accent was more deliberate, dismissively aloof. "We are safe

from discovery here, for a long time. I have supplies—
enough for myself for twice as long. If you wish to
drink and eat, you must learn the art of compromise."

"You English bastard—what do you *want?*" It was
the outrage of Afrikaanerdom, of membership of the
Broederbond, of sleek wealth and real power. This
could not, in Johannesburg, be happening to him; he
refused to believe it.

"Information," Anderson sighed. Van Vuuren
wasn't ready, but his own impatience prompted. He
dragged a chair opposite van Vuuren and straddled it,
leaning his forearms on its back, the bottle in one
hand. He stared at his prisoner. "Information that will
enable me to destroy Blantyre—pull the house down
around even Paulus Malan. I want to know about the
shipments and the KGB officer who died in the DC–3
and who owns what and what is being smuggled. *And*
why my wife was murdered." He watched van Vuuren
as he sipped at the bottle's narrow neck. Clicking his
tongue in satisfaction, he stared at the man once more.
"I am deadly serious, but you're beginning to sense
that, aren't you?"

"You think *you* can take us on—take on MLC—
and win?"

"I am"—he swallowed—"a man without a future,
van Vuuren." He spoke with soft, plausible menace.
The involuntary brightening of his eyes added its
penn'orth of conviction. "I am . . . bereft, lost. I don't
suppose you understand, do you, not with that plain
wife of yours and your habits of occasional congress
with good-looking blacks and coloreds?" He stood up
suddenly, as if his emotions were too betraying. Facing
the window, he said: "My wife was classified as colored, van Vuuren. Did you know that? Ironic, isn't it?
Having lost her, I have lost, as the poet said, the better
half of myself." He turned to face van Vuuren, the
light from the window behind him. "I have nothing

more to lose, and a single purpose. Justice, revenge—
you may use which term you prefer. And I will have
that justice." He was leaning over van Vuuren now. "I
doubt you've ever killed anything bigger than a gazelle,
van Vuuren. I have killed a lot of people. Recently, I
killed Blantyre's man in Swakopmund. Discovered it
could still be done, quite easily. Therefore, either you
assist me or I destroy you, and bury you behind this
shed, or throw you into one of the underground stor-
age tanks out there"—he gestured at the window—"or,
I don't. An alternative would be to allow the first kaf-
fir-dominated government to bring you to trial for rape
and assault." He turned his back quickly and moved
again to the window. "That would ruin you utterly. A
fate worse than death, surely?" He chuckled softly,
then listened, his back still to van Vuuren.

Eventually van Vuuren said, "I don't know what
you mean, man. You won't kill me."

"I might have to, if you're not afraid of disgrace."
He stared at the reddish earth lying like a range of low
hills in the haze. The Reef; the power. He turned. "You
really have forgotten, haven't you? Forgotten me and
forgotten Veronica Mokesi, too."

The girl's name evidently was forgotten. Van
Vuuren strained toward Anderson in the gloom of the
hut, which creaked softly in the sun, then shook his
head.

"You've got some grudge against me, man—why
didn't you say? I don't even remember you! Did I get
you the sack, you lose your pension rights, or something?"

"Nothing like that. Bright, Seaward, Seaward &
Anderson, solicitors to the powerful, white and
wealthy. You really don't remember?"

Slowly, van Vuuren shook his head, in disbelief
rather than at a failure of memory. Anderson sighed.

"The Englishman? The house Englishman in that

firm? *You?*" Van Vuuren could hardly believe it. "So, you're that bloke? So what? You've got a bill I haven't paid?" He laughed, but his voice was becoming more hoarse. Anderson offered the bottle and van Vuuren shook his head vehemently.

"Suit yourself. Now you remember me, do you recall Veronica?"

"Who? Is that your wife's name? Might have guessed you'd have married a kaffir girl. Yes, I remember Bright told me they kept you on as the firm's conscience. The respectable, liberal front man."

"You think I was unaware of that?"

"Doesn't matter. Your efforts weren't worth elephant dung, man—and you know it. You were just salving your English conscience."

"Agreed. It was wasted time. No, Veronica Mokesi was not the name of my wife. Veronica was one of your secretaries. She didn't work for you for long. Didn't enjoy the little attentions you paid her."

Van Vuuren's face was puzzled, and he frowned for memory like a child. When he did remember, his confidence seemed undiminished.

"I remember something." His smile was lascivious. "So what, man?" He shrugged in his restraints.

"So what? I have the files—from Bright, Seaward & Seaward, no less. Her statements to me, photographs which were taken at the time—she was very bruised. And your statement transcribed from a tape recording."

"What can you do with them?"

"Ruin you. Paulus Malan would be deeply embarrassed—MLC would be outraged. The boys in the Bond"—he smiled—"oh, dear, wouldn't they be upset. Mandela and the ANC would press for your arrest—a quid pro quo for dear Winnie's misbehavior and her sentence, hm?" Van Vuuren's eyes began to see, quite lucidly, the possible future. "At the least, your wife

would have to sue for a messy and public divorce.
Things have changed, Piet. You would be a cause
célèbre, as they say. A fate worse than death."

Van Vuuren shook his head. "You don't mean it."

"Oh, but I do. I assure you I do."

"Why?"

"Oh, you mean why should I care? I don't really. I
admit that. It serves my purpose. The ANC would care,
though, wouldn't they?"

Van Vuuren's mouth opened slightly, like a widen-
ing settlement crack in fresh plaster. The slow, inexorable collapse had, perhaps, begun. Then he shook his
head defiantly. "It would be hushed up, man. It would
still be hushed up."

"Perhaps." Anderson shrugged. Van Vuuren's
voice was very hoarse now, and he tilted the bottle
invitingly in the man's direction. A few drops of Evian
fell to the linoleum, disturbing foraging ants, who
returned to inspect the droplets. At Blantyre's insistence
or even that of Malan, the police would already be
scurrying like the ants, looking for him. "Perhaps."
Van Vuuren could not be disabused of belief in a rescu-
ing cavalry bugle which would sound at any moment.
"I shouldn't count on a burial other than your own—
unless you cooperate. The files are in my briefcase, on
the counter there." Van Vuuren's head swung quickly,
possessively. "You may take them with you when you
leave. If you give me what I want. If you don't, of
course, then you won't be leaving at all. I couldn't risk
my own safety by letting you survive, could I?"

Godwin sat in the rear of the taxi, behind the indifferent driver who lit another cigarette as soon as he
tugged on the hand brake and picked up his newspaper. The dust settled around the car. *English private
eye, huh? Divorce?* Godwin's nod had been sufficient

to still any vestigial curiosity. The cypresses and cedars were dark against the sky, reaching back from the high, closed gates toward the white stuccoed villa. The dark green shutters were opened back, and there was a glint of distant water from a high fountain.

The limousine had turned in, after the gates had opened electronically, taking Malan and Michael Davies inside. The dust was settling from the vehicle's passage along the ochre drive.

Godwin got out of the taxi and lumped himself to comfort on his crutches. Thus propped, he studied the gates, the dark stains of the trees and the large, elegant residence beyond them. In the distance and the midday haze, the Eugenean hills struggled to possess more substance than in a painting of themselves. The villa was on the Padua road, fifteen miles from Mestre. Hyde had suspected it might once have been a KGB R&R house. It might well have been. Certainly, Babbington was now inside, awaiting his lunch guests. Godwin rubbed his sheened forehead and pushed back his hair with a large hand. The traffic was light off the main highway to Padua and Verona. He'd followed Davies out of the exhibition hall, and recognized Paulus Malan. He grabbed the taxi—*follow that car*—and it had drawn him all the way out here, to the place Babbington had been brought the previous night.

Not that he was going to creep up to the house for his evidence. A photo opportunity beckoned whenever they left the villa again.

He reached back into the rear of the taxi with a smile of satisfaction and lifted out the cellular phone. *I've told you not to ring me while I'm at work,* Patrick would probably complain. Still, he shouldn't be in a position to be overheard talking. He dialed the number. No ringing out, just a flashing light. If he couldn't answer, he wouldn't. The tiny answering machine in the casing of the receiver would tape his message. *I'll get back to you.* Wonderful thing, science. He leaned against the trunk of a stringy-looking sycamore at the side of the road. There were other villas dotting the landscape, small as cattle in their neat grounds, behind their tiny fountains. Vineyards and orchards stretched away toward the bruise-colored hills to the west. He scented lemon on the slight, dust-sifting breeze. He stretched luxuriously. Naughty Mike Davies—shame, really. He quite liked the guy. Must have had some bad breaks, needed funds to save the company, photographed with another woman, a man . . . Whatever it was, Babbington and Malan had gotten their hooks into him. And Aubrey would have to decide what to do about it, not him, thank God. Come on, Patrick, check the light on your phone, you idiot. Aubrey could gut Davies like a haddock, get every shred of proof they needed. Now, it was just a matter of stopping whatever was in Warehouse 14 from going any further east or south. He leaned his cheek against his shoulder, the receiver trapped there, and rubbed his hands. Look at your light, you silly bugger or switch on the answering machine. Science might be wonderful, but Hyde's inattention to detail wasn't. Poor old Davies; it could be his last nice lunch for a long time. Perhaps the old man would fly out—

"Yes? Where the hell have you been, in the bog?"

"I'm on the roof of a fucking warehouse, watching our old Czech mate pissing about below me. Arrived with a couple of bodyguards half an hour ago."

"Where? Number 14?"

"No, next door. I wonder why?"

"I'm out at that villa. Davies is here with Malan."

"Tell Aubrey. He'll have apoplexy."

"Listen, I got our Italian friends to check on Novak's room, his reservation, tickets, et cetera."

"Yes?"

"He tried to get hold of van Vuuren—his home number, office, car phone, anything he could think of—more than two dozen times this morning. Must have got into a panic when he couldn't find him."

"Is van Vuuren on his way here?"

"Room's booked at the Cipriani, same as Malan. Expected today some time."

"That's all right, then."

"Novak wants van Vuuren but not Malan—he hasn't been near him."

"So?"

"I just wondered. Novak did have a call from Johannesburg, just before he left for the warehouse. It was Blantyre. What the message was no one knows. Blantyre and van Vuuren; makes you think, what with *another* warehouse being used. I wonder if Babbington knows?"

"Doesn't matter, does it?"

"I don't know, but you'd better find out what's in there. Perhaps there's something wrong with van Vuuren?"

"Maybe. Anderson was going after him. Perhaps the bugger got to him?"

"Just see what's in that warehouse, will you, that's so important to van Vuuren, Blantyre and Novak?"

"Don't give me the nerve gas story, please."

"It's a side deal, whatever it is. And there are people who'd like it on hand—even like to use it—in South Africa."

"All right, all right. You take some pictures and ring the old man. Find out when he wants us to lift Davies, what we do about Babbington—and Warehouse 14."

"OK. See you."

He switched off the phone and then stared at it. Time to call the old man, then. He wouldn't like it. Apoplexy was right. Poor old Davies; Aubrey's disapproval would make him squirm more than the thought of twenty years inside!

There was a moment, seated in van Vuuren's study, with the gazelle-skin rugs on the deep carpet and the kaffir bric-a-brac clinging to the paneled walls, when he realized that he detested van Vuuren. As well as most of their mutual associates in the Bond, even Paulus Malan. It was little more than a moment, but very real, like an indigestive pain. Then Robin Blantyre continued dialing the number of Novak's car phone, having failed to contact the Czech at his hotel. It was all slightly unclean. No, not that—it had been unclean for a long time. He had retreated south from Rhodesia to South Africa and had spent years in the South-West fighting SWAPO with the Defense Forces and the Selous Scouts. Even then, he felt his integrity had been soiled by others. It was nothing but the protection of profit, of gold and diamonds.

The phone rang in Novak's car.

Van Vuuren's wife had slipped through the study door like a black servant, leaving him alone. The police had been briefed, they had Anderson's picture to distribute, his own people were mining the man's background and raking over abandoned buildings. They knew what car to look for, who to look for. The rest was a matter of time. He would be run down, dug out and got rid of. Van Vuuren? It would depend, he thought, as he forensically examined the study and its whispers of money and self-satisfaction. Even Anderson had the right idea: the Bush was better than all this.

"Novak? Blantyre," he said when the phone in Novak's car was answered. He listened for a moment to the Czech's earlier nerves being regurgitated, a twist of contempt on his mouth. Then he said, "The money's there, man. No, van Vuuren's got stomach trouble, I

told you. He's been delayed. The plan goes ahead . . .
yes. *You* do what's necessary, man—do it. Yes,
tonight. Everything's arranged. *Then* I release the
funds, yes . . . "

He looked at the ceiling. It was a constant process
of corruption, backsliding, impropriety. Novak had a
villa in Majorca, he was renovating a palace in the
Czech countryside, he had the Swiss account. And, like
van Vuuren, it was always more that he wanted. Van
Vuuren's arrangement with Novak was bringing them
money—that was their shared motive. Fuck the
Republic, fuck South Africa and the white man, so
long as we have the money to get out!

It applied to Paulus, too, he reacknowledged as he
murmured to Novak: "Yes, that's right. Once the shipment touches down and I've inspected it, the authoriza-
tion will be sent to Zurich." Don't worry, you bastard,
you'll get the money.

Paulus, too. Cozying with the fucking Communists
and a traitor, Babbington—thinking about moving
MLC out of South Africa because he wouldn't stay and
fight for what he'd always believed.

"No!" he snapped at Novak. "You watch out for
Hyde, and for the cripple, Godwin. You've been sent
the photographs. Don't get near them, or let them near
you or the shipment. Other than that, Novak, I don't
give a fuck with a gazelle what you do or what happens to you. Yes, that's right. Just business. If this first
shipment's good, then there'll be new orders. Sure."

He put down the receiver and glanced around the
room. These white men who filled their places with
African rubbish. Did they think that made them
belong? Paulus and van Vuuren—running out, one way
or another. Not him, though—oh no, not him.

He almost admired Anderson, and his motive. You
killed my wife, I'll get back at you any way I can. It
was clean, comprehensible. It had nothing to do with

money, or traitors, or servants of the Crown like fucking Hyde, who he would like to meet again, just once more.

Mrs. van Vuuren sidled her face around the study door, as if she might be asking whether he would like tea or when he would be leaving. Blantyre stood up. Look at her, he thought, fat, white and forty-five. Needs a hairdo, some makeup, and she'd still be ugly as sin. No wonder van Vuuren preferred the kaffir girls, the little shit.

"I'll be going now," he announced, passing her. "You've got my number if he calls. And"—he turned, looming over her—"if he calls, make sure you tell me. Understand, Mrs. van Vuuren?" The woman nodded dumbly, terrified by his bulk in her hall, reflected from the polished mahogany floor.

Blantyre went outside, squinting in the noon sun. When and if van Vuuren called, then it would be neater, tidier, if he died. Anderson could be blamed. A sudden and only half-expected rage of contempt for his acquaintances rose into his chest. They rocked the secure cradle of his world more violently than the ANC and Mandela and the de Villiers government had ever been able to do. Bastards.

He'd find Anderson and van Vuuren and kill them both.

12

STRIKE ON THE
TINDER

"Yes, Westfield and I will be with you by late afternoon...yes, yes. No, I'll use our Italian friends when it becomes necessary. You say there's no sense of immediate removal of the goods from either warehouse?"

Godwin squinted in the afternoon sun, toward orchards, vineyards and olive groves stretching away in distant hills.

"No, sir, I don't think so."

"Then Patrick has time to make a closer inspection, if he can gain ingress to the target area. Is that possible?"

"He thinks he can get in from the roof."

"Then let him do so. In safety. For yourself, I see no real necessity for photographs of anyone except Davies, so you'd better hang on there in the hope of obtaining something picturesque and incriminating. Then you may detain him. At least restrict his movements until I have a chance to confront him. That other warehouse, by the way . . . "

"Patrick's still sniffy about the nerve agent scenario."

"Naturally. I wonder if Michael Davies can help us there?" There was a pause. "I would not have believed it of him."

Godwin grinned. Nothing like righteous indignation. Davies was up shit creek. The old man's wrath and technique would fall on him like a ton of bricks. "No, sir. He might have got stuck in the mud like Reid himself."

"Perhaps, perhaps."

"Are we rounding them all up, sir? Making a big splash?"

"I, the Cabinet Secretary and—other informed opinion would prefer not. Arrest whom we must, but quietly."

"There's a bloody warehouse full of high-tech, sir. It'll take more than a Ford Transit—"

"I have a thought regarding that aspect of the matter. It would be better if it—disappeared. *Not* east or south, of course. I'll consider. Where is Priabin?"

Godwin looked at the tall gates. Priabin had gotten out of a small, hired Alfa half an hour earlier, bent toward the entryphone, grinned up into its lens, and the gates had been opened for him. The woman had been driving the car.

"He's here, too. Nice lunch laid on, I expect."

"But there is no sign that matters might be coming to an immediate head—*no* sign?"

"No, sir. I'd say tomorrow."

"Priabin must have been *running* Davies!" Aubrey suddenly burst out. "Clever young man!"

"Aren't they all, sir? But we've got them by the short and curlies now."

"Tell Patrick that the warehouses are of the utmost importance. And tell him to be *certain* what they contain. *Each* of them."

"Worried it's going too smoothly, sir?"

"Perhaps. Ah, the car is here. Maintain contact. But get hold of Davies as soon as he is separated from his friends."

The receiver purred and Godwin hung up, letting it dangle from his wrist by its cord. Hyde was certainly going to *love* his afternoon on a hot tin roof.

Distantly, Venice floated in the haze and glitter of the Lagoon. Mestre sprawled, its thrown-together ugliness softened by the heat. The Lido lay like a sandbank across the steel-colored water. Godwin brought a plastic packet containing cheese sandwiches from his pocket, ripped its plastic covering and began eating. The taxi driver had had wine, salami and thick, crusty bread—without offering him any.

It'd be better if they burned the bloody warehouses down—not if there's nerve gas though. Patrick had better check the sprinkler system, if there is one. Chewing on the indigestible, soapy bread—did the Italians import British white sliced for these bloody sandwiches?—he dialed Hyde's cellular phone.

"Keep down!" Anderson whispered fiercely as van Vuuren struggled in his grip like a frightened cat, his eyes bulging and his lips attempting to form a shout behind the gag. He drew the pistol and pressed it against van Vuuren's temple, and the man's efforts subsided into still resentment, a lassitude of desperation. "That's better."

He raised his head and looked over the grass-clumped sandy knoll, back down toward the abandoned petrol station. The police car had passed, then slowed and turned on the dusty road, heading back toward them. He had stifled van Vuuren's first attempt to cry out, gagged him, released his legs and dragged him out of the rear door and up the slight rise behind the hut. Their footprints were as big as those of some huge, maddened animal in the soft sand. If the two policemen—one of them was still in the patrol car—searched for signs, they'd find their tracks at once.

Van Vuuren squirmed beside him, belly down on the sand. Anderson pressed the barrel of the pistol harder against his sweating temple. Quietude almost at once, except for the shiver of fear that trembled through the man's body. The policeman peered through the cracked, grimy windows, then pulled open the door. He paused on the step—Anderson could just see him, around the edge of the long hut. The supplies he had bought were in the kitchen behind the main room, the empty Evian bottles lay on the floor. There was the chair . . .

The policeman disappeared, then almost at once reappeared around the corner of the building, his cap pushed back on his head, his stride unsuspicious, unhurried. He glanced up at the knoll, shading his eyes for a moment, then turned on his heel and headed back to the patrol car, drawn up under the dappling shade of the forecourt's decaying roof. He shook his head as he climbed back into the car.

Anderson's relief as the car pulled out into the road was a cattle prod to van Vuuren, who rose to his knees and bullied Anderson aside. He toppled himself over the lip of the incline, rolling before getting to his feet and beginning to run, his head flailing from side to side and his legs floundering, as if they were waving to attract attention because his arms were still tied behind his back. He raised the pistol, then realized the futility of the noise and the risk of killing van Vuuren. Instead, he tumbled after him, leaping on the man's back and dragging him flat. Sand was in his eyes and mouth as he looked up. Blinking away wetness, he saw the police car begin to hurry away down the road toward Diepkloof. He was breathing violently as he rolled off the man and lay facing him, the pistol aimed at van Vuuren's face. The eyes died as if some light had been switched off behind them.

Now, Anderson told himself, now, while he's deflated, feels his last chance has gone. He stood up, dragging van Vuuren to his knees by gripping his pajama collar; he then dragged him by one bound arm toward the lee of the building, thrusting him inside as if throwing the man away like a sack of rubbish. He slammed the rear door behind them, pushing van Vuuren ahead of him into the main room and onto the chair. The violence of his breathing was an added terror to the South African as he was tied to the chair. Anderson stood back, making sure the pistol was in plain sight as he deliberately opened another bottle of water and swallowed greedily, then used more of it to wash the sand from his face and eyes. Van Vuuren watched with impotent malevolence, as Anderson poured some onto the floor, then shouted: "Listen to me, you Afrikaaner *shit!*" His body was bent toward van Vuuren, the pistol waggling beside his thigh, as if it might accidently fire at any moment, discharged by the force of his rage. "Listen to me! I want to know things, and I want to know them *now*. Understand? Either you start telling me, or I won't wait to ruin you the legitimate way. You'll be reading about your divorce from your wheelchair! Understand me van Vuuren?" He moved closer in a quick, pouncing step. "*Understand?*"

Van Vuuren was terrified, as if he believed Anderson insane. His eyes flicked from the pistol to his face, to the pistol. He tried to swallow, even attempted to speak, but only hoarse, tired gobbling noises came from behind the gag—

—which Anderson roughly removed. There were no words, even then, only louder scrapings and swallowings. Hefting the Evian bottle from the counter, he tilted it to van Vuuren's lips and the man swallowed greedily; then Anderson snatched it away.

Narrow hatred flared in van Vuuren's eyes. "What do you *want?*" he wailed hoarsely. "Why are you doing this to me, you bastard?" Veins stood out on his temples, and the cords of his neck were drawn taut.

Anderson realized he must possess the appearance of some malevolent ghost, and employed even that to his advantage.

"I want *you!*" he bellowed, his own neck tightened, his temples throbbing. "If I can't bring down Malan, then I'll settle for you—and kill Blantyre from a distance some dark night!" He held up his hands in front of van Vuuren, palms inward. "See these fingernails? My partners always asked me to keep my hands out of sight whenever we had important clients! The KGB pulled the nails out in the cellars of the Lubyanka. They never grew straight or clean again!" Theatrically, he dipped his hand into the briefcase and pulled out a pair of pliers, still polyethylened onto their manufacturer's cardboard rectangle. "You'll be luckier, van Vuuren! Your hands are behind your back— you won't have to watch while I do it to you!"

He paused and drank from the bottle again. What had Aubrey wanted to know, precisely? It was, of course, difficult to recall everything he and Aubrey had discussed over the telephone, from that phone booth half a mile away toward Diepkloof. There was so much detail. How long, how much, by what means? It seemed to have very little to do with justice, with *his* satisfaction.

"I lost my first wife to lovers and finally to cancer. I lost my second to a faked atrocity meant to kill me! Do you think I give a fuck what happens to *you?*" He grinned, then took up the pliers and pulled away the polyethylene case. He held them up, then picked up the file on Veronica Mokesi, waving them both loosely in his fingers. "One or the other, van Vuuren. Of course, choose the wrong one and you won't even be able to hold the other when I hand it over, will you?"

Aubrey had said it was urgent. There was something he could hardly bring himself to speak of. Nerve gas. For van Vuuren's friends? Whoever they were— the boys in the Bond, the AWB. Yes, he had replied, they'd like the insurance of something like nerve gas. They'd like to wear a VX canister slung under their pot bellies instead of a mere pistol. Oh, yes . . .

All the moments he was silent, he stared at the ceiling, dragging in large, threatening, unstable breaths. Then he looked down at his prisoner.

"See? Who cares, van Vuuren? I can do it. I've killed men with guns, explosives, booby traps, piano wire—anything I could lay my hands on." He snorted. "Who's the nerve gas for?"

It was true, he realized, in the betraying instant before van Vuuren shook his head. "I don't know what you mean!"

He laid down the file and kept the pliers very visible, as he said, "But we know that's a lie, don't we? How can you convince me you're telling the truth?" He made a dart behind van Vuuren's back, the pliers extended and open in his right hand.

"No!"

He closed them firmly on the nail of the right forefinger.

"No—no!"

He leaned caressingly against van Vuuren's shoulder and cheek, like a lover. "Tell me, then . . . tell me," he whispered.

Van Vuuren's head dropped, shaking from side to side, but the denials meant nothing. "How did you know?"

He smoothed van Vuuren's hair and neck like a whore, then tilted the Evian bottle against the man's lips. Van Vuuren's frame shivered, like a frail dwelling in a violent storm. When he had finished drinking, he took the bottle away gently, then patted the man's shoulder.

Nerve agent. Last man in the *laager*. While ninety percent of white South Africans were either resigned, accepting or even optimistic, the other ten percent would do *anything* to change their world back to what it had been. Nerve gas, guns . . . it fitted.

"How—why did you get involved?" Anderson asked.

Van Vuuren stared at the floor.

"They're selling us down the river, man." He looked up, glaring. "Who could expect *you* to understand? This is *our* country, man!"

"Theirs, too."

Van Vuuren snarled: "Most of the kaffirs have been here less time than the English. You think—man, you really *think*—they'll play by the rules, once they get their hands on power? They're shooting each other in the townships because they're Zulu or non-Zulu right now! You think *we* would stand any chance?" He coughed, and Anderson nursed the bottle to his lips. Best to leave him to fulminate. He stepped back, and van Vuuren glared at him, straining forward against the rope.

"Man, you English are so bloody ignorant! Years now since they let that kaffir bastard Mandela out of prison, and there's more people dying every day— blacks!—than during the state of emergency. That's what you call progress, is it?" He shook his head in contempt. "You think we're all pig-ignorant Afrikaaners with rotten fucking accents, I know your kind! But we know, man. We know how it will be, people like me and Robin Blantyre and some of our politicians and businessmen. Unless the kaffirs can get their house in order, then we're not prepared to hand everything over to them, just like that! Whatever it takes, whatever we can get our hands on, we'll use— just like you English would if it was *your* bloody country!"

The silence that followed seemed endless, punctuated only by their mutually ragged breaths and the droning of some large insect up near the corrugated roof of the hut. Eventually, recalling Aubrey's conversation, Anderson said: "And this is where Novak comes into the picture, is it? You met him through EuroCon and you realized he had things you could make use of. At least hoard for a rainy day? Is that it?"

"You know a hell of a lot, Englishman." Van Vuuren was genuinely disorientated by the extent of his information.

"You think I'm entirely alone, van Vuuren?" He shook his head. "I sent some evidence from the crash to London. To people I know. It tied in with what they know. I said you'd be able to fill out the picture, in exchange for your life. So, nerve gas is the answer, is it? To *all* our problems?"

"You think we'd use it if we didn't have to?"

"I've no idea. It'll be stopped in Venice, anyway." Van Vuuren appeared dumbstruck. "Oh, yes, it's not coming here." Pray God. "It's dealt with. It's the penetration—extent, persons, purposes—that people want from you in exchange for your life. Get it now?"

Van Vuuren's features were charted with conflicting fear, doubt, contempt—and the overriding sense of being tricked.

"You don't know anything!" he snapped, straining forward, the rope across his chest imbedded in his flesh. "You're just piss-assing about, hoping to catch something on the end of the line!"

Anderson had no notion of how much bluff there was in his defiance. He said coldly: "You think I'm just an agent, do you, van Vuuren? The people in London—you think I'm restrained in some way, people to answer to, that kind of thing. Well, maybe I was once . . . " He had begun to circle van Vuuren's chair, not touching him, rather abstracted and diffident, if anything. But as regular and inexorable as the ticking of a clock toward an explosion. "I was something like you imagine—once, a long time ago . . . but you know that. I don't work for them now, haven't for years." Van Vuuren had sunk back on the chair, uneasy with the pedagogic tone. "It was pure accident—finding the wreckage. Maybe I sent them the stuff because of auld lang syne. But I'm here because I choose to be. Understand? I want to ruin Malan and Blantyre for what they did to *me*. To begin with, there is a great desire in me"—he turned to face van Vuuren, stopping in front of him, holding out the pliers once more—"to do it now. Your schemes, the ones you've admitted to, killed my wife, van Vuuren. There really isn't anything more to say, is there?" The gleam of his eyes was hardly pretended. It was true, he could strike out this moment, hurt and humiliate and revenge himself. "Why don't I have fun with you, for my wife's sake?"

Van Vuuren appeared to be listening. There was the hard, sharp intrusion of bird song for a moment from outside, and the mutter of a receding car. Almost half a minute later, another car. Anderson watched the plump, collapsed figure in the chair. More quietly, he said: "I have nothing more to lose. I am one of those desperate people usually encountered in fiction. I have nothing left, van Vuuren."

He did not even look at the man; rather he stared at the fly-specked ceiling and the still fan and grubby striplight; then at the abandoned, empty shelving and the greasy counter and rusty till. He could almost hear the termites in the structure. Another car passing outside, as if its noise was funneled from a great distance, then in the ensuing silence, the sift of sand against the planking of the walls. His throat was dry with talking, constricted with memory, and his eyes felt tight, squeezed. Margarethe was coming back, out of the tidy darkness at the back of his mind.

Looking down, having blinked his eyes wide, he murmured: "You see, van Vuuren, I'm everyone's fantasy of freedom of action. No consequences."

Then he moved swiftly, gritting his teeth as he passed behind van Vuuren, and gripped one of his fingers with the pliers, tugging at once at the nail, wincing against the scream as blood poured from the damaged hand. He let the freed nail drop from the grip of the pliers, themselves bloody at the bright tips, then clamped his hand over the open, screaming mouth, shuddering at what he had done. The cellars of the Lubyanka; he'd crossed more than a Rubicon. Then he remembered nerve gas and Veronica Mokesi and Margarethe. His stomach began to settle, and eventually van Vuuren's shudders lessened and there seemed to be no stifled noises vibrating against his wet palm. Then he released the man and moved to confront him, bending over him, the Evian bottle tilted against his lips. His dampened hand patting the man's flinching brow.

"Now?" he asked, eventually. "Without any more of it." He felt cold in the fetid air of the shedlike building, which smelt of rat-droppings and sand and van Vuuren's loosened bowels. He suppressed a shiver.

Van Vuuren was sobbing with pain and shock. And nodding, rhythmically as a pendulum, without thought. For the moment, he would do anything. It was time to disinfect and bandage the finger. The flies had deserted their sweating foreheads—they'd already have settled on the blood. Time to put the savage away until required, for Blantyre and Malan.

Now that van Vuuren would talk, he could feel a certain narrow sympathy for him. And relief, too.

* * *

Godwin slapped his insensitive thighs with his large hands, and glared at the camera he had thrown down on the rear seat beside him. Bloody waste of time! Bloody tinted windows that half-obscured Malan—and Davies traveling back on his own with that bloody woman Valentina! They already had pictures of those two cozying.

The taxi drifted in the settling dust behind the small Alfa which the woman was driving. Godwin looked at his watch again. Three-thirty. Hyde still on the roof, complaining about the heat and the delay—and the security that prevented him from going through a skylight and checking either warehouse. The old man had said Patrick could go in. He just couldn't *get* in, that was the trouble; too many people about.

Which meant Davies. The road straightened from its twists, and emerged from beneath ranks of oaks then dipped toward a Venice becalmed and glittering. Davies—he'd have him in straight away—might even be able to persuade him to cooperate, let them see inside at least one of the warehouses.

He sat back against the hot plastic, feeling his shirt stick to it and slide greasily as buttered paper around a baking tin. He grinned. He did feel hungry, in fact. Coffee and a piece of rich cake wouldn't go amiss. Davies could have room service bring some up while they discussed his immediate future.

The Alfa reached the causeway out to the city and the taxi followed, after Godwin waved the driver to proceed. His shrug was stereotypical. It was too hazy to make out the airport to the north from the Ponte della Liberta. The islands of Murano and San Michele were basking whales, without contour or feature. A train, pulling out of the city, passed them on the parallel railway bridge. Then they had reached the first *campanile* and *palazzo*, and modernity threatened to vanish until they reached the Piazzale Roma and the vast parking lots. The Alfa drifted away beneath a barrier as his driver pulled into the taxi rank. Godwin heaped bright Italian currency into his hand and got out of the hot interior into the humid afternoon. Davies wouldn't walk in this—he'd take a water taxi or even a gondola. He'd meet them there, save looking for the Alfa in that crowd.

However, he waited until he saw Davies, attentive to the Russian woman, perhaps overly so, leaving the parking lot, the jacket of his suit trailing over his shoulder. The woman seemed indifferent, even as if she were pretending not to be his companion. Godwin hobbled after them, obscured by a crowd that had emerged from coaches, down a narrow *calle* toward the landing stage. Presumably, Davies' efforts at ingratiation implied they were returning to the Gritti Palace—Davies was not described as monogamous in his file. The woman looked as if she wouldn't be spending the afternoon in his suite. Godwin hesitated. The *vaporetti* and the smaller *motoscafi* ran every ten minutes from the Piazzale Roma. He could afford to wait for the next one, whichever route they took. He waited, in the narrow entrance to the *calle,* behind the milling passengers.

Thought so . . . Davies was taking the *Accelerato* route along the Grand Canal—give the woman a sightseeing tour, soften her up, probably. If he took the *Diretto* route via the Rio Nuovo—no scenery—he'd reach San Marco before them, maybe even get as far as the Gritti Palace before they did.

He shuffled forward on his crutches as the *vaporetto* pulled away from the landing stage toward the first long bend of the Grand Canal. He reached the end of the queue, hot, but satisfied. Anticipating the shocked look on Davies' face—*who's been a naughty boy, then?*—as he opened the door of the suite. He touched the pistol in his pocket. Just in case. The *motoscafo* churned the languid gray water of the canal and bumped against the landing stage. Godwin shuffled behind a jabbering family—three children who communicated only in high-pitched screams—up the gangway onto the deck.

The tired dusty trees of the Gardino Papadopoli, then a stretch of dank, high houses before the single church until the Rio Foscari emptied them into the Grand Canal. The city eventually reassumed its weary beauty and much recorded face as he looked ahead from the stern of the *motoscafo* over heads and lenses. He saw Santa Maria della Salute like a mound of grubby snow in the haze and the *palazzos* that had become hotels lining the route toward the church.

Godwin disembarked at the San Marco landing stage and struggled through the heat and crowds past the artists and their daubs, and into the crowded narrow *calle* up to San Moise. Finally, he reached the rear entrance of the Gritti Palace, and the chance to lounge in brief shade as gratefully as one of the thin dogs or thinner cats. The crowds drifted past, most of them organized, some in smaller groups, even couples. Suited men entered the Gritti Palace, and one or two sleek with more casual wealth. He hefted the sports bag on his broad shoulder and was content to wait.

Eventually, Davies and Valentina. She was laughing now, even touching at his arm as at something she might examine more closely. The woman who had tried, very hard, to murder Patrick. Good job it was him, not Hyde, standing in the shade of Santa Maria, as they went into the foyer of the hotel. Godwin was puzzled. The woman had demonstrated the indifference of a taxi driver. Now, rearing its ugly head, the beast with two backs. On the other hand, maybe they had mirrors on the ceiling in the Gritti Palace, or something else just as intriguing . . . or perhaps a canal-view suite and a drink heavily iced was sufficient for her to be pleasant to Davies. What's a bonk between friends, after all? He prepared to wait, looking at his watch. Four-ten. The old man would be landing soon, flustered, dark-suited, insistent as a Dalek that his enemies be exterminated. Godwin laughed aloud, to the alarm of a Japanese with a huge lens and a small woman.

Four-fifteen . . . four-twenty. *Have another, why don't you? Are you trying to get me drunk, Mr. Davies?* Four twenty-five.

And then, the thought of Shapiro as the woman, Valentina, emerged with a studied casual haste from the hotel and turned right over the little hump of a bridge toward the Via 22 Marzo. Shapiro's death was superimposed upon a sense of her professional persona and her proximity to Davies—and there was the hotel, the imagined suite overlooking the Grand Canal and now, very vividly, Shapiro's dead face looking up at the ceiling of his London hotel room. The girl had done it, to stop a leak.

Godwin all but started after her, then shambled violently toward the foyer doors, which slid open to receive him. Take Davies in now, anyway, assuming he wasn't . . . Jesus, he couldn't be, could he? He jabbed the button of the lift. Suite 302–303. The lift doors opened. An American voice behind him complained at the price charged at Florian's for two coffees. His wife seemed unimpressed. Godwin grinned shakily when silently appealed to, then lurched out of the lift as it reached the third floor. He knocked on Davies' door and waited, then rang the bell before knocking again.

"Mike—are you OK? Mike, open up. Tony Godwin—Mike?"

He pressed his head against the door and listened. Nothing. No running of a shower, no splashes from a bath. Then the noise of a *vaporetto* through open windows. On the balcony? He glanced wildly around. A maid appeared from another room, her arms laden with soiled towels.

"Quick—please!" he called. "I think my friend may be ill—Mr. Davies. Open the door for me, would you? Please hurry!"

Startled into compliance, the crutches an emblem of Godwin's harmlessness, she turned her master key in the door and Godwin blundered past her. Shapiro was so strongly in his mind he looked into the bedroom first, expecting to find a body. Davies was, however, lying facedown on the floor of the suite's sitting room, his legs twisted one beneath the other, one arm stretched out as if he had sought some last support from the armchair near which his head lay. His other arm was beneath his body, his hand spread against his chest. The maid was quietly appalled. Godwin managed to turn over Davies' body. The spread hand fell away from the chest. Beautiful. A heart attack. A half-empty bottle and his breath smelled of the spirit. Oh, you *cow!*

"I want to see the manager—*manager*," he repeated to the maid. "Go and fetch him—*prego*."

She nodded and left the room. Godwin heard her slithering hurriedly along the corridor to the service lift.

He closed Davies' eyes. His face was twisted with pain. There was no harm in the local police being called in. An autopsy wouldn't find anything if Valentina's skills were up to their usual standard! No connections. He looked at his watch. Just after four-thirty. The ancient Dalek would soon be getting off the plane with young Darren, to find he'd been beaten to it.

To find that it was all in danger of being up the spout again, bugger it! Davies had been the best way in. Which left Patrick, perched up on the warehouse roof like one of the bloody pigeons. He'd wait for Aubrey's OK, but Patrick had to go in now, whatever the risks.

* * *

The first heavy drops of rain splashed against the rear window, beside Aubrey's cheek, and bounced on the roof of the limousine put at his disposal by Giovanni Calvino of Italian Intelligence. A nightlike darkness had spread across the Lagoon, and the city seemed subdued. Suddenly, it was lit by a jagged flash of lightning, as the rain intensified, drumming against the windows.

"Yes, Tony, yes," he murmured through the storm's static, the receiver of the car phone pressed against his ear. "Quite damnable . . . and, yes, I agree with your assessment. Matters are coming to a head. Patrick must go in immediately, if he can do so with safety. No, I'll talk to him myself." He scribbled the number on a pad on his knee. "No, Tony, you simply cooperate. I'll inform Giovanni Calvino. Stick to your story—" He flinched at another yellow-blue streak of lightning and the sudden image of La Serenissima as a ship in distress. Then only the afterimage of the light remained as the darkness of the storm crowded back. "It must be stopped," he added. "No, Tony. I have nothing positive from South Africa. I feel I'll have to drag someone unwillingly from some cocktail party, to protect Richard and his prize. Our only prize, as of this moment. Goodbye, Tony."

He put down the telephone and glanced at Darren Westfield, who seemed fascinated by the storm and the sudden, defenseless appearances of Venice out of the darkness. The rain beat on the limousine as on corrugated iron. Hyde, up on the roof . . .

It *was* at a head, like some monstrous boil to be lanced. Priabin and Babbington must intend sudden action; they had precipitated the situation by murdering Davies, who was evidently of no further use to them and too closely watched by Hyde and Godwin. He rubbed his cheek. Anderson was a narrow thread, with Blantyre doubtless seeking him with efficient desperation, at Malan's orders. Tony had echoed his own decision when he had suggested that *destruction was the easiest choice, sir*. Once they were certain of what the warehouse contained, then it should be put to the torch.

He picked up the receiver once more and dialed Hyde's number.

"Christ, about fucking time!" he heard almost at once. "It's *pissing* on me, Godwin!"

"Patrick—Aubrey."

"At bloody last!" Hyde repeated. "I've spent the bloody afternoon roasting up here, hopping from roof to roof like a bloody pigeon, and now I'm being drowned! Have you seen the weather?"

"Can you go in, with any degree of safety, Patrick?"

"Which bloody one?"

"Warehouse 14—I think the urgency lies there. I want identification of just *one* smuggled item of equipment from Reid Group—one photograph, one piece of evidence. Then it may all be put to the torch."

"You think it would burn in this bloody weather?"

"You must advise me."

"You've got the authority?" Hyde's voice sounded filled with effort, and seemed to move too, as if it were a weak, drifting radio signal.

"Longmead and Orrell have been informed that Babbington is here. They fear the mocking laughter that would be occasioned by *his* getting the better of us—and of them. I am commanded to do what must be done—to be *tidy*." A gasp from Hyde. "Are you all right?" Aubrey blurted.

"Just fucking slipped on the bloody ladder, that's all!" A few moments, then, "Down now."

"Is there any sign of urgent activity?"

"Couple of trucks drew up a few minutes ago.

Outside 14. There's no hurry, though. Not at the moment. I'm crossing open ground now—hang on." Aubrey could hear Hyde's rapid, hoarse breathing as he sprinted what must be the space between the two warehouses. Then, breathlessly, "OK—it's OK!"

"Davies is dead, Patrick—the woman killed him."

"Great—oh, fucking great! No wonder you want me to have a look inside. We've got bloody nothing at the moment, then, have we?" His breathing was stertorous, concentrated again from the effort of climbing up to the roof of the larger warehouse. Lightning flashed once more over the Lagoon, the dotted islands looking like spars and fragments ripped from the city by the storm's violence. "Bloody gang of dick-pullers, my old Granny could do better," he heard Hyde muttering. "Right, I'm on the roof. There's one skylight at this far end. I might be able to get down behind some of the crates, or even the container load that's intact. With luck. Look—sir, am I getting any backup? I don't really like to ask, but it might help." The sarcasm was elated, almost wild. Hyde was, as they said, psyching himself up. "There's another container arrived. Three now—the drivers are still in their cabs. I guess at four people inside, at most. I've loosened the studs holding the skylight . . . yes, I can get down, *if* they're at the other end of the warehouse."

"Our interest must have provoked Babbington to action. It won't be long. Go carefully, Patrick."

Aubrey replaced the receiver, then tapped the driver's shoulder. "Take us to Commander Calvino now," he said.

Lightning poured like the rain, making the whole area of the Lagoon blaze for a moment. Then the thunder bellowed.

Once Hyde had firm evidence that the smuggled material was in Warehouse 14—that which had left Birmingham airport or had reached Venice via Dumas

or other MLC subsidiaries—then he would have the
place surrounded. One of Calvino's people could dis-
charge some kind of incendiary device, destroying as
much as possible in a terrible "accident." So much
neater, with so much less to explain. He closed his
hand. The operation was in one place, almost in one
dimension. He was suddenly impatient at the blinding
rain hardly disturbed by the wipers, the flashes of lightning and the booming of the thunder, and the slow
traffic in which they were caught.

He flinched against another tumult of light, hunched
against the beat of the rain and then clapped his hands
against his ears as the thunder came. The rain stung,
even through the black waterproof cape buttoned
around his throat that had been with the equipment in
the boot of the Mercedes. He felt immersed. Anything
was better than the jagged stab of the lightning or its
sudden, repetitive incandescence, and the deafening
thunder. Glimpses of Venice were of a liner tilting bow-
first into the Lagoon.

He had padded to the other end of the warehouse
roof, then returned. The three trucks—two cabs and
only one with a trailer—were drawn up in front of the
warehouse, the windows still fogged by their drivers.
For the moment, no one was interested in loading. The
rain ran into his ears and eyes and his hair was flattened against his skull. He looked down through the
wet skylight, rubbing it continuously like a windshield
wiper. No one. He'd seen three different people, one
older than the other two, and one of them recognizable
as one of his pursuers from the *zettere*. Priabin's people, then. There was no one at this far end of the warehouse now.

Carefully, he eased the glass and frame of the skylight away from its base, dragging his cape over the

empty little rectangle, and peered in. Rain from his hair and neck dropped away into the hardlit gloom as he lowered his head. He stared like a bat along the dustily illuminated ranks of crates and boxes, past the intact container, then strained to see beneath the lighting suspended from the ceiling, and could just make out the offices inside the main doors. Listened as well as he could—

—shuffled the glass back into place as the lightning flashed again and the thunder rolled immediately after it. Shivering, he clasped the edges of the skylight frame in his hands, until the thunder had rolled away inland, toward the Eugenean hills. He clipped the rope to one of the struts just below the skylight, and dropped it away into the dusk. He hesitated, then balanced the tool bag on one shoulder and lowered himself through the hole of the skylight, dragging his cape across the opening to keep out the rain as he slithered through, clinging to the strut and the rope.

He hung there, turning slow as a top above the crates and boxes and the regimented alleys of concrete between them. The rain drummed on the cape, which seeped but which wouldn't have to matter—better than half an hour working the glass back into place, ballocks to that. But the acreage of the warehouse seemed artificially silent, dumbstruck by the weather outside. Gradually, he heard a radio reedily piping at the far end of the warehouse, smelled the cardboard and wood and plastics and polystyrene and oil, and began lowering himself into a gloom—

—which became hardlit, spotlighted, as soon as he passed beneath the nearest of the rank of shaded bulbs strung from the ceiling, so that his throat constricted. He dropped quickly down the rope until he became masked by the high-stacked crates labeled REID DAVIES—adjacent to DUMAS ELECTRONIQUES stenciled on other crates and vast cartons. Recognitions warmed him. He looked up at the rope, and heard the occasional drip of water before the cry of thunder. As it rolled, he tugged the rope on its clip along the strut into the shadow against the warehouse wall. DUMAS, REID GROUP, REID DAVIES, springing out of the dusty gloom and his memory like emblems. He looked down at his feet. Water surrounded them. Never mind. He opened the bag and removed the camera, then the jemmy and the screwdriver. Then he padded along the corridor formed by the crates and the outside wall. Old packaging littered the floor and the dilapidated, grubby shelving. Signs of haste in disturbed dust, handprints, footmarks, the untidy stacking of shelves, the lack of system. No one was coming here to draw exhibits or samples, this was all going somewhere else.

He levered one plank of wood out from its crate, then a second, exposing nothing much. He moved on quickly, his footsteps no longer slippery or audible, and opened the side of another crate, and found anonymous wood beneath it which he also jemmied into splinters. Found his treasure. Godwin would have wet himself at the sight. Transputers and WSI microchips, neatly boxed and labeled. Stepping back, having tugged out a single box and opened it, he photographed the package and the crate's labeling. The lightning would account for any superfluous flashes of light. Then a Dumas crate, hardly recognizing the French on the boxes it contained, except that Dumas wouldn't legitimately be supplying those avionic parts to anyone except the French air force. He felt elated, an excitement that was at last tangible. *Eureka.* The flash of the camera detonated in the gloom. Nice, neat—

The buzzer of the main doors sounded beelike through the warehouse, startling him. Through another small canyon of crates and shelving, he saw that the intact container rested in an amphitheatre of dull light. He shouldered the camera and climbed the stack of crates until he was looking over the top, toward the doors. And *she* walked through the small judas door in her shiny raincoat, shaking her spotted umbrella, as casually coming from a death as a prostitute might have come from a client. She shook her wet hair like a dog, in all innocence. Priabin was behind her, then the sloping shoulders of overalled or T-shirted men, the drivers. The door closed behind them with a distant clatter. Lying on the crates now, flattened and tense, he recognized the shadow who had closed the door before the man walked into the first dusty hardness of light. God bless you, Sir Andrew. Babbington, unused and uncomfortable yet also commanding, expecting and receiving deference.

Where was Malan?

The drivers of the three container trucks drifted away into shadow. Through the skylights, lightning gouged at the warehouse and the thunder volleyed behind it, deafening. Babbington began a processional toward the undisturbed container. It had been backed into the warehouse—and would be driven out, presumably, by one of the trucks. The girl and Priabin clung to Babbington's progress like moths drawn after a light. The divvy-up needed Malan, but then perhaps Babbington, prodded by Davies' execution, wouldn't wait and would just order the stuff to be loaded and taken to Marco Polo or even overland through Yugoslavia, seals intact.

If Aubrey wanted this lot put to the torch, easiest would be one of the American portable flame-grenade launchers. No setting of charges, fuses, just fire away. Babbington reached the container and leaned toward Priabin in intent conversation. Beyond the two men, and the container beside which they had all halted, was a second container. A forklift, arms laden with crates, was resting at the lip of its tailgate. Christ, he hadn't seen that second load from the skylight. They must have been loading that container most of the afternoon. Babbington was inspecting its interior now, hands on his hips, face pursed into disapproval. He motioned to Priabin, who called back along the corridor of shelving and crates. The drivers slouched into a distant light, followed by other overalled figures and two men in shirtsleeves. Babbington waved his arms, then spoke in a chill, authoritative voice. One man climbed onto the forklift and started its engine humming. It lurched into the interior of the container and almost at once Hyde could hear its hydraulics lowering the crates. The bloody thing was well over half-full already. Lightning flashed again and the lights in the warehouse flickered, like the waving of fragile old hands, then their light steadied again. Babbington looked up toward the whalelike ribs of the ceiling. The forklift came out of the container's stomach and nuzzled away toward more crates, as Priabin and Babbington directed it. The increase in tension was tangible, the hurry unmistakable. Fuck a fire in here, Hyde thought, there wasn't going to be time. He must get closer.

He began lowering himself down the cliff-face of crates toward the concrete floor. Then he slipped along the narrow corridor between them and the corrugated wall, then through stacked boxes, more crates, moving with exaggerated caution, as if stepping through thick mud. The forklift passed close to him, along another alleyway, then a second truck nudged the crates behind which he had paused. He ducked and moved on, then found himself down on one knee, peering through dusty boxes on metal shelves at Babbington and Priabin; their legs and shoes confronting one another. Babbington's replies were hesitant and soothing. Hyde could get no closer.

" . . . had to be done," he heard Priabin assure.

" . . . acceleration—don't like . . . " from Babbington." . . . what we can, then!" he burst out, his rain-wet shoes striding a pace or two away, then returning.

"... most, anyway."

"... *dislike!*"

Then Babbington's shoes strode away toward the tires of one of the forklifts. Hyde breathed steadily, quietly, then he looked down at the bag beside him. Call Aubrey, get the place under surveillance, sealed. Too late to be tidy.

Footsteps, even as he made to move. His hand, in the mouth of the bag, closed around the Browning automatic's grip. He turned, and confronted a man opening his mouth, one of the shirtsleeved KGB men. Hyde fired twice. The shells spat on the concrete, their glasslike noises drowned by the clatter of nuts and bolts from an open box, as the man collapsed against the shelves. He fell facedown on the floor and Hyde stood up as if in response to the first shout of surprised alarm.

He ducked through one alleyway of shelves, then another. The noises of the forklift trucks ceased, and he heard his own breathing and the blood racing in his ears—then he heard someone shouting orders before all noise was drowned by thunder.

He had to call Aubrey. They had to come now—

It was as if the air bed that Anderson had brought from the car and inflated with a foot pump was some species of psychiatrist's couch; a confessional. His detachment, too, was a pastiche of some professional manner. Van Vuuren had drunk the whisky greedily, and now clutched the bottle against his chest with his bandaged hand. Through the grimy window, the quick African dusk settled over the forecourt and the dusty, empty perspective beyond it; at least, it seemed to. It might be a storm darkening the sky, he thought, as he looked at his watch as if measuring van Vuuren's pulse.

It had been a rambling confession—more a denouncement, a cry of betrayal accompanied by the catalogue of infidelities and compromises of the government, MLC, Paulus Malan, all except a few brave white spirits who would not let the past go. Self-justification, ego, bigotry, hatred, anger and despair.

Arms had been brought in, from Eastern Europe, for some months, mostly rifles and handguns, grenades, even flamethrowers. Not in great numbers, Anderson surmised, but with a threatening acceleration and growing recklessness. *Some of us are prepared to resist . . . I began to realize it could be done. There's so much stuff just lying around over there, man—cheap, too.* Van Vuuren had become voluble with the drink, its effect magnified by his body coming out of trauma after the—

Anderson avoided looking at the bandaged hand, the occasional grimaces of pain on van Vuuren's face, his nursing of the hand against his chest.

. . . then I found Novak, made it easier. Never used MLC money, only our own, he affirmed with incongruous rectitude.

There was nerve gas—*make the buggers blink, that will*—waiting to be transported. *Why I was needed in Venice,* he had complained as if some kind of small domestic crisis had detained him, shipwrecking his plans. He had glared as he made the pronouncement. *Novak will get it here.* He seemed certain of that. Anderson had learned from the rambling, oblivious denunciations and accusations that Malan was not implicated in the arms or nerve gas smuggling.

Such had been Anderson's borrowed detachment that he was hardly stirred by the information. He would, eventually, pass it to Aubrey, who would stop the consignment, but there were no images of twisted black shapes on the ground or poisoned water supplies or armageddon blackmail—just his own, narrower concerns.

Eventually, van Vuuren had admitted, *Malan ordered your killing. Blantyre would have done it anyway, but Malan gave the order. You'd stumbled on the pipeline for MLC's share of the profits.* Now, he did see the bodies—one body, really, just one. At that point, he had needed only Blantyre to satisfy his revenge. Interrupted, and surprised by the question regarding the faked atrocity in Etosha, van Vuuren had eventually nodded, confirming Malan's part in Margarethe's murder.

Nothing else mattered. The Broederbond and the AWB and the Conservatives and the two-bit white resistance groups . . . only Malan's guilt, Blantyre's culpability. He had found the man *behind* things, the only things that were of any significance.

He would inform Aubrey, after dark when it was safer to find a telephone, of the consignment of nerve gas—VX or Sarin or whatever filthy rubbish they had got their hands on in Czechoslovakia. And, with that call, resign; walk away to confront his own concerns, *his* probity, *his* demand for justice. Malan and Blantyre. He would kill them both.

Van Vuuren continued to mutter confession and contempt and rage and cunning, more distantly and intermittently now, as if his transmitter was fading, its batteries run low. Anderson paid him no attention. He had learned everything he wished. Van Vuuren, should he have attempted to escape, might have been allowed to walk out, wander off down the road.

A ragged blind blew in the increasing wind that rattled sand against the grimy window. The dust was a dust storm, the spoil from the Rand blowing over the Johannesburg suburbs. Ashes to ashes. . . . It might take months, certainly weeks, but it would be done. *Lex talionis.* The sand sifted in through the rotting window frames and loose planking. Van Vuuren appeared not to have noticed the approaching storm.

Occasional, bleary headlights passed on the road. Anderson turned his future in his hand, like a child's glass ball. Upside down, the snow fell on the tiny scene within the glass. Whichever way he turned the prospect of his future, it invariably bore the same distinct outline. There was nothing, absolutely nothing, to stop him. An eye for an eye. That would give him the illusion of peace, make sense of it, give her rest . . .

Headlights turned off the road and splashed through the flying sand and dust over the forecourt. The shadowy vehicle behind them slowly came to a halt. The headlights remained on, probing the building.

Hyde was crouched near the office inside the main doors, in deep shadow. The doors were opened to the storm, and the torrential rain diffused the headlights of one of the truck cabs as it turned toward the warehouse. A KGB man, in overalls, stood beside the open door, the headlights illuminating the Makarov pistol in his left hand. Inside the hutlike office, another man peered over his spectacles as he completed the faked inventories of the container loads. His hesitations, his small, neat handwriting and figures, tingled nerves on Hyde's arms and neck. It was a salvage operation now. Snatch up the goodies, the alarm's gone off. He shuffled back into the shadows. The truck rolled into the warehouse, its lights blazing.

He edged his way along the wall, hearing nothing other than the engine and the renewed drumming of the rain after organlike thunder. When he was wedged between two small steeples of crates, he fished the cellular phone out of the bag and dialed Aubrey's number. You'd better have the cavalry organized, sport—

The red light on the phone blinked its ringing-out rhythm, then was interrupted.

"Just listen!" he whispered fiercely. "I'm identified. The target area's about to be abandoned. Get here with the troops. *Now.*"

"Yes," Aubrey murmured from a great distance. Hyde thrust the phone back into the bag, then considered leaving the bag, but knew he might need the phone again, and *would* need the spare clips of ammunition. Better hang on to it.

He listened now that the truck's engine was no more than idling, and heard Babbington's raised voice, urging matters ahead, Priabin calling to his people, then the woman's higher-pitched reply. It wouldn't take long now. Lightning through the open doors, then the thunder, now perhaps a couple of miles away. The woman would be commissioned with killing him while Babbington and Priabin organized the looting. Two containers?

Yes, they were still loading the second one. He breathed as steadily as he could after climbing skeletal shelving and peering over it at the ampitheater glaring in the headlights of the truck shunting in reverse gear toward the waiting, loaded container. The warehouse seemed denuded, far less full, as if to deliberately mock his surveillance. He clung on, scanning the remaining columns of boxes and crates. The logos were familiar even if indecipherable now—REID GROUP, REID DAVIES, DUMAS. Being cleared like Harrods on the first morning of a sale. The forklifts could hardly get off the ramp of the second container now, Santa had stuffed the stocking so full. One of them chugged backward, then the other mounted and deposited its crates. Sweating men shuffled them more closely together, Babbington waving his arms like a maddened traffic warden, while Priabin was hurrying toward the office. Through the doors, the second truck was nosing inside, as if looking for its companion, its engine noise obscuring everything else.

Metal dented near his hand, and was hot as he touched it, but he had not heard the bullet or its ricochet. Wildly, he glanced around. One man knelt atop a heap of crates thirty yards away, with his arms stiffly extended, gripping a pistol in his curled hands.

Hyde dropped from the shelves and buckled into a crouch while the gunman's shouts, eager as those of a huntsman, rang through the warehouse. This was Brum fucking airport all over again, having the bloody stuff snatched away from under his nose! He scuttled to the end of the shelving. Pausing for a moment, he opened the bag and withdrew the two extra clips of ammunition. Then left the bag. The telephone was useless now.

He heard the next shot, but had no sense of its direction. Then a third. He could see no one, not even the man on top of the crates. He heard calls, back and forth, from invisible hunters, heard the directions being given to the truck driver as he attempted the linkup between his vehicle and the container, heard the idling of the second truck's engine. Then a glare of blue light burst through the open doors and the skylight, and the preliminary rasp, then growl, of the retreating thunder—in which noise he moved, scurrying like a rat for deeper shadow, seeing one figure briefly, from the corner of his eye. Whether the man had seen him he had no idea. Another flicker of lightning, less dazzling, and a breath of thunder. The rain struck more reticently on the roof.

He crouched beside cardboard boxes. REID DAVIES, PART OF THE REID GROUP PLC. Fax machines. He wiped his forehead with the back of the hand that held the Browning, then rested the barrel against his heated cheek. He couldn't stop the container truck leaving, not even by shooting the driver. To do that, he'd have to be exposed and they'd kill him easily. Boxes falling somewhere made him start, his hand gripping the edge of a damaged crate—neat stacks of mainframe computer tapes, cushioned in polystyrene wedges, wrapped in polyethylene; huge program spools.

One of them, a man's footsteps by the sound of it, was moving toward him. Then, at a shout, the footsteps halted. "Bag here!" he heard. Then, more loudly and clearly, "Camera, telephone!" The footsteps that had been approaching hurried away.

Closer than he had guessed, he heard Babbington's voice, realizing the significance of the telephone. Stupid sod, leaving it for them to find. It would invoke greater urgency in them, an almost manic scramble to find and destroy him. Possibly Priabin's voice, but distorted by a megaphone. Then scattering noises, like the barks and scampering of eager dogs. He shivered. The walls had shrunk inward and the zealous voices seemed louder, the calling back and forth of the small expert pack. The rain was lessening and the thunder was grumbling away inland. The chugging truck engines were impatient to move. The second container's doors slammed shut in a kind of panicky triumph.

—footsteps. He turned, shaking, arms extended in front of him, and fired. The man ducked back, then something tore a sliver of wood from a crate near him. He watched, with a kind of slowed-down, filmic shock, as the splinter of wood cartwheeled out of the light into shadow. Then he turned and fired again, swiveling on one knee like someone in a training demonstration.

Arms up, the second man fell back, gun skittering on the concrete. He swung back again and fired a third shot. The man ducked out of sight once more without being able to fire. Then Hyde scrambled up a stack of cardboard boxes, treacherous as a loose dune slope, and rolled as he felt the impact of two bullets into the untidy, slipping mound. Bright coins of transputer chips spilt into the dusty light like a fortune lost. More shots, but he was rolling, amid boxes. Then he was half-buried by their weight. He struggled free, gun extended, turning even as he sat amid the wreckage, firing again two-handed. At no one, he realized, when he had the composure to look. He scrabbled away on hands as well as feet, into the shadow of high shelving.

Then she was there—Valentina, less surprised than himself, her hands seeming to move more quickly, but her features distracted between the megaphone in her left hand and the gun in her right—so that it was he who fired first, twice, then once more, like someone beating a venomous snake long after it was dead. Then the cold frenzy of a fourth shot. The woman was quite still, her right leg twisted under her body, her skirt rucked to her thighs, her hair gleaming with rain.

Calls were shouted out again, but they were less confident, quietened by the succession of shots he had fired. He tugged out the empty clip and thrust in a new one, jerking the first round into the chamber. He was shivering, sweating profusely. Then, slowly, he backed away from the woman's body and into deeper shadow, while her name was called—even her rank—but there were no sounds of Babbington or Priabin, no assumptions of command. Then he heard the noise of the truck's engine growling forward toward the doors.

He began running. You'd better shoot the driver, sport, even if it only holds them for a couple of minutes. Shoot the driver, shoot the driver . . . over and over as he raced along one of the long corridors of shelving, all but oblivious to voices behind him. If someone blurted out of a side passage behind him, they'd have a running target, could take their time. Perhaps they'd paused having found the woman's body and been subdued into indecision.

He was at the doors as was the truck with the first of the containers—

—he raised his gun, aiming at the high window of

the cab. The driver wasn't even looking at him, he was looking directly ahead to—where the doors were blocked by a truck. In front and to either side of which men with Uzis and rifles were waiting for the driver's decision—which was to halt, pull on the brake loudly, and raise his hands in the cab. Hyde sank into a squatting position on the concrete, shivering uncontrollably.

Even before the driver had had time to obey the order, in Italian, repeated in English, and then in Russian, to climb down from his cab, Aubrey was bending over him, shaking him as if he had failed some test, been a disappointment to a doting parent.

"Who emptied the other warehouse—when?" Aubrey demanded. "Patrick—there's nothing there. Novak has cleaned it out!"

PART THREE

ONLY IN AFRICA, PEACE

Ex Africa semper aliquid novi—
"There is always something new out of Africa"

—*Pliny the Elder*

13

ANOTHER LEAN UNWASHED ARTIFICER

The sunlight streamed in on the intent, concentrated, vivid faces of the loadmaster and her crew as the rear cargo ramp opened like the tailgate of a huge truck. The engine noise from the Hercules was louder, but there was a strange illusion of windless silence, too. Then the drogue chute cracked open behind him with an explosive sound and his head was jerked against the vehicle's seat. He was flung backward, away from the aircraft's cargo crew, the Land Rover hurtling out of the diminishing tunnel of the C–130's dark interior into the African sun. Then he felt nauseously jolted as the shock-absorbing pallet struck the sand of the Kuiseb Canyon. The scene was obscured by the dust storm thrown up behind it by the aircraft's passage at no more than fifteen feet above the desert. The wild, surreal sense of the impact followed, then the pallet slowed, slewing sideways and braking in the reddish sand—sand which settled on him, on the Land Rover, and above which the Hercules would lift lumberingly into the dark blue of the dawn.

London to Brighton in four minutes—Jesus Christ, it had been just like that. Coughing in the chill, dust-laden air, he released the straps that had secured him in the Land Rover's driving seat. Jesus, the things I do for England.

He squinted above the slowly settling dust, picking up the Hercules as it leveled after its turn and came back toward the flat, ages-dry riverbed they had selected for the drop. The aircraft would, after its second drop, recross the Namibian coast and drift up into radar view once more, pursuing its journey from Ascension Island to the Falklands. It had flown below radar height most of the way from Ascension across the darkened ocean, while he slept. It came on again, dropping lower, undercarriage lowered, ramp open. It was slightly to starboard of the original track—*I don't want to be dropped on from a great height, everyone else has already done that*—and then it passed, the dust roiling behind it, into which a chute vanished, a gleaming metal canister dragged out of the cargo bay behind it. He thought he saw a hand wave whitely, then the ramp and the undercarriage both came up together and the Hercules banked away toward the coast, south of the Walvis Bay enclave, its engine noise diminishing into—

—a silence that seemed to press on his ears, palpable as the pressure created by a small concussion. He jogged into the settling dust and dragged the canister toward the Land Rover. He released the cords of the parachute and wrapped it into a bundle, then heaved the canister into the rear of the vehicle—*not to be opened before Christmas*—and then began releasing the 4WD from the restraints that attached it to the pallet. Straightening at last, he looked around him. He was perhaps three or four miles from the C 14 road to

Aruvlei and Walvis Bay, which was sixty miles north-west. A fingernail of sun rose above the closest lip of the canyon. The low escarpment's edge became gilded, and the worn, dessicated, empty hills reddened lividly from their bruised night color. Hyde shook his head. *Welcome to Mars.* The sun struck warmly and immediately in its milder winter anger. A lizard scuttled away across the coarse, gravelly sand toward the shade of rocks. As he started the Land Rover, the noise of the engine bellowed back at him from the low canyon walls, shapeless and gradual as a mudslide. The vehicle bucked across the uneven ground, and he looked back at the forlorn pallet and its half-buried drogue parachute. Anyone who saw it would think it was South African Defense Forces equipment, abandoned after some exercise. *Who* would see it? Empty as the moon. He nudged the vehicle, in four-wheel drive, up the twisting, low incline, heaving on the wheel as he followed the bed of a sometime stream which had once emptied into the dry riverbed of the Kuiseb. A few stunted acacias, the discoloration of lichen—or perhaps even minerals— decayed on the rocks. As he reached the canyon lip, he looked west toward the frozen march of dunes out in the Namib; more solid-seeming than the pale, stunted hills around him.

He looked down at his shorts, heavy boots, the already sweatstained bush shirt with its faded corporal's insignia. The bush hat was clamped down on his forehead. SADF. Corporal bloody Hyde . . . couldn't give him an officer's uniform, could they? He slowed the Land Rover and turned off the engine. There was a streak of dust along the northern horizon which might have marked the passage of a heavy truck along the road. The silence pressed around him once more, heavy as a blanket, and as disorientating as the loss of hearing.

Stop it at any cost, Aubrey had impressed upon

him, without adding *to yourself,* but it was what he had meant. Anderson said it was nerve agent, so nerve agent it was. *Stop it inside Namibia. By any means.*

Short of blowing it up, of course, and releasing it. Slight drawback to that. Priabin and Babbington had got away from Venice without a hitch, and that same night someone had Semtexed Warehouse 14, reducing its contents to scorched and melted rubbish. Under the noses of the Italians. It destroyed a man's faith in the EC, really. So, it had all gone back under the carpet, and was no longer a matter of proof, investigation or counteractivity, just of stopping a consignment of Czech nerve agent reaching the lunatics on the fringes of Afrikaanerdom.

Hyde tossed his head, squinting in the hard light to where the road passed across the endless, bleak gravel plains of the northern desert. He looked down at the map again. The MLC complex outside Walvis Bay was where they would have shipped the stuff from Venice, on the Italian cargo charter that had taken off half an hour before he and the Italians had reached Marco Polo in the cool aftermath of the storm. Two days ago. Find the plane, which hadn't reappeared despite being scheduled to return to Milan with imported MLC nuts and bolts or whatever. Aubrey assumed it was still sitting on the airstrip. Expensive way to find out, hiring a whole aircraft to get him there. The aircrew had been highly amused at the idea of shooting him out of the back of the Hercules—and more excited then they would have been pushing grain out over Ethiopia or supplies over Kuwait. They'd looked at him as at some exhibit in a museum—a reconstruction of a dinosaur. A *spy?* What's that?

He studied the terrain, nodding to himself, then started the engine. The hood of the Land Rover dipped as he began descending a shallow slope toward the flat, drab, gravel plain. If it's all that's left—and Aubrey

wasn't going to get far now with Longmead and half
the Cabinet trying to keep the boat steady and HM
Secretary of State for Trade and Industry shitting bricks
in case anything nasty stuck to his untarnished image—
then he'd better give it his best shot. At least stuff van
Vuuren and Blantyre and their plan!

The Land Rover bounced and crabbed over the
gravel and small, pebbly boulders. Aubrey was back on
the fringes again: overzealous behavior, the blight on
his career. Hyde grinned sourly. The old bugger was,
really, immensely naive, always assuming that people
wanted to hear the unpalatable truth. More dust hanging in the air a little to the north—the road, for sure.
Reid Davies was going to carry the whole heavy can—
David Reid was going to go on smelling of roses
because there were too many people who saw him as
the heir apparent, and no one wanted to rock the
Pretoria boat just now, with Mandela and de Villiers
engaged in their long courtship dance.

Then he shivered slightly in the hot air, his hands
gripping the wheel more fiercely, as if for reassurance.
It *was* nerve gas—Jesus. And you're the night-soil man,
come to clear up the fucking mess.

Nothing of this must touch David Reid, Longmead had
pronounced with unctuous gravity. *None of it is of his
making, and none of it should cloud his career . . .*
though, for certain David had long known where the
funds and orders that had rescued Reid Group had
originated—with Malan and even the KGB!

Aubrey glanced through the aircraft window as the
747 banked over one of the neat, dusty suburbs of
Johannesburg and began its approach to Jan Smuts airport. His empty glass of orange juice—*no champagne,
thank you, a little early for my stomach*—had been
taken away by the attentive stewardess, and his small

table folded beside him into its slot. First class was all but full, mostly British businessmen confident and legitimate in their business trips to the new South Africa. Champagne? There was nothing to celebrate.

Some kind of botched blackmail scenario would be attached to the uxorious Michael Davies, Reid Davies would be cleansed, to use Longmead's word, and Malan would remain at large. *Can't rock any boats at the moment in South Africa.* From the snatches of conversation he had overheard during the flight, he understood the reluctance of the Cabinet committee to implicate Malan. Such pressing business reasons, such imperatives of trade.

The aircraft began sliding through thin, gauzy morning clouds toward the gleaming city below. A cricket team would undoubtedly follow the businessmen within months, with the MCC's blessing.

Malan will be forbidden all dealings with Reid Group. That should satisfy you, Kenneth. Connections between Reid Group and this French company will be severed—the French can clean their own house. If necessary, Reid Group will be broken up.

Longmead at his most obsequious, most Victorian. Close one's front door and there was no way the plague could affect one, hm? It was all such rubbish. He heard his dentures grinding and glanced at the seat beside him. His traveling companion—a machine-tool manufacturer from the Midlands—had evidently vanished to the toilet, to return smothered in expensive aftershave, no doubt. Aubrey's embarrassment dissipated. *Embarrassment to the de Villiers government by activity directed at MLC is inconceivable. There is always a point at which to stop, and that point has been reached.*

For two days and nights he had pressed his own imperatives, only for them to be dismissed, overruled. His claim regarding the shipment he believed to be

nerve agent had been ridiculed, and time had made
David Reid innocent. There was nothing more to be
said—except, *Stop it, at any cost*. To Hyde. He had
abused the last of his authority to place Hyde in
Namibia. It had been a desperate, final decision. His
reputation and career would, in all probability, never
recover from it, but it simply *had* to be done. It had to
be stopped because disbelief in Whitehall would not
make it go away. It was not a nightmare to be avoided
by putting heads under safe blankets; it was real. It
would be used to kill. Even to destabilize South Africa.
He could not let it happen. Even to the extent of coming to Johannesburg himself, to confront Malan, to
attempt to bend him to his will. Blackmail him.

The Midlands businessman slipped back into his
seat, clouded in aftershave, his cheeks shinily smooth,
almost accusatory of Aubrey's own lack of toilet. He
smiled and Aubrey returned the expression, before
glancing down toward the nearing city with a sensation
of fluttery nerves in his stomach.

The seatbelt and NO SMOKING signs were illuminated. Tiredly, he fiddled with his seatbelt. Richard
Anderson was out there somewhere, utterly free and
entirely dangerous, with a single purpose—to kill
Malan. Nothing except his own demise would stop
him. Malan had to be blackmailed and used to prevent
a catastrophe before Richard got to him. Malan had to
help him locate, and stop, the consignment from
Venice, and stop Blantyre and whoever else might be in
on things, especially van Vuuren.

After that—he nodded grimly—Richard could have
Malan or anyone else he wished to kill.

The Zil swept past the television tower and the uglier,
older domes and crosses of the Donskoi monastery,
down the M4, the Lyusinovskaya ulitsa, toward the

M5 and Domodedovo airport. Babbington stared sullenly at the bright noon beyond the passenger window, the sun gleaming off the monastery's inevitable, barbaric onion towers. Determined as he was not to glance in Kapustin's direction, for fear of betraying his overwhelming sensation of relief, he continued to stare through the window. Having collected Kapustin from the glass-enclosed offices of the KGB's Chairman, they were beyond the Sadovaya ring road and making good time. Another monastery reflected in a loop of the river. They were like confrontations with upbraiding spirits.

" . . . behind us," Kapustin was growling, staring at the back of the driver's neck beyond the glass partition of the limousine. "When it came to it, we were recognized as indispensible . . . even *you*. Someone who understands how they think, who was once one of them . . . " He'd survived because of a former identity, because he was *still* the Englishman, *Sir* Andrew Babbington. "So, the failure in Venice was easier to pass off than I expected." The sense of favors done, obligations incurred.

"Thank you," Babbington murmured.

Kapustin shrugged. "It was necessary. Get rid of that interfering old shit, Aubrey. Make sure what is done is done under *your* auspices, not Malan's. We need Malan—and power over him, as before. You assure me the British will drop this business like a hot stone without Aubrey—prove your case."

Babbington looked toward the vain towers of churches which had become museums. The traffic toward the airport was thicker, wilder as it always was on Moscow's motorways. The courts filled with drunken drivers and petitioners for dead men's pensions— *killed in a road accident, your honor*. The traffic clotted, swerved, raced. Their driver's shoulders were stiff with concentration and anticipated avoidance. A minor collision between two old Moskvas resulted in upspringing hoods and steam from burst radiators, and an almost immediate scuffle in the motorway's slow lane. Less than a quarter of a mile farther on, another car, burned out, lay on the side of the road. Babbington was unnerved by the insistent evidence of *accident*, of disruption.

"We have been blamed—*you* have been blamed—for that appalling screw-up in Venice, but Priabin may be made to carry some of your temporary burden. *If* you get rid of Aubrey." He shook Babbington's arm roughly, so that he was obliged to turn his head and look at Kapustin. The burning eyes seemed retreated into innumerable lines of age and cunning. "Andrew, do your job. Malan's asked for our assistance and advice. Render him the necessary service." He laughed throatily, shaking Babbington's arm now as if in apology, even affection. "We are indispensible. Mother Nikitin can't run the show without us. Malan helps us to sustain our crucial importance. Let nothing happen to him. Just get *rid* of Aubrey."

It dropped slowly, almost elegantly out of the hot, windless afternoon sky, like a pale seabird seeking the coast behind him. Then it took the form of an aircraft and he heard the note of its engine—almost the first noise since the retreating engines of the Italian cargo plane had vanished eastward a little after twelve. Gradually, the aircraft became a Cessna wobbling in the air currents as it floated above the airstrip and then landed, throwing up a cloud of dust behind it. It slowed, then taxied, and the cabin door opened before it came to a halt. A stubbled man slewed to a halt in a 4WD beside the aircraft and—oh, yes . . .

Blantyre, saluted with cheerful mockery by the driver of the Japanese 4WD, returned the salute with a grin. The Cessna taxied away to its hangar as the vehicle bristled toward the administrative building of the MLC compound. Hyde watched through binoculars, squinting against the glare from chrome and sand, until Blantyre had passed into the air-conditioned, enviable interior of the main building. The driver lit a cigarette and the first exhaled smoke hung above his head like a small cloud. Then Hyde rolled on his back on the isolated dune and stared, satisfied, up at the sky. Until that moment, he had merely hoped that nothing had left by road. Now, he knew for certain. Blantyre had arrived to supervise, command. The consignment of nerve agent and small arms was in one of the low warehouses. The Italian plane that had brought them had been the same one that had taken off from Venice, just before they'd got to Marco Polo, with a flight plan filed that would bring it to Walvis Bay. The registration tallied. The shipment had come in, but it hadn't left—oh no, no show without Punch, and Punch had just arrived. A beaut . . .

The Land Rover was hidden half a mile away, in the shallowest of gravelly depressions, overhung by a sorry, lean clump of dessicated bushes. Clever old bastard, Aubrey—good guesser, anyway.

Then the sense of the desert and the glittering ocean and the silence now that the 4WD's noise had died—all impinged, then pressed. Dunes to the south, the escarpment to the east, the gravel desert to the north, the sea to the west; himself on the solitary dune. Blantyre, two container trucks at least, perhaps three in each cab, escort of maybe two vehicles, three or four to each 4WD—and they might drive nonstop, taking turns at the wheel. He would have to follow alone, and without rest. Until they were all isolated enough by desert or mountain or canyon for *no* alternative arrangement to be made. No plane, no other trucks, no helicopter, no boat . . . so that there was no way out.

He shivered. It wasn't a beaut, not really. It was something else entirely.

He remained patient, self-possessed—so habitual had the mood become that he no longer remarked it. It was of no significance to him that perhaps weeks, even months, stretched ahead of him; evasions, disguise—even the lying-low of a hunted animal—nothing dismayed him. There was an accepted sense of duty that sustained him much as a faith might have done, something evangelical. Malan had given the order, or sanctioned it at the least. So van Vuuren had said. *QED*—Malan had murdered Margarethe in trying to remove him. Malan would honor the debt he had incurred.

Even the surveillance no longer niggled, and hadn't become mere routine. He left his car parked where it was all day, only leaving the parking deck when Malan left MLC. He returned to the exact place early each morning, so that the vehicle occupied the same position on the same floor of the multistorey deck, overlooking Malan's suite of offices. Overlooking, too, the adjoining executive parking lot for the MLC building, where he could remain aware of the movements of Malan's long, cream-colored Mercedes and its driver. Eventually, he would have to hire another car. It was the best he could maintain without drawing attention to himself, to that *white extremist responsible for the kidnapping and death of Piet van Vuuren, respected senior executive, loving husband and . . .* blah, blah, blah. He was dedicated to this one thing and it would be accomplished. The police were looking for him, old pictures and more recent but bearded pictures of him had been shown, his background had been slandered and his history curried and spiced by interviews with people like Bright. Dangerous psychopath, outraged

and demented sympathizer with black violence, and
fifty other darkened images of him. He knew he could
avoid the police if he was careful enough. And, if he
was patient enough, he could kill Malan.

He rested his elbows on the rough, gray concrete
sill of the parking deck, his small binoculars sufficient
to give him the assurance of movement in Malan's
office. He caught glimpses of the man's heavy frame at
his desk or moving about his office in shirtsleeves,
through the slits of the vertical blinds. Moving the
glasses, he checked the executive parking lot. The driver was washing the Mercedes, soaping its hood as gently as he might have done a child's back, after the dust
of Malan's drive to the Wanderers Club and his return
after nine holes of golf with two senior government
advisers and the chairman of Anglo.

He swung the binoculars back to the office suite.
Malan was seated on the edge of his huge desk, papers
in one hand, admonishing or instructing a seated trio
of senior subordinates. The subject of their conversation was irrelevant, just as it was of no consequence
that security men had prevented Anderson from
approaching anywhere near the golfers that morning.
He required knowledge only of a physical body—
where it went, how it traveled, where it came to rest,
and when it might be left alone, isolated. When he
knew all those things he would be in the position he
wanted.

A moment later, Malan was left alone in his main
office, after his secretary had cleared some coffee cups
and poured Malan more from a percolator jug. He
might, perhaps, kill from long range. The window
might, at the least, deflect or slow any bullet sufficiently for it only to wound—unsatisfactory. Somewhere, at
some moment, the physical frame, the vulnerable
head—bending now over the desk, studying papers—
would be devoid of caution and bodyguards, just for a

moment. Then he would have *his* moment.

He poured himself tea from a thermos into the cup-shaped screwtop, then sipped it meditatively, or so it might have appeared. His mind was empty. Through the glass of the roof over the shopping mall, he saw the crowds of bright dresses and shirts drift like leaves. Beyond the MLC building, the day was winterly hot, a pale sky without clouds. In the far distance, the slag heaps of spoil from the old mines, from the ancestry of Anglo and MLC. There was no sting to any of it now. He did not believe, as Aubrey evidently did, that Malan might move his operations out of South Africa. No one abandoned gold and diamonds, whatever else they acquired . . . unless the mines were nationalized.

Beyond the red-ochre, artificial hills, thin remnants of smoke hung in the distance, over Soweto. More township violence. Palls of smoke in the windless air, like the signals of encircling savages surrounding a white man's fortification. And probably only as real as a Western film. Zulu and ANC, AWB against the government, MLC and Anglo watching the price of their shares, even the vast, irresistible tide of genuine progress—none of it was of any significance. He finished his tea and flicked away the last drops from the cup before screwing it back on the thermos. Then he placed it in the back of the car before resuming his surveillance of Malan's offices.

Blantyre had killed van Vuuren, or had him killed. Blaming himself was of secondary importance. Van Vuuren had talked. That much would have been evident from the bandaged, nailless finger. It had been Blantyre in the car that had drawn up, in the increasing darkness of the dust storm, with two other men. Anderson presumed that the police patrol had, after all, been suspicious and had acted under orders not to alarm him. He had left van Vuuren to them, uncaring as to his fate, because he knew everything he needed to know. He had escaped by the back door, staggered through the wind and the blown sand to the dilapidated garage, started the car and driven violently toward the road, disappearing into the gloom of the storm which had swallowed the noise of his engine and discouraged and confused any pursuit. Side roads, the boundary of a golf course, the Reef, all half-seen, blurred by the dust outside the car. They had not been able to tail him. Eventually, he had found a cheap boarding house in the Hillbrow district, had gone to earth. And had awoken to newspapers and radio and TV accusations and libels that were so exaggerated and urgent as to be laughable.

He had tracked the movements of the physical body that was Malan for the past two days. The afternoon sun was entering the man's office from another window, striped like the coat of a tiger by the blinds. Malan sat in what seemed a hot, glaring dusk, his head bent over the papers on his desk. Then he looked up. His secretary's legs, then the gray trousers of a man's suit, which became the jacket and then the profile of an old man as the figure sat in the chair indicated by Malan, next to a glass coffee table. Anderson watched the old man, his shock dissipating almost immediately, with a detached, grim amusement. Observing life on another world, or from the strangest and most remote of habitats. Aubrey confronted Malan, who now perched on the edge of his desk. Aubrey and Malan . . . he had no interest in their business together. Aubrey would not tell Malan what he intended, of that he was certain. Therefore he could not come between them.

The light was behind Malan as he perched on the desk, discomfiting Aubrey, who had to squint to make out the man's features. He steeled himself to appear patient, relaxed, however difficult the assumption of calm. He cleared his throat and said, "How is your father?"

"Not good. You should call on him—talk about old times," Malan replied dismissively.

"Yes, I must," Aubrey murmured.

The secretary brought coffee cups and a pot, smilingly poured for Aubrey, then left. His delicate demitasse rattled softly in its saucer as he lifted it from the table. He sipped like an anxious bird, deliberately remaining silent.

Malan brushed his right hand across his hair and said, "You called, asking for a meeting. From London. I agreed, but I'm busy, Sir Kenneth." Even his politeness was abrupt. "What is it you want with me?"

"I see, from the newspapers and television at my hotel, that you have just, hm, lost a senior executive of the company."

Malan laughed, then in the ensuing silence, Aubrey heard the air-conditioning's steady murmur. Malan shook his head. "You wouldn't have had anything to do with that, of course," he observed, leaning slightly forward on the edge of the desk, as if poised to attack. Then he rocked back, shaking his head and crossing one leg over the other, folding his arms across his broad chest.

"No, I would not," Aubrey replied primly. He put down his tiny blue-and-gold cup and saucer.

"But you know—or perhaps knew—the man involved. He was working for you, I imagine."

Aubrey flicked his hand. "In a sort of unofficial capacity."

Malan smiled. Through the windows across the room from Aubrey was a multistorey parking deck; beyond that the vast sky and the first heavy late afternoon shadows falling from high buildings on other office complexes.

"I understand, Sir Kenneth. What I don't understand is, why? Any why here? We played to some kind of draw, didn't we? In Venice. The game's over." His smile was assured, even serene in a chiseled, sculpted way; the expression of some benevolent dictator in celebratory stone or bronze.

"I don't really think it is. Your old colleague Andrew Babbington may have destroyed the evidence, but there was much else that led us to Venice, and which implicates you. MLC, certainly. Matters that amount to considerable embarrassment, even outrage, in the present climate."

"You want me to get out my check book now, man?" Malan replied scornfully. "And you fill in the amount, right?"

"I am not blackmailing you, Malan."

"Not yet." He sighed, arms still folded. "Go on. *Embarrassment,* you said."

"We have a great deal of proof regarding the network of companies, previous shipments, funding, takeovers—that kind of thing."

"From here, it looks like good business."

"Would such 'good business' include nerve gas, Malan? I ask not merely from curiosity, you understand."

Malan appeared genuinely perplexed, his brow creasing, then smoothing into jocular disbelief.

"I don't understand. Explain."

"Your much-regretted late senior executive had begun a sideline to your mutual interests in Eastern Europe and the U.K. Van Vuuren had arranged—am I telling you much that is new?—had arranged various smallish shipments of arms that followed the same route through Dumas Electroniques and then to Namibia as did the material so urgently sought by MLC and the Soviet Union." Malan was shaking his head, but his eyes were bright with attention. "I am not certain how many such shipments there were. The latest of them contained nerve gas, in some quantity. Of that I *am* certain."

"Nerve gas? Why?"

"I presume he intended supplying it to extremist white organizations here. As he did the small arms. I am here to find out *who* the intended recipient is, and *where* its destination is."

"Where is it now? No, I can't believe you. It's an easy deception to foist on a dead man."

"There I agree with you."

"This is from the crazy man who wandered out of the Bush, isn't it?"

The intercom buzzed. Malan snapped down the switch and growled into the machine. Then he looked up again as Aubrey shook his head.

"Not entirely. Agreed, van Vuuren confessed as much to him—"

"Before he killed him."

"He assures me that van Vuuren was alive when he left."

"Robin Blantyre assured *me* that he was dead. After being tortured."

"Ah, yes. I'm afraid that was likely. But I believe that crazy man, as you call him. Which leaves Blantyre, who at this moment is . . . ?"

Malan was about to speak, then shook his head, and said, "I know where Blantyre is." It was evident that he believed what he said, and yet was disconcerted; like a man moving boxes that contained stolen goods and finding a decayed, skeletal body behind them, evidence of a viler, unacceptable villainy.

"Good. I'm glad you do. I believe that Blantyre has to be involved—though there I must in part take the word of the crazy man." Aubrey smiled thinly as Malan slipped from the desk and half-crossed the room to him. His folded arms and stance now seemed less assured. "The fact remains, I have come to make a bargain with you."

"On the basis of blackmail?" Malan said. Aubrey

merely shrugged and stirred the brown sugar in the delicate bowl with the silver spoon. "I don't think so, Sir Kenneth."

"Hear me out." Aubrey did not look up. "I have no doubt that you believe yourself immune from my small stings. You assume that I am at the end of my career, and probably at the limit of other people's indulgence. You may, in that assumption, be correct." He looked up. "But I can make a great deal of trouble for you—with your government and the ANC, if not in the U.K. That much I can promise you. Self-driven, if necessary, by more personal motives. You understand me? It is all in the past now, my niece's unfortunate death, but I have never ceased to hold you responsible in some important way." He cleared his throat of memory. "I am as much a crazy man as the man from the Bush. I may become reckless. Unless you agree to help me."

Malan was silent for some time, standing at the windows as if contemplating the architecture of the parking deck and the city beyond. Then he said, without turning: "You might—just might—be troublesome."

"Were there to be some 'atrocity,' some use made of this nerve agent—and we both know there are men mad enough in any country to use it, perhaps especially here—then I could certainly implicate MLC, van Vuuren, probably Blantyre—and, thus, by a causal chain, yourself. I would do that, I assure you."

Malan whirled round, moving lightly, almost boxerlike toward Aubrey; his face gratified by Aubrey's tiny flinch. "Christ, man, you must hate me," he announced, shaking his head, hands thrust into his pockets. "You really must hate me. I had nothing to do with your niece's death." Then he straightened. "No, it's not just that, is it? Even if you wanted it to be. It's something else—you want what? Things to be *right*?

Aboveboard, straight? You're out of your depth, Aubrey. Even Babbington, who went to the same kind of school and belonged to the same kind of clubs, knows it doesn't work like that!"

"I can't change the world, Malan. I realize that." He smiled. "With some reluctance, I accept it. But I will *not* ignore this!"

Malan raised his hands, palms outward, in front of his chest. "All right, all right, Aubrey. I knew nothing of this. What is it you want, in exchange for your silence, your lack of interest? You'll die soon, anyway, just like my father. Make the air a little less choked with moral exhaust."

Aubrey shivered. "I dare say. But however much you intend abandoning this country—"

"Is that what you think, man?" Malan scoffed. "All you've seen or guessed is insurance, nothing more or less. I work with the Russians because it suits, as it always has done. So *if* the kaffirs nationalize the mines, freeze the assets, *I* won't choke to death! Now do you understand, *royneek?*" He slumped into the opposite chair with a shrug, and added: "What do you want me to do?"

"It is quite simple. I need your assistance in stopping that shipment reaching the Republic and being distributed. I need to know to whom, and to where."

"From where?"

It was Aubrey's turn to shrug. "I guess at Walvis Bay, but I am not certain of that."

"I'll check. It left Venice when?"

"When you did—when Babbington did."

"OK. Who's it intended for?"

"Again, I'm uncertain. The AWB—people closely connected with van Vuuren, in any event."

"Piet was a fool—and disloyal. I'm no longer angry your man killed him."

"Or whoever."

Malan glared at him, then scribbled something on a pad he had dragged from the table onto his knee. "Give me the rest of the day, and tonight," he said. "I'll call you tomorrow. Which hotel—the Carlton?" Aubrey nodded. "OK." Malan stood up quickly. "I think that takes care of our business, Aubrey. I'll do this for you because you can apply pressure—*this* time. Do anything else, overstep this request, and I'll do you harm. Do we understand each other?"

"We do. I think well enough not to shake hands, don't you? Thank you, Malan. I'm grateful for your time."

He collected his cane and allowed himself to be walked to the door. Malan's frame loomed beside him.

"You stay out of everything else, Aubrey. Understand?"

"Agreed. I will be kept out of much—as for the remainder, I will not embarrass you to your government, providing this business is satisfactorily concluded. Goodbye, Malan."

The door closed on Malan's unsmiling features, his eyes hard with anger and contempt. Malan was barely in control of himself, but Aubrey realized that he was in no sense in control of Malan. But there had been no other way, none whatsoever. For himself, he had made a devil's bargain indeed! Necessity was certainly not the parent of probity.

He smiled at Malan's principal secretary, the young woman who had brought his coffee, as he passed her desk.

Babbington slid into the rear seat of the Mercedes beside Malan, his jacket over his arm, his tie loose. Together, they completely occupied the rear seat, almost touching after Malan had folded up the arm rest. The airport lights glowed in the cool of midnight.

There was a bitterly amusing irony in the multiplicity of 747s from a great many of the world's airlines. Welcome to South Africa—moral smallpox has been eradicated. The big jets brought planeloads of businessmen every day. Even Russian businessmen, though Babbington could hardly be said to qualify—especially as he appeared now, unkempt and tired and angry with more than the irritation of aircraft incarceration.

"Good flight?" Malan murmured. They had hardly shaken hands.

Babbington glowered in the dusky interior of the car, his eyes preternaturally bright, as if he were drugged. "What?" he snapped.

"Doesn't matter."

The limousine glided toward the airport exit, passed through the perimeter and then, ahead of them, Johannesburg glowed as if set on fire. The city's lights overwhelmed those of Alexandra township. The ranks of hostels for migrant male workers were all but dark. They'd even begun pulling them down, rebuilding "family" homes. They said de Villiers had been outraged when he'd made his first visit to Alexandra, rounding on his staff and accompanying ministers *in front of kaffirs* and berating them. Aubrey and the nerve gas . . . there was some point to van Vuuren's lunacy. At least it was understandable.

"He came to see me this afternoon."

"Aubrey?" There it was, the Englishman's habitual shock at a world not behaving according to his precepts. "Why?"

"To ask for my help." Malan grinned.

"Help? To destroy yourself. He gave you a revolver and told you to do the decent thing, I presume?" The sarcasm was cool, recovered, as if Babbington had transmuted from some traveling persona that was less assured.

"Not quite. Something else. There was another

consignment, one I didn't know about, just as you didn't." Babbington's stare was suspicious. The Mercedes moved smoothly down the outside lane of the motorway toward Gillooly's Interchange. "Nerve gas," Malan announced. "One of my people, trying to supply some of his friends, so Aubrey told me."

"And you knew *nothing* of this?" Babbington asked accusingly.

"Should I have? The shipment came from Czechoslovakia or somewhere. Van Vuuren—"

"What have you done with him?"

"Van Vuuren's dead." Babbington nodded and Malan added no details. Instead, he remarked: "Aubrey wants to trace the shipment. That's why he's here and why he asked to see me and why I informed you he was coming."

Babbington rubbed his chin. The beard rasped.

"I see nothing to concern us in this nerve gas matter. I will find out, however. People *I* use must be involved. It is, of course, typical of Aubrey, to come haring out here in pursuit of it! That man's impossibly grand sense that he is the moral arbiter of international affairs never ceases to amaze."

"He's just an old man."

"People have underestimated him on such grounds before. His appearance *is* deceptive." Babbington's face was grim with admission.

"He's here," Malan remarked impatiently. "That's all that matters—apart from the method. I've stalled him until tomorrow. Then I can spin him any line we wish. That *is* why you've come?"

Babbington appeared challenged, even insulted. Then he nodded and smoothed his creased jacket on his lap like a pet animal. He was nodding at some inward satisfaction. Then he said, "Yes. It was necessary before—vital now. I am—*charged* with ridding ourselves of that odious little man!" The contempt did not quite efface the anger at being the recipient of a direct order—some kind of *field agent,* his lips almost expressed. Babbington's fury amused Malan. He knew Aubrey's suite number, had people watching him, *knew* the man was alone and had made no effort to contact any South African intelligence officer or politician, however sympathetic they might have been to his story. The old man actually believed, in the blindness of his rectitude and self-esteem, that Malan could be bent to his will, would actually assist him in response to his threats. His mistake, then.

After the interchange's clusters of high, overhanging lights, the motorway looked down on neat suburbs and the oddly symmetrical dark shapes of golf courses and parks. The city had brightened ahead, vinelike lights climbing into the night. Malan considered mentioning van Vuuren's death once more, then remained silent. The crazy man from the Bush was of little or no account. There had been no contact between Aubrey and Anderson, or whatever his name was. He must have been slaked by van Vuuren's murder. Traffic thickened, coming away from the city. Headlights glow-wormed along quiet suburban streets on either side of the motorway. The Reef was invisible in the night. A detached glow, like a source of radiation, burned away to the south. Soweto.

"You'll want my people's help. Tell me tomorrow what you need," Malan said. "You won't be using your people, I assume." Babbington shook his head. "Better if you implicate me in everything, uh?" Malan smiled, then shrugged. "I don't mind, Andrew. Just assure me that Aubrey makes a full stop, not just a comma, will you?"

Babbington's right hand formed a fist in a spasm-like movement. He opened it slowly, as if expecting the moth he might have caught to be dead. "I am in receipt of assurances. From the London rezident. Aubrey's powers of investigation, the scope of the inquiry, have both been drastically curtailed, from all the available evidence." Again, he worried at his beard, as if it were no more than stage makeup, a disguise. "People like Longmead, people in the Cabinet, don't want to rock the boat here, *nor* do they wish even the slightest breath of scandal to touch David Reid. Both are powerful considerations, of far greater import than Aubrey and his theories. Without Aubrey, it will all dribble away into the sand."

Malan nodded, as if he had just achieved possession of a potential fortune. "Good. Right, man. We'll get you home, you can take a shower and have a sleep, then we'll decide what to do with Sir Kenneth." He chuckled.

"It must be accidental."

"Accidents are easy to arrange, uh, Andrew? An old man, alone in a strange city—not too much of a challenge for you and I." His laughter was full and genuine, even infectious.

He struggled awake, clumsily putting on his spectacles and switching on the bedside lamp. The digital clock proclaimed two in the morning. He felt drugged with jet lag. The nightcap whisky was salty on his palate. Levering himself into a sitting position in the bed, he snatched up the telephone.

"Kenneth—Richard."

"Richard—what—where are you? *Here?* My dear fellow—"

"Kenneth, I know your instantaneous charm of old. Just listen to me."

Aubrey swallowed and rubbed his eyes beneath his spectacles, pushing them up almost to meet the strands of hair that had invested his forehead. He frowned. The room was quiet beyond the light's spillage. "Yes, Richard. But we must talk—meet."

"I don't think so, Kenneth. You'd try to dissuade me. And you should not be the one to talk of putting heads into lions' mouths, coming here alone." Anderson sounded tired but detached.

"Richard, I can only *understand,* not disapprove. But your effort and safety concern me." He hunched over the receiver, as if he were on the point of whispering. "I have come to an understanding with Malan. I must stop that consignment reaching the Republic, Richard. Your help was invaluable—"

"You don't want harm to come to Malan until your little job's all done, eh?"

"No, not that. Just that there are other ways!"

"You think so? Kenneth, I rang simply to warn you. I followed Malan's car to the airport this evening—midnight, to be precise. Not long ago I got back. He collected someone and took him out to the estate. Andrew Babbington. I recognized him."

"What?" Aubrey whispered.

"Andrew Babbington is here in Johannesburg, in Malan's company. I wouldn't say it boded well for your little plan, would you, Kenneth? And you alone. Be careful, Kenneth. I don't really think you understand the kind of people you're dealing with. I'm sorry I can't help further. I have my own priorities. Goodnight, Kenneth. Sleep well."

The noise, whatever it was, woke him from his doze, making him flail his arms inside the quilted blanket he had wrapped around his body against the chill of the night. It was still dark, only a pencil-line of light on the horizon, sketching the distant escarpment. He struggled his way out of the blanket, cursing, the sand clinging to his damp, warm palms. He'd fallen bloody asleep for Christ's sake!

He rolled onto his stomach and wriggled to comfort on the lip of the dune, the binoculars extricated from the folds of the quilt. He shivered. It was bloody cold at night, and this was bloody Africa! Tropic of Capricorn right overhead . . .

Through the infrared binoculars, he saw the movements in the fenced compound as the shifting of solid gray ghosts and bulks. Even the exhaust fumes writhed grayly, like windblown curtains. Two container trucks, two 4WDs, one a scout car, the other a *bakkie,* pickup truck. He counted the men. Two to each cab—thank Christ, they might stop, then, once in a bloody while. He felt warmer, encouraging his anger, his cursing. Four men in the *bakkie*—must carry the supplies, that—and two men in the scout car. Ten. Then he saw two more men—he could even see the rifles they carried—climb into the rear of the pickup. All of them wore bush shirts and shorts or khaki trousers, and floppy bush hats. Twelve good men and true, then.

The gates of the compound were opened and the leading XR 311 scout car—that must be Blantyre, it was the set of his body and head—passed through and out onto the gravel road. Its headlights swung east. The *bakkie* followed—call it a ute, mate, and I'll know what you're on about—then the first of the container trucks.

Hyde scrambled to his feet, folding the quilt awkwardly beneath one arm, the glasses slung around his neck and the automatic rifle in his right hand. He scrabbled down the slope of the dune, wading with big, balancing strides until he reached level ground. He'd moved the Land Rover closer, but very quietly and carefully, during the small rush hour of departures by the MLC staff, just before dusk. He began running, carefully dodging the pebbles and small rocks scattered across the gravelly sand. Then he found the shallow depression and the vehicle, which nudged over the lip as if curious as to his whereabouts. He threw the quilt in the back, then listened in the near-silence . . . the noise of retreating engines and the rumble of heavy vehicles, like the sound of a distant storm.

Twelve good men and true—Jesus wept. He started the Land Rover's engine, slipped into four-wheel drive and lurched out of the shallow depression, the sand churning beneath the tires, the vehicle emerging like something from a swamp in a very cheap movie. Then it leveled and he accelerated gently toward the gravel road, without headlights. The escarpment along the horizon was tinged with reddish gold and the lip of the dune was already ochre in color. A tall radio mast rose silvery into the lightening sky above the MLC buildings.

He bounced onto the road and turned the Land Rover eastward. The dust from the convoy hung ahead of him like a pillar of cloud. He glanced at the dashboard clock. Six-ten. It would take them—with regular stops, please God—two days to reach the South African border, whichever route they took. Once they crossed it, action against them would become suicidal at best. It had to happen in the next two days, in Namibia, in the silence and emptiness. Twelve men versus the mighty . . . him. Jesus.

14

TO BE SAFELY THUS

Around midmorning, they had passed through some place called Solitaire that was no more than a street of shops, one hotel and a couple of bars. Its few inhabitants were dressed in working clothes or print dresses and scattered amid a few weary cars; the black faces had far outnumbered the white. Then the isolated, cramped little place had settled invisibly into the dust behind him. The spike of its German church thrust up out of his dust trail, making him shiver. Solitaire. This was Blantyre's country and he was being drawn farther and farther down a narrowing tunnel in the man's wake.

Then, around one in the afternoon, the convoy was no longer ahead of him and he had to slow suddenly and slip off the road onto a dirt track that skirted the village of Maltahöhe. The two container trucks and their escort had halted at the petrol station. Then he lost sight of them as he passed behind a string of low houses. A black gardener looked up in surprise and some chickens stirred nervously on a greener patch of dust.

Corrugated roofs flashed in the sun. White, red-roofed houses, a wooden German church, the white blur of goats, until eventually he halted in the shade of a dusty, spreading acacia, its lower bark protected from grazing animals and the depredations of dogs by a leaning, rusty iron railing. The square was small and quiet, as if the center of the tiny town had moved a few hundred yards away, to the wider square ahead of him around which a small supermarket and a new, low hotel and a few shops had gathered.

The dust settled on his clothes. A bar winked at him from the corner of the forgotten square, constricting his dry throat. People drifted near the shops, their colors mingling. A white man engaged in conversation with two black men and a willowy young black woman under a shadowy awning. The mannequins in the window were as still and posed as the people on the pavement. A woman's face peered from the side of ornate net curtains behind a shabby wooden fence as he swilled water from a plastic bottle and then rubbed his lips with the back of his hand.

He had waited all morning, as he trailed behind their dust-signals, for some sight or sense of a place where he might halt their progress. As they had climbed gently up the escarpment onto the plateau, everywhere had been flat and open. There had been nowhere he could pull the landscape over them like a net. Certainly, it couldn't be done here, in Maltahöhe, which sat on the plateau like a sullen, abandoned member of a wagon train that had ventured farther inland.

He glanced round. The old white face had removed itself from the window of the low bungalow and the net curtain had fallen back into place. A dog relieved itself against the rear, nearside tire. The heat settled as

certain as the dust. He unfolded the map on his knee
with a quivering hand. Reaction from gripping the
wheel . . . except that he knew better. It was reaction
to Blantyre, as if the man had been seated beside him
throughout the morning, not up ahead and invisible in
the dust cloud. He had been *there*—every memory of
him. Hereford, the Brecon Beacons, even Oman for
one short tour of duty. Blantyre, who had been more
efficient, more ruthless, more competent during their
mutual training. More of a bastard, perhaps because he
didn't have two aging aunts in the East End who were
quietly appalled at the changes being wrought in their
nephew by SAS training. The nephew who had joined
the army from an undistinguished progress through a
certainly undistinguished state school. Blantyre had
attended the best school in Salisbury—Rhodesia—to
where he had eventually returned, to enlist in the
Selous Scouts. Moving, after Rhodesia became
Zimbabwe, to Namibia. Hyde stared at his knuckles as
they gripped the steering wheel. Blantyre, the world's
biggest bastard; his head prefect, his tormentor, who
had despised more than anything else the indifference
Hyde had always displayed toward him.

Not now, though . . .

He looked down at the map on his dusty thighs,
and flicked open the neatly labeled album of prints that
rested on the passenger seat. RAF enlargements, tourist
snapshots, color photocopies culled from coffee-table
books, all so hurriedly assembled that his first opportunity to study them had been aboard the Hercules. His
forefinger traced along the road they had traveled that
morning, the C14. If Blantyre chose to stay on it, then
follow the C13, he would head directly south through
the Schwarzrand range of hills and then the Rooirand.
He flicked the album's polyethylene-folder pages.
There was an airport at Aus, which meant that relief
could be flown in, reinforcements. But, after Aus, the

Namib opened out again, inland of the diamond mining area at Lüderitz—from which MLC could reinforce
Blantyre. Anyway, the desert was far too open for a
successful ambush.

His finger followed the major road, the B1, east.
Better going—more flat land, more airports. The landscape conspired with Blantyre. MLC was everywhere in
Namibia, as close as radio contact and an hour's flying
could make them.

He rubbed his arms. *Stop them,* Aubrey had said,
as if it was a matter of traffic and nothing more. *Cause
a road block, perhaps? I leave it to you, Patrick.* Only
because, you old bugger, you couldn't think of any way
of doing it. Now, the old man was fiddling in
Johannesburg while Hyde burned! His *good luck* and
nervous handshake had been furtive and quick. His
manner had been strange, though. As if he were looking over Hyde's shoulder all the time, at something or
someone else. If he didn't watch himself, the old bugger'd be as much in the shit as he was! The old white
face was back at the window of the bungalow, wrin-
kled like the surface of a moon. The net curtain was
hitched up like a long, Victorian petticoat. Hyde smiled
and the old woman flicked out of sight. *You wouldn't
want to see the rest of the story anyway, darling.*

He would have to scout ahead of them, just as
soon as he was certain which road they were taking.
After that, they could be left for hours, heading in one,
unchanging direction. He rubbed his stubbled chin and
pulled his bush hat lower over his eyes. All he had to
do was find one ambush point along the four hundred
miles that remained to the border with South Africa.
He idly flicked through the album of photographs,
shaking his head again and again as he checked the picture with the map on his knee, looking up at the noise
of an aircraft. A small Cessna, red and white, floated
toward Maltahöhe's landing strip.

   As he looked down, Blantyre's 4WD, then the rest
of the small column, passed across the main square
ahead of him. Heading east, toward Mariental. He started the engine. The face appeared again at the window
and he waved at it. It paused before removing itself, as if
it might break out of the egg of its routine and return
the gesture. He let out the clutch. The dust of the convoy
was beginning to settle as he reached the main square. A
few miles along the road, there was a track that the
container trucks couldn't use but he could in the Land
Rover. It cut like a hypotenuse across flattish escarpment to join the B1 forty miles south of Mariental. He
could scout down as far as Keetmanshoop before dark,
if he got a move on.

   He turned left across the main square. The convoy's dust column rose ahead of him, beyond the town.

It was a harsh, arid place now slipping quickly into
evening, and was sparsely littered with karakul sheep
and listing fences. Hyde rubbed his forehead. His skin
was dry and gritty with dust, his lips powdery and
cracked. Inwardly, he was enraged. There was
nowhere—*nowhere*. Even a leopard couldn't have
ambushed its prey with any certainty out here. He had
driven the main road south through Namaland, passing a scattered succession of sheep stations, tiny villages and outposts, the open country spreading
depressingly out around him for most of the journey.
Sheep, the occasional herdsman in a woolly hat, the
odd vehicle or three. The road followed the easiest land
and the railway ran beside it for most of its length. He
had pressed on to Keetmanshoop, deeply frustrated
and angry.

   He looked down now from a rocky outcrop
toward the main road, as the sun's red disc was swallowed by the ridged, toothed horizon and the open,

scrubbily grassed landscape darkened. Sheep drifted away toward shelter and the first jackal was snouting through clumps of stiff grass only hundreds of yards away. What might be a dust column wavered in the distance, thrown up by more than one vehicle. If Blantyre had maintained the morning's pace, it would be them. The rocks around him were reddened by the sun's last touch before it dropped into the horizon's grasp and darkness pounced on the landscape. He could make out the pinpricks of headlights approaching along the dusty snake of the road. His throat constricted. In one day, they'd already traveled more than four hundred miles. The first big, soft stars bloomed overhead and the thin moon, now visible, was already high. The sky was blue-black.

The vehicles were already as big as toys as a slight cool breeze sprang up. The headlights were foggy inside the dust cloud thrown up by the convoy. They would make their overnight stop—please God—in Keetmanshoop or somewhere close by. If they didn't, then he'd need the pills just to stay awake—just to keep going.

He slipped the strap of the Nova night-vision goggles over his head, adjusting the eyepieces to comfort. The goggles fitted like a diver's facemask, but they were heavy. They made neck muscles ache with the effort of keeping the head upright against the weight of the single lens barrel that jutted out like the horn of a unicorn. He switched the goggles on, and immediately the fog of the dust cloud seemed to clear, so that he could see tiny, ghostly figures in the leading vehicle and obscure shapes behind the windshield of the leading truck. Even the figures in the fourth vehicle were visible, small black dots of heads. Twelve good men and true. He removed the goggles and placed them on the passenger seat, then started the engine. There had been one scouting jackal, a gray, swift shape, near the road and another closer to the hillock on which he was concealed. Hyde let out the clutch and the Land Rover bounced down the slope. He replaced the goggles—he was getting tired, forgetting simple things. Clumps of grass, tussocky bushes and thorny scrub, the occasional leaning aloe. A hunting bird rushed whitely across his path and disappeared into bushes with the vigor of attack. Then he bumped onto the road and turned toward Keetmanshoop in the wake of the convoy.

He had to do something tonight, whether they stopped or not. It meant declaring his presence, unless he could make any action of his look like an accident. Disabling one of the vehicles, perhaps?

He drove beneath stunted acacias on either side of the road. They thrust up from the ground like wind-flattened, small clouds on thin poles. The lights of the convoy were sharp amid the aura of the town's lights, which glowed like the heat from a fire. He glimpsed the sliding shape of something that might have been a leopard beside the road, then it vanished with a gleam of eyes. Then the quiver trees replaced the acacias, strange low aloes with pineapplelike bark and tufted with leaves that jutted like starfish spines. He realized he was overtaking the convoy and slowed to a crawl. The kokerbooms—quiver trees—crowded the road threateningly, and they seemed ever thicker as he halted at the side road where the convoy's lights had turned off into the forest. It had to be their overnight camp, there was nothing on the map except a farm and a few scattered homesteads. Blantyre was taking no chance of drinking or indiscretion in Keetmanshoop.

Hyde waited until the glow of the headlights diminished into meteorlike flickerings. He could make out the jutting debris of boulders, as if some great stone temple had collapsed and the aloes had slowly encroached onto consecrated ground. Off the track, there'd be little chance of making progress in the Land Rover.

Then the lights seemed to halt and gather together. They must have found a clearing they could use to set up camp. He accelerated and drove carefully along the main road, looking for—

—a shallow, long ditch that dipped away from the road and from which the trees seemed to have drawn back. He switched on the headlights as the Land Rover bumped off the tarred road. It lurched like a drunk over rocks he could not avoid, then the aloes began to close overhead once more. Eventually, he drew to a halt and pulled on the hand brake, turning off the engine. The silence rushed in against his ears like the pressure from an explosion. Then he heard something die in the darkness away to his left, its surprise choked off by the asphyxiating bite of a big cat. Perhaps it was the leopard he had seen beside the road. He shivered and looked up. The sky was pearl gray as silk and the stars shone through the cloth like small tears. His eye sockets ached from the pressure of the goggles and he rubbed his stiff neck. *Might just save your life. . . .* Who'd said that, Aubrey or the armorer? He stepped out of the Land Rover onto a rock as big and smooth as a hippo, standing with his hands on his hips. He could make out no source of light in the direction he knew Blantyre to be—trees too close together, or some rocky outcrop masking them from him.

An accident, then.

You'll be bloody lucky to convince Blantyre of *that,* sport. He jumped down from the rock into tussock grass, overbalancing and steadying himself against the door of the Land Rover. The trees were little more than twenty feet high, their bark rough as the skin of a tropical fruit. He slapped his hand softly against one of the trunks, pondering. By the time they'd set up camp and eaten, it would be hours before they relaxed into sleep and routine. He reached into the vehicle for a water bottle, drank from it, then ate chocolate. Cold beans later, even some compressed cheese and hard biscuits. No time to risk a fire and some soup.

When he had finished eating the chocolate, he climbed into the Land Rover and fished a second sweater out of one of the bags, drawing it clumsily on over the goggles. Then, irritated with their weight and pressure, he removed them. The manufacturer liked them but most of the soldiers who used them didn't. Removing them because of discomfort had killed quite a few who'd tried to rely on their own unassisted night vision. He rubbed his eye sockets. The African night pressed close around him and he thought of the leopard. It would be eating now, but it was still difficult to ignore. Two hours. He'd try to rest, and it would give them time to cook and whatever they—

He heard a shot. Whatever they'd just killed, he told himself, calming the ragged nerves that had twitched at the noise of the rifle. Settle down, relax . . .

He jerked awake and at once looked at his watch and listened to the silence of the night. More than two hours. He'd dozed, even slept soundly for a time. He massaged his cold arms and thighs, yawned and rubbed his eyes. Then he got down from the Land Rover and drew the Heckler & Koch G3 rifle from the rear of the vehicle, weighing it in his hands for a moment. Nice lot of plastic parts, it didn't make much noise in contact with other surfaces. Then he checked the pistol and slipped it into his belt. Then the spare clips of ammunition. The VP 70 was half plastic, too— clever buggers, the Krauts. He slung the rifle across his chest, its butt folded beneath the barrel. Then he slipped his arms through the straps of a small pack and adjusted its weight on his hips and shoulders.

He began walking in the direction of Blantyre's camp, oriented by the glow of a passing vehicle's headlights on the main road. The stars were like great damp eyes in the darkness. Something small skittered near his feet through the scrub, then careered away. A shrew?

The camp was, indeed, in a small clearing. He reached it after twenty careful minutes of walking, coming first upon their casual, incautious noises and conversation. Then the glow he had seen ahead hardened into the illumination of lanterns. He skirted the clearing until he was downwind of it. He climbed a knoll of crumbly rock that overlooked their camp and lay down on his stomach.

A man was bent into the hood of the pick-up truck, the nearest vehicle. He heard the clatter and scrape of tools against engine parts, and the scratch of utensils against tin plates and cups. The man being swallowed by the truck was whistling, unworried. There was no way the vehicle wouldn't be able to continue in the morning. Hyde dragged the goggles over his head and the bright firelight and lamplight grayed once more, becoming detached and strange. The two container trucks were turned toward one another like large cats sleeping at either side of a fire. Beside the remaining vehicle, he saw four people gathered, Blantyre the tallest of them. On the hood of the scout car, a map lay spread like a tablecloth. At the edge of the clearing, the single man on patrol seemed to leer envyingly into the gray firelight, which someone else fussed around, cooking meat Hyde could smell.

He swung his head ponderously, like a much larger creature because of the nightsight, back toward Blantyre at the 4WD, greedy for a glimpse of the sheet of paper that was tapped so insistently. They gesticulated and talked . . . and evidently agreed. The route for the following day, their rendezvous in the Republic—which road? If he could only . . .

The smell of roasting buck over the roaring fire, the burning of its fat as its carcass hung from a spit, churned at his stomach. The assured noises of the camp nibbled at his confidence like a wearing, repeated question. If he could risk—take one look at the map—that Blantyre now folded away as he grasped a bottle of beer from a corporal and grinned. The cook was using a long, glinting knife on the buck's flesh, and there was impatience even from the patrolling sentry. The mechanic had emerged from the jaws of the small truck with a positive signal and vociferation. There was an impregnability about the place, despite his aerie above it. He'd try to disable the scout car or at least get at the map. Then he'd know what Blantyre intended. He watched them settle into easier routines, into harmlessness. He shrugged himself to greater comfort, one hand supporting the bulk of the Nova sight, the rifle placed noiselessly at his side, the pistol in the small of his back, his thighs and knees less conscious of the rock on which he lay. The perimeter guard was waved toward the bright fire and the buck's carcass diminished with the flashing and cutting of the long knife. The truck's hood was slammed shut and the mechanic wiped jelly over his hands, cleaning them, before joining the others around the fire.

Shit, two of them were placing about the camp's perimeter, at each imagined corner of the clearing, what might have been wheeled stands for hi-fi speakers, or skeletal, closed camera tripods. Leads snaked away from them toward one of the tents. Blantyre watched the two men setting up the microwave fence with minimal interest. British manufacture. He recognized it. The invisible fence between the scattered stands with their letterboxlike shutters at the top would be two and a half meters high and the same in width. In the tent, the leads would be connected to a control unit and an audible alarm. His head flicked between the stands. Tight as a fucking drum, impenetrable. It was as if the scene around the fire had become a framed picture beyond a security cord, valuable and unapproachable. The two container trucks, the scout car and the pickup truck were contained within a mushroom circle, protected by the fucking fairies! Blantyre's laughter over the beer and the meat irritated him further.

Shorrock's—ballocks. He'd used that bloody equipment time and again—light, portable, mobile, effective. He'd even had his and Ros' flats secured by Shorrock alarm systems. He'd paid the buggers money and now they'd sold this fucking setup to Blantyre, keeping him out! He took off the goggles and wiped his sweating face, trying to calm himself. One needed to be a fucking monkey to jump over that. Eight feet high, eight feet thick, and invisible. But he *needed* that bloody map! The conversation occasionally burst out in laughter or mockery. Behind him in the trees, something moved stealthily away from him. He heard the rustle of grass as either it or its intended prey accelerated. One of the men in the clearing, hearing the noise, looked up, then shook his head, returning to the buck and potatoes.

A slender, twisted aloe, like a young girl with a limp, dragged itself out over the clearing, approaching a large quiver tree like a supplicant. Need to be a bloody monkey, his thoughts repeated. Would it bear his weight? He judged the distances, the stoop and halt of the smaller tree, the upright sturdiness of the larger. It was the only possibility. Getting out would be—well, they'd know by then, wouldn't they? It wouldn't matter *afterward*. He rolled silently onto his back, staring at the slim trunk of the bent, crippled aloe—winked at it. You're all I've got. Below him, in the clearing, the noise of companionship and safety continued unabated. He had to wait . . .

He jerked awake, aware he must not move, then squinted at his watch, his arm held close to his eyes. Just after two in the morning.

He rolled stiffly onto his stomach, ignoring the

companionable aloe for the moment, looking down into the clearing, which brightened as he dragged on the goggles. Gray ash where the fire had been, gray shapes of the tents, gray shapes of sleeping men, two of them out in the open near the trucks. And the damnable little stands of the microwave fence, dotted about as if no more than lumber to be thrown away. He rubbed his arms cautiously, the night's chill deep in his flesh and bones. He sat upright, facing the clearing, rubbing his cold legs into suppleness as he stared up at the bent aloe. Then he checked down in the clearing—a patch of gray, footprinted sand to cushion his landing, muffle any noise. Blantyre was in the tent with the control unit of the microwave fence, the rest of them outside or scattered in two other tents. He listened, heard the noise of something splashing, then one of them came sleepily back into view from the bushes, zipping his fly. Hyde watched him return to the tent, where his snoring began almost at once. They'd be breakfasting and leaving before dawn.

He picked the rifle up carefully and drew its strap over his head, the butt retracted. It nuzzled against his chest. He checked the spare clip, then the pistol, finally the knapsack, tightening the straps further. Then he approached the aloe, hands reaching for it, feet moving softly across the rock of the outcrop. The roots of the tree thrust down into a cleft in the rock. He tested its strength. Slowly, he began sliding himself up the trunk, across the gritty, knobbled bark. The tree shivered at his weight and movement. Gradually, gently, it bowed toward the invisible fence as he eased forward, out over the sand. He was sweating profusely and blinking the moisture from his eyes. He inched forward again, straddling the tree, pushing with his hands and scraped knees. Estimating—head back and forth, still wearing the goggles—the line of the invisible beams. The tree became more suppliant, bending into a cower. The closest receiver was fifty meters from its companion transmitter, and the tree was bowing and fucking scraping like a menial just over the bloody fence! His hands were slippery on the rough bark, his knees trembling. The tree quivered with his exertions and panic and its wood began to groan—monkey, all fours, poised—

—he thrust out, twisting in the dark air, managing to land on his feet. His whole frame and mind were hunched and tense against the noise of the alarm as he curled to one side in a parachute landing, and rolled, his hands cushioning the goggles. The two black stands glowered silently at one another, *behind* him—

—*inside*. His chest pumped but he held his breath, staring up at the tree as it shuddered above him. He grinned, and he rolled onto his stomach, shivery with adrenalin at the slight noise of someone stirring on a campbed. The tents remained dark, their flaps closed. The two in sleeping bags near the trucks remained oblivious, unmoving. The starlight and the sheen from the paring of moon seemed to fall tiredly into the clearing. Hyde got to his feet in a crouch, then skittered like an elephant shrew toward the scout car. The map first, then any damage he might disguisedly do to that vehicle or the truck.

He moved across the clearing, spinning on his heel occasionally, then obliterating the professional marks, watching the tents, the vehicles, the sleeping bags. Somewhere in the trees, a monkey grumbled in its sleep. More distantly, the bark of a wild dog or jackal. The sounds flowed into the clearing more coldly and sharply than the starlight. He reached the XR 311 scout car. Blantyre had put the map back in the glove compartment. Gingerly, he touched the door handle, paused, then opened the passenger door.

Through the goggles, the map, as he carefully unfolded it, seemed distant, featureless. Then he saw the snail track drawn from Keetmanshoop, south and then southwest, tomorrow's route. His breath caught. They were going the way he wanted. It was the only likely place, the only terrain suitable for an ambush that would immobilize them and cut them off from outside help. He breathed out gratefully. He stowed the map inside his shirt. It had to be the scout car then, to cover the missing map—

He heard the tiny noise of metal moving against metal. He whirled around, seeing the man and beyond him one of the sleeping bags, opened. The man was holding an R5 rifle at his hip and grinning, as if he found the froglike mask of the goggles disarmingly amusing. Hyde fired twice, the pistol in his right hand, the map still held in his left. The silencer made the faintest of noises. He ran, pouncing on the slumping body and catching the man's weight against him, trapping the loosely held rifle under his armpit. Immediately, he squeezed the trigger of the rifle, certain the angle was correct for the scene behind him. The magazine, on automatic, emptied immediately with a terrifying noise. The goggles were steamed up with his effort and the rifle's barrel was hot against his side and arm. Then he dropped the body and ran, until he was thrust forward by the explosion behind him. He felt the heat from the scout car's exploding petrol tank on his back and shoulders.

He hardly heard the alarm he triggered as he blundered through the beams of the fence, or the voices that rose in surprise and panic above the crackle and roar of the flames.

Malan snapped angrily, "He believes me because I've told him the truth! Those bastards in that junkyard are waiting for Blantyre and what he has to deliver." The statement amounted to a confession—of Blantyre's working independently, of having conceived and executed this business with the Czech nerve gas. An admission to Babbington of all people! "They've been promised nerve gas," he continued with an effort at calm, "for a great deal of money. I found them because Aubrey would not have believed anything but the truth." He scowled, then continued, "There are bound to be consequences if you kill Aubrey now—here."

Babbington spread his hands in a mockery of benediction.

"It cannot be any other way, Paulus," he murmured. "We have come this far. There's no other solution." He sipped at the whisky he had held like the Host as he spread his arms in blessing and certainty.

"Aubrey's not some nameless black from Alexandra," Paulus argued. "People will interest themselves in his death. My government"—the contempt was undisguised—"will interest itself." He turned away momentarily from Babbington's implacable confidence, then snapped his head round and said, "*Your* masters want him dead—the ears of the bull, right, man? But why not wait and see? He might lose interest, be sidetracked or called home, for all I know!"

"No, Paulus, I'm afraid not. Our safety depends on Aubrey's overdue demise. It has to be done and done quickly. Tomorrow night, for certain."

Malan turned from the liquor cabinet on the far side of the spacious, lamplit room to find the same pretense of utter confidence on Babbington's features, daring him to dissent. And the hatred of Aubrey, the greed for it to be done, glittered in Babbington's eyes. Malan detested his subordination to the Englishman.

"I don't work for the KGB!" he snapped.

"Your interests are as well served by his death as are mine—and the people I represent. Stop wriggling under the inevitable, Paulus." Babbington smiled loftily.

Malan slumped back into his armchair. Eventually,

his features stilled from their vigorous mastication of his anger and he murmured: "Very well, Andrew. All *right*."

Why was he now reluctant? He saw, for God's sake, just as clearly as Babbington did, the necessity of Aubrey's death. He would enjoy it as Babbington did, but then it wasn't personal. Was it?

It was like some kaffir curse put on another black, he admitted reluctantly. Aubrey's niece, his own father, the connections between himself and Aubrey . . . there was a sense of it going wrong, of not working out . . .

He was aware of Babbington's studious gaze, his intent scrutiny. Fuck Babbington. He hardly needed the continuing links with the KGB. They'd be coming to him in twelve months, desperate to unload vast amounts of diamonds on the market for hard currency. He could afford to wait . . . except that he couldn't. Aubrey was getting closer and closer. He looked up, to find Babbington still studying him. Then the Englishman smiled.

"I mean to have it done, Paulus." He looked at his empty glass. "I mean to have that infernal, interfering old man dead—and I intend to be there to see it done." He yawned through his cold smile. "Past my bedtime, I'm afraid. I'm not certain I shall sleep, but I think I had best try." He stood up and stretched luxuriously. "You'll see those people first thing, Paulus—just to make certain?"

Malan looked up angrily, then merely murmured: "Yes, I'll see to all the *arrangements*. Stage manage the last little act of your overlong drama, Andrew."

"Thank you, Paulus, thank you." His sigh of satisfaction was stomach-turning. "Goodnight, then."

When he had closed the door behind him, Malan sat on, unable to calm himself, unable even to adopt a pretense of relaxation. He almost gagged on his drink as he swallowed it.

What he hated was being *subject* to Babbington, having to obey him, to fulfill another's priorities, not his own, even if it was inevitable, and altogether better, if Aubrey died tomorrow night.

He drew to a halt near the outskirts of Alexandra. He was aware of the former bachelor township just beyond the ragged horizon of spoil-heaps from the mines. Its history pressed against the windows of the car like a wild crowd bent on mischief. He stared across the road at the scrapyard and its heaped cars, still retaining on his retinae the image of Malan's red Porsche turning through the rickety, corrugated metal gates a few moments earlier.

Anderson rubbed his cheeks and yawned. Lights still glowed in a grubby halo around the township. He had been surprised from a doze as Malan's car had turned out of the electronic gates of his estate. It had been difficult to keep up with him, but easy to keep him in sight in the necessarily red sports car. Then the Porsche had slewed aside from this winding road in a decaying suburb into the scrapyard outside which Anderson had drawn to a shocked halt. DE VRIES was the name daubed untidily in black paint on the corrugated gates. The name meant nothing to Anderson.

He pulled forward perhaps three hundred yards, from his position opposite the gates, onto a grubby, weed-strewn patch of concrete that masqueraded as a parking lot and warned against black customers. The bungalow motel behind its parking lot wished to remain in the past. He opened the door and got out. The early morning was cool, fresh, and he felt his curiosity come awake like hunger. On the faint breeze, he smelt frying bacon, and his stomach protested. The distant factories and mines, on which everything depended, belched smoke and dust into the lightening sky. He opened the trunk and took out his pistol, camera and the directional microphone. Blacks moved along the pavement or tottered in the road itself, either going to work or away from shibeens, with irremovable grace.

The place was flat, seedy, and the scrapyard's heaped contours of wrecked or old cars and trucks provided its immediate horizon. He crossed the road and looked through the gates. There was no sign of Malan's Porsche. He moved inside, adrenalin itching in his stomach, his body expressing the aches gathered during his night's uncomfortable sleep. He was met by cranes, crushers, great suspended grabs—like the little cranes in glass boxes in amusement arcades from his childhood holidays in Bournemouth or Weston-super-Mare; tiny cranes whose grabs were suspended over chocolate bars and trinkets. Money in the slot, turn the wheel furiously, guide the crane before the time the pennies had bought ran out. . . . Now, these grabs that hung poised over last year's models, eager to seize and deliver them to the crusher, might catch him Malan, a far greater prize. He moved with exaggerated care around and through anthills of rusted metal, the long microphone dibbing ahead of his steps like an extravagant gardening tool—

—to find, after avoiding the few blacks and even fewer whites who worked in the scrapyard, Malan and two other men paused on the steps of a leaning, disheveled caravan which seemed parked against a portable lavatory. Which he could scent on the morning air. The two men were caricatures; stubbled, potbellied, thick-necked. Anderson rested his elbow on the dented wing of a red, rusting Ford and adjusted the focus of the heavy telephoto lens attached to the camera. Malan and the two men jumped into closeup. He snapped the photographs, concentrating on the other two but always including Malan in profile in the shots, as if concerned merely with composition.

Why not kill him now? But he knew the answer. He wanted to survive. He was almost ashamed to admit it. Despite Margarethe and his grief, he didn't really want to die in the process of killing Malan.

Malan was gesticulating angrily at the other two, causing Anderson to raise the directional mike quickly and steady it on the hood of the Ford, thrusting it toward the dilapidated caravan. He fitted the earpiece of the mike and heard: "I'm bringing the Englishman here tonight—I want it finished then. My people will take care of it." Malan was using his hand in chopping, assertive motions. "—no problem." The muttering of one of the Afrikaaners was masked to the microphone, but seemed to be conciliatory at the mention of reward. He gestured Malan inside the hut and they went in together, closing the door behind them.

Anderson, cursing, could see them moving excitedly to and fro like insects behind glass, but the murmur of their voices was drowned by the upstart of a crane and the hoisting of the first of the day's ruined cars into the sunlight; it gleamed and shone before being dropped into the crusher, whose eating noises made him lower the microphone as he realized that Aubrey must be the subject of their conversation. Malan moved into view inside the hut, smiling, his arms moving in decisive gestures. It was a setup. They intended Aubrey's death, Malan and Babbington. A disposal job, Aubrey ending up in the scrapyard. He glanced around him, at the mounds of cars and tires and other metal piled like termite mounds of disposable technology.

Then, Malan emerged from the hut and stood posed on its steps as if for assassination. Anderson realized he could kill Malan that night *and* have a margin for escape.

He allowed Malan to move down the steps and reach his car with a luxury of confidence. He knew now, and that was all that mattered. The metal around him began to warm with the slanting rays of the run, and the dust and smog over the city started to dissipate. It was the nearest to a good dawn since Margarethe's death. Malan smoothed the Porsche away from the noisome hut, down another channel between the great, untidy flexed muscles of the car heaps. The crusher continued to chew as another mangled car was dropped into its throat. He shivered as he thought that someone must have died in that, the wreckage was so maimed and twisted. Then he regained confidence as he remembered that Malan was walking into a trap. Not Aubrey—Malan. If Aubrey had to be the tethered goat, then so be it. He owed Aubrey almost nothing. If he hadn't remembered Aubrey when he'd discovered the crashed Dakota, then she would not now be dead.

He moved cautiously down one of the alleyways between the walls of dead cars, the mike trailing like a spade in the hands of a weary gardener, the camera around his neck. A black man near the main gate alarmed him, but the man was intent upon worrying at something that glowed dully like copper from the middle of a hive of broken cars. Above him, the sky was cleanly blue. Anderson scuttled toward his car, the dust from Malan's Porsche already settled on the road. He threw the mike and the camera carelessly into the trunk. He needn't even follow Malan. The time between now and tonight mattered nothing. He started the engine and turned the car. He could go back to the cheap boarding house and the lumpy mattress and sleep. He'd put on the traveling alarm clock as if he needed to wake simply to go to work—which is what it would be, just a job, the *last* job.

The road bustled with drivers heading for city work. An accident, a car mangled and scorched beneath the cab of a truck, hardly disturbed his mood.

Two more fragments of the newest heap in the scrap-yard where, that night, Malan would become his victim, where he would fall backward with a little hole in his forehead before his mouth opened in shock and final exhalation. It would do—it would do very well.

The city gathered about him, straggly suburbs eventually becoming more dense, clotted. Not wealthy, just small front lawns or apartment buildings and old, decayed bungalows. Almost a shabby gentility in places. The golf courses and the parks and the white, stuccoed houses were masked by grubby lines of houses, like washing taken in from the wealthier areas, as he moved closer to the center of Johannesburg. Neat estates became leaning, crowded boarding houses and twisting, mean-faced streets. Hillbrow. Translation into the dialect of tourists, hitchhikers and migrant workers of sallow complexion: cheap lodgings.

He turned into a narrow, curving street where old cars jostled each other in the gutters and the stained pavements fronted tall, narrow houses with pinched expressions, undernourished and deprived of sunlight. The boarding house at which he was registered under another name was on the left, where he looked for a parking space—

—and found police cars, their occupants spilt onto the pavement and into the road. Blue lights whirled slowly, hypnotically above the cars. Guns. Outside *his* boarding house, cutting it off. The mean street of lodging houses, snack bars, fleabags and shops leered at him, as if it had planned this shock.

Malan's power and influence. They'd found him.

Hyde had had to wait outside Holoog, to be certain that they stuck to the route sketched on the stolen map. Then, once they were on the winding, climbing road through the hills toward the Fish River Canyon, he had scuttled ahead of them in the Land Rover, giving himself perhaps an hour before the container trucks and the now cramped pickup truck arrived . . . just here.

The winter afternoon weighed on his shoulders and stuck his sweatstained shirt to his damp torso. He had hidden the Land Rover almost a mile from the canyon, forcing it up a narrow track further along the road, which wound through the maze of hills that lay to the southwest of the canyon. Then he had scrambled and urged himself back here, to *this* spot. Where he could ambush them, could pull rock and earth down in front of them and behind, boxing them in, with no escape except on foot.

He looked down from the road to the bottom of Fish River Canyon. A few scattered water holes, nothing more in the dry season. The river only ran in spate during the wet season—if the rains came. There were a few buck, some zebra and a couple of baboons scattered around the nearest and largest of the water holes. The canyon snaked out of sight within a couple of miles in either direction, twisting its way through a tumbled, mountainous landscape. He looked up. Hills and flat-topped plateaus stretched away in every direction, blue and hazed in the afternoon. The whole landscape was fingered with canyons and narrow valleys, and was dry and empty, red brown or flint blue under the sun. A mountain desert in Namibia, no more than forty miles from the border with South Africa—the last place and the only place he could hope to stop them. Here, on this narrow dusty strip of road, he could do it.

Here the road dropped below the lip of the canyon for a distance of some miles, sagging like a rope-bridge suspended alongside the cliff face. Rock overhung the road, rock that could be blown down in a landslide.

One of the two overhangs he had selected was hidden from the other by a bend in the road. Which meant

he would have to be somewhere in the middle, concealed by no more than rubble beside the road, and he
would have to be quick and certain. He looked at his
watch after staring up at the sun. Their speed along this
stretch of the road—for the last ten miles or so—would
be about twenty-five. He had three or four minutes. He
sensed the ground beneath his feet. Nothing yet, no
quiver of the approaching weight of the two container
trucks.

And, once he'd declared his hand, they'd try to
reverse out of the trap, back toward *you,* sport, standing in the middle of the road like a fucking lemon. He
glanced back the way he had come, but there were
other twists in the road that hid their approach. No
column of dust, not yet.

He rubbed his hands through his hair, his temperature jumping as if he had been pricked by a needle. He
moved to the side of the road and knelt beside the two
fiberboard boxes he had brought from the Land Rover.
Twenty-five kilos, combined weight. His arms ached as
much from hurry and tension as from the effort of car
rying them. The ground beneath his foot and bent knee
seemed to quiver, as if warning of an imminent earthquake. It was them.

He fumbled open one of the boxes and withdrew a
short tube, laying it on the ground beside him. The dust
trembled underneath his fingertips as he did so and
sweat broke out on his forehead. He removed the second tube from the box and then opened another one,
laying two more tubes on the ground, then four closed-
finned rockets beside them. Feverishly, bent over his
work as if secretive, he loaded each of the tubes with a
rocket, after first extending the inner tube of each
launcher and hearing the cocking mechanism operate—
he just heard the last as the noise of approaching heavy
vehicles grinding against their brakes seemed to rush
against him.

He checked the sight on one of the tubes, and then flung himself flat against the shaking earth, behind the shelter of a scrubby little thorn bush and a litter of small boulders as the noise of the two trucks became deafening. The ground shuddered against his body. He thrust his hands over his ears as the dust rolled over him and then a vast shadow cut off the sunlight. He glanced sideways and saw—

—a small, old green car, overawed by the dust from the first of the trucks. A white-haired man drove, with a white-haired woman in the passenger seat, traveling at twenty miles an hour, their faces agape with the view and the drop to the right. Then the first truck passed, then the second, its shadow cold. He glanced up again, and imagined Blantyre in the pickup as it passed. He sprang to his feet in the swirling dust and, gripping a tube, ran out into the road after the convoy. Shit, why did those two silly old buggers have to be there just *now?* They'd have to be trapped, that was all, have to be . . . maybe the old green car wouldn't be buried . . .

He felt exposed by the settling dust and raised the tube to his shoulder, pressing the rocket launcher's crude, effective sight to his eye. He saw nothing but dust for a moment, then the stadia lines and crosses enclosed the shadowy bulk of the pickup truck. He raised the tube slowly, his hand cupped over the trigger bar, the safety handle pushed to the armed position. He glimpsed the green car for an instant before he focused on the overhang. Range, two-fifty meters. Target stationary.

He squeezed the trigger bar. There was the slightest jolt. He sensed the six spring-loaded fins snap out from the missile, then saw the small jet of flame from the motor before he lost sight of the tiny, inadequate projectile. Then he saw the impact, detonation and explosion, and the burst of rock and debris from the overhang. He snatched up the second tube, discarding the first, armed it, sighted, paused. The rock was falling out of a cloud of dust, like the collapse of slums being pulled down. It was almost as if he anticipated a bathroom's weary wallpaper to be exposed rather than raw rock. He fired the second missile. The green car, for Christ's sake—poor old buggers . . .

He heard the noise of violent braking, he even heard voices, coming out of the slow roar of the landslide. Then the second explosion obscured everything in more dust, the noise recoiling from the walls of the canyon. The dust rolled along the road toward him like a sea fog coming inland. Perhaps the green car had slipped through . . .

He lurched to the side of the road as if nauseous and picked up the third and fourth tubes. The noise of the explosions seemed to growl back from the landscape. He saw brown hills and blue mesas for a moment before the dust enveloped him. Then he heard the screech of reversing tires. He ran back along the road toward the second overhang. It might not be enough. He couldn't know how much of each landslide would fall off the road and into the canyon. He came blunderingly out of the dust cloud into the blinding sunlight. Tires squealed and shifted and there were human shouts behind him. He passed beneath the overhang, turned and paused to breathe deeply. His throat was thick with dust. Then he sighted the tube and fired. Flame, fins, diminishment—explosion. Rocks grumbled, even screamed in protest as they began to tumble. Then the pickup truck reversed out of the dust and he saw wild faces watching the road and the drop beside it before they saw him. At once, there was yelling and the movement of the black sticks of rifles.

He ducked onto one knee and fired again into the maelstrom of dust and rock tumbling down the cliff face. He did not see the flame of the explosion, but heard the detonation. The rock face slithered viscously like mud onto the road between himself and the truck. One shot whined harmlessly near him.

Hyde heard cries and the roar of an engine accelerating away from the landslide. Then he turned and ran ahead of the rolling cloud of dust. He reached the narrow, slitlike crevice that ate into the cliff face and wound jaggedly to its top. Get up there, look down on them, check the damage. Green car, two old people . . .

As he began climbing, feet and back braced against rock, sweat bathing his body and dust choking his throat and nostrils, he saw the landscape open out beyond the rolling dust. The G3 rifle clinked against the rocks. He'd begun it now—not with the murder of two civilians, please—but begun it he had. The canyon was a deep, twisting scratch in the arid land which tumbled and jutted away from him in every direction, hills and plateaus empty and barren under the afternoon sun.

He pushed himself higher up the crevice, his muscles quivering with effort.

Green car. Poor old buggers.

15

DARE ME TO THE DESERT

The lift climbed the floors of the parking deck with asthmatic, shuddering difficulty. The graffiti of hatred and inconsequence jostled against each other on the metallic walls. Anderson glanced down at the briefcase he carried, containing the rifle, the nightsight, the spare ammunition and clothing, and felt himself settled by it. It had been easy to drive past the boarding house in Hillbrow, ignoring the police cars and the small crowd of loungers and gawpers on the opposite pavement. Easy, too, to return to the car, almost easy to eat breakfast. By lunchtime, it was different, extending his nerves to breaking, because they were ever more intent in their search. The midday editions of the evening papers all carried his picture. He had spent much of the afternoon checking and rechecking that he was not being tailed, that he could survive without being immediately recognized.

The lift jolted and Anderson's temperature jumped

like an insect, feeding on his anxieties. It *was* closing in, like this scarred metal box of a lift. Malan had gone to see Aubrey at the Carlton, no doubt confirming the arrangements for the setup. That night they would get rid of the inquisitive old man. He rubbed the arm that carried the briefcase with his free hand. The lift dragged to a halt and the door opened. He stepped out into the shadowy air-raid shelter of the deck.

He had to use Aubrey. But the old man had his own reasons for being there. Only his ignorance would be used. His quiet footsteps echoed above the hum of the city's traffic. The hot afternoon sun hardly intruded, except to emphasize shadow. He had his reservations, but Aubrey's death would hardly weigh, after all, beside Margarethe's.

He noted slabbed glimpses of hard afternoon light beginning to mellow toward evening, and rainbow pools of oil and petrol, the scent of fuel. Far below, impatient tires screeched, turning a sharp corner from one floor to another. He'd remain here, watching Malan's office, until the man left for home or for the Carlton to collect Aubrey.

A memory of the old man's impatient, irresistible moral outrage caused him to stumble. He righted himself and shook his head. That was then, this is now, he told himself. He spotted the trunk of the car jutting out near the end of the row of vehicles, and began to hurry toward it.

He opened the trunk to place the briefcase inside and take out the binoculars. One small suitcase, a second handgun, night-vision binoculars—all he needed. The sun began to slant into the upper floor of the deck, spilling across the scarred hood of the car, its dusty paintwork.

Hand poised to slam the trunk, hand making prints on the paintwork, just like the hand that had made an impression on the edge of the hood, which was normally tightly closed. But there was another smudgy print near the first, as if two hands had closed the hood very carefully. The sun exposed the intrusion. His hand quivered on the trunk lid, still holding it aloft, his fingertips sweaty, his brow prickling with damp. Smell of petrol, sharp as a winter morning's exhaust fumes. His stomach churned as the hood threatened to bulge like a frog, explode—

Carefully, with a huge effort of will, he lowered the lid of the trunk until it touched the knuckles of his other hand. He let it rest on its hinges and moved carefully toward the front of the car. The smudged signals of interference vanished until he bent, cocking his head sideways, and caught them again. Two thin-gloved hands closing the hood after . . .

He knelt on the stained concrete and peered beneath the car. Sump, gearbox, exhaust—and a cancerous tumor sprouting wires. Trembler trigger or mercury switch or radio controlled. He bolted upright, staring wildly around him. No one. Sure? Again, his eyes swept the parking deck floor. No one. He was sweating profusely. He wiped savagely at his face, shuddering with anxiety. His death was to have been just another terrorist outrage, his body never identified . . .

He opened the trunk carefully, and took out the briefcase as the first silenced bullet sprang with a wasplike noise off the trunk lid. Pistol, low velocity, only denting the metal. He jerked round but his hand did not forget to lower the lid carefully as he ducked beside the car, crouching against the rear wheel, his knee in a pool of damp, grubby oil. A second shot shattered the rear window above his head, showering his hair and neck with fragments. He was shudderingly aware that he was on the same level as the bomb, that any impact might trigger it. Oh, Christ . . . A third shot—from where? *Where?* He wanted to scream. No muzzle flash from a silenced gun. The third bullet broke into the car next to his, frosting both the side window and windshield. How many? He bent forward and drew the briefcase toward him, and the concrete puffed up dust near his hand. One gunman? The bullets seemed to be coming from the same direction. Silence, except for tires moving on a lower floor and the hum of the traffic, the occasional impatient horn.

He slid behind the nearest car, moving closer to the gunman, squeezing his crouched body between the bumper and the concrete sill of the parking deck wall. Then a second car, then a third—flinching at a shot whining away off the roof of his car. The briefcase clutched to his chest, he eased past another radiator—Volvo grille and badge. The pistol in the small of his back, under his jacket, scraped silently along the concrete wall, over which seeped the noises of Johannesburg's indifferent afternoon. He wiped his forehead and eyes—

—footsteps, scuttling like rat noises in a cellar. He raised his head above the parapet of a BMW and glimpsed a shadowy figure, one arm clutching a blunt little shape, the other hand pressing something against an indistinguishable face. Calling for help. Unconsciously, he drew the pistol from his belt and slipped a round into the chamber and the safety off. Slight thumb movement, nothing more. The bulk of an American limousine hid the man for a moment, then he was a stronger shadow jutting above the curve of the Cadillac's roofline, just for . . . elbows resting on the BMW's roof, gun extended, finger squeezing twice. Spit of bullets onto concrete, the kick of the gun, the jerk of the struck head and shoulders and the skitter of the dropped handgun across the concrete. The screech of tires shut out all other noise, even that of his breathing as he ran for the exit door and the stairs.

* * *

He threw himself down at the top of the crevice, elbows jarring as he raised the glasses to his eyes. The lenses clouded for a moment, then cleared. The speck of green at the periphery of the binoculars' vision drew him with a surge of relief and he focused on the old car and the older couple doddering out of it, dazed at the sight of the collapsed cliffside behind them. Christ, they'd escaped, thank God. The old man and woman clung together as if amid the wreckage of their home. His thin, shaking hand kept patting her shoulder and cheek. It was strangely affecting, so that he flicked the glasses aside—

—to see Blantyre, arms waving, pointing. Hyde's shirt began drying on his back, stuck unwelcomely to it. The cab of the leading truck was crushed inwards, like a beer can that had been closed in an angry fist, but the container itself, thank Christ, was intact, merely scarred and dented by the falling rocks. Two men were trying to open the door, flinching against any escape of the cargo, goaded by Blantyre's yelled instructions. The door wouldn't open. His heart continued to thud against the rock on which he lay prone. The road ahead of them was completely blocked with tons of rock and debris above which dust seemed reluctant to settle. He swung the glasses hesitantly past Blantyre's angry bulk and the rest of his troops, one of whom seemed to be nursing an arm, toward the other fallen outcrop. Much of it had spilled over the canyon, down toward the dry river, but a great, dull mound of rocks lay across the road, perhaps twenty feet high. Impenetrable. Both ways out were blocked, they were in the box. Thank Christ.

Blantyre had glasses up to his eyes now and was scanning each broken outcrop in turn. He must be able to smell the explosives even through the amount of dust in the air. He'd know—and know who—even if they had persuaded themselves that SWAPO remnants or bandits had killed the patrolling guard and destroyed the scout car. Blantyre's mind must already be forming the name and the accompanying expletives, and before long he'd react—

—waving at the clifftop, and yelling. Hyde shuffled, as if flinching, a yard farther from the edge. One of them, the driver of the second truck by the look of it, was gesticulating as he argued with Blantyre, whose face was suffused with rage. Then he calmed, his shoulders relaxing, his head beginning to nod, as the driver pointed beyond the fallen outcrop that blocked their route.

Blantyre ordered them around him and began gesturing at the wall of rock. Then he hurried toward it. Hyde shifted the glasses and caught the speck of green that was the old couple's car. She was holding the top of a thermos flask in both hands, sipping at something that smoked hotly. He was holding her upper arms and talking to her with slow gestures of his head. Christ— witnesses. Blantyre was scrabbling up the slope of fallen rock, dust billowing around him. Two others, with Uzis or something else blunt and dangerous slung across their backs, were climbing in his wake. The old woman went on sipping obliviously. The hot drink evidently calmed her. They stood close together, *were* together. Blantyre had scrambled to the top of the mound, then paused. The other two joined him, and there was instant gesticulation at the two elderly people. Witnesses, that was all they were, to be eliminated. He saw in the faces of the two old people a growing sense of concern at what might have happened to the convoy which had been behind them in their cautious progress, so that they turned, as Blantyre's two companions leveled their submachine guns.

Oh, you bastard. It was futile to call out. They could not escape their execution. Hyde bit his bottom lip as his body flinched against the noise of the two Uzis. He watched the two slowly collapsing bodies. They fell apart as they would never have wished, one to either side of a scattering of small boulders. Blantyre immediately clambered over the lip of the rubble and raised dust as he slid invisibly down the other side. Hyde's reaction was instinctive, even stupid. He raised the rifle, the butt extended against his shoulder, a round carried in the chamber. He fiddled quickly with the adjustments to the telescopic sight. A sweat-streaked back enlarged, became clear—and he fired. Then he transferred his aim to the other man as he glimpsed Blantyre come back into view as he reached the bottom of the mound and glanced back at the noise of the first shot. Hyde fired again, then a third time because his finger had jumped on the trigger rather than squeezed. The second sweat-stained shirt slumped against the rocks as if exhausted. Two dead, for the older two.

Blantyre had already ducked away from the suspected line of fire toward a scatter of boulders, leaving the two old bodies. It was somehow obscene that the old woman's skirt had ridden above her narrow thighs when she fell and their outstretched arms had no hope of reaching each other. They were lying only yards from the green car. The cliff above Blantyre's hiding place was bathed in late afternoon sunlight.

On this side of the trap, men scurried for cover like ants. He had invaded their nest. He fired three shots, cartridges puffing out of the right cheek of the rifle, and then the scene went silent. Lack of movement, stillness. They were all, suddenly, hidden from him.

And now it began. Keeping them here, in the trap. The silence pressed against his ears, drumming. The two old bodies on the road, the two bodies on the rubble mound like dirty clothes drying in the sun. He had to keep them *all* here.

*   *   *

His rain forest had gone, his natural habitat of anonymity had been razed. Every evening newspaper carried pictures of him with banner headlines in thick black type, blazoning his fictitious crimes. In a paranoid moment in a paranoid country, he had become a right-wing terrorist plotting to overthrow the government and the process of peaceful change. He had murdered an unarmed policeman who had been keeping his car under surveillance. There was even to be an inquiry as to why defenseless police officers were forced to risk their lives to confront men as dangerous and mad as he. His face was everywhere; he could not risk confronting anyone—car rental firms, cheap lodging-house clerks, waitresses in dingy cafés. He was the last lion on a scorched veldt, exposed to the hunt.

Anderson leaned against the warm brick of an alley wall, the lights from one of the city's main thoroughfares leaking into it. Car headlights and the flicking spray of red or blue from police patrols flashed frequently into the darkness. Somewhere farther along the alley, a black man had discovered oblivion in a bottle and was snoring. Occasionally, the noise of a radio or a quarrel, laughter passing the end of the alley where a restaurant's rubbish attracted thin cats with its smell. His whole body quivered in a spasm as one of the cats knocked off a dustbin lid and it rolled along the alley. He wiped his sheened face, feeling on his skin the shiver of his fingers. Christ . . . oh, *Christ!* The briefcase was at his feet, the small of his back was numb where the gun had been pressed between cloth and brick. There was no way of going on and little or no possibility of getting out. He stared at his hands in the splashed light of a passing car. There was nothing he could do, not now. He could never get to Malan and survive. He would be lucky to get out of Jo'burg alive.

Because your bottle's gone, old boy. His courage, determination, whatever name you gave it, had slipped away. He couldn't find revenge any longer, nor even hatred. Their superiority was too evident, too omnipresent as he had skirted a newspaper stand or lighted shop window; too evident each time a patrol car or a policeman on foot passed him. Finally, having fled into this drunk-inhabited, cat-roamed alley at the siren of yet another patrol car, he had surrendered to his body's spasms and vomited with fear. He could smell that, too, mingled with the alleyway's other scents.

All he could do, he admitted—if he could get up the nerve to move at all—was to call Aubrey. At least warn him what Malan had planned for him. Sign off, bow out with a little face-saving gesture. He pressed the face of his watch close to his eye. Nine-twenty or thereabouts. The night enlarged, extended, making him shiver.

It was nine-forty before he had pushed his way along the wall to the end of the alley. One of the cats had inspected his shoes because he must have stepped in something fleshy and enticing. The lights made him flinch, the people passing possessed loud, accusing voices. A patrol car forced him into a runner's crouch for a long moment. Eventually, he straightened, back pressed against familiar brick, hands spread so that his palms were comfortingly gritty with brick dust. If he waited until the streets emptied, Aubrey would be dead for certain—

The telephone booth was perhaps fifty yards along the well-lighted, crowded street. Nine forty-five. A blue-shirted police back, a streak of sweat darkening the uniform in a ragged stripe from neck to waist. Hands on hips, the armed policeman was no more than six or eight yards beyond the telephone booth—which was empty. He touched the handle of the briefcase with numb fingers, then picked it up, wiped his forehead brusquely and stepped out of the alley into the drifting crowd, allowing himself to be shunted toward the telephone and the oblivious policeman. Thirty yards, then twenty, the scene joggling in his vision. He gripped the briefcase unfeelingly. A minute, no more, just enough time to blurt out, *They're going to kill you tonight, don't go anywhere with Malan*—then he could try to get out of the city, out of the country, find some desolate border crossing into Botswana or even Namibia.

A black lifted the telephone off its hook and began dialing. Anderson halted and the crowd jostled before parting around him. The policeman scanned the street and the pavement and Anderson bolted against a shop window, staring unseeingly at trinkets and watches behind a heavy grille. When he glanced round at the telephone booth, the black was gesticulating, arguing with whomever he had called. Time ran as slowly as the beads of cold sweat down Anderson's sides. The black man continued to bellow silently into the receiver. A patrol car passed, slowed, then drew across to the pavement and the relaxed policeman. Its headlights remained on, as if looking for Anderson. The black left the phone booth, throwing aside a cigarette butt before moving angrily away. The policeman was leaning into the patrol car, then he emerged, nodding and grinning. A smell of frying onions. The policeman nudged his way to the front of the small queue at the vendor's cart and returned to the patrol car with two dull buns around fat, shining sausages and one polystyrene cup. He handed the food and drink into the car, which slid casually out into the traffic. Anderson darted to the booth and dialed the Carlton Hotel. The policeman had drifted back to the vendor and planted himself once more at the head of the queue.

"Sir Kenneth Aubrey," he blurted. "Quickly!" The heat of tension mounted in his frame, burned on his cheeks and forehead. He glanced at the policeman, his mouth blocked with some kind of burger. The stench of frying onions was utterly nauseating. His fist punched harmlessly at the directory on its chain. Come on—

"Yes?" he heard. There was a palpable tension in Aubrey's voice.

"Kenneth—Richard."

"Richard—please listen to me. I've seen the news, you must not—"

"What—not do anything to upset your plans, Kenneth?" His anger was delaying him. "Christ, do you realize Malan's about to have you killed?" He heard his own breathing and smelt onions and petrol fumes. He felt sick.

"Richard, you must be careful, you're in considerable—"

"Christ, don't tell me, Kenneth!" A car drew up, a small BMW, and the driver got out almost close enough to nudge against the glass of the booth. He strolled to the vending cart, passing the chewing, bovine policeman. "I'm in danger now! This minute. But you can't go with—"

"I have to, Richard. I don't yet know what I need to. Thank you, however."

"I'm getting out, Kenneth. Before they get me."

The keys were in the BMW's ignition. The policeman had finished chewing and was being asked directions. The driver was still behind one other person in the queue, casually smoking.

He slapped the receiver back onto its hook and picked up the briefcase. It was a sign, a gift. Before the number could be circulated and watched for, he'd be beyond the city's outskirts and into the night. On a road out of the country, the damned *fucking* country! He threw the briefcase into the rear of the car as he glanced at the driver, who was studying two young women. The policeman's arm was gesticulating at some destination streets away. Anderson started the engine, slipped the car into gear and skidded out with a screech of tires into the street's traffic. In the driving mirror, the owner of the car only slowly became aware. He swung north onto a narrower street that would take him toward the nearest motorway.

He was getting out.

Aubrey slowly put down the disconnected telephone, then straightened in his chair and sighed. He shivered as if a chill breeze had penetrated the warm sitting room of his suite—which itself seemed to diminish, as if he were suddenly outside it, looking at a photograph of its furniture and carpet and drapes. He sighed again and clutched his thighs with his fingers. He felt a sharp concern for Anderson . . . and perhaps regret that matters could not be settled in the way that Richard would have wished, by a quick strike, an execution. He knew it to be wrong—and shortsighted, of course. *He*, Aubrey, had to know, to discover more before Malan could be consigned to the flames of whatever hell he admitted. That was paramount. Malan would offer him real people, real conspiracies, as the price of silencing him.

He puffed out his cheeks and exhaled, then rose and poured himself a small whisky, returning with it to one of the suite's ample sofas. Ten o' clock. Malan had called an hour before, arranging to collect him at twelve. He had been circumspect and devious, but he *had* located the destination of Blantyre's cargo of nerve gas, however he had arranged matters since. Malan himself would put those people to the sword, but it was essential that Aubrey play his part as innocent seeker-after-truth and victim.

He sipped at the glass and his fingers quivered it

against his dentures. He adjusted them and a mirror caught his action dimly on the other side of the sitting room. He shook his head at himself. Why not walk away? He couldn't. He thought of the Prime Minister he had served for so long going out in her own blaze of immolation; of her deep and genuine rage against circumstance. The man who succeeded her was not half the man she was, as a tabloid had recently claimed. And he could acknowledge that, despite her abiding distrust of him. His rage was similar, one of entire rectitude. He had to ensure that it was stopped. He glanced across at the drawer of the desk where the pistol lay. He hardly knew how to use it, such a modern weapon. Malan had been responsible for so many deaths—Kathryn, his niece, in California all those months ago, Michael Davies, whose company had been the conduit for the smuggled high technology, and Terry Chambers, who was knifed to death in a quiet Midlands street. It had poetic, just symmetry, at least.

He rubbed his creased forehead and stared into the whisky glass. Such memories seemed to hurt and tire these days—that was part of the problem. When Paulus Malan came for him, he would get into the car—to be taken wherever, like a seeker after knowledge and a lamb to the slaughter.

Thus resolved, he nodded to himself and rose to replenish the whisky in his glass. He poured the drink from the bottle of malt whisky. The neck clinked against the tumbler. He knew that Babbington was on a course of action that must result in the death of one or both of them. Here, or in London, or at the cottage in Oxfordshire, even in a street or field somewhere, Babbington would have him killed. He swallowed the whisky calmly and dedicatedly. It might as well be here, in Johannesburg—tonight.

He touched the drawer and pulled it out, exposing

the gun. Be *damned* to you, Andrew Babbington—and to you, Paulus Malan.

He finished the whisky. What was the bloodstream's capacity to absorb alcohol, for someone hoping to kill a man at close range? He shook his head. Better not risk another drink.

Had it been childhood, they would have made coyote or whippoorwill calls and would have been Apaches or Comanches, as they moved in the rocks and amid the stiff, rattling vegetation. They would have been his friends from other dusty frame houses along the barren street of the suburb where he had spent the years before his mother died. Hyde shrugged. It wasn't any old game, it was *the* old game, the wild hunt, the one he had played most of his adult life.

At the latest count, there were six of them. He could never be certain, of course, because they were scattered in their search for him. But there were four dead or wounded: the bloke he'd killed beside the scout car, two on the scree slope from his landslide, at least one injured when the cliff had fallen on the cab of the leading truck. That left eight in total, and two of those were guarding the stranded vehicles. Six out looking for him. Once he had been forced, by their fire and their attempt to outflank him, to retreat from the lip of the canyon back into the hilly country southwest of the river.

But the passage of time had adjusted the odds and even two of them would be an army if they kept out of sight and were certain their opponent was alone. And they were aware that he had begun to horde his ammunition, that they were safe if they kept out of sight. Safer still, after nightfall. They only existed for Hyde as occasional calls, or in brief skirmishes with no outcome, as he had gradually retreated from the canyon, along dry gullies, up crevices in steep hillsides, across plateaus, drawing them after him. Now, it was eleven at night and the moon was thin, like a nail paring, low over the silent landscape. The land stretched away from his vantage point toward the canyon, lumped and bald and ravined, a maze in which he had not yet lost them—or killed any more of them, either.

He listened intently, disregarding the occasional calls of harmless, night-hunting creatures that moved among the hills. Someone—it was human by its clumsiness and the slow progress it was making—was climbing up the gully he had used himself to reach this ledge. He heard small explosions of breath and the scrape of metal on rock. He leaned out and looked over the lip of the ledge, but could see no glint of weaponry in the weak moonlight. The man was thirty feet away at most, and coming closer.

His Land Rover was still hidden in the gully he'd found a mile from the road. He had led them away from it, circuitously and slowly, but always away. He had with him food and water, an emergency kit. And it wasn't going to be long or drawn out, not unless he could keep them distracted and scattered and away from the road. As soon as they managed to kill him, they'd return to the guarded vehicles and summon assistance to get the nerve gas out.

He touched the barrel of the G3 rifle at his side as he might have done a child's comforter, once more hearing the scratch of metal on rock. Then came an involuntary, breathed curse. The climber did not know he was there. Hyde grinned. Soon will, mate, soon will.

He knew they would have to eliminate him that night. Blantyre wouldn't want to risk the morning and the chance of more traffic on the road, the report of the landslide, other people taking an interest in the vehicles and their cargo.

The goggles hung unused around his neck. From

time to time, he had glimpsed their shapes, less ghostly than those of zebra and occasional monkeys on the lower slopes of the canyon. But never for long enough to *load-aim-fire*. He hadn't seen Blantyre, not once. He'd only heard his voice shouting in the darkness, taunting him.

Hyde strained to listen. A careful footstep, the slither of dry fingers seeking purchase, the creak of muscles hoisting a man's weight to a higher perch. He withdrew the knife from the sheath strapped beneath his arm. Its blade was darkened. He raised himself slightly on his haunches, seeking an aggressive balance. He could hear each breath now as the man moved upward unaware of him.

"Come on, Hyde!" the megaphone bellowed, distorting Blantyre's mockery. "You can't take all of us on. You haven't got a hope, man!"

The still darkness boomed with his voice, to the left somewhere, perhaps four or five hundred feet away. He leaned out from his perch, but could still discern nothing, could still hear nothing now, until Blantyre's noise erupted again, breaking like another wave as the echoes ebbed: "You crazy bastard—you can't stop it, Hyde! You were *never* good enough!"

Hyde's hands twitched as they held the knife. Where was the bugger climbing up toward him? He couldn't hear anything. Had he paused?

"Before midnight, Hyde—before the midnight hour, you'll be falling down here somewhere! We'll look for the body in the morning!"

Hyde opened his lips, as if to shout back. Where was the—? An arm snapped closed like a jaw across his throat, pulling his head back. A broad hand clamped on his right wrist even in the instant that he reacted by raising the knife. The arm across his windpipe tightened and his vision flashed with lights. He was unable to breathe.

"Quick, Dirk—*here,* man!" his attacker grunted like a huge animal.

The climber was scrambling noisily the last few yards up the dry gully like a startled goat. There was a silence outside the small, rocky perch, as if the others were listening in the darkness for the scuffling noises of the kill. Hyde was dragged backward on his haunches as the man pressed his weight down on him and tightened his grip. The hand holding the knife was becoming numb. His left hand clawed behind his head, gripping the man's shirt, his skin, shoulder—not hurting the man. Lights flashed and the climber came out of them, heaving himself over the lip of Hyde's perch as if to fall heavily on him.

After an attempt to thrash his body free, Hyde relaxed suddenly. His weight slumped, surprising the man behind him for a moment, halting the climber's rush at him. The grip on his wrist did not slacken for an instant. He allowed his hand to relax. White teeth flashed in a black-streaked face. Hyde's left hand flopped feebly at his side. He felt a rock under his left hand as the arm across his throat started to slacken, then it tightened again. He tried not to struggle. The climber was drawing his knife slowly, enjoying the strength of his companion, the ease with which Hyde was being asphyxiated. The sharp-edged rock was in his hand, but his throat ached and he was beginning to black out. The man choking him was breathing angrily against his cheek and temple. Head just *there*—? In his oblivion, the climber seemed to swim away from him as if falling backward from the cliff, the arm across his throat was simply a numbness, his right hand holding the knife numb, too. He thought he still held the knife but could not be certain . . . the rock was in his left hand . . . where's the *head?* he screamed at himself. He couldn't feel his legs any longer, or see the warm stars, if they were anywhere in the same blackness as himself.

He moved his left arm as slowly as if he were merely flexing the muscles after sleep, and clashed the rock against the man's elbow, whose scream of pain was a drawn-out, electronic version of a human cry. The numbness around his throat, which seemed to have spread to his cheeks and temples, eased. The climber moved a half-step back in surprised slow motion. Hyde's hand retained control of the rock and flung it upward again, to where the attacker's head breathed and salivated against his temple. The noise of contact was subterranean, then the man fell away and Hyde collapsed on top of him, and the man's legs buckled under him. His right arm was still numb as the climber came toward him, cursing loudly. The man blundered forward onto Hyde's knife, which impaled him. Blood spurted from his stomach into Hyde's eyes. He dropped the knife because his still-numb arm could not support the man's sudden weight. The climber fell aside, his face dropping below the level of Hyde's eyes, then away altogether as Hyde rolled aside from the thrashings of the man beneath him. His left hand raised the rock twice and smashed downward, breaking the dimly seen face.

He was not aware of dropping the rock or of collecting the knife and wiping it on the dead man's shirt. He slumped to one side, as if himself wounded.

He heard Blantyre's distorted demands for information billowing toward him from somewhere hundreds of feet away. He massaged his throat and tried to breathe so shallowly that it would not feel like swallowing sharp crystals of ice. The climber was dead, the other man's body heaved with tormented breathing. Blantyre's orders continued, more concentrated and urgent than before. Answering calls, as if they were an enlivened and blood-smelling pack of wild dogs. He raised himself to look. Torches flashed around and below him as they attempted to converge.

Out of the blur of sight and reason, he heard a radio which terrified him, until he realized it must be in one of their pockets, close to him. *If you can't locate the bastard, find his vehicle* repeated the message.

Hyde sheathed the knife, checked the pistol and the G3, and dizzily stood up, leaning against the rocks for support. Torches flicked in their eagerness, he could hear noises of ascent and clambering down, of running. He stepped forward and looked over the ledge, down the dry gully. Nothing there. Hefting his pack for comfort, shaking his head to clear his vision, he began to descend the gully.

Hyde worked his way carefully along the old, dry watercourse, avoiding contact with the jagged, stiff bushes and stunted trees that littered the sandy gully. His footprints were broken by rocks and pebbles. Blantyre's people were well behind him now, as far as he could determine, slowed by the shock of another of their number dead and a second incapacitated. The paring of moon had risen higher in the sky, loitering like a narrow spectator. The temperature had dropped, but he felt hot with exertion and the necessity of silence and stealth. It was a little after midnight, and he was still alive. Blantyre had stopped employing the megaphone. Hyde needed more food, water, ammunition. He intended to survive.

Something, probably a scorpion, crackled like a blown dead leaf across a small rock near his feet. It disappeared into the darkness and he moved on, ducking beneath the stiff, sticklike arms of a weathered bush that jutted out from the bank of the dry gully. He was a mile from the canyon itself. And holding them. Blantyre and five others now. He had to hold them until Aubrey turned the hunt on Blantyre.

He could now make out the bulk of the Land

Rover beneath a lolling tree in a narrow jaw of the gully. He squatted on a rock, watching, listening. Aubrey needed to achieve *control* over Malan, then arrange assistance. He forbade himself to sniff disdainfully. He listened to the night's distant noises—the disturbed or dreaming animals, the sudden creak of rocks, the scuttle of large insects—and declared them harmless. He hunched in the barely moonlit dark, the rifle between his knees, the pack light against his shoulders and the pistol at the base of his spine. The Land Rover was safe, he could wait another minute or two. Then he slouched, half-bent, along the distance that separated him from the vehicle. His hand touched metal and he rose into a taller crouch over the Land Rover, at once beginning his harvest of water, a pack of chocolate, an ammunition clip, then a second, his hands playing as cleverly as those of a blind pianist, by familiarity. He opened packets, compartments, zipped-shut packs; the zips sounded like tears in the night, startling him each time. His hands thrust his supplies into his pack like the paws of a greedy squirrel—

The windshield cracked an inch from his hand, which jerked away, his body dropping beside the vehicle. Another silenced bullet careened off the hood, making him leap with tension.

He heard a voice summoning others by walkietalkie. He hurriedly slipped his arms through the straps of the backpack, his breathing hard, preparatory. He rested his weight against the panel of the Land Rover. Another shot struck, thudding like a blow and burying itself somewhere in the upholstery. Then the silence flowed back, and Hyde flung himself to his feet and away along the gully. He was cuffed from behind by the first ripple of disturbed air, then lifted and flung forward by the wave of the detonation. As his hands clamped over his ears and the ground lit up to receive the impact of his body, he heard the explosion of a grenade, then the second, immediate detonation of the petrol tank. The rocks flared red as if dyed, and the ground quivered climactically beneath his body. He then scrabbled away from the light, his shadow dancing like that of a hunchback. Shots whined, the noise of the rifle now evident, the silencer removed for greater muzzle velocity.

Hyde dropped exhausted behind a rock, dimly hearing the first delighted cries from others, and the gradual decline into disappointment and recrimination. Then he heard only his own pulse, thudding in his ears. He rolled onto his stomach and then got to his haunches, then to a crouch. They'd have night-vision goggles, at least nightsights. He was hidden by a jutting rock around which the ancient stream must have run. He scrabbled away from the place, farther up the gully, back the way he had entered it in the Land Rover, whose fire was burning down now, the air chilly again and darkening. He continued like some apelike ancestor, almost on all fours, scrambling toward evolution and two legs.

He straightened eventually, his back aching, the unbalanced weight of the pack against his neck dropping away to settle on his hips. He climbed quickly out of the gully, onto the edge of a mesa, which seemed no more than a vantage to look at rising, craggy hills stretching away. The canyon was—that way. A light flashed briefly some hundreds of yards away, then flicked off at a snarled command. He couldn't see their shapes against the stars or the dismal, impoverished moon. He scrabbled silently across the mesa until he reached its edge. Gently, as if getting into a too-hot bath, he lowered himself over the edge, feet testing for firm purchase, then began to slide slowly, gently, down the steep slope toward inky shadows, using his feet as brakes.

His feet touched bottom. He stood up, and saw

himself in a sharp knife-cut of a ravine, one that sloped in the direction of the canyon. If he followed it down, he might find the narrow track that led back to the road. The floor of the Fish River Canyon would be safer now, filled with scrub, water holes, vegetation, caves. Up here, he felt exposed. He patted his equipment again. Pack, gun, pistol—he thrust that back into his belt, it had begun to work loose—knife. Goggles—

No. He'd dropped them somewhere—farther up the slope? He looked wildly upwards. No, he hadn't had them when the Land Rover exploded, had just forgotten about them. Damn—fuck it. He adjusted the pack, making at once for the steep twist of the gully. As he started down it, he heard distant voices.

They seemed to be shouting, giving and taking orders. He stumbled in his haste, rolling over, scraping hands and bare knees and then his side against rocks, bouncing on pebbles and sharp, small stones, trying to grip hold of some rock that wouldn't move after filling his fingernails with dirt.

Halted, breathless, skewed almost upside down, legs above his head, hand holding onto a rock, the rubble sliding and puffing past him and rattling on down the gully. The stars joggled above and the moon swayed like a drunk. His breathing bellowed—

—above a scrabbling noise too delicate for the stones that had been disturbed by his fall. The rifle, butt folded, was in his right hand, saved from loss. His left hand held the edge of a creased rock, halting him. He raised the rifle butt—

—the hunting scorpion was too quick. Hyde had disturbed and angered it. He saw its twin stings protruding from the black bud at the end of its tail, raised in an arch above its back, its claws ceasing to click and knit on the rock as it steadied itself to strike. As he moved the scorpion struck, its sting burying itself in his left forearm. He crushed the life from it with the rifle's

blow, hurting his knuckles against rock as the barrel
cracked the scorpion open. His left arm was immediately on fire.

Aubrey glanced surreptitiously at his watch. The leaning, cranelike lights of the motorway heading toward
the northern suburbs winked at the watch's face.
Twelve-thirty. He let his wrist fall casually away so
that his hand rested on the edge of the cream leather
seat of the long Mercedes limousine. Malan's physical
bulk and intent loomed against his nerveless side, even
though the man looked unconcernedly out of his own
window. The driver's neck, just in front of Aubrey, was
slim and clean-shaven. Both he and Malan seemed as
unconcerned as if they were transporting livestock
across the Channel to some European abattoir.

Aubrey calmed the nervous little twitch of his fingers against the seat's leather. Oh, yes, Malan certainly
was offering him some right-wing extremists who actually were involved with van Vuuren and Blantyre and
the nerve agent shipment. After all, he'd had to find
them simply so that they did not exist outside his gravi-
tational pull. Unknown, they were dangerous, and
could cause him embarrassment with the de Villiers
government. Now, he could offer them up patriotically
at a moment's notice, or use them to his advantage. For
he certainly did not intend that Aubrey should expose
them.

The dark blotches of unlit parks and golf courses
flashed by, surrounded by rows of streetlights which
semaphored the presence of neat, orderly suburbs.
Ahead, beyond the motorway lights, the darkness
spread more widely. He felt, under the circumstances,
rather calm, surprising himself. The suburbs slipped
aside like a stage curtain and the darkness spread as the
lights tried less successfully to signal to each other. A

moment later, the Mercedes purred away from the comfort of traffic, down onto a sliproad, then at once onto a wide, sparsely lit avenue lined by small factory units and dim housing. A few moving cars, some others parked, the occasional pedestrian, some dogs. He settled his shoulders to disguise a shiver of anticipation.

"These people . . . " he began, clearing his throat. Malan's head twitched toward him, his eyes gleaming. "These people, Malan—they will believe my cover?"

Malan grinned and nodded. "You worry too much. They're not very smart. They'll think you're the money man. You look like a shriveled accountant, after all." His grin broadened and Aubrey attempted to respond to it.

"And afterward? After I—*we're*—certain of them?"

"We drive quietly away and you can talk to whomever you like." The streets around them became shabbier and darker, people flitting out of the shadows between the sparse streetlights. "I've given you two names. They'll listen quickly and they'll understand. You won't have any problems." He sighed. "Satisfied?" Then he seemed to remember his lines in a play in which he had lost interest, and added: "This clears our debt, our *account?*"

Aubrey nodded. "Agreed. It is all I can do, or wish to do. Anything else would now be beyond me." His hand flapped loosely, like that of an invalid speaking from his bed. "I shall leave you to your own devices, if you give me these people."

"Your man may not finish off Robin Blantyre," Malan observed. "Probably won't, in fact. Robin's a hard man."

"What?" Aubrey asked dispassionately.

Malan grinned, and seemed to relax. "Oh, I know where Blantyre is, and that's where you've sent your wild dog, Hyde. Otherwise, he'd be here, watching your back. After Venice. He killed the girl, Valentina, I heard?"

"That—is true." Aubrey rubbed his chin. "Yes," he murmured. "*I* shall stop Blantyre. With your assistance tonight, of course." He smiled. "Even though you wish your contribution to remain anonymous, like all the best charitable donations."

Malan turned away. Aubrey, too, resorted once more to gazing out of the tinted window that made the few lights even more distant and small. He could just make out a handful of stars overhead.

He did not need to steel himself further. He had entered the situation and had heard the key turn in the lock behind him. He could not withdraw. It was simply a matter of keeping his nerve, remaining calm. How he might escape was unclear, but he had the gun, of which he believed Malan remained unaware. The car passed a telephone kiosk. There would be telephones. He had not rung the embassy or any of the few people he vaguely knew in South African Intelligence. Any contact would have only invited restraint, complications. If necessary, he would come away as he arrived, with Malan as his companion, at the point of a gun.

Malan, of course, was right. It might prove impossible for Patrick to remain alive, let alone prevent the nerve agent from reaching Johannesburg. Malan assured him it had not yet arrived. That, at least, he believed. Malan could be ruined by news of its smuggling, its purchase by employees of MLC. No, there was still time, providing he—and Hyde, but mostly it seemed to depend upon himself—could remain alive.

The Mercedes hurried off an ill-lit street of low houses, empty lots and factory units, through gates of corrugated tin, into—

Startled, he saw in the darkness, outlined by the glow from Alexandra township, the car's headlights reflected from buckled metal. Bumpers, hoods, hubcaps, trunks. Cars were heaped upon one another as if to simulate the orgy of a million frogs or crabs. He shivered and Malan's laugh at his discomfiture was hard. Then the South African opened the door of the limousine. Aubrey, too, got out. The night was cool, windless, the stars glittering above the slag heaps and temples of broken vehicles. He shuddered. It was too easy to imagine how many lives had ended or been ruined or distorted inside the crumpled metal boxes.

"This way," Malan announced, steering him by the elbow.

Ahead of them, light showed grubbily in slitted lines and scratches around something which, as his eyes became accustomed, appeared to be a low trailer.

"Yes," he murmured. "Very well."

The driver remained beside the car, his cap pushed back on his head. The scrapyard was silent. A crane loomed over the city of wrecks like a long-necked vulture. Aubrey cleared his throat and his hand involuntarily gripped the gun in his coat pocket.

How many of them would there be? Too many, he suspected, for one old man.

16

THE BLANKET OF
THE DARK

Anderson raised his body from a stiff, awkward crouch, his fingers crooked on the sill of one window of the lopsided trailer, and squinted into the dim, shadowy interior. There were rough mugs on a stained, narrow table, greasy cushions, abandoned clothing. Crockery lolled unwashed at the edges of the metal sink.

Why in God's name had he come *back* here? There had been no sign from heaven, no pointing finger instructing him that he couldn't leave Kenneth Aubrey to his fate, just the old man's face and resolution, pricking at him. So that, eventually, he had had to turn back, far along the northbound road and against every conscious thought or wish.

Because *her* face had been against the windshield, not just that of Aubrey, as if she were trying to break into the car. He had slewed the BMW violently, as if avoiding a child caught suddenly in the headlights, and had sat for a long time at the side of the road, his face in his hands, his whole body shaking and reluctant . . . revolting against what he knew must be done . . . until he had admitted it, and turned in the road and headed back toward Johannesburg.

As his eyes probed the trailer's interior, he eventually realized that a foot was jutting out from behind the lumpy armchair drawn close to the table. Then he saw that the other foot—leg—was sprawled toward the kitchen sink. The rest of the body was hidden by the chair. There was no sign of any other body. Those who had been here to meet Malan's people had probably been thrown into wrecks, ready to be given to the crusher. Then a harder light was switched on inside the trailer and he ducked out of sight, his breathing suddenly loud and hoarse.

He realized he was illuminated by the greasy light. Malan's people were waiting for Aubrey—one of them was inside now. They'd killed already, and would have been warned to watch out for him, for anyone.

Headlights flashed along the road outside the scrap yard, then glared their way into it. Aubrey, being brought to the slaughter by Malan. He heard the big engine slow to a halt some distance away, crouching into himself as much as possible, his back against the trailer's peeling paint, his arms wrapped around his knees with the rifle resting across his forearms. Then he heard only silence—

—into which dropped the separate pebbles of a car door closing, a brief murmur of voices, then footsteps. He drew the nightsight from his windbreaker and crept silently toward the corner of the trailer. Then he raised the sight to his eye and focused it. Two figures came into focus, one tall and bulky, the other more hesitant in its movements, with a walking stick. They were moving side by side down an aisle of wrecked cars. Aubrey's breath was visible around him. He flicked the tube of the nightsight rapidly over the cathedral of broken vehicles, until—

There. One of them, dressed in black, face smudged with shoe polish, his stained hand gripping the barrel of a rifle as if he might turn it into a club. Anderson felt the adrenalin course through him like old, familiar music. The cold, urban landscape pressed against him like a place he knew well, his hunting ground. *There*. The backup man, moving with utmost purpose and quiet into a position to cover the flank of the trailer. Neither man was ready to fire. Evidently, Aubrey was to be gloated over, was to meet the man who had turned on the light inside the trailer . . . before he was murdered. He wanted to confirm his suspicions, but remained still, watching Malan and Aubrey slowly approach. He heard the creaks of settling metal, their footsteps, the whisper of the bottled gas supply beneath the trailer. Carefully, he slipped the first round into the breech of the sniper's rifle, unfolding the butt so that it came easily and at once against his shoulder like the reassurance of a friend. He fitted the nightsight and adjusted its focus on the first gunman, whose head peered from between the crushed radiator grille of a Japanese car and the open-mouthed trunk of a rusting Citroën. The clouding of excitement cleared from the lens, and he refined the focus. Then he transferred the sight to Aubrey's face, adjusting into focus his grim features, carved and stony. Malan was beside him, his face inexpressive. His finger tightened involuntarily on the trigger, now, *now*—

He forced himself to ease the trigger back and slacken his grip on the rifle. Not yet, not until you can ensure your escape, and perhaps Kenneth's. His hands were shaking. Aubrey and Malan were murmuring together as they reached the trailer. Margarethe's face intruded for a moment, but it was distant and lifeless and had no business in this place with him in his present mood. Later, later . . .

Tears, unexpectedly, dripped into his throat because he could not noisily sniff them away. *Later,* he snapped angrily at himself.

He heard movement inside the trailer, in anticipation of Aubrey's arrival. He lurched to his feet and scuttled bent double to the window, peering inside. He recognized at once a bearded profile, as he also recognized the gleam of light on a pistol. Jesus, they weren't going to savor killing Aubrey, they were just going to do it now.

The pistol moved upward, to point at the door of the trailer, waiting for it to be opened.

As Malan held his elbow, as if assisting him to cross a busy street, Aubrey sensed his alertness. Aubrey puffed smoky air like an impatient little steam engine. Malan's feral attentiveness trembled through the old man's arm.

"What is it?" Aubrey murmured.

"I thought I heard something. Just wait a moment."

Aubrey had seen an outlined shadow appear inside the trailer, just before the main light had come on. The whole trailer listed like a boat going down in the dark. He suppressed a shiver of anticipation. The night was windless but the scrapyard creaked around him like condemned tenement blocks in a gale. Eerie, the noises of old vehicles, as if murmuring their separate demises.

"What is it, Malan?" he repeated with some impatience.

"I'm just looking after your health, Sir Kenneth." There was confidence in the man's voice again, a belief that everything was in place, a trap poised to snap shut. "Shall we go in? Someone awaits us."

Aubrey quailed as Malan removed his hand. It had to be his oldest enemy. Babbington. Dear Andrew, his personal Alberich, consumed by unenacted revenges.

As *yet* unenacted. He gripped the butt of the pistol more firmly in his coat pocket. Given the opportunity, he *could* kill Andrew Babbington, as easily as Babbington could dispense with him.

"Yes," he murmured.

The scurrying of something that might have been a rat delayed his reply.

"Let's go in, then."

Aubrey squared his shoulders and stepped onto the creaking steps of the trailer. He must now continue this charade, though he expected to learn nothing more. There was the startling noise of breaking glass and he stumbled back from the steps. He heard a voice that he recognized as Anderson's bellow out: "Kenneth, it's a trap! Watch yourself!" Then: "Babbington, stay where you are or I'll kill you now!" Finally, even louder: "Kill the old man and Malan dies—do you hear me? Babbington, *stay where you are!*"

You never fucking die of a scorpion sting, it says so in the rules. Oh, Christ, this *hurts!*

Hyde lowered his arm once more into the water that seeped down one wall of the cave before trickling along the narrow channel beside which he lay stretched out, exhausted. The noise of the water made the cave seem larger, hollower than it was. The low night temperature had no effect on the burning pain in his stiff, swollen arm. The aspirin he had taken against an insistent sense of survival had had no effect, either. He had no antivenom because *some bastard forgot to pack it!* You don't die of scorpion stings, not unless you're a baby or a heart case aged three hundred . . . you just feel like one!

Try to rest the affected area, the book said. He'd applied a pressure bandage to slow the spread of the venom, and had doused the arm in cold water. There were no other remedies available. Not even lying still. He flicked on the thin beam of the flashlight, then immediately switched it off. Best not to look at the swollen, almost immovable limb. He felt nauseated, close to fever. He lay on his back, staring at the invisible roof of the cave. That the scorpion had cracked like thin ice beneath the blow from the rifle was of no consolation. Damn fucking scorpion.

He flicked on the flashlight once more, then returned himself to the darkness. Something whirred away like a windblown leaf—a bat, probably.

He shouldn't have tried to reach the road, shouldn't have climbed down to the floor of the Fish River Canyon, abseiling with his one good arm, spinning like a top, feeling sick and wanting to bellow with pain and effort. The venom had been pumped round his system by his exertions—but the only other choice was to wait for Blantyre and his people, who were even more poisonous than the scorpion. He was—whatever shape he was in—still alive. He stifled a groan of pain as he attempted to move his arm. Then he lay back again, letting his arm rest in the trickling water it could barely feel. The water was brackish, salty. He couldn't drink it, but it had, initially, cooled his face and forehead. And his arm, for a few moments. Now, it was burning again like a small, intense bonfire. He couldn't stop shivering.

He flicked on the flashlight and looked at his watch. Almost one in the morning. He switched off the beam, and the bat rustled and chittered back to its roost above his head. He knew he'd have to move soon.

It was as if the scorpion sting had been an electrical shock, goading him into frenzied activity. He had blundered away into the darkness, hearing their cries of surprise and puzzlement clear on the night air. He'd struggled in a maze of gullies and ravines and eventual-

ly found the track and made better time down to the
road, half a mile from the landslide. He was terrified
contemplating his only means of escape, down the
canyon wall to the riverbed. It had taken him a long,
nauseating time. His swollen arm was just able to grip
the rope and let it slide through stiff, lumpy fingers up
to the good hand, which had had to take all his weight,
as he eased himself down the canyon wall.

Eventually, exhausted, he had reached a litter of
boulders and the rope had come tumbling about him
like the coils of a python. He had rested for a few minutes, then moved out across the canyon. Up on the
road, he had seen the faint glow of a fire from the
vicinity of the two container trucks.

Then he had scouted along the canyon until he
knew he must rest or collapse, and had found this bat-
invaded cold darkness and the noise of dribbling water.
And isolation.

He forced himself to sit up. His head whirled and
in his vision small, separate lights flashed like fireflies.
He held his brow with his right hand, draping his left
arm into the water once again. You're not going to get
any better, sport, so get used to it. Blantyre, of course,
had the perfect antidote, though unacceptable. He got
painfully to his knees and heard, above his dry retch-
ing, the distressed bats whirr and click and rustle like
old umbrellas being opened. Using the G3 as a stick, he
levered himself to his feet and turned dizzily around to
face the dim starlight seeping from the entrance.
Something skittered across the rocky floor, then was
muffled by its passage across sand. Scorpions, like
lightning, never strike twice.

He hauled himself toward the opening of the cave.
The pack was heavy on his back and the strap over his
left shoulder bit into swollen flesh. He slipped the rifle
into a submachine gun position against his hip, the
strap over his right shoulder. He saw flashlights, hun-

dreds of yards away, creeping down the cliff face on the other side of the canyon. Tiny lights, insubstantial and wavering. Either they'd found the marks of his descent or were still working on supposition. Either way, they were right.

Eventually, he made out six separate lights bobbing and wobbling down the cliff. Above them, the headlights of one of the trucks spilt over the lip of the canyon like poured silver. Hyde leaned heavily against the curve of the cave mouth, the rock pressing into his side and back, his arm jutting out as if held by a plaster cast. The rifle now hung in his right hand like shopping and the pack at his back was heavier than ever.

It wasn't that he couldn't respond—not physically, anyway. He could do that. There was plenty of rock to steady himself against. The sliver of moon shone in a gap of water out in the middle of the canyon. He shook his head carefully, but could not avoid the dizzy nausea. He was shivering continually now. It wasn't even that. He could manage to still the shakes for long enough to kill one or two of them. It was *beginning* it. All field agents demanded to go into the final phase of any operation fit and well, no more than weary or strung out. *Not* with scorpion stings or bullet wounds. The moon slipped across the pool of water to which cats and their prey would be drawn at dawn—as to other pools dotted along the canyon's umbilical extent. In the morning, too, there would be traffic up on the road. Investigation, assistance—

—not for *you*. Blantyre's advantage entirely. He was sweating violently. The small lights on the opposite cliff danced in and out of focus. The first man had reached the canyon floor and his light was extinguished. Blantyre would be second or third in the descent, just in case Hyde was still *compos*. Six against one. He glared blearily at his swollen, hanging arm. He dreaded beginning it: The Finale. Once he announced with a rifle shot that he was fit enough to kill or wound, it wouldn't stop until they had him or he had finished them, *all* of them. He felt sick at the prospect and hung his head, the floor beginning to turn under him like the earth's rotation. Then he sniffed, the noise seeming to carry. He raised the rifle against his side and checked the nightsight. As he unfolded the stock with one hand, the muzzle scraped against rock. Then he moved, feeling a screech of pain and the sweat of effort, using his right hand to lift the left limb into position, to take the weight of the rifle in the inflamed hand. He watched his hand close around the forward grip as slowly as a crustacean making an attack on an immobile prey. It had to be a tight enough grip. He adjusted the nightsight. Light sprang into the circle of the sight, flaring gray. Amid its pale, dead glow was a figure shunting itself down the cliff in little repeated bounces. His brow was wet and he blinked furiously. His arm was on fire and the fingers of his left hand were entirely numb. He squeezed the trigger as much because his arm *had* to be moved, as for any reason. Almost at once, the figure amid the gray light seemed to shudder against the cliff, then fall dreamlike out into the air, which let him fall.

It had begun, then. He heard their alarm, their orders and sudden, fierce application. He shivered aside from the cave mouth, sliding into shadow.

Babbington had turned in the doorway, enraged, and glared back toward the shattered window as Anderson was shouting. But something had halted his first quick step, made him thrust his hands into his pockets and strive for calm and calculation. He heard Aubrey's voice, which stung him like a lash, his shoulders twitching at the sound.

"Richard? *Richard!*" with the greatest relief.

"Babbington!" he heard Malan bark, then some muffled curse. He had to get to the other side of the trailer—and be picked off like a fly?

"Kenneth, there are two snipers somewhere!" Anderson shouted. "Be careful!"

Babbington stared into the muzzle of the rifle that was poked through the broken window as if failing to recognize it and seeing some other, closer enemy on the frayed strip of carpet in front of his feet. His pockets worked like glove puppets over his knuckles. Then he heard: "I'm all right, Richard—warn them, Malan— warn them!"

Babbington shuffled, as if distracted, toward the rifle muzzle and the shattered window, his breath smoking in the trailer's suddenly reduced temperature. Anderson glared at him, nudging the rifle in threatening gestures.

"Stand there!" he snapped. "Just there, and turn around and face the door."

Babbington seemed like a child, the rage of disappointment and the sense of having been cheated so evident on the distorted features. His handsomeness declined into cunning, wizened frustration. Then he turned reluctantly to present his back to Anderson.

Aubrey called: "Richard, what now?" in a confused, lost voice.

Anderson grimaced. "I've got Babbington covered, Kenneth. You and Malan get inside. Come forward, but be careful."

Anderson's hand reached along the rusty flank of the trailer and touched the handle of the door on that side. He waited until the door on Aubrey's side clicked open and he could see Malan's bulk lumbering into the interior, Babbington cautiously making way for him, waited until Aubrey's smaller frame made the trailer even more cramped and the door shut behind him. Then he opened the door on his side and darted inside, shutting it quickly and noisily behind him.

Aubrey's face gleamed palely like a puzzled moon. Malan glowered at him. Babbington's hatred was undiminished. Anderson listened. They hadn't risked firing even one shot, whether or not they had him in their sights. A bullet could enter the flimsy tin wall of the trailer and kill—anyone; the bullet could even pass right through the wallet that would pay them for the job. Bad for business. He grinned, surprising himself. Outside, one of them called to the other, but he could not make out the words. What he really heard was his own breathing and pulse rate, and almost a noise of tension between the three men at whom he pointed the rifle, their mutual hatred and mistrust rubbing like the friction of metal on metal.

He leveled the rifle on Malan. He'd be the first to die anyway, just in case there was no time for a second shot. If the two outside adopted an independent assessment of the situation, decided on taking a risk or got close enough to distinguish their legitimate targets, he'd have to ensure that Malan was going into the dark. That much was certain.

"Hello, Kenneth," he announced softly. Then he added with a mocking nod, "Shall we all sit down, gentlemen?"

He stood between two bunk beds, facing the three of them, grouped as tightly as guilty schoolboys around the narrow table. He saw the legs of the dead man sticking out from behind the chair, in which Malan sat unconcernedly.

"Kenneth, up here, please," he ordered. "Stay out of the firing line."

Aubrey sidled with exaggerated caution to Anderson's end of the trailer and sat down at a nod from him on one of the bunk beds. Babbington perched himself with massive reluctance on the edge of a hard chair beside the table, his right hand at once fiddling and twitching amid sugar grains and the untidy pages of a tabloid newspaper. He glanced at Aubrey, who smiled loose-toothed in gratitude.

"Good," Anderson said, then he flicked the switch and doused the trailer's lights. At once, there was a jackallike response from outside. Inside, Anderson heard their collective breathing like the noise of wolves as yet curious, undecided. But hungry. He heard Babbington's chair scrape, then said, "I can see both of you. Don't provide me with an excuse so soon." His calm was studiedly chilling amid the claustrophobia of the confined space and their pressing rage.

Aubrey murmured: "Thank you, Richard." His relief was deep.

"Not for you," he replied, so that Malan could understand his meaning. Then he added, "I came back for Malan. It's him I want."

The trailer was lighter now. The glow from the surrounding streets and from the township seeped through the smashed window. Babbington's haughty profile was more that of a woman in deep *hauteur*, excepting the beard. Malan slouched harmlessly and cunningly in the armchair, his face turned to Anderson, who lowered himself onto the other unmade bed opposite Aubrey, their knees almost touching. He patted Aubrey's arm with his left hand, holding the rifle against his right side, pointed always at Malan. Except, he decided, he would nudge it occasionally toward Babbington, whom he failed to understand; the man was from Aubrey's drama, not his own, but it might prove fatal to ignore him. So he calmly said, "I know you're armed, Sir Andrew. Put the pistol on the floor, please."

Babbington growled, then withdrew the gun from his coat and lowered it by the butt to the floor, kicking it away before commanded to do so. We all know the routines, Anderson thought with a smile. Even Malan, probably. Gradually, the trailer's occupants became more firmly penciled by the growth of his night vision. The tension was as palpable as the condensation on the metal walls.

How should he finish it, since he wanted to survive? Malan had to be killed—he couldn't settle for less. Aubrey's breathing was shallow beside him. There were two marksmen outside, with nightsights and sniper's rifles. He suppressed a shiver. But the nightsights couldn't penetrate. All they would be able to see, through the broken window, was Malan. It would take them some time to convince themselves that he and Aubrey were just where they were, at the other end of the trailer.

Then Malan ventured, sarcastically, "This is cozy. But what now?"

His words seemed to release Babbington's furious concentration on Aubrey, and he growled: "What went wrong? What the hell went wrong?" The chair creaked as he leaned heavily forward. Anderson tensed himself.

"Nothing," Malan replied sullenly. Then he looked toward Anderson. "Just a wild card. The unexpected."

Babbington's arm pointed stiffly at Anderson. "*He* should have been found and disposed of *days* ago! I warned you of the man's past for God's sake—what he might do."

"I know that. He wasn't taken care of. That's all."

Babbington was staring at him and Aubrey now, and the old man's hand quivered on Anderson's arm. He felt, depressingly, like the relative of a very old person on whom the duty of visits and care had fallen.

"Well, Anderson, what now?" Malan growled.

"It's called a standoff. The problem is simple—how to kill you and still get out alive." Malan's face was composed entirely of lines and planes, dull surfaces amid which his eyes glittered.

"Impossible." Babbington placed his hands flat on

the stained table as if he had declared a winning hand. "Malan's car is too far away for either of you to get to it unhurt, Anderson."

"Perhaps we should telephone the driver?"

"You'd still have little chance of surviving."

Babbington was studying him as if attempting to match his features to those in some old, sepia-toned photograph. His body was stiff as he suppressed the evidence of a diseaselike rage. The hairs on Anderson's neck and arms tickled with nerves. Malan was obviously angry, like a wild animal behind bars.

"Therefore, what shall we do to amuse ourselves, in these temporary circumstances?" Babbington taunted.

"Now that you can't kill Aubrey?"

"I shouldn't be too certain of that, were I you."

The patently assumed drawl infuriated Anderson. It reminded him of past debriefings, all of which he had exorcised for so many years. And made him more alert to the prowling marksmen outside, who must by now be in debate, frustrated by the constant shadowy reappearances of Malan and Babbington. Soon, they might decide it would be worth their while to place a few shots into *his* end of the trailer. He glanced sideways at Aubrey.

The old man appeared to be watching Babbington with the stillness of a cat, with an infinite patience that bore the appearance of sorrow. He did not seem to be fearful on his own or anyone else's account; so still was he, he seemed the result of taxidermy. Then his old eyes blinked once behind his spectacles, slow as those of a fish.

Malan stirred again, snorting and impatient as the captured animal he was. "All right, Anderson—what do you want? What happened to your woman—I'm sorry it happened. Now—how *much?*"

"Your apology is *not* accepted," Anderson replied

through clenched teeth. Then, "My *wife*, by the way."

Malan was silent, but remained urgently alert for possible activity outside. Babbington appeared unconcerned, as if recognizing that Anderson was no more than a minimal, transitory interruption of his own strategy. He continued to glower at Aubrey, the author of all his woes. Given the slightest opportunity, Babbington would try to kill the old man.

Anderson leaned toward Aubrey and whispered: "Are you armed?" Aubrey nodded. "You can kill either of them if necessary?" After some hesitation, Aubrey nodded again. "OK. You may have to. Babbington won't let you go without some attempt."

"I understand, Richard. He and I understand each other perfectly." Then he cleared his throat and, raising his voice, said, "I take it, Malan, that our dead friend was one of those expecting the shipment of nerve gas."

"What? Yes, he was. There are a couple more of them out there in the dark, prematurely deceased. They were real enough. You might not have come otherwise." He grinned.

"Then you've satisfactorily cleared up this end of the business, saving your government both time and money. Thank you, on their behalf and mine."

"A pleasure, man."

Aubrey leaned toward Anderson. "Richard, I need Malan alive," he whispered.

"No," Anderson replied with utter conviction, shaking his head.

Aubrey sat back, studying Anderson—the motive force trapped inside the box of the trailer—and admitted that the man was approaching the point at which he might well sacrifice his own life to ensure Malan's death. It was the confinement, the claustrophobia, that was affecting him. Affecting himself, too. It would be easier, now, to shoot Babbington, should the man make any slight, suspicious move. And Andrew had long reached the same conclusion. His pistol lay on the floor, closer to Aubrey than to himself, but there was no real safety in mere distance. Babbington would risk anything to ensure he killed his oldest enemy. *Any* action, so long as it brought about Aubrey's death.

Aubrey sat back, recognizing that he could hope to persuade neither Babbington nor Anderson. But he had to engineer something that allowed him to remove himself from this situation and get assistance to Hyde. He was the only one in the trailer with any shred of rationality left. He did not hate Babbington, after all, he merely despised him. He did not need any of them dead as the fulfilment of his purpose. Which only made him impotent, unable to prevent—

—what was already beginning to happen. He sensed, then heard, a slight, ratlike noise outside the trailer. It alerted Anderson, even before the other two appeared to become aware. He realized, from Anderson's reaction as Malan was stung into hopeful awareness, that events could no longer be prevented. Anderson hesitated for only an instant, then fired at the window where, momentarily, there had been a dim shadow. Malan continued to his feet and blundered like a bull toward and through the door, even as Aubrey was still raising his hands in supplication, like a child attempting to prevent the tide from demolishing his sand castle.

Babbington hunched down as Anderson turned the rifle on Malan's disappearing bulk. Malan was bellowing something into the night about his identity and not shooting as Anderson fired again, the noise deafening in the cramped space. Aubrey expected Malan to lurch sideways, or be thrust forward, then he realized that Anderson had not fired at his quarry, but down at the floor. He was dazzled by the muzzle flash and by the time he could see through the dancing lights, he saw Babbington scrabbling near his feet. His body straightened slowly, as if the man felt tired after vigorous exercise and chose to lie, straightened and quiet.

The black rectangle of the doorway was empty, and Aubrey heard above the reverberations of a third shot, and the partial deafness it induced, the clump of running footsteps and the cry from Malan of: "Kill him, kill him!"

Aubrey looked up at Anderson, who hesitated for no more than a moment to glance at Babbington's prone form, before bundling himself through the trailer's rear door. It slammed behind him, and Aubrey heard two shots.

He slipped from the bed into a sitting position on the floor, dragging the thin mattress down beside him as inadequate protection. More protection was to be had from the fact that Malan and Anderson were both outside, and the gunmen were concerning themselves with them. He heard further shots from outside, close upon more running footsteps. He reached forward as if toward a wounded wild animal and felt for the pulse in Babbington's neck. Faintly there. He got slowly to his knees and turned Babbington's heavy frame, so that his pain-clenched features stared up at the low, grubby ceiling. Then, breathing heavily, Aubrey crawled with the utmost caution toward the still-open door of the trailer and squinted into the chilly night's dull glow.

In the dipped headlights of the distant Mercedes, he saw an enlarged shadow that was Malan fleeing toward the limousine. There was something awkward and wounded about his shuffling, hunchback gait. There was a body, too small to be that of Anderson, lying fifty yards away. The doors of the Mercedes were open and the driver crouched behind one of them, probably armed. There was no sign of Richard.

Malan reached the car and flung himself desperately into the rear of it. The driver at once got in and slammed the doors, reversing wildly toward the gate in a flurry of dust that looked frosty in the headlights. The limousine skidded through the gates and turned violently before accelerating out of sight toward the city.

Almost at once, a smaller car squealed into view, following Malan. Aubrey had heard shots muffled by the noise of the Mercedes' engine. He strained to see . . . yes, something once human was lying near the gates. It had fallen away from the second car after a desperate attempt to hold on. It did not move.

He knew that Malan was finished. Anderson had killed both marksmen, and would not now let go. The shark had tasted blood, and was moving in for the kill. It might take hours, even days—no longer than a few days—but he knew with utter certainty that Anderson would kill Malan. Settle *both* their accounts. *Nothing,* not even Babbington's dying, was more certain.

Which, he realized light-headedly, rendered him safe. Bereft of proof, but safe.

He looked down, sighing before he crawled back toward Babbington's heaving chest. His face was twisted with the growing fear of the nature of his wound, which was from a high-powered rifle, at close range. The bullet was probably buried six inches in the dirt beneath the trailer. It had passed through Babbington's middle. His frame was already stiff long before the heart and mind accepted the fact. He sat beside him.

There was spittle on Babbington's beard, bright as tears. Blood glistened as well on his coat and shirt. He was bleeding to death and it was pointless to try to staunch the bleeding. The effort would be no more than cosmetic—and it was a gesture Aubrey had no intention of making. Instead, he and the dying man seemed mutually exhausted.

The two of them were alone in the vast scrap yard. Then Babbington groaned, the sound seeming much more like a quiet scream of protest, not so much at his end but at business left unfinished. Aubrey stared at the ceiling, as if embarrassed, as Babbington gargled blood.

Consummatum est—it is finished.

Eventually, Babbington's liquid throat was quiet again, and the eerie creaks of the scrap yard once more intruded. Aubrey's breath smoked, but he did not feel the cold. Babbington's intermittent puffs of clouded breath were like vain attempts to strike a spark as he went headlong into the dark. The noise of cars in flight and pursuit had long faded, sounds from a distant past.

Then the ugly, wet noises in Babbington's throat became more desperate. Aubrey looked down. Andrew's eyes glared like those of some enraged revenant, a corpse not yet dead. His lips worked mutely, his voice spluttering like a mechanism that refused to start. Then, most strangely, as if surrendering to his fate, his clawed fingers reached out and touched Aubrey's sleeve. Aubrey watched the hand crawl down the cloth of his coat, then attempt to grasp his hand. He opened his fingers and gripped Babbington's hand. The gesture was little enough, after all. Babbington was all but dead. It was hardly forgiveness, just company, for a brief moment. He shook his head at the vivid image of the darkness above which Babbington was poised.

Gradually, Babbington's features lost their expression of baffled malevolence and growing terror. They relaxed not into peace or resignation, but into familiarity. Strange meeting, he thought, after so long a time. *It seemed that out of battle I escaped. . . .* Their feud, and the war in which they had so vigorously engaged, were both over, at least for them. *Piteous recognition. . . .* He looked down at Babbington's ghostly, bearded features. He had never particularly warmed to Wilfred Owen, but now the lines of one of his poems came unbidden and freshly out of the back of his head. *Wisdom was mine, and I had mastery. . . .* He must once have had to learn it as an imposition, set by a pre-fect somewhat like Babbington, the eternal Head of House—and gone to the bad, like so many of them had. *I am the enemy you killed.* . . . No, he felt nothing for the man, no pity or sorrow, not even a small regret such as toward a stranger whose name one had heard or read.

He tightened his grip on Babbington's hand, aware that the man's ruined chest still fluttered after breath—a few minutes now, at most. He was not holding the hand of some alter ego, he refused such identification between the two of them; he was just holding the hand of someone whose history might have been identical, but had not been because of vanity and appetite—and treason.

He felt very tired, but continued to hold the man's hand, until the end. *Let us sleep now.* . . .

He sensed the moment when Babbington's muscles relaxed and his hand became heavier. Nevertheless, Aubrey did not release his grip; instead he continued to listen to the creaking silence outside, indulging a sense of completion and an almost fey, detached mood. Even Patrick Hyde's fate failed to concern him.

Hyde sat cross-legged amid the stiff, rustling reeds that surrounded a small water hole, hugging his wounded arm across his chest with his good hand. They were less than a mile behind him now, following his progress like a drift net, confident that he was ahead of them. They checked out each cave, each water hole. Blantyre would have found the signs, long ago, of his frequent halts, his numerous falls and stumblings. And he would know that he was wounded.

They'd overtake him long before dawn . . . what time was it? He shook his hanging head. Not worth the eye strain. It wasn't important. They'd have him before it got light, and that was all that mattered.

He shuddered with shock at the explosion behind him. He turned and saw the afterglow, and heard the slow growl of falling rock. Someone had thrown a grenade or fired a rocket into one of the caves. In the starlight, he saw the dust puff out less than half a mile behind him.

If he was remembering the map accurately, the canyon ahead of him twisted like a wounded snake, again and again, narrowing, too. He probably wouldn't get that far. And he couldn't climb out, not with his immobilized arm and as dizzy as he was. There were tracks up to the cliff top, but he'd be more than lucky to find one in the dark. He just had to try to keep ahead of them.

Why? At dawn, if he lived that long, there'd be at least one helicopter, maybe more. Blantyre would organize people he could trust and get them up from Oranjemund or from inside the Republic. And, if Aubrey hadn't got Malan by the balls, then even *he* might think it worth a cover-up—after all, he had only to eliminate one wounded soldier and a nosy old man.

He rubbed his face. The next twist of the canyon would hide him from them for a while. Even though reluctance seized him like nausea, he knew it was time to attempt some kind of ambush. He touched his arm. No way, son, no fucking way. He got wearily to his feet, using the rifle to lever himself upright. There was no one outlined against the dying fire of scrubby bushes and there were no noises of walkie-talkie communication. Five of them still fit and well, and goaded on by Blantyre. Hyde struggled off in a caricature of rapid movement that Hollywood might associate with a hunchback and call characterization.

He'd seen headlights moving along the road up on the cliff perhaps an hour earlier. They'd ducked out of sight in a twist of the canyon long before reaching the landslide. Now, the driver and whoever else were probably camped beside the mound of fallen rocks, perhaps even sharing food and laughter with those Blantyre had left on guard. No help for *him,* whoever they were.

He turned the twist in the riverbed and the cliffs seemed to crowd mockingly above him. He huddled against a large boulder, his head spinning. He pressed the rifle against his cheek to cool himself, but the barrel was hot from his feverish grip. Gradually, the stars slowed once more and his breathing calmed. The dotted water holes gleamed blackly like a wet, tarred road in the starlight as they skulked behind beds of reeds or low, stunted bushes. Otherwise, the landscape was bouldered and pebbly and hollowed with low, narrow caves like the one in which he had hidden.

Wise to that halt, they'd already grenaded or rocketed three caves during the night. Each of the caves he had passed had tempted him, but he wasn't that far gone. At the slightest noise or suspicion, they'd blown caves apart, liking the destruction, the noise and light feeding something.

Slowly, carefully, he eased himself back into the rocks, his feet scrabbling heels first up the slightest of inclines until he was twenty feet or more above the riverbed. Only during a flood would the river reach the rocks around and behind him. The place was desiccated, lunar.

Blantyre liked inflicting fear and pain. There had always been a few of them in SAS, more in the Selous Scouts and the Rhodesian SAS. And the SADF. Blantyre had followed a trail of certainties, a trek down through southern Africa, always looking for another border, another incursion, another set of niggers becoming uppity and being armed by the East Germans and the KGB. Christ, what a terrible redundancy had faced him until he'd signed up with MLC!

The anger and contempt cleared Hyde's thoughts

and enabled him to concentrate, so that he could squint into the nightscope on the G3 without feeling woozy. There was nothing coming, yet. He unscrewed the top of a water bottle and swilled the tepid liquid in his mouth—don't drink from the water holes until you have to, leopards and zebra might have pissed in them, although the guide books didn't quite put it like that. He screwed back the top. Not much wider than a quarter of a mile here, a narrow waist of canyon between two hips of rock. Yes, Blantyre had trekked all the way, following the Promised Land of violence and destruction, from Hereford and the Brecon Beacons and Oman and a few other places, down through Rhodesia and South Africa to—

—here. A figure appeared in the nightscope, stalking in a crouch and moving with expert speed, ducking quickly behind the nearest available cover so that the gray ghost of a bush masked his gray shadow. Then came a second man slightly more upright.

He fired. The shadow's arms went grayly up and then it tumbled back and out of sight behind the dust thrown up by a pebbly slope. He heard their voices exclaim and protest, and then knew he had made a mistake as the first rocket burst behind him, an instant after he had seen the small spit of flame. The stovelike pipe slung over the man's shoulder had hardly registered until then. Rock screeched, then roared outward above his head. He pressed back, feet scrabbling, his arm shrieking again as his fingers clawed backwards.

The starlight disappeared in rock fragments, boulders and dust, which were flung away from him by the narrow jut of rock under which he sheltered. The rocks bounced away, terrifyingly enlarged in the lens of panic. The dust choked him, caught at his throat, made him cough. They'd come in concertedly and quickly now, like a pack of hunting dogs. He edged his way beneath the overhang. The dust was thinning.

Movement made nighttime shadows easier to see in the sniperscopes. *Four* of them. The barrel rested like a hot blade on his injured arm as he shuffled the rifle to some kind of readiness, ducking behind another clutter of boulders, gagging on, then swallowing, the gritty dust.

Wait for them.

"Where is he? Can you see him, Pik? You, Danie?"

"The bastard's killed Danie!" someone yelled back.

"Shut up, you cretin!" Blantyre shouted. No radios now.

Hyde's arm ached beneath the impossible weight of the rifle barrel and he gritted his teeth against the pain. He even forced the numb, swollen arm to raise itself until the barrel could rest on top of the boulder and he could lever himself into something like a firing position. His head, with great luck, would look like a jut of rock through a nightsight—until he fired. He squinted into his own scope.

"Give the bastard another!" Blantyre yelled, and there was almost at once an obedient spit of flame, then the cliff erupted again, the rocks splitting and tumbling thirty yards or more to his left. He ducked, terrified, as a huge boulder flung itself toward him, then bounced over his hiding place, careering toward the nearest water hole, where it startled invisible animals. The dust pall dragged itself toward their positions, and the noise reverberated. The slight scrape of his rifle on the rock would not be noticed.

He fired at the bush, twice. A cry, and the stretching of a shadowy leg. Hurt, not killed.

"Pik?"

"The bugger's shot me!"

"Keep your fucking voice down or he'll kill you!"

That was from behind that rock there—shoulder, head for an instant? Hyde fired again, saw rock splin-

ters fly up and something move quicker than an animal. He fired twice more, then the returned fire drove
him behind the rock. Three fit, one wounded. He
turned awkwardly, studying the terrain. There were
enough littered boulders, if he was quick, to afford him
enough cover, were he fit and in control. He slung the
rifle's strap around his neck, holding it against his chest
with the injured arm. The pressure was appalling. He
shook his head, and blundered toward the nearest
cover, paused, then moved again. Bullets skipped
behind him like flung stones, rock slivers grazed and
slit his legs and back—*cover!* He fell rather than
stretched behind it, gasping for breath, his arm aflame
and his chest heaving.

"Did you get the bastard?"

"Might have winged him, Colonel?"

No you bloody didn't . . .

"Not good enough!" he heard Blantyre cry. "Get
up there and take a look!"

"Look your fucking self—sir!"

"Vermaak, either get up there or *I'll* finish you
off!"

Come on, Vermaak. Come and have a look. You
can make it across forty yards of open country against
an injured man with good night vision. Come on. Was
that effort in Blantyre's voice, a shortness of breath
more to do with pain than anger? Too much to hope
for, that he'd slowed the bastard down, even caused
him grievous bodily. Hyde shook his head. Bastards
like Blantyre never died that easily. Enough people had
got the shitty end of the stick already, trying to kill
him. Come on, Vermaak, follow the officer's order —
there!

He fired a ten-round burst, then returned the G3 to
single shot, moving the fire lever back into position.
Then he fumbled a new, twenty-round magazine from
a pocket and clipped it onto the rifle. One up the spout,

ready to go again—not knowing whether he'd hit Vermaak or not.

"Vermaak?"

"Yes, Colonel—go your fucking self, sir!"

He'd missed. Shit.

Blantyre suddenly scrabbled from cover toward the bush that had masked the man with the rocket launcher. Hyde fired once before ducking down from their returned fire. Had Blantyre been carrying one shoulder higher than the other, as if protecting it? He couldn't be certain. Hyde raised his head again, very slowly, and squinted through the night sight. There was activity behind the bush, the bodies of Blantyre and Pik hotter than the bush, but indistinct. He didn't have another magazine to waste on a burst of automatic fire. Two shots flicked off the rock near his face and he ducked out of sight.

He rose, fired once toward the bush, then dropped down. More shots skittered off the rock. They've got you pinpointed. *Move*—

He scuttled in a crouch to his right, where he would be well covered by rocks, and where they would expect him to move, in the direction he had always taken—go left! Left, you stupid sod, *left!*

He scrambled back to the rock that had hidden him and then beyond it, back through the litter of newly fallen rock. Sweat bathed his body and his arm thudded with the impact of his racing blood. The explosion seemed overhead, then, as he stumbled and half-turned, he saw the hiding place he would have chosen disappear in rubble and dust. Bastard. Blantyre had almost been right. He'd have buried Hyde, for certain. He got to his feet and moved again, picking his way across the new scree slope, using the cover of boulders and the enveloping dust. They'd hesitate now, for a few seconds at least, confident that there was no hurry, that he was under half a ton of rock.

The rifle scraped against a boulder as he lost his balance on loose rock. There were shots immediately, and he returned fire because there was one solid shadow that was too clear to miss. Then he ran again, the noise of his movements amid the tumbled boulders hardly audible above the sound of his heart and lungs. His injured arm was detached from him, its pumping ache as he blundered along happening to someone else. He ran, off balance, down a shallow, rippling slope of pebbles toward the riverbed, the canyon suddenly seeming to enlarge and spread out around him. His arms flailed, his feet were noisy, the slope rumbled and muttered behind him. Then he turned suddenly, when he could no longer bear the tension of anticipating their fire.

He flicked the rifle to automatic and emptied the magazine in a fraction of a second. The noise was deafening as he fired up the slope at the starlit shapes giving chase. Then, without waiting and dropping the now-useless rifle, he fled on down the slope, dodging and weaving as if running with a ball in some lunatic sport. There was silence behind him, but his skin slowly stretched tighter and tighter across his shoulderblades like drying leather as he waited for their first shot. His feet stumbled again, clumping like those of a heavy child learning to walk, legs threatening to give way. He clutched his injured arm against his chest with his other hand, his shoulders hunched, as if he carried some weighty treasure he refused to drop.

Still silence. Then he thought he heard a rocket burst harmlessly a long way behind; if it had, then someone was still alive. But he heard only the one detonation, and that might have been illusory. Then he fell as if hit, his injured arm stretched out in front of him and finding an element that moved aside, that splashed back to wet his face and neck. Things rustled and scraped against his stubbled face. Reeds. Water. He scrabbled into the reeds and they bent obsequiously, masking him. He dimly realized his arm was in water, and his body was quivering against spoored and printed earth. Water hole, he thought as he blacked out, the adrenalin failing like a light going out.

Behind you . . . they're still behind you, still there . . .

The realization was not sufficient to keep him conscious. He sensed himself curling into a ball, cradling his injured arm, as the blackness he welcomed engulfed him.

He was curled fetally, he realized, as he opened his eyes. He even remembered that that was how he had surrendered to unconsciousness. He saw the big male leopard fifteen yards away, in the reeds, lying with its front paws extended like a harmless domestic cat. Around him—he suppressed a shiver—were its prints, and he could almost sense its big, rough tongue on his skin. There was a smug certainty on the leopard's streaked and blotched facial fur. It was very big— about a hundred thirty pounds. Hyde realized that it was almost dawn, that the landscape was gray now, no longer dark, and the sky was empty of stars, dotted instead with high clouds already pinking with the rising sun. He forced himself not to move, clenching his arms into his body, clenching his watery bowels.

Oh, Christ, has the fucking thing killed? Has it eaten?

He knew it hadn't. Leopards were night hunters when they could afford to be, secretive, lone. It wouldn't be waiting now if its belly was full. If it had already killed, it would have dragged off its prey to whatever cave it lived in. It was still waiting for a meal. Oh, Christ . . .

The leopard was watching him with lordly indifference. It was waiting for the first buck, even monkey, to come to the water. Prey that moved, evoked curiosity and hunger. Had it been starving, it might have eaten him as he'd slept. Oh, Jesus, keep your fucking imagination under control! Perhaps it had been the defensive, harmless crouch in which the leopard had found him that had disarmed it—in which he still lay, terrified into immobility.

He swallowed drily, with the utmost care. He was too weary to move, too unnerved to even twitch. He was certain that any move would be the last, fatal one. The pistol was still nestled in the small of his back—he could shoot the leopard, if he was quick enough. One shot was all that he would be allowed. He didn't feel capable, not yet. It was easier to remain still, breathing shallowly, becoming accustomed to the leopard's proximity.

And he would have to hit it in an eye, or straight through the heart, or it would bully through the impact of the bullet as if shrugging off insects.

The leopard's ear flicked, not against the first of the day's flies, but attentively. No one as shagged out as you, as slow to react, takes on a big male leopard at fifteen paces. Its ears were now twitching attentively. Zebra, buck or monkey—something was moving toward the water hole. Hyde could hear nothing. The leopard's ears strained back, exactly locating the source of the sounds. Hyde kept his arms still, his hands pressed together between his thighs. Now that the big cat was alert, he knew that soon the scent of his fear would distract the leopard away from its anticipated prey and toward himself.

Then he would have to be quick and certain enough to kill it with one shot. He had to reach behind him, draw the VP 70, chamber a round, sit up, aim and fire—Christ, he'd never do it, not one-handed.

He could smell his fear now, sour and rank. The leopard's staring eyes watched him intently, even though its ears were still alert to pick up the noises of the approaching animal—the *other* prey. Oh, dear Jesus! Somewhere out there, however many of them were still alive were looking for him. They'd find the bloody bones, or rags of flesh and clothing, the marks of his being dragged off.

Then he, too, heard the noise of an animal blundering incautiously through the reeds surrounding the water hole. The leopard tensed, a slight alteration of shape and readiness. It released his own tension— which immediately began to build again. The bloody animal would hear his heartbeat if it got any louder. Best bloody shot of your life, sport, the very best—

An upright human form blundered through the reeds to the water's edge. Blantyre grinned with immense, pained satisfaction as he saw Hyde's body curled by the pool. There was a slow, awkward but inexorable movement of the pistol from his side to an extended, one-handed aim. Hyde could see a big dark stain of blood on his bush shirt—on almost the whole shirt. The gun quivered and Blantyre seemed about to lose his balance. He tottered slightly—

—before the leopard, excited out of caution by the smell of blood, knocked Blantyre off his feet as it sprang on him. The pistol discharged into the air and then Blantyre screamed, high and loud like an animal caught in a mantrap. Then his screams were drowned by the snarling roars of the leopard. The reeds, which masked both bodies, thrashed and swayed with the throes of something that was not a contest. Blantyre was half again as big and heavy as the leopard, but the animal had known he was wounded.

Hyde heard one last scream as he got to his knees and stumbled away. Then he glanced briefly back. What remained of Blantyre was striped and stained with blood. He was dead now. The leopard was beginning with the stomach, since the man had no fur to be fastidiously picked off before it ate. The leopard was oblivious to Hyde, its facial fur deeply dyed with Blantyre's blood.

Hyde walked carefully, slowly away from the water hole, holding his wounded arm against his chest, the pistol in his right hand. There was no one else in sight on the floor of the canyon. The others must be dead or wounded. Only Blantyre had come after him, determined to finish him. The leopard would spend most of the morning dragging the bastard to its cave or up a tree. Jesus Christ—

He retched drily, then moved on, his throat sore, his arm throbbing and woodenly stiff, hugely swollen. But the pain was diminishing, very slowly. All he had to do was find a path up to the road and wait. He stood, right hand still holding the pistol and pressed to his forehead to shield his eyes from the first glimpse of sun. He saw a path less than a quarter of a mile away, like a pale parting in reddish hair, wavering up to the cliff road. The canyon was silent. A single vulture circled on the earliest thermal.

At the top of the path, he saw a parked 4WD. And the flash of the first sunlight on field glasses and chrome. A vehicle and two people, distant and small as toys. The smaller of the two—a woman?—pointed toward him, then he saw her tiny, matchstick arm raised in a greeting. He waved wearily back. Civilians. Tourists. He waved again. Now, there was no hurry, no urgency at all.

He sat down on a rock as the dawn slid down the opposite wall of the canyon, golden and clean. Glad morning.

POSTLUDE

Since he means to come to a door he will
*   come to a door,*
Although so compromised of aim and
*   rate*
He may fumble wide of the knob a yard
*   or more,*
And to those concerned he may seem a
*   little late.*
                    —*Robert Frost*, Willful Homing

Dear Prime Minister,

It is with the utmost regret that I tender my resignation as Chairman of the Joint Intelligence Committee. Reluctantly, I feel the time has come for younger minds and hands to take up such arduous tasks as an uncertain future might place before our country.

I wish to thank you most warmly for your support and trust during our too-brief acquaintance.

Yours most sincerely,

Sir Kenneth Aubrey

Sir Kenneth Aubrey

Here is an excerpt from Craig Thomas' latest hardcover, PLAYING WITH COBRAS, coming from HarperCollinsPublishers in June 1993.

Philip Cass nudged the Japanese four-wheel-drive out from behind the sightseeing bus wheezing up the road, and slid carefully past it. The road dropped away to his left, into the smeared, scented darkness of pines. Pines loomed above, too, marching down towards the twisting, dusty track wriggling tiredly up towards Gulmarg. The bus, its asthmatic engine belching exhaust fumes, disappeared from the mirror as he rounded a twist of the road. Nanga Parbat, for a moment, hunched to the north, snow-peaked. The Kashmir valley's orchards and ricefields, in the haze of late summer, spread out to his left then behind him as the road climbed and twisted again.

The smell of the pines. He sighed. Not long now, not much of such things left, unless he came back as a tourist. The steering wheel struggled in his hands against the potholes and stones of the road, before his vehicle levelled and confronted the old hill-station of Gulmarg. New ski lifts against the sky, new hotels and bungalows beached amid grass and wild flowers. The sensation of imminent departure not only from Kashmir but from India suddenly hurt him, like emotions he might have felt beside a terminal sickbed. He passed two backpacked trekkers, utensils rattling at their shoulders above the noise of the vehicle's engine. Bright shirts and slacks on the highest golf course in the world. A necklace of tourists mounted on ponies emerged from the crowding pines. They paused to appreciate their first glimpse of the resort afloat in its meadow, with the Pir Pangal range pushing up to the south and the outriders of the Himalayas to the north, cupping the place in a great rock embrace. Cass smiled with something approaching bitterness. He spoke Hindi, Urdu, a smattering of Punjabi, could stumblingly read Sanskrit—all of which meant that his tour of duty in India was over and that SIS would probably send him to Washington or Moscow, where the last four years would immediately be redundant.

He tossed his head. He had another couple of months, why so sad already? He sniffed like a hound at the clean, sharp air. Delhi was still like a cauldron, even Srinagar behind him in the valley had been sticky, oppressive—but up here. . .

Up here was the real source of his melancholy, and it was human. Sereena. Waiting for him in her husband's bungalow just behind Gulmarg, perched on the edge of a cliff and facing north towards Pakistani Kashmir and the great mountain, Nanga Parbat— Sereena the Indian film star and the wife of the Minister of Tourism and Civil Aviation, V.K. Sharmar. He rubbed his hand through his breeze-blown hair as if embarrassed, grinning at the awakened sense of danger, the effrontery of their months-long liaison, the locales of their encounters in Delhi or here in Kashmir. The dangerous, exhilarating joke of it, the added earnestness that risk gave to their lovemaking. When he left India, he'd leave her behind, too.

The resort trickled tourists along its main street. There was noise from cafés, music blaring from open-

topped cars and flung-open doors. Then he was climbing the short, winding, narrow track up towards the
long wooden bungalow that once housed, beneath
elaborately carved eaves and in scented-wood rooms,
memsahibs for each summer of the Raj. He slowed the
vehicle and dragged on the brake, disappointed that
she was not posed in the shadow of the verandah, then
at once pleased in anticipation of her waiting for him
in the minister's kingsize bed in the long, low-beamed
main bedroom. The fan would be turning cooly above
her, its arms waving in encouragement rather than
reproach. He cocked his head, listening. The hi-fi was
playing some of the American country rock Sereena
incongruously enjoyed; even as he preferred ragas and
the sitar. She was, because of her status as one of the
Hindu deities of the cinema, more Western than he,
sometimes. She was in bed, then. It would all be done
with titillating, cinematic cliché; the iced champagne,
the silk sheets, the seductive underwear, the acted
whore—everything. He smiled, rubbing his cheeks. He
was in the intelligence service, after all; Sereena had
merely changed his name to Bond, glamorizing their
relationship within the conventions of celluloid.

And, if it was a fantasy, then he enjoyed that too. It
was *every* man's sexual fantasy, after all. Experienced
Asian beauty, exotic settings, the delicious-lubricious,
the element of risk. Enough to make him all but rub his
hands in anticipation.

Or remember that she'd become more than a fantasy, an appetite. Awkwardly, he had begun to love
her. At least to be with her, and to want not to end it.
He climbed out of the vehicle and breathed deeply,
slowly. He could just see the spray of a fountain at the
rear of the bungalow. Jesus, it was close enough to par-
adise, every aspect of the situation. He dragged his
overnight bag out of the four-wheel-drive and hurried
into the cool, purple shadow of the verandah. Maybe,

just maybe, he'd wangle another extension to his tour of duty. Trouble was, with Aubrey gone, there was no one who would just okay it with a slight smile. Pete Shelley was stuffed to the gills with pompous rectitude since taking over the Director-General's job. He might well not give him an extension.

Sod that for the moment, anyway. He called out: "Sereena—it's me! The flight was on time."

She must be teasing, some new game. Wanted him to go straight into the bedroom, be surprised by what she was wearing, or the way her body was posed in the bed or perhaps against the late afternoon light from the window, the mountains behind her. He hurried, dropping his overnight bag and cotton jacket on the living-room sofa. Scented woods, carved cornicing, heavy old furniture, deep, complex rugs. He plucked up a glass of still-bubbling champagne from a small table, sipping it as he grinned. Sipped again, the drink's coldness tightening his throat pleasurably. A broken champagne glass crackled into shards beneath his shoe as he approached the bedroom door. He could smell, above the usual scents and incenses of the bungalow, the Chanel he'd bought for her last birthday.

He looked down at the broken glass beneath his feet. She was getting careless in her eagerness. Perhaps she'd heard his engine note approaching and dropped it in her hurry. He stepped through the open door of the bedroom, rubbing his temple against a sudden dizziness. She was lying on the silk sheets—saried though, as if she'd flung herself on the bed in a modelling pose, her hair strayed out like a black cloud across the pillows. There was a great deal of blood, a great deal. It had soaked into the sheets and the pillows. There was even a splash of it on the wall behind the elaborate carving of the headboard. Blood everywhere.

The room whirled, even before he could vomit in horror, the smear of blood on the wall spinning like a firework, fiery in the slanting sunlight coming through the window, which was moving, circling the room, then floating above him as he fell into the darkness.

Window. He realized the opaque area of dull light was the window. It was unmoving. He was lying on the bed. The window was where it should be, if he was lying on the bed. Nanga Parbat's flanks were golden as the sun began to go down. His hand and forearm, stretched out to where she would be across the bed, were sticky. His fingers—he wriggled them—were weblike, stuck to one another. His head lurched like a loosely-stowed cargo as he attempted to sit up and look as his hand. Red?—hand—why red, *sticky*? Flies buzzed in the room beneath the revolving, slow fan. He turned. Her body was covered with them, feasting on the drying blood that covered her, the sheets, his hand, his shirt, and the knife that lay on the bed between them. He lurched across her body, waggling his arms, beating at the air around the flies, his head aching, his stomach revolted. His mind seemed pierced by a silent scream attempting to bully itself into his awareness. He stared at the gashes in the glowing, bloodstained sari, then at his reddened hands. He was stilled with shock, unable to move, his throat fighting back the bitter vomit he could taste. The flies settled on her again, advantaged by his paralysis.

The hi-fi continued its drool of country rock from the living room, the noise pressing against his throbbing temples. Then, gradually loudening as it approached from Gulmarg, the noise of the police siren drowned out the music as Cass continued to stare, immobile, at the woman's body.

Look for PLAYING WITH COBRAS by Craig Thomas. Available in June, 1993 from a bookseller near you.